Davenport Dunn
A Man Of Our Times
Vol. II

By

Charles Lever

Davenport Dunn
A Man Of Our Times
Vol. II
by Charles Lever

Copyright © 2023

All Rights reserved.

ISBN: 978-93-61154-36-2

Published by

DOUBLE 9 BOOKS

2/13-B, Ansari Road
Daryaganj, New Delhi – 110002
info@double9books.com
www.double9books.com
Tel. 011-40042856

ABOUT THE AUTHOR

Lever and Boyle earned pocket money by singing their own ballads in Dublin's streets and engaging in a variety of other pranks, which Lever dramatized in his novels O'Malley, Con Cregan, and Lord Kilgobbin. In 1833, he married his first love, Catherine Baker, and in February 1837, after a number of experiences, he began publishing The Confessions of Harry Lorrequer in the newly created Dublin University Magazine. In 1833, he married his first love, Catherine Baker, and in February 1837, after a number of experiences, he began publishing The Confessions of Harry Lorrequer in the newly created Dublin University Magazine. During the previous seven years, popular taste had turned toward the "service novel," examples of which include Frank Mildmay (1829) by Frederick Marryat, Tom Cringle's Log (1829) by Michael Scott, The Subaltern (1825) by George Robert Gleig, Cyril Thornton (1827) by Thomas Hamilton, Stories of Waterloo (1833) by William Hamilton Maxwell, Ben Brace (1840) by Frederick Chamier, and The Bivouac (1837), also by Maxwell. Lever had met the genre's nominal founder, William Hamilton Maxwell.

CONTENTS

CHAPTER I
THE TELEGRAPHIC DESPATCH

When Mr. Davenport Dunn entered the drawing-room before dinner on that day, his heart beat very quickly as he saw Lady Augusta Arden was there alone. In what spirit she remembered the scene of the morning,—whether she felt resentment towards him for his presumption, was disposed to scoff down his pretensions, or to regard them, if not with favor, with at least forgiveness, were the themes on which his mind was yet dwelling. The affable smile with which she now met him did more to resolve these doubts than all his casuistry.

"Was it not very thoughtful of me," said she, "to release you this morning, and suffer you to address yourself to the important things which claimed your attention? I really am quite vain of my self-denial."

"And yet, Lady Augusta," said he, in a low tone, "I had felt more flattered if you had been less mindful of the exigency, and been more interested in what I then was speaking of."

"What a selfish speech!" said she, laughing. "Now that my forbearance has given you all the benefits it could confer, you turn round and say you are not grateful for it. I suppose," added she, half pettishly, "the despatch was not very pressing after all, and that this was the cause of some disappointment."

"I am unable to say," replied he, calmly.

"What do you mean? Surely, when you read it—"

"But I have not read it,—there it is still, just as you saw-it," said he, producing the packet with the seal unbroken.

"But really, Mr. Dunn," said she, and her face flushed up as she spoke, "this does not impress me with the wonderful aptitude for affairs men ascribe to you. Is it usual to treat these messages so cavalierly?"

"It never happened with me till this morning, Lady Augusta," said he, in the same low tone. "Carried away by an impulse which I will not try to account for, I had dared to speak to you of myself and of my future in a way that showed how eventful to both might prove the manner in which you heard me."

"Well, Dunn," cried Lord Glengariff, entering, "I suppose you have made a day of work of it; we have never seen you since breakfast."

"On the contrary, my Lord," replied he, in deep confusion, "I have taken my idleness in the widest sense. Never wrote a line,—not looked into a newspaper."

"Wouldn't even open a telegraphic message which came to his hands this morning," said Lady Augusta, with a malicious drollery in her glance towards him.

"Incredible!" cried my Lord.

"Quite true, I assure your Lordship," said Dunn, in deeper confusion, and not knowing what turn to give his explanation.

"The fact is," broke in Lady Augusta, hurriedly, "Mr. Dunn was so implicit in his obedience to our prescription of perfect rest and repose, that he made it a point of honor not even to read a telegram without permission."

"I must say it is very flattering to us," said Lord Glengariff; "but now let us reward the loyalty, and let him see what his news is."

Dunn looked at Lady Augusta, who, with the very slightest motion of her head, gave consent, and he broke open the despatch.

Dunn crushed the paper angrily in his hand when he finished reading it, and muttered some low words of angry meaning.

"Nothing disagreeable, I trust?" asked his Lordship.

"Yes, my Lord, something even worse than disagreeable," said he; then flattening out the crumpled paper, he held it to him to read.

Lord Glengariff, putting on his spectacles, perused the document slowly, and then, turning towards Dunn, in a voice of deep agitation, said, "This is very disastrous indeed; are you prepared for it?"

Without attending to the question, Dunn took the despatch from Lord Glengariff, and handed it to Lady Augusta.

"A run for gold!" cried she, suddenly. "An attempt to break the Ossory Bank! What does it all mean? Who are they that make this attack?"

"Opponents—some of them political, some commercial, a few, perhaps, men personally unfriendly,—enemies of what they call my success!" and he sighed heavily on the last word. "Let me see," said he, slowly, after a pause; "to-day is Thursday—to-morrow will be the 28th—heavy payments are required for the Guatemala Trunk Line,—something more than forty thousand pounds to be made up. The Parma Loan, second instalment, comes on the 80th."

"Dinner, my Lord," said a servant, throwing open the door.

"A thousand pardons, Lady Augusta," said Dunn, offering his arm. "I am really shocked at obtruding these annoyances upon your notice. You see, my Lord," added he, gayly, "one of the penalties of admitting the 'working-men of life' into your society."

It was only as they passed on towards the dinner-room that Lord Glengariff noticed Miss Kellett's absence.

"She has a headache or a cold, I believe," said Lady Augusta, carelessly; and they sat down to dinner.

So long as the servants were present the conversation ranged over commonplace events and topics, little indeed passing, since each seemed too deeply impressed with grave forebodings for much inclination for mere talking. Once alone—and Lord Glengariff took the earliest moment to be so—they immediately resumed the subject of the ill-omened despatch.

"You are, at all events, prepared, Dunn?" said the Earl; "this onslaught does not take you by surprise?"

"I am ashamed to say it does, my Lord," said he, with a painful smile. "I was never less suspectful of any malicious design upon me. I was, for the first time perhaps in all my life, beginning to feel strong in the consciousness that I had faithfully performed my allotted part in the world, advanced the great interests of my country and of humanity generally. This blow has, therefore, shocked me deeply."

"What a base ingratitude!" exclaimed Lady Augusta, indignantly.

"After all," said Dunn, generously, "let us remember that I am not a fair judge in my own cause. Others have taken, it may be, another reading of my character; they may deem me narrow-minded, selfish, and ambitious. My very success—I am not going to deny it has been great—may have provoked its share of enmity. Why, the very vastness and extent of my projects were a sort of standing reproach to petty speculators and small scheme-mongers."

"So that it has really come upon you unawares?" said the Earl, reverting to his former remark.

"Completely so, my Lord. The tranquil ease and happiness I have enjoyed under this roof—the first real holiday in a long life of toil—are the best evidences I can offer how little I could have anticipated such a stroke."

"Still I fervently hope it will not prove more than inconvenience," said he, feelingly.

"Not even so much, my Lord, as regards money. I cannot believe that the movement will be general. There is no panic in the country, rents are paid, prices remunerating, markets better than we have seen them for years; the sound sense and intelligence of the people will soon detect in this attack the prompting of some personal malice. In all likelihood a few thousands will meet the whole demand."

"I am so glad to hear you say so!" said Lady Augusta, smiling. "Really, when I think of all our persuasions to detain you here, I never could acquit us of some sort of share in any disaster your delay might have occasioned."

"Oh, Dunn would never connect his visit here with such consequences, I 'm certain," said the Earl.

"Assuredly not, my Lord," said he; and as his eyes met those of Lady Augusta, he grew red, and felt confused.

"Are your people—your agents and men of business, I mean," said the Earl—"equal to such an emergency as the present, or will they have to look to *you* for guidance and direction?"

"Merely to meet the demand for gold is a simple matter, my Lord," said Dunn, "and does not require any effort of mind or forethought. To prevent the back-water of this rushing flood submerging and engulfing other banking-houses; to defend, in a word, the lines of our rivals and enemies; to save from the consequences of their recklessness the very men who have assailed us,—these are weighty cares!"

"And are you bound in honor to take this trouble in their behalf?"

"No, my Lord, not in honor any more than in law, but bound by the debt we owe to that commercial community by whose confidence we have acquired fortune. My position at the head of the great industrial movement in this country imposes upon me the great responsibility that 'no injury should befall the republic' Against the insane attacks of party hate, factious violence, or commercial knavery, I am expected to do my duty, nay, more, I am expected to be provided with means to meet whatever emergency may arise,—defeat this scheme, expose that, denounce the other. Am I wrong in calling these weighty cares?"

Self-glorification was not usually one of Davenport Dunn's weaknesses,—indeed, "self," in any respect, was not a theme on which he was disposed to dwell,—and yet now, for reasons which may better be suspected than alleged, he talked in a spirit of even vain exultation of his plans, his station, and his influence. If it was something to display before the peer claims to national respect, which, if not so ancient, were scarcely less imposing than his own, it was more pleasing still to dilate upon a theme to which the peer's daughter listened so eagerly. It was, besides, a grand occasion to exhibit the vast range of resources, the widespread influences, and far-reaching sympathies of the great commercial man, to show him, not the mere architect of his own fortune, but the founder of a nation's prosperity. While he thus held forth, and in a strain to which fervor had lent a sort of eloquence, a servant entered with another despatch.

"Oh! I trust this brings you better news," cried Lady Augusta, eagerly; and, as he broke the envelope, he thanked her with a grateful look.

"Well?" interposed she, anxiously, as he gazed at the lines without speaking, — "well?"

"Just as I said," muttered Dunn, in a deep and suppressed voice, — "a systematic plot, a deep-laid scheme against me."

"Is it still about the Bank?" asked the Earl, whose interest had been excited by the tenor of the recent conversation.

"Yes, my Lord; they insist on making me out a bubble speculator, an adventurer, a Heaven knows what of duplicity and intrigue. I would simply ask them: 'Is the wealth with which this same Davenport Dunn has enriched you real, solid, and tangible; are the guineas mint-stamped; are the shares true representatives of value?' But why do I talk of these people? If they render me no gratitude, they owe me none, — my aims were higher and greater than ever *they* or *their* interests comprehended." From the haughty defiance of his tone, his voice fell suddenly to a low and quick key, as he said: "This message informs me that the demand upon the Ossory to-morrow will be a great concerted movement. Barnard, the man I myself returned last election for the borough, is to head it; he has canvassed the county for holders of our notes, and such is the panic that the magistrats have sent for an increased force of police and two additional companies of infantry. My man of business asks, 'What is to be done?'"

"And what *is* to be done?" asked the Earl.

"Meet it, my Lord. Meet the demand as our duty requires us."

There was a calm dignity in the manner Dunn spoke the words that had its full effect upon the Earl and his daughter. They saw this "man of the people" display, in a moment of immense peril, an amount of cool courage that no dissimulation could have assumed. As they could, and did indeed say afterwards, when relating the incident, "We were sitting at the dessert, chatting away freely about one thing or another, when the confirmed tidings arrived by telegraph that an organized attack was to be made against his credit by a run for gold. You should really have seen him," said Lady Augusta, "to form any idea of the splendid composure he manifested. The only thing like emotion he exhibited was a sort of haughty disdain, a proud pity, for men who should have thus requited the great services he had been rendering to the country."

It is but just to own that he did perform his part well; he acted it, too, as theatrical critics would say, "chastely;" that is, there was no rant, no exaggeration,—not a trait too much, not a tint too strong.

"I wish I knew of any way to be of service to you in this emergency, Dunn," said the Earl, as they returned to the drawing-room; "I'm no capitalist, nor have I a round sum at my command—"

"My dear Lord," broke in Dunn, with much feeling, "of money I can command whatever amount I want. Baring, Hope, Rothschild, any of them would assist me with millions, if I needed them, to-morrow, which happily, however, I do not. There is still a want which they cannot supply, but which, I am proud to say, I have no longer to fear. The kind sympathy of your Lordship and Lady Augusta has laid me under an obligation—" Here Mr. Dunn's voice faltered; the Earl grasped his hand with a generous clasp, and Lady Augusta carried her handkerchief to her eyes as she averted her head.

"What a pack of hypocrites!" cries our reader, in disgust. No, not so. There was a dash of reality through all this deceit. They *were* moved,—their own emotions, the tones of their own voices, the workings of their own natures, *had* stirred some amount of honest sentiment in their hearts; how far it was alloyed by less worthy feeling, to what extent fraud and trickery mingled there, we are not going to tell you,—perhaps we could not, if we would.

"You mean to go over to Kilkenny, then, to-morrow, Dunn?" asked his Lordship, after a painful pause.

"Yes, my Lord, my presence is indispensable."

"Will you allow Lady Augusta and myself to accompany you? I believe and trust that men like myself have not altogether lost the influence they once used to wield in this country, and I am vain enough to imagine I may be useful."

"Oh, my Lord, this overwhelms me!" said Dunn, and covered his eyes with his hand.

CHAPTER II
"THE RUN FOR GOLD"

The great Ossory Bank, with its million sterling of paid-up capital, its royal charter, its titled directory, and its shares at a premium, stood at the top of Patrick Street, Kilkenny, and looked, in the splendor of its plate-glass windows and the security of its iron railings, the very type of solvency and safety. The country squire ascended the hall-door steps with a sort of feeling of acquaintanceship, for he had known the Viscount who once lived there in days before the Union, and the farmer experienced a sense of trustfulness in depositing his hard-earned gains in what he regarded as a temple of Croesus. What an air of prosperity and business did the interior present! The massive doors swung noiselessly at the slightest touch, meet emblem of the secrecy that prevailed, and the facility that pervaded all transactions, within. What alacrity, too, in that numerous band of clerks who counted and cashed and checked unceasingly! How calmly they passed from desk to desk, a word, a mere whisper, serving for converse; and then what a grand and mysterious solemnity about that back office with its double doors, within which some venerable cashier, bald-headed and pursy, stole at intervals to consult the oracle who dwelt within! In the spacious apartment devoted to cash operations, nothing denoted the former destiny of the mansion but a large fireplace, with a pretentious chimney-piece of black oak, over which a bust of our gracious Queen now figured, an object of wonderment and veneration to many a frieze-coated gazer.

On the morning of the 12th August, to which day we have brought our present history, the street in front of the Bank presented a scene of no ordinary interest. From an early hour people continued to pour in, till the entire way was choked up with carriages and conveyances of every description, from the well-equipped barouche of the country gentleman to the humblest "shandradan" of the petty farmer. Sporting-looking fellows upon high-conditioned thoroughbreds, ruddy old squires upon cobs, and hard-featured country-folk upon shaggy ponies, were all jammed up together amidst a dense crowd of foot passengers. A strong police-force was drawn up in front of the Bank, although nothing in the appearance of the assembled mass seemed to denote the necessity for their presence. A low murmur of voices ran through the crowd as each talked to his neighbor, consulting, guessing, and speculating, as temperament inclined: some were showing placards and printed notices they had received through the post; some pointed to newspaper paragraphs; others displayed great rolls of notes; but all talked with a certain air of sadness that appeared to presage coming misfortune. As ten o'clock drew nigh, the hour for opening the Bank, the excitement rose to a painful pitch; every eye was directed to the massive door, whose gorgeous brass knocker shone with a sort of insolent brilliancy in the sun. At every moment watches were consulted, and in muttered whispers men broke their fears to those beside them. Some could descry the heads of people moving about in the cash-office, where a considerable bustle appeared to prevail; and even this much of life seemed to raise the spirits of the crowd, and the rumor ran quickly on every side that the Bank was about to open. At last the deep bell of the town-hall struck ten. At each fall of the hammer all expected to see the door move, but it never stirred; and now the pent-up feeling of the multitude might be marked in a sort of subdued growl,—a low, ill-boding sound, that seemed ta come out of the very earth. As if to answer the unspoken anger of the crowd,—a challenge accepted ere given,—a heavy crash was heard, and the police proceeded to load with ball in the face of the people,—a demonstration whose significance there was no mistaking. A cry of angry defiance burst from the assembled mass at the sight, but as suddenly was checked again as the massive door was seen to move, and then, with a loud bang, fly wide open. The rush was now tremendous. With some vague impression that everything depended upon being amongst the first, the people poured in with all the force of a mighty torrent. Each, fighting his way as if for life itself, regardless of the cries of suffering about him, strove to get forward; nor could all the efforts of the police avail to restrain them in the slightest. Bleeding, wounded, half suffocated, with bruised faces and clothes torn to tatters, they struggled on,—no deference to age, no respect to condition. It was a fearful anarchy, where every thought of the past was lost in the present emergency. On they poured, breathless and bloody, with gleaming eyes and faces of demoniacal meaning; they pushed, they jostled, and they tore, till the first line gained the counter, against which the force behind now threatened to crush them to death.

What a marvellous contrast to the storm-tossed multitude, steaming and disfigured, was the calm attitude of the clerks within the counter! Not deigning, as it seemed, to bestow a glance upon the agitated scene before them, they moved placidly about, pen behind the ear, in voices of ordinary tone, asking what each wanted, and counting over the proffered notes with all the impassiveness of every-day habit. "Gold for these, did you say?" they repeated, as though any other demand met the ear! Why, the very air rang with the sound, and the walls gave back the cry. From the wild voice of half-maddened recklessness to the murmur that broke from fainting exhaustion, there was but one word,—"Gold!" A drowning crew, as the surging waves swept over them, never screamed for succor with wilder eagerness than did that tangled mass shout, "Gold, gold!"

In their savage energy they could scarcely credit that their demands should be so easily complied with; they were half stupefied at the calm indifference that met their passionate appeal. They counted and recounted the glittering pieces over and over, as though some trick were to be apprehended, some deception to be detected. When drawn or pulled back from the counter by others eager as themselves, they might be seen in corners, counting over their money, and reckoning it once more. It was so hard to believe that all their terrors were for nothing, their worst fears without a pretext. Even yet they couldn't imagine but that the supply must soon run short, and they kept asking those that came away whether they, too, had got their gold. Hour after hour rolled on, and still the same demand, and still the same unbroken flow of the yellow tide continued. Some very large checks had been presented; but no sooner was their authenticity acknowledged than they were paid. An agent from another bank arrived with a formidable roll of "Ossory" notes, but was soon seen issuing forthwith two bursting little bags of sovereigns. Notwithstanding all this, the pressure never ceased for a moment; nay, as the day wore on, the crowds seemed to have grown denser and more importunate; and when the half-exhausted clerks claimed a few minutes' respite for a biscuit and a glass of wine, a cry of impatience burst from the insatiable multitude. It was three o'clock. In another hour the Bank would close, as many surmised, never to open again. It was evident, from the still increasing crowd and the excitement that prevailed, how little confidence the ready payments of the Bank had diffused. They who came forth loaded with gold were regarded as fortunate, while they who still waited for their turn were in all the feverish torture of uncertainty.

A little after three the crowd was cleft open by the passage of a large travelling-barouche, which, with four steaming posters, advanced slowly through the dense mass.

"Who comes here with an earl's coronet?" said a gentleman to his neighbor, as the carriage passed. "Lord Glengariff, and Davenport Dunn himself, by George!" cried he suddenly.

The words were as quickly caught up by those at either side, and the news, "Davenport Dunn has arrived," ran through the immense multitude. If there was an eager, almost intense anxiety to catch a glimpse of him, there was still nothing that could indicate, in the slightest degree, the state of popular feeling towards him. Slightly favorable it might possibly have been, inasmuch as a faint effort at a cheer burst forth at the announcement of his name; but it was repressed just as suddenly, and it was in a silence almost awful that he descended from the carriage at the private door of the Bank.

"Do, I beg of you, Mr. Dunn," said Lady Augusta, as he stood to assist her to alight; "let me entreat of you not to think of us. We can be most comfortably accommodated at the hotel."

"By all means, Dunn. I insist upon it," broke in the Earl.

"In declining my poor hospitality, my Lord," said Dunn, "you will grieve me much, while you will also favor the impression that I am not in a condition to offer it."

"Ah! quite true,—very justly observed. Dunn is perfectly right, Augusta. We ought to stop here." And he descended at once, and gave his hand to his daughter.

Lady Augusta turned about ere she entered the house, and looked at the immense crowd before her. There was something of almost resentfulness in the haughty gaze she bestowed; but, let us own, the look, whatever it implied, well became her proud features; and more than one was heard to say, "What a handsome woman she is!"

This little incident in the day's proceedings gave rise to much conjecture, some auguring that events must be grave and menacing when Dunn's own presence was required, others inferring that he came to give assurance and confidence to the Bank. Nor was the appearance of Lord Glen-gariff less open to its share of surmise; and many were the inquiries how far he was personally interested,—whether he was a large stockholder of the concern, or deep in its books as debtor. Leaving the speculative minds who discussed the subject without doors, let us follow Mr. Dunn, as, with Lady Augusta on his arm, he led the way to the drawing-room.

The rooms were handsomely furnished, that to the back opening upon a conservatory filled with rich geraniums, and ornamented with a pretty marble fountain, now in full play. Indeed, so well had Dunn's orders been attended to, that the apartments which he scarcely occupied for above a day or so in a twelvemonth had actually assumed the appearance of being in constant use. Books, prints, and newspapers were scattered about, fresh flowers stood in the vases, and recent periodicals lay on the tables.

"What a charming house!" exclaimed Lady Augusta; and, really, the approbation was sincere, for the soft-cushioned sofas, the perfumed air, the very quiet itself, were in delightful contrast to the heat and discomfort of a journey by "rail."

It was in vain Dunn entreated his noble guests to accept some luncheon; they peremptorily refused, and, in fact, declared that they would only remain there on the condition that he bestowed no further thought upon them, addressing himself entirely to the weighty cares around him.

"Will you, at least, tell me at what hour you'd like dinner, my Lord? Shall we say six?"

"With all my heart. Only, once more, I beg, never think of us. We are most comfortable here, and want for nothing."

With a deep bow of obedience, Dunn moved towards the door, when suddenly Lady Augusta whispered a few rapid words in her father's ear.

"Stop a moment, Dunn!" cried the Earl. "Augusta is quite right. The observation is genuine woman's wit She says I ought to go down along with you, to show myself in the Bank; that my presence there will have a salutary effect. Eh, what d'ye think?"

"I am deeply indebted to Lady Augusta for the suggestion," said Dunn, coloring highly. "There cannot be a doubt that your Lordship's countenance and support at such a moment are priceless."

"I'm glad you think so, glad she thought of it," muttered the Earl, as he arranged his white locks before the glass, and made a sort of hasty toilet for his approaching appearance in public.

To judge from the sensation produced by the noble Lord's appearance in the Bank, Lady Augusta's suggestion was admirable. The arrival of a wagon-load of bullion could scarcely have caused a more favorable impression. If Noah had been an Englishman, the dove would have brought him not an olive-branch but a lord. I say it in no spirit of sarcasm or sneer, for, *coteris paribus*, lords are better company than commoners; I merely record it passingly, as a strong trait of our people and our race. So was it now, that from the landed gentleman to the humblest tenant-farmer, the Earl's presence seemed a fresh guarantee of solvency. Many remarked that Dunn looked pale,—some thought anxious; but all agreed that the hearty-faced, white-haired old nobleman at his side was a perfect picture of easy self-satisfaction.

They took their seats in the cash-office, within the counter, to be seen by all, and see everything that went forward. If Davenport Dunn regarded the scene with a calm and unmoved indifference, his attention being, in fact, more engrossed by his newspaper than by what went on around, Lord Glengariff's quick eye and ear were engaged incessantly. He scanned the appearance of each new applicant as he came up to the table; he listened to his demand, noted its amount, and watched with piercing glance what effect it might produce on the cashier. Nor was he an unmoved spectator of the scene; for while he simply contented himself with an angry stare at the frieze-coated peasant, he actually scowled an insolent defiance when any of higher rank or more pretentious exterior presented himself, muttering in broken accents beneath his breath, "Too bad, too bad!" "Gross ingratitude!" "A perfect disgrace!" and so on.

He was at the very climax of his indignation, when a voice from the crowd addressed him with "How d' ye do, my Lord? I was not aware you were in this part of the country."

He put up his double eyeglass, and speedily recognized the Mr. Barnard whom Dunn mentioned as so unworthily requiting all he had done for him.

"No, sir," said the Earl, haughtily; "and just as little did I expect to see you here on such an errand as this. In *my* day, country gentlemen were the first to give the example of trust and confidence, and not foremost in propagating unworthy apprehensions."

"I'm not a partner in the Bank, my Lord, and know nothing of its solvency," said the other, as he handed in two checks over the counter.

"Eight thousand six hundred and forty-eight. Three thousand, twelve, nine, six," said the clerk, mechanically. "How will you have it, sir?"

"Bank of Ireland notes will do."

Dunn lifted his eyes from the paper, and then, raising his hat, saluted Mr. Barnard.

"I trust you left Mrs. Barnard well?" said he, in a calm voice.

"Yes, thank you—well—quite well," said Barnard, in some confusion.

"Will you remember to tell her that she shall have the acorns of the Italian pines next week? I have heard of their arrival at the Custom-house."

While Barnard muttered a very confused expression of thanks, the old Earl looked from one to the other of the speakers in a sort of bewilderment. Where was the angry indignation he had looked for from Dunn,—where the haughty denunciation of a black ingratitude?

"Why, Dunn, I say," whispered he, "isn't this Barnard the fellow you spoke of,—the man you returned to Parliament t' other day?"

"The same, my Lord," replied Dunn, in a low, cautious voice. "He is here exacting a right,—a just right,—and no more. It is not now, nor in this place, that I would remind him how ungraciously he has treated me. This day is *his*. *Mine* will come yet."

Before Lord Glengariff could well recover from the astonishment of this cold and calculating patience, Mr. Hankes pushed his way through the crowd, with an open letter in his hand.

It was a telegram just received, with an account of an attack made by the mob on Mr. Dunn's house in Dublin. Like all such communications, the tidings were vague and unsatisfactory: "A terrific attack by mob on No. 18. Windows smashed, and front door broken, but not forced. Police repulsed; military sent for."

"So much for popular gratitude, my Lord," said Dunn, as he handed the slip of paper to the Earl. "Fortunately, it was never the prize on which I had set my heart. Mr. Hankes," said he, in a bland, calm voice, "the crowd seems scarcely diminished outside. Will you kindly affix a notice on the door, to state that, to convenience the public, the Bank will on this day continue open till five o'clock?"

"By Heaven! they don't deserve such courtesy!" cried the old Lord, passionately. "Be as just as you please, but show them no generosity. If it be thus they treat the men who devote their best energies, their very lives, to the country, I, for one, say it is not a land to live in, and I spurn them as countrymen!"

"What would you have, my Lord? The best troops have turned and fled under the influence of a panic; the magic words, 'We are mined!' once routed the very column that had stormed a breach! You don't expect to find the undisciplined masses of mankind more calmly courageous than the veterans of a hundred fights."

A wild hoarse cheer burst forth in the street at this moment, and drowned all other sounds.

"What is it now? Are they going to attack us here?" cried the Earl.

The cry again arose, louder and wilder, and the shouts of "Dunn forever! Dunn forever!" burst from a thousand voices.

"The placard has given great satisfaction, sir," said Hankes, reappearing. "Confidence is fully restored."

And, truly, it was strange to see how quickly a popular sentiment spread its influence; for they who now came forward to exchange their notes for gold no longer wore the sturdy air of defiance of the earlier applicants, but approached half reluctantly, and with an evident sense of shame, as though yielding to an ignoble impulse of cowardice and fear. The old Earl's haughty stare and insolent gaze were little calculated to rally the diffident;

for with his double eyeglass he scanned each new-comer with the air of a man saying, "I mark, and I 'll not forget you!"

What a contrast was Dunn's expression,—that look so full of gentle pity and forgiveness! Nothing of anger, no resentfulness, disfigured the calm serenity of his pale features. He had a word of recognition—even a smile and a kind inquiry—for some of those who now bashfully tried to screen themselves from notice. The great rush was already over; a visible change had come over that vast multitude who so lately clamored aloud for gold. The very aspect of that calm, unmoved face was a terrible rebuke to their unworthy terror.

"It's nigh over, sir," whispered Hankes to his chief, as he stood with his massive gold watch in the hollow of his hand. "Seven hundred only have been paid out in the last twelve minutes. The battle is finished!"

The vociferous cheering without continued unceasingly, and yells for Dunn to come forth and show himself filled the air.

"Do you hear them?" asked Lord Glengariff, looking eagerly at Dunn.

"Yes, my Lord. It is a very quick reaction. Popular opinion is generally correct in the main; but it is rare to find it reversing its own judgments so suddenly."

"Very dispassionately spoken, sir," said the old Lord, haughtily; "but what if you had been unprepared for this onslaught to-day,—what if they had succeeded in compelling you to suspend payments?"

"Had such been possible, my Lord, we would have richly deserved any reverse that might have befallen us. What is it, Hankes?" cried he, as that gentleman endeavored to get near him.

"You'll have to show yourself, sir; you must positively address them in a few words from the balcony."

"I do not think so, Hankes. This is a mere momentary burst of popular feeling."

"Not at all, sir. Listen to them now; they are shouting madly for you. To decline the call will be taken as pride. I implore you to come out, if only for a few minutes."

"I suppose he is right, Dunn," said Lord Glengariff, half doggedly. "For my own part, I have not the slightest pretension to say how popular demonstrations—I believe that is the word for them—are to be treated. Street gatherings, in my day, were called mobs, and dispersed by horse police; our newer civilization parleys to them and flatters them. I suppose you understand the requirements of the times we live in."

The clamor outside was now deafening, and by its tone seemed, in some sort, to justify what Hankes had said, that Dunn's indifference to their demands would be construed into direct insult.

"Do it at once!" cried Hankes, eagerly, "or it will be too late. A few words spoken now will save us thirty thousand pounds to-morrow."

This whisper in Dunn's ear decided the question, and, turning to the Earl, he said, "I believe, my Lord, Mr. Hankes is right; I ought to show myself."

"Come along, then," said the old Lord, heartily; and he took his arm with an air that said, "I 'll stand by you throughout."

Scarcely had Dunn entered the drawing-room, than Lady Augusta met him, her cheek flushed and her eyes flashing. "I am so glad," cried she, "that you are going to address them. It is a proud moment for you."

When the window opened, and Davenport Dunn appeared on the balcony, the wild roar of the multitude made the air tremble; for the cry was taken up by others in remote streets, and came echoing back, again and again. I have heard that consummate orators—men practised in all the arts of public speaking—have acknowledged that there is no such severe test, in the way of audience, as that mixed assemblage called a mob, wherein every class has its representative, and every gradation its type. Now, Dunn was not a great public speaker. The few sentences he was obliged to utter on the occasions of his health being drunk cost him no uncommon uneasiness; he spoke them, usually, with faltering accents and much diffidence. It happens, however, that the world is often not displeased at these small signs of confusion—these little defects in oratorical readiness— in men of acknowledged ability, and even prefer them to the rapid flow and voluble ease of more practised orators. There is, so to say, a mock air of sincerity in the professions of a man whose feelings seem fuller than his words,—something that implies the heart to be in the right place, though the tongue be but a poor exponent of its sentiments; and lastly, the world is always ready to accept the embarrassment of the speaker as an evidence of the grateful emotions that are swaying him. Hence the success of country gentlemen in the House; hence the hearty cheers that follow the rambling discursiveness of bucolic eloquence!

If Mr. Dunn was not an orator, he was a keen and shrewd observer, and one fact he had noticed, which was that the shouts and cries of popular assemblages are to an indifferent speaker pretty much what an accompaniment is to a bad singer,—the aids by which he surmounts difficult passages and conceals his false notes. Mr. Hankes, too, well understood how to lead this orchestra, and had already taken his place on the steps of the door beneath.

Dunn stood in front of the balcony, Lord Glengariff at his side and a little behind him. With one hand pressed upon his heart, he bowed deeply to the multitude. "My kind friends," said he, in a low voice, but which was audible to a great distance, "it has been my fortune to have received at different times of my life gratifying assurances of sympathy and respect, but never in the whole course of a very varied career do I remember an occasion so deeply gratifying to my feelings as the present. (Cheers, that lasted ten minutes and more.) It is not," resumed he, with more energy, — "it is not at a moment like this, surrounded by brave and warm hearts, when the sentiments of affection that sway *you* are mingled with the emotions of my own breast, that I would take a dark or gloomy view of human nature, but truth compels me to say that the attack made this day upon my credit — for *I* am the Ossory Bank — (loud and wild cheering) — yes, I repeat it, for the stability of this institution *I* am responsible by all I possess in this world. Every share, every guinea, every acre I own are here! Far from me to impute ungenerous or unworthy motives to any quarter; but, my worthy friends, there has been foul play — (groans) — there has been treachery — (deeper groans) — and my name is not Davenport Dunn but it shall be exposed and punished. (Cries of "More power to ye," and hearty cheers, greeted this solemn assurance.)

"I am, as you are well aware, and I glory in declaring it, one of yourselves. (Here the enthusiasm was tremendous.) By moderate abilities, hard work, and unflinching honesty — for that is the great secret — I have become that you see me to-day! (Loud cheering.) If there be amongst you any who aspire to my position, I tell him that nothing is easier than to attain it. I was a poor scholar — you know what a poor scholar is — when the generous nobleman you see now at my side first noticed me. (Three cheers for the Lord were proposed and given most heartily.) His generous patronage gave me my first impulse in life. I soon learned how to do the rest. ("That ye did;" "More power and success to ye," here ran through the mob.) Now, it was at the table of that noble Lord — enjoying the first real holiday in thirty years of toil — that I received a telegraphic despatch, informing me there would be a run for gold upon this Bank before the week was over. I vow to you I did not believe it. I spurned the tidings as a base calumny upon the people, and as I handed the despatch to his Lordship to read, I said, 'If this be possible — and I doubt it much — it is the treacherous intrigue of an enemy, not the spontaneous movement of the public.' (Here Lord Glengariff bowed an acquiescence to the statement, a condescension on his part that speedily called for three vociferous cheers for "the Lord," once more.)

"I am no lawyer," resumed Dunn, with vigor,—"I am a plain man of the people, whose head was never made for subtleties; but this I tell you, that if it be competent for me to offer a reward for the discovery of those who have hatched this conspiracy, my first care will be on my return to Dublin to propose ten thousand pounds for such information as may establish their guilt! (Cheering for a long time followed these words.) They knew that they could not break the Bank,—in their hearts they knew that our solvency was as complete as that of the Bank of England itself,—but they thought that by a panic, and by exciting popular feeling against me, I, in my pride of heart and my conscious honesty, might be driven to some indignant reaction; that I might turn round and say, Is this the country I have slaved for? Are these the people for whose cause I have neglected personal advancement, and disregarded the flatteries of the great? Are these the rewards of days of labor and nights of anxiety and fatigue?"

They fancied, possibly, that, goaded by what I might have construed into black ingratitude, I would say, like Coriolanus, 'I banish you!' But they little knew either you or me, my warm-hearted friends! (Deafening cheers.) They little knew that the well-grounded confidence of a nation cannot be obliterated by the excitement of a moment. A panic in the commercial, like a thunder-storm in the physical world, only leaves the atmosphere lighter, and the air fresher than before; and so I say to you, we shall all breathe more freely when we rise to-morrow,—no longer to see the dark clouds overhead, nor hear the rumbling sounds that betoken coming storm.

"I have detained you too long. ("No, no!" vociferously broke forth.) I have spoken also too much about myself. ("Not a bit; we could listen to ye till mornin'," shouted a wild voice, that drew down hearty laughter.) But, before I go, I wish to say, that, hard pressed as we are in the Bank—sorely inconvenienced by the demands upon us—I am yet able to ask your excellent Mayor to accept of five hundred pounds from me for the poor of this city— (what a yell followed this announcement! plainly indicating what a personal interest the tidings seemed to create)—and to add—(loud cheers)—and to add—(more cheers)—and to add," cried he, in his deepest voice, "that the first toast I will drink this day shall be, The Boys of Kilkenny!"

It is but justice to add that Mr. Dunn's speech was of that class of oratory that "hears" better than it reads, while his audience was also less critically disposed than may be our valued reader. At all events, it achieved a great success; and within an hour after its delivery hawkers cried through the streets of the city, "The Full and True Account of the Run for Gold, with Mr. Dunn's Speech to the People;" and, sooth to say, that though the paper was not "cream laid," and though many of the letters were upside down, the literature had its admirers, and was largely read. Later on, the city was illuminated, two immense letters of D. D. figuring in colored lamps in front of the town-hall, while copious libations of whiskey-punch were poured forth in honor of the Man of the People. In every rank and class, from the country gentleman who dined at the club-house, to the smallest chop-house in John Street, there was but one sentiment,—that Dunn was a fine fellow, and his enemies downright scoundrels. If a few of nicer taste and more correct feeling were not exactly pleased with his speech, they wisely kept their opinions to themselves, and let "the Ayes have it," who pronounced it to be manly, above-board, modest, and so forth.

Throughout the entire evening Mr. Hankes was everywhere, personally or through his agents; his care was to collect public sentiment, to ascertain what popular opinion thought of the whole events of the morning, and to promote, so far as he could with safety, the flattering estimate already formed of his chief. Scarcely half an hour elapsed without Dunn's receiving from his indefatigable lieutenant some small scrap of paper, with a few words hastily scrawled in this fashion:—

"Rice and Walsh's, Nine o'clock.—Company in the coffee-room enthusiastic; talk of a public dinner; some propose portrait in town-hall."

"A quarter to Ten, Judy's, Rose Inn Street.—Comic song, with a chorus:—

"*'If for gold ye run,*
Says the Shan van Voght;
If for gold ye run,
I'll send for Davy Dunn,
He's the boy to show ye fun,
Says the Shan van Voght!'"

"Eleven o'clock, High Street.—Met the Dean, who says, 'D. D. is an honor to us; we are all proud of him.' The county your own when you want it."

"Twelve o'clock.—If any one should venture to ask for gold to-morrow, he will be torn to pieces by the mob."

Assuredly it was a triumph; and every time that the wild cheers from the crowds in the street broke in upon the converse in the drawing-room,

Lady Augusta's eyes would sparkle as she said, "I don't wonder at your feeling proud of it all!"

And he *did* feel proud of it. Strange as it may seem, he was as proud as though the popularity had been earned by the noblest actions and the most generous devotion. We are not going to say why or wherefore this. And now for a season we take our leave of him to follow the fortunes of some others whose fate we seem to have forgotten. We have the less scruple for deserting Davenport Dunn at this moment, that we leave him happy, prospering, and in good company.

CHAPTER III
A NOTE FROM DAVIS

Am I asking too much of my esteemed reader, if I beg of him to remember where and how I last left the Honorable Annesley Beecher? for it is to that hopeful individual and his fortunes I am now about to return.

If it be wearisome to the reader to have his attention suddenly drawn from the topic before him, and his interest solicited for those he has well-nigh forgotten, let me add that it is almost as bad for the writer, who is obliged to hasten hither and thither, and, like a huntsman with a straggling pack, to urge on the tardy, correct the loiterer, and repress the eager.

When we parted with Annesley Beecher, he was in sore trouble and anxiety of mind; a conviction was on him that he was "squared," "nobbled," "crossed," "potted," or something to the like intent and with a like euphonious designation. "The Count and Spicer were conspiring to put him in a hole!" As if any "hole" could be as dark, as hopeless, and as deep as the dreary pitfall of his own helpless nature!

His only resource seemed flight; to break cover at once and run for it, appeared the solitary solution of the difficulty. There was many a spot in the map of Europe which offered a sanctuary against Grog Davis. But what if Grog were to set the law in motion, where should he seek refuge then? Some one had once mentioned to him a country with which no treaty connected us with regard to criminals. It began, if he remembered aright, with an S; was it Sardinia or Sweden or Spain or Sicily or Switzerland? It was surely one of them, but which? "What a mass of rubbish, to be sure," thought he, "they crammed me with at Rugby, but not one solitary particle of what one could call useful learning! See now, for instance, what benefit a bit of geography might be to me!" And he rambled on in his mind, concocting an educational scheme which would really fit a man for the wear and tear of life.

It was thus reflecting he entered the inn and mounted to his room; his clothes lay scattered about, drawers were crammed with his wearables, and the table covered with a toilet equipage, costly, and not yet paid for. Who was to pack all these? Who was to make up that one portmanteau which would suffice for flight, including all the indispensable and rejecting the superfluous? There is a case recorded of a Frenchman who was diverted from his resolve on suicide by discovering that his pistols were not loaded, and, incredible as it may seem, Beecher was deterred from his journey by the thought of how he was to pack his trunk; He had never done so much for himself since he was born, and he did n't think he could do it; at all events, he wasn't going to try. Certain superstitious people are impressed with the notion that making a will is a sure prelude to dying; so others there are who fancy that, by the least effort on their own behalf, they are forecasting a state of poverty in which they must actually work for subsistence.

How hopelessly, then, did he turn over costly waistcoats and embroidered shirts, gaze on richly cut and crested essence-bottles and boot-boxes, whose complexity resembled mathematical instruments! In what manner they were ever conveyed so far he could not imagine. The room seemed actually filled with them. It was Rivers had "put them up;" but Rivers could no longer be trusted, for he was evidently in the "lay" against him.

He sighed heavily at this: it was a dreary, hopeless sigh over the depravity of the world and mankind in general. "And what a paradise it might be," he thought, "if people would only let themselves be cheated quietly and peaceably, neither threatening with their solicitors, nor menacing with the police. Heaven knew how little he asked for: a safe thing now and then on the Derby, a good book on the Oaks; he wanted no more! He bore no malice nor ill-will to any man breathing; he never wished to push any fellow to the wall. If ever there was a generous heart, it beat in *his* bosom; and if the world only knew the provocation he had received! No matter, he would never retaliate,—he 'd die game, be a brick to the last;" and twenty other fine things of the same sort that actually brought the tears to his own eyes over his own goodness.

Goodness, however, will not pack a trunk, nor will moral qualities, however transcendent, fold cravats and dress-coats, and he looked very despondently around him, and thought over what he half fancied was the only thing he could n't do. So accustomed had he been of late to seek Lizzy Davis's counsel in every moment of difficulty, that actually, without knowing it, he descended now to the drawing-room, some vague, undefined feeling impelling him to be near her.

She was singing at the piano, all alone, as he entered; the room, as usual, brilliantly lighted up as if to receive company, rare flowers and rich plants grouped tastefully about, and "Daisy"—for she looked that name on this occasion—in one of those charming "toilettes" whose consummate skill it is to make the most costly articles harmonize into something that seems simplicity itself. She wore a fuchsia in her hair, and another—only this last was of coral and gold elaborately and beautifully designed—on the front of her dress, and, except these, nothing more of ornament.

"Tutore mio," said she, gayly, as he entered, "you have treated me shamefully; for, first of all, you were engaged to drive with me to the Kreutz Berg, and, secondly, to take me to the opera, and now, at half-past nine, you make your appearance. How is this, Monsieur? *Expliquez-vous.*"

"Shall I tell the truth?" said he.

"By all means, if anything so strange should n't embarrass you."

"Well, then, I forgot all about both the drive and the opera. It's all very well to laugh," said he, in a tone of half pique; "young ladies, with no weightier cares on their hearts than whether they ought to wear lilac or green, have very little notion of a man's anxieties. They fancy that life is a thing of white and red roses, soft music and bouquets; but it ain't."

"Indeed! are you quite sure?" asked she, with an air of extreme innocence.

"I suspect I am," said he, confidently; "and there's not many a man about town knows more of it than I do."

"And now, what may be the cares, or, rather, for I don't want to be curious, what sort of cares are they that oppress that dear brain? Have you got any wonderful scheme for the amelioration of mankind to which you see obstacles? Are your views in politics obstructed by ignorance or prejudice? Have you grand notions about art for which the age is not ripe; or are you actually the author of a wonderful poem that nobody has had taste enough to appreciate?"

"And these are your ideas of mighty anxieties, Miss Lizzy?" said he, in a tone of compassionate pity. "By Jove! how I'd like to have nothing heavier on my heart than the whole load of them."

"I think you have already told me you never were crossed in love?"

"Well, nothing serious, you know. A scratch or so, as one may say, getting through the bushes, but never a cropper,—nothing like a regular smash."

"It would seem to me, then, that you have enjoyed a singularly fortunate existence, and been just as lucky in life as myself."

Beecher started at the words. What a strange chaos did they create within him! There is no tracing the thoughts that came and went, and lost themselves in that poor bewildered head. The nearest to anything like, consistency was the astonishment he felt that she—Grog Davis's daughter—should ever imagine she had drawn a prize in the world's lottery.

"Yes, Mr. Beecher," said she, with the ready tact with which she often read his thoughts and answered them, "even so. I do think myself very, very fortunate! And why should I not? I have excellent health, capital spirits, fair abilities, and, bating an occasional outbreak of anger, a reasonably good temper. As regards personal traits, Mr. Annesley Beecher once called me beautiful; Count Lienstahl would say something twice as rapturous; at all events, quite good-looking enough not to raise antipathies against me at first sight; and lastly, but worth all the rest, I have an intense enjoyment in mere existence; the words 'I live' are to me, 'I am happy.' The alternations of life, its little incidents and adventures, its passing difficulties, are, like the changeful aspects of the seasons, full of interest, full of suggestiveness, calling out qualities of mind and resources of temperament that in the cloudless skies of unbroken prosperity might have lain unused and unknown. And now, sir, no more sneers at my fancied good fortune; for, whatever *you* may say, I feel it to be real."

There was that in her manner—a blended energy and grace—which went far deeper into Beecher's heart than her mere words, and he gazed at her slightly flushed cheek and flashing eyes with something very nearly rapture; and he muttered to himself, "There she is, a half-bred 'un, and no training, and able to beat them all!"

This time, at all events, she did not read his thoughts; as little, perhaps, did she care to speculate about them. "By the by," said she, suddenly approaching the chimney and taking up a letter, "this has arrived here, by private hand, since you went out, and it has a half-look of papa's writing, and is addressed to you."

Beecher took it eagerly. With a glance he recognized it as from Grog, when that gentleman desired to disguise his hand.

"Am I correct?" asked she, "am I correct in my guess?"

He was too deep in the letter to make her any reply. Its contents were as follows:—

> "Dear B.,—They 've kicked up such a row about that affair
> at Brussels that I have been obliged to lie dark for the last
> fortnight, and in a confoundedly stupid hole on the right
> bank of the Rhine. I sent over Spicer to meet the Baron,
> and take Klepper over to Nimroeguen and Magdeburg, and
> some other small places in Prussia. They can pick up in

this way a few thousand florins, and keep the mill going. I gave him strict orders not to see my daughter, who must know nothing whatever of these or any like doings. The Baron she might see, for he knows life thoroughly, and if he is not a man of high honor, he can assume the part so well that it comes pretty much to the same thing. As to yourself, you will, on receipt of this, call on a certain Lazarus Stein, Juden Gasse, Nov 41 or 42, and give him your acceptance for two thousand gulden, with which settle your hotel bill, and come on to Bonn, where, at the post-office, you will find a note, with my address. Tramp, you see, has won the Cotteswold, as I prophesied, and 'Leo the Tenth' nowhere. Cranberry must have got his soup pretty hot, for he has come abroad, and his wife and the children gone down to Scotland. As to your own affairs, Ford says you are better out of the way; and if anything is to be done in the way of compromise, it must be while you are abroad. He does not think Strich can get the rule, and you must n't distress yourself for an extra outlawry or two. There will be some trouble about the jewels, but I think even that matter may be arranged also. I hope you keep from the tables, and I look for a strict reckoning as to your expenses, and a stricter book up as regards your care of my daughter. 'All square' is the word between pal and pal, and there never was born the man did n't find that to be his best policy when he dealt with

"Your friend,

"Christopher Davis.

"To while away the time in this dreary dog-hole, I have been sketching out a little plan of a martingale for the roulette-table. There's only one zero at Homburg, and we can try it there as we go up. There's a flaw in it after the twelfth 'pass,' but I don't despair of getting over the difficulty. Old Stein, the money-changer, was upwards of thirty years croupier at the Cursaal, and get him to tell you the average runs, black and red, at rouge-et-noir, and what are the signs of an intermitting game; and also the six longest runs he has ever known. He is a shrewd fellow, and seeing that you come from me will be confidential.

"There has been another fight in the Crimea, and somebody well licked. I had nothing on the match, and don't care a brass farthing who claimed the stakes.

"Tell Lizey that I 'm longing to see her, and if I didn't write it is because I 'm keeping everything to tell her when we meet. If it was n't for her picture, I don't know what would have become of me since last Tuesday, when the rain set in."

Beecher re-read the letter from the beginning; nor was it an easy matter for him to master at once all the topics it included. Of himself and his own affairs the information was vague and unsatisfactory; but Grog knew how to keep him always in suspense,—to make him ever feel that he was swimming for his life, and he himself the only "spar" he could catch at.

"Bring me to book about my care of his daughter!" muttered he, over and over, "just as if she was n't the girl to take care of herself. Egad! he seems to know precious little about her. I 'd give a 'nap' to show her this letter, and just hear what she 'd say of it all. I suppose she 'd split on me. She 'd go and tell Davis, 'Beecher has put me up to the whole "rig;"' and if she did—What would happen then?" asked he, replying to the low, plaintive whistle which concluded his meditation. "Eh—what! did I say anything?" cried he, in terror.

"Not a syllable. But I could see that you had conjured up some difficulty which you were utterly unable to deal with."

"Well, here it is," said he, boldly. "This letter is from your father. It's all full of private details, of which you know nothing, nor would you care to hear; but there is one passage—just one—that I'd greatly like to have your opinion upon. At the same time I tell you, frankly, I have no warranty from your father to let you see it; nay, the odds are he 'd pull me up pretty sharp for doing so without his authority."

"That's quite enough, Mr. Beecher, about *your* scruples. Now, *mine* go a little further still; for they would make me refuse to learn anything which my father's reserve had kept from me. It is a very easy rule of conscience, and neither hard to remember nor to follow."

"At all events, he meant this for your own eye," said Beecher, showing her the last few lines of the letter.

She read them calmly over; a slight trembling of the lip—so slight that it seemed rather like a play of light over her face—was the only sign of emotion visible, and then, carefully folding the letter, she gave it back, saying, "Yes, I had a right to see these lines."

"He *is* fond of you, and proud of you, too," said Beecher. A very slight nod of her head gave an assent to his remark, and she was silent. "We are to leave this at once," continued he, "and move on to Bonn, where we shall find a letter with your father's address, somewhere, I take it, in that neighborhood." He waited, hoping she would say something, but she did not speak. And then he went on:

"And then you will be once more at home,—emancipated from this tiresome guardianship of mine."

"Why tiresome?" asked she, suddenly.

"Oh, by Jove! I know I'm very slow sort of fellow as a ladies' man; have none of the small talents of those foreigners; couldn't tell Mozart from Verdi; nor, though I can see when a woman is well togged, could I tell you the exact name of any one part of her dress."

"If you really did know all these, and talked of them, I might have found you very tiresome," said she, in that half-careless voice she used when seeming to think aloud. "And you," asked she, suddenly, as she turned her eyes fully upon him,—"and you, are you to be emancipated then,—are you going to leave us?"

"As to that," replied he, in deep embarrassment, "there 'a a sort of hitch in it I ought, if I did the right thing, to be on my way to Italy now, to see Lackington,—my brother, I mean. I came abroad for that; but Gr—your father, I should say—induced me to join *him*, and so, with one thing and the other, here I am, and that's really all I know about it."

"What a droll way to go through life!" said she, with one of her low, soft laughs.

"If you mean that I have n't a will of my own, you 're all wrong," said he, in some irritation. "Put me straight at my fence, and see if I won't take it. Just say, 'A. B., there's the winning-post,' and mark whether I won't get my speed up."

What a strange glance was that which answered this speech! It implied no assent; as little did it mean the reverse. It was rather the look of one who, out of a maze of tangled fancies, suddenly felt recalled to life and its real interests. To poor Beecher's apprehension it simply seemed a sort of half-compassionate pity, and it made his cheek tingle with wounded pride.

"I know," muttered he to himself, "that she thinks me a confounded fool; but I ain't. Many a fellow in the ring made that mistake, and burned his fingers for it after."

"Well," said she, after a moment or so of thought, "I am ready; at least, I shall be ready very soon. I 'll tell Annette to pack up and prepare for the road."

"I wish I could get you to have some better opinion of me, Miss Lizzy," said he, seriously. "I'd give more than I 'd like to say, that you 'd—you 'd—"

"That I'd what?" asked she, calmly.

"That you 'd not set me down as a regular flat," said he, with energy.

"I 'm not very certain that I know what that means; but I will tell you that I think you very good tempered, very gentle-natured, and very tolerant of fifty-and-one caprices which must be all the more wearisome because unintelligible. And then, you are a very fine gentleman, and—the Honor-Able Annesley Beecher." And holding out her dress in minuet fashion, she courtesied deeply, and left the room.

"I wish any one would tell me whether I stand to win or not by that book," exclaimed Beecher, as he stood there alone, nonplussed and confounded. "Would n't she make a stunning actress! By Jove! Webster would give her a hundred a week, and a free benefit!" And with this he went off into a little mental arithmetic, at the end of which he muttered to himself, "And that does not include starring it in the provinces!"

With the air of a man whose worldly affairs went well, he arranged his hair before the glass, put on his hat, gave himself a familiar nod, and went out.

CHAPTER IV
LAZARUS, STEIN, GELDWECHSLER

The Juden Gasse, in which Beecher was to find out the residence of Lazarus Stein, was a long, straggling street, beginning in the town and ending in the suburb, where it seemed as it were to lose itself. It was not till after a long and patient search that Beecher discovered a small door in an old ivy-covered wall, on which, in irregular letters, faint and almost illegible, stood the words, "Stein, Geldwechsler."

As he rang stoutly at the bell, the door opened, apparently of itself, and admitted him into a large and handsome garden. The walks were flanked by fruit-trees in espalier, with broad borders of rich flowers at either side; and although the centre spaces were given up to the uses of a kitchen garden, the larger beds, rich in all the colors of the tulip and ranunculus, showed how predominant was the taste for flowers over mere utility. Up one alley, and down another, did Beecher saunter without meeting any one, or seeing what might mean a habitation; when, at length, in a little copse of palm-trees, he caught sight of a smalt diamond-paned window, approaching which, he found himself in front of a cottage whose diminutive size he had never seen equalled, save on the stage. Indeed, in its wooden framework, gaudily painted, its quaint carvings, and its bamboo roof, it was the very type of what one sees in a comic opera. One sash of the little window lay open, and showed Beecher the figure of a very small old man, who, in a long dressing-gown of red-brown stuff, and a fez cap, was seated at a table, writing. A wooden tray in front of him was filled with dollars and gold pieces in long stately columns, and a heap of bank-notes lay pressed under a heavy leaden slab at his side. No sooner had Beecher's figure darkened the window than the old man looked up and came out to meet him, and, taking off his cap with a deep reverence, invited him to enter. If the size of the chamber, and its curious walls covered over with cabinet pictures, might have attracted Beecher's attention at another moment, all his wonderment, now, was for the little man himself, whose piercing black eyes, long beard, and hooked nose gave him an air of almost unearthly meaning.

"I suppose I have the honor to speak to Mr. Stein?" said he, in English, "and that he can understand me in my own tongue?"

"Yaas,—go on," said the old man.

"I was told to call upon you by Captain Davis; he gave me your address."

"Ah, der Davis—der Davis—a vaary goot man—my vaary dear friend. You are der rich Englander that do travel wit him,—eh?"

"I am travelling with him just now," said Beecher, laughing slightly; "but as to being rich,—why, we 'll not dispute about it."

"Yaas, here is his letter. He says, Milord will call on you hisself, and so I hold myself—how you say 'bereit?'—ready—hold myself ready to see you. I have de honor to make you very mush welcome to my poor house."

Beecher thanked him courteously, and, producing Davis's letter, mentioned the amount for which he desired to draw.

The old man examined the writing, the signature, and then the seal, handing the document back when he had finished, muttering to himself, "Ah, der Davis—der Davis!"

"You know my friend very intimately, I believe?" asked Beecher.

"I belief I do,—I belief I do," said he, with a low chuckle to himself.

"So he mentioned to me and added one or two little matters on which I was to ask you for some information. But first this bill,—you can let me have these two thousand florins?"

"And what do he do now, der Davis?" asked the Jew, not heeding the question.

"Well, I suppose he rubs on pretty much the same as ever," said Beecher, in some confusion.

"Yaas—yaas—he rub on—and he rub off, too, sometimes—ha! ha! ha!" laughed out the old man, with a fiendish cackle. "Ach, der Davis!"

Without knowing in what sense to take the words, Beecher did not exactly like them; and as little was he pleased with that singular recurrence to "der Davis," and the little sigh that followed. He was growing impatient, besides, to get his money, and again reverted to the question.

"He look well? I hope he have de goot gesundheit—what you call it?"

"To be sure he does; nothing ever ails him. I never heard him complain of as much as a headache.

"Ach, der Davis, der Davis!" said the old man, shaking his head.

Seeing no chance of success by his direct advances, Beecher thought he 'd try a little flank attack by inducing a short conversation, and so he said,

"I am on my way to Davis, now, with his daughter, whom he left in my charge."

"Whose daughter?" asked the Jew.

"Davis's,—a young lady that was educated at Brussels."

"He have no daughter. Der Davis have no daughter."

"Has n't he, though? Just come over to the 'Four Nations,' and I 'll show her to you. And such a stunning girl too!"

"No, no, I never belief it—never; he did never speak to me of a daughter."

"Whether he did or not—there she is, that's all I know."

The Jew shook his head, and sought refuge in his former muttering of "Ach, der Davis!"

"As far as not telling you about his daughter, I can say he never told me, and I fancy we were about as intimate as most people; but the fact is as I tell you."

Another sigh was all his answer, and Beecher was fast reaching the limit of his patience.

"Daughter, or no daughter, I want a matter of a couple of thousand florins,—no objection to a trifle more, of course,—and wish to know how you can let me have them."

"The Margraf was here two week ago, and he say to me, 'Lazarus,' say he,—'Lazarus, where is your goot friend Davis?' 'Highness,' say I, 'dat I know not.' Den he say, 'I will find him, if I go to Jerusalem;' and I say, 'Go to Jerusalem.'"

"What did he want with him?"

"What he want?—what every one want, and what nobody get, except how he no like—ha! ha! ha! Ach, der Davis!"

Beecher rose from his seat, uncertain how to take this continued inattention to his demand. He stood for a moment in hesitation, his eyes wandering over the walls where the pictures were hanging.

"Ah! if you do care for art, now you suit yourself, and all for a noting! I sell all dese,—dat Gerard Dow, dese two Potters, de leetle Cuyp,—a veritable treasure, and de Mieris,—de best he ever painted, and de rest, wit de land-schaft of Both, for eighty tousand seven hundred florins. It is a schenk—a gift away—noting else."

"You forget, my excellent friend Stein," said Beecher, with more assurance than he had yet assumed, "that it was to receive and not spend money I came here this morning."

"You do a leetle of all de two—a leetle of both, so to say," replied the Jew. "What moneys you want?"

"Come, this is speaking reasonably. Davis's letter mentions a couple of thousand florins; but if you are inclined to stretch the amount to five, or even four thousand, we 'll not fall out about the terms."

"How you mean—no fall out about de terms?" said the other, sharply.

"I meant that for a stray figure or so, in the way of discount, we should n't disagree. You may, in fact, make your own bargain."

"Make my own bargain, and pay myself too," muttered the Jew. "Ach, der Davis, how he would laugh!—ha! ha! ha!"

"Well, I don't see much to laugh at, old gent, except it be at my own folly, to stand here so long chaffering about these paltry two thousand florins. And now I say, 'Yea or nay, will you book up, or not?'"

"Will you buy de Cuyp and de Wouvermans and de Ostade?—dat is the question."

"Egad, if you furnish the ready, I 'll buy the Cathedral and the Cursaal. I 'm not particular as to the investment when the cash is easily come at."

"De cash is very easy to come at," said the Jew, with a strange grin.

"You 're a trump, Lazarus!" cried Beecher, in ecstasy at his good fortune. "If I had known you some ten years ago, I 'd have been another man to-day. I was always looking out for one really fair, honester-hearted fellow to deal with, but I never met with him till now."

"How you have it,—gold or notes?" said Lazarus.

"Well, a little of both, I think," said Beecher, his eyes greedily devouring the glittering little columns of gold before him.

"How your title?—how your name?" asked Stein, taking up a pen.

"My name is Annesley Beecher. You may write me the 'Honorable Annesley Beecher.'"

"Lord of—"

"I 'm not Lord of anything. I'm next in succession to a peerage, that's all."

"He call you de Viscount—I forget de name."

"Lackington, perhaps?"

"Yaas, dat is de name; and say, give him de moneys for his bill. Now, here is de acceptance, and here you put your sign, across dis."

"I 'll write Annesley Beecher, with all my heart; but I 'll not write myself Lackington."

"Den you no have de moneys, nor de Cuyp, nor de Ostade," said the Jew, replacing the pen in the ink-bottle.

"Just let me ask you, old boy, how would it benefit you that I should commit a forgery? Is that the way you like to do business?"

"I do know myself how I like my business to do, and no man teach me."

"What the devil did Davis mean, then, by sending me on this fool's errand? He gave me a distinct intimation that you 'd cash my acceptance—"

"Am I not ready? You never go and say to der Davis dat I refuse it! Ah, der Davis!" and he sighed as if from the very bottom of his heart.

"I'll tell him, frankly, that you made it a condition I was to sign a name that does not belong to me,—*that* I 'll tell him."

"What care he for dat? Der Davis write his own name on it and pay it hisself."

"Oh! and Davis was also to indorse this bill, was he?" asked Beecher.

"I should tink he do; oderwise I scarce give you de moneys."

"That, indeed, makes some difference. Not, in reality, that it would n't be just as much a forgery; but if the bill come back to Grog's own hands—"

"Ach, der Grog,—ha! ha! ha! 'Tis so long dat I no hear de name,—Grog Davis!" and the Jew laughed till his eyes ran over.

"If there's no other way of getting at this money—"

"Dere is no oder way," said Lazarus, in a tone of firmness..

"Then good-morning, friend Lazarus, for you 'll not catch me spoiling a stamp at that price. No, no, old fellow. I 'm up to a thing or two, though you don't suspect it. I only rise to the natural fly, and no mistake."

"I make no mistake; I take vaary goot care of dat," said Lazarus, rising, and taking off his fez, to say adieu. "I wish you de vaary goot day."

Beecher turned away, with a stiff salutation, into the garden. He was angry with Davis, with himself, and with the whole world. It was a rare event in his life to see gold so much within his reach and yet not available, just for a scruple—a mere scruple—for, after all, what was it else? Writing "Lackington" meant nothing, if Lack-ington were never to see, much less to pay the bill. Once "taken up," as it was sure to be by Grog, what signified it if the words across the acceptance were Lackington or Annesley Beecher? And yet, what could Davis mean by passing him off as the Viscount? Surely, for such a paltry sum as a couple of thousand florins, it was not necessary to assume his brother's name and title. It was some "dodge," perhaps, to acquire consequence in the eyes of his friend Lazarus that he was the travelling-companion of an English peer; and yet, if so, it was the very first time Beecher had known him yield to such a weakness. He *had* a meaning in it, that much was certain, for Grog made no move in the game of life without a plan! "It can't be," muttered Beecher to himself, — "it can't be for the sake of any menace over me for the forgery, because he has already in his hands quite enough to push me to the wall on that score, as he takes care to remind me he might any fine morning have me 'up' on that charge." The more Beecher ruminated over what possible intention Davis might have in view, the more did he grow terrified, lest, by any short-comings on his own part, he might thwart the great plans of his deep colleague.

"I never met his equal yet to put a fellow in a cleft stick," muttered Beecher, as he walked to and fro in intense agitation, "and he's just the man also, whenever anything goes wrong, not to listen to a word of explanation. 'Why didn't you do as I bade you?' or, 'As I ordered you?' for that's his phrase generally. 'Who told *you* that you had any option in the matter? Did *I* take you into consultation? Play up to *my* hand!' that's his cry. 'Play up to *my* hand, and never mind your own!' Well, I have been doing so some ten or twelve years back, and a nice game I've made of it! Break with him! — of course I'd break with him, if any one would tell me how! Egad, sometimes I begin to think that transportation and the rest of it would not be a bit harder to bear than old Grog's tyranny! It wears one out, — it positively drains a man's nature dry!" There are volcanic throes, that, however they may work and struggle, throw up no lava; so with Beecher. All his passionate indignation could not rouse him to action, although his actual suffering might have prompted energy to any amount. He took out Davis's letter and re-read it. One line which had escaped his attention before, now caught his eye on the blank leaf. It ran thus: "Take care that you do not delay at Aix after receipt of this. Benson's fellows are after you." A cold shudder came over Beecher as he perused the line. Benson's fellows meant bailiffs, detectives, or something of the like. Benson was a money-lender of the most inveterate villany, — a fellow who had pursued more men of station and condition than any one living. He was the terror of the "swells." To be in Benson's hands meant ruin in its most irretrievable shape; and at the very moment he stood there his minions were on his track!

Ere he was well aware of it, he was back at the little window of the cottage.

"I must have this money on your own terms, Stein," said he. "I find that Davis has some urgent need of my presence. I can't delay here another day."

"How many tousend gulden, milord?" asked the Jew respectfully, as he dipped his pen in the ink-bottle.

"Davis says two—I should like to say four, or even five."

"Five if you wish it, milord; to me is it all as one—five, fifteen, or fifty; whatever sum you want."

Beecher put his hand on the other's wrist to detain him while he took a moment's counsel with himself. Never had such a golden opportunity as this presented itself. Never before had he seen the man who so generously proffered his services. It was ask and have. Was he to reject such good fortune?—was he to turn his back on the very first piece of luck that had ever befallen him? What heartburnings might he be storing up for future years when he looked back to the time that, with a word, he might have made his fortune!

"But are you quite sure, friend Lazarus, that if I say eight or ten thousand,—for I don't want more,—Davis will be as willing to back the bill?"

"I am quite sure."

"Well, now, I am not so very certain of that; and as it is Davis will have to book up, it might be safer, perhaps, that I did n't go beyond the amount he mentions,—eh?"

"As you will,—as you please yourself. I only say, dere is der Herr Davis's name; he send it to me and say, 'Milord will do de rest.'"

"So that he sent you a blank acceptance?" cried Beecher, in amazement.

"Yaas, Just as you see,—'Christopher Davis,' and de flourish as usual. Ach, der Davis!" and he sighed once more.

The man who held Grog's signature on a blank stamp assumed no common shape in Annesley Beecher's eyes, and he continued to gaze on the old man with a strange sense of awe and astonishment. If he had not the document there before him on the table, he would not have believed it. The trustful courage of Van Amburgh, who used to place his head in the lion's mouth, seemed poor in comparison with such heroic boldness as this; and he gazed at the writing in a sort of fascination.

"And Grog actually sent you that over by letter?" asked he again.

"Yaas, as you see," was the calm answer.

"Well, here goes then, Abraham—Lazarus, I mean; make it out for a matter of—five—no, eight—hang it, let as say ten thousand florins when we are about it! Ten thousand, at six months,—eh?"

"Better at tree months,—we can always renew," said Stein, calmly.

"Of course; and by that time we may want a little more liquor in the decanter,—eh! old boy?" said Beecher, laughing joyfully.

"To be sure, vaary mush more liquor as you want it."

"What a brick!" said Beecher, clapping him on the shoulder in all the ecstasy of delight.

"Dere!" said the Jew, as he finished writing, "all is done; only to say where it be paid,—what bank at London."

"Well, that is a bit of a puzzle, I must own!" said Beecher, rubbing his chin with an air of doubt and hesitation.

"Where do de Lord Lackington keep his account?" asked the Jew; and the question was so artfully posed that Beecher Answered promptly,—

"Harmer and Gore's, Lombard Street, or Pall Mall, whichever you like."

"Hanper and Gore. I know dem vaary well,—that will do; you do sign your name dere."

"I wish I could persuade you that Annesley Beecher would be enough,—eh?"

"You write de name as der Davis say, and no oder!"

"Here goes, then! 'In for a penny,' as the proverb says," muttered he; and in a bold, dashing hand, wrote "Lackington" across the bill.

"Ah!" said the Jew, as he examined it with his glass, and scanned every letter over and over; "and now, vat you say for de Cuyp, and de Mieris, and de Ostade,—vill you take 'era all, as I say?"

"I 'll think over it,—I 'll reflect a bit first, Master Stein. As for pictures, they 're rather an encumbrance when a man has n't a house to hang them in."

"You have de vaary fine house in town, and an oder vaary fine house in de country, beside a what you call box—shoot-box—"

"Nothing of the kind, Lazarus. I haven't a thing as big as the crib we are standing in. Your mind is always running upon my brother; but there's a wide difference between our fortunes, I assure you. He drew the first ticket in the lottery of life; and, by the way, that reminds me of something in Grog's letter that I was to ask you." And Beecher took the epistle from his pocket and ran his eye over it. "Ah! here it is! 'Ask Stein what are the average runs at rouge-et-noir, what are the signs of an intermitting game, and what are the longest runs he remembers on one color?' Can you answer me these?"

"Some of dem I have here," said Stein, taking down from a shelf a small vellum-bound volume, fastened with a padlock and chain, the key of which he wore attached to his watch. "Here is de grand 'arcanum,'" said he, laughing; "here are de calculs made in de experience of forty-one year! Where is de man in Europe can say as mush as dat? In dis book is recounted de great game of de Duc de Brancas, where he broke de bank every night of de week till Saturday,—two million tree hundred tousand francs! Caumartin, the first croupier, shot hisself, and Nogeot go mad. He reckon de moneys in de casette, for when he say on Friday night, 'Monseigneur,' say he, 'we have not de full sum here,—there's one hundred and seventy tousand francs too little,' de Duc reply, 'Never mind, mon cher Monsieur Nogeot, I am noways pressed,—don't distress yourself,—only let it be pay before I go home to bed.' Nogeot lose his reason when he hear it. Ah! here is de whole 'Greschichte,' and here de table of chances."

Beecher gazed on the precious volume as Aladdin might have done on the lamp. It was the mystic key to untold riches. With that marvellous book a man needed no more in life; there lay all the "cabals," all the "martingales," that years of intense toil and deep study had discovered. To win that knowledge, too, what hearts had been broken, what desolation, what death! It was a record of martyrs in his eyes, and he really regarded it with a sort of rapturous veneration.

Old Lazarus did not fail to detect the expression of wonderment and admiration. He saw depicted there the glowing ecstasy that all the triumphs of high art could not call up. The vigorous energy of Wouvermans, the glowing coloring of Cuyp, the mellow richness of Mieris, had not touched that nature which now vibrated in every chord to the appeal of Fortune. It was the submissive worship of a devotee before some sacred relic! Stein read that gaze, and tracked its every motive; and with a solemn gesture he clasped the volume and locked it.

"But you are surely going to show me—I mean, you are about to tell me the answer to these questions?"

Stein shook his head dubiously, as he said: "Dat is my Kleinod, my idol,—in dat book lie de secret of secrets, and I say to myself, 'Lazarus, be poor, be destitute, be houseless to-morrow, and you know how to get rich if you will.' De great law of Chances—de rule dat guide what we call 'Luck'— dere it is written! I have but to say I will have, and I have! When I die, I will burn it, or have it lay wit me in my grave."

"It's not possible you could do this!" cried Beecher, in horror: far less of indignation had it cost him to hear that any one should carry out of the world with him the cure of cancer, of cholera, or some such dread scourge of poor humanity. The black-hearted selfishness of such a crime seemed without a parallel, and for a second or two, as he looked at the decrepid object before him, and saw the lonely spot, the isolation, and the propitious moment, a strange wild thought flashed across his mind that it might be not only pardonable, but praiseworthy, to seize upon and carry it off by force.

Whether the old man read what was passing within him is hard to say, but he returned the other's look as steadily and as fiercely, and Beecher felt abashed and cowed.

"I' ll tell you what, Stein," said he, after a pause, "I 'll buy that same old volume of yours, just for the curiosity of the thing, and I 'll make you a sporting offer,—I 'll give you ten thousand francs for it!"

A low wailing whistle of utter contempt was all the Jew replied.

"Well, it's a splendid bid, if you come to think of it; for, just suppose it be everything you say—and I own I can't believe it is,—but suppose it were, who is to guarantee the continuance of these great public play-tables? All the Governments of Europe are setting their faces against them,—not a year passes without one or two being closed. This very spring there was a talk of suppressing play at Baden. Who can tell what the first outbreak of fanatic zeal may effect?"

"No, no. So long as men live, dey will do tree tings,—make love, make war, and gamble. When dey give up dese, de world shut up."

There was a truthful force about this Beecher felt could not be gainsaid, and he stood silent and confuted. There was another appeal that he had not tried, and he resolved to neglect nothing that gave even the faintest chance of success. He addressed himself to the Jew's goodness of heart,—to the benevolence that he knew must have its home in his nature. To what end, therefore, should he carry to the grave, or destroy, a secret that might be a blessing to thousands? He depicted, not without knowledge, some of the miseries of the man "forgotten of Fortune,"—the days of fevered anxiety,—the nights of agonizing torture, as, half maddened by his losses, he played wildly, recklessly on,—suicide in all its darkest forms ever present to his aching faculties, while all this time one glance within that little book would save him. And he wound up all by a burst of enthusiastic praise of a man who could thus transmit happiness to generations unborn.

"I never wish to sell dat book. I mean it alway to die wit myself! but if you will give me one tousand pounds, it is yours. If you delay, I will say two tousands."

"Done—I take it. Of course a bill will do—eh?"

"Yaas, I will take a bill,—a bill at tree months. When it is yours, I will tell you dat you are de luckiest man in all Europe. You have dere, in dat leetle volume, all man strive for, fight for, cheat for, die for!"

As he said this, he sat down again at his desk to write the acceptance Beecher was to sign; while the other, withdrawing into the window recess, peered eagerly into the pages of the precious book.

"Mind," said the Jew, "you no let any one see de 'Cabal.' If it be once get abroad, de bank will change de play. You just carry in your head de combinations, and you, go in, and win de millions dat you want at de time."

"Just so," said Beecher, in ecstasy, the very thought of the golden cataract sending a thrill of rapture through him. "I suppose, however, I may show it to Davis?"

"Ach, der Davis, yaas,—der Davis can see it," said the Jew, with a laugh whose significance it were very hard to interpret. "Dere now," said Stein, handing him the pen, "write de name dere as on de oder."

"Still Lackington, I suppose—eh?" asked Beecher.

"Yaas,—just de same," said Stein, gravely.

"'Just as good for a sheep as a lamb,' as the proverb says," muttered Beecher. And he dashed off the name with a reckless flourish. "I 'll tell you one thing, Master Stein," said he, as he buttoned up the magic volume in the breast of his coat, "if this turn out the good dodge you say it is, I 'll behave handsomely to you. I pledge you my word of honor, I'll stand to you for double—treble the sum you have got written there. *You* don't know the fellow you're dealing with,—very few know him, for the matter of that,—but though he has got a smart lesson or two in life, he has good stuff in him still; and *if*—I say *if*, because, of course, all depends on *that*—*if* I can give the bank at Hamburg a spring in the air with the aid of this, I 'll not forget *you*, old boy."

"You make dem all spring in de air!—Ems, Wiesbaden, Baden—all go up togeder!" And the Jew laughed with the glee of a demon.

"Not that I want to hurt any one,—not that I 'd like to squeeze a fellow too hard," broke in Beecher, suddenly, for a quick thrill of superstitious fear—the gambler's innate conscience—shot through him, and made him tremble to think that by a chance word or thought he might disgust the Fortune he would propitiate. "No, no; my motto is, 'Live and let live!' There's room for us all!" And with the utterance of a sentiment he believed so truly generous, he took leave of the Jew, and departed.

CHAPTER V
A VILLAGE NEAR THE RHINE

It was at a little village called Holbach, about fifteen miles from the right bank of the Rhine, Grog Davis had taken up his quarters while awaiting the arrival of his daughter. Near as it was to that great high-road of Europe, scarcely out of earshot of whizzing steamers and screaming trains, the spot was wonderfully secluded and unvisited. A little trout-stream, known to a few, who treasured the secret like fishermen, made the inn resorted to in the months of May and June; but for the rest of the year the "Golden Hook" had few customers, and the landlord almost abdicated his functions till spring came round again. The house, originally intended for a mill, was built over the river itself, so that the indolent angler might actually have fished from the very window. The pine-clad mountains of Nassau enclosed the narrow glen, which straggled irregularly along for miles, now narrowing to a mere strip, now expanding into little plains of fertile meadow-land, with neat cottages and speckled cattle scattered around them. A narrow belt of garden flanked the river, on whose edge a walk of trellised vines was fashioned,—a charming spot in the sultry heat of summer, with its luxuriant shade above and the rippling stream below. Davis had seen the place years before in some hurried Journey; but his retentive mind carried a full memory of the spot, and he soon found that it comprised all he was in search of,—it was easy of access, secret, and cheap.

Only too well pleased to meet with a guest at this dead season of the year, they gave up to him the choicest apartment, and treated him with every solicitude and attention.

His table was supplied well, almost luxuriously; the good wine of Ettleberg given in liberal profusion; the vine alley converted into a pistol gallery for his use; and all for such a sum *per diem* as would not have satisfied a waiter at the Clarendon. But it was the calm seclusion, the perfect isolation that gratified him most. Let him stroll which way he would, he never chanced upon a traveller. It was marvellous, indeed, how such a place could have escaped that prying tribe of ramblers which England each year sends forth to wrangle, dispute, and disparage everything over Europe; and yet here were precisely the very objects they usually sought after,—

beautiful scenery, a picturesque peasantry, and a land romantic in all its traits and traditions.

Not that Grog cared for these: rocks, waterfalls, ruins, leafy groves, or limpid streams made no appeal to *him*, He lived for the life of men, their passions and their ambitions. He knew some people admired this kind of thing, and there were some who were fond of literature; others liked pictures; others, again, fancied old coins. He had no objection. They were, if not very profitable, at least, harmless tastes. All he asked was, not to be the companion of such dreamers. "Give me the fellow that knows life," would he say; and I am afraid that the definition of that same "life" would have included some things scarcely laudable.

If the spot were one to encourage indolence and ease, Davis did not yield to this indulgence. He arose early; walked for health; shot with the pistol for practice; studied his martingale for the play-table; took an hour with the small-sword with an old maître d'armes whom he found in the village; and, without actually devoting himself to it as a task, practised himself in German by means of conversation; and, lastly, he thought deeply and intently over the future. For speculations of this kind he had no mean capacity. If he knew little of the human heart in its higher moods, he understood it well in its shortcomings and its weaknesses; to what temptations a man might yield, when to offer them, and how, were mysteries he had often brooded over. In forecastings of this order, therefore, Davis exercised himself. Strange eventualities, "cases of conscience," that I would fain believe never occurred to you, dear reader, nor to me, arose before him, and he met them manfully.

The world is generous in its admiration of the hard-worked minister, toiling night-long at his desk, receiving and answering his twenty despatches daily, and rising in the House to explain this, refute that, confirm the other, with all the clearness of an orator and all the calmness of a clerk; but, after all, he is but a fly-wheel in that machine of government of which there are some hundred other component parts, all well fitting and proportioned. *Précis* writers and private secretaries cram, colleagues advise him. The routine of official life hedges him in his proper groove; and if not overcome by indolence or affected by zeal, he can scarcely blunder. Not so your man of straits and emergency, your fellow living by his wits, and wresting from the world, that fancies it does not want him, reward and recognition. It is no marvel if a proud three-decker sail round the globe; but very different is our astonishment if a cockboat come safely from the China Seas, or brave the stormy passage round the Cape. Such a craft as this was Grog, his own captain: himself the crew, he had neither owner nor underwriter; and yet, amidst the assembled navies of the world, he would have shown his bunting!

The unbroken calm of his present existence was most favorable to these musings, and left him to plan his campaign in perfect quiet Whether the people of the inn regarded him as a great minister in disgrace come, by hard study, to retrieve a lost position, a man of science deeply immersed in some abstruse problem, or a distinguished author seeking isolation for the free exercise of his imagination, they treated him not only with great respect, but a sort of deference was shown in their studious effort to maintain the silence and stillness around. When he was supposed to be at his studies, not a voice was heard, not a footfall on the stairs. There is no such flattery to your man of scapes and accidents, your thorough adventurer, as that respectful observance that implies he is a person of condition. It is like giving of free will to the highwayman the purse he expected to have a fight for. Davis delighted in these marks of deference, and day by day grew more eager in exacting them.

"I heard some noise outside there this morning, Carl," said he to the waiter; "what was the meaning of it?" For a moment or two the waiter hesitated to explain; but after a little went on to speak of a stranger who had been a resident of the inn for some months back without ever paying his bill; the law, singularly enough, not giving the landlord the power of turning him adrift, but simply of ceasing to afford him sustenance, and waiting for some opportunity of his leaving the house to forbid his re-entering it. Davis was much amused at this curious piece of legislation, by which a moneyless guest could be starved out but not expelled, and put many questions as to the stranger, his age, appearance, and nation. All the waiter knew was that he was a venerable-looking man, portly, advanced in life, with specious manners, a soft voice, and a benevolent smile; as to his country, he could n't guess. He spoke several languages, and his German was, though peculiar, good enough to be a native's.

"But how does he live?" said Davis; "he must eat."

"There's the puzzle of it!" exclaimed Carl; "for a while he used to watch while I was serving a breakfast or a dinner, and sallying out of his room, which is at the end of the corridor, he 'd make off, sometimes with a cutlet,—perhaps a chicken,—now a plate of spinach, now an omelette, till, at last, I never ventured upstairs with the tray without some one to protect it. Not that even this always sufficed, for he was occasionally desperate, and actually seized a dish by force."

"Even these chances, taken at the best, would scarcely keep a man alive," said Davis.

"Nor would they; but we suspect he must have means of getting out at night and making a 'raid' over the country. We constantly hear of fowls carried off; cheese and fruit stolen. There he is now, creeping along the gallery. Listen! I have left some apples outside."

With a gesture to enforce caution, Davis arose, and placed a percussion-cap on a pistol, a motion of his hand sufficing to show that the weapon was not loaded.

"Open the door gently," said he; and the waiter, stealing over noiselessly, turned the handle. Scarcely had the door been drawn back, when Grog saw the figure of a man, and snapped off the pistol. At the same moment he sprang from the spot, and rushed out to the corridor. The stranger, to all seeming, was not even startled by the report, but was gravely occupied in examining his sleeve to see if he had been struck. He lifted up his head, and Davis, with a start, cried out,—

"What, Paul!—Paul Classon! Is this possible!"

"Davis—old fellow!—do I see you here?" exclaimed the other, in a deep and mellow voice, utterly devoid of irritation or even excitement.

"Come in,—come in here, Paul," said Davis, taking him by the arm; and he led him within the room. "Little I suspected on whom I was playing this scurvy trick."

"It was not loaded," said the other, coolly.

"Of course not"

"I thought so," said he, with an easy smile; "they 've had so many devices to frighten me."

"Come, Paul, old fellow, pour yourself out a tumbler of that red wine, while I cut you some of this ham; we 'll have plenty of time for talk afterwards."

The stranger accepted the invitation, but without the slightest show of eagerness or haste. Nay, he unfolded his napkin leisurely, and fastened a corner in one buttonhole, as some old-fashioned epicures have a trick of doing. He held his glass, too, up to the light, to enjoy the rich color of the wine, and smacked his lips, as he tasted it, with the air of a connoisseur.

"A Burgundy, Davis, eh?" asked he, sipping again.

"I believe so. In truth, I know little about these wines."

"Oh, yes, a 'Pomard,' and very good of its kind. Too loaded, of course, for the time of year, except for such palates as England rears."

Davis had now covered his friend's plate with ham and capon, and, at last, was pleased to see him begin his breakfast.

We are not about to impose upon our reader the burden of knowing more of Mr. Classon than is requisite for the interests of our story; but while he eats the first regular meal he has tasted for two months and more, let us say a word or so about him. He was a clergyman, whose life had been one continued history of mischances. Occasionally the sun of prosperity would seem disposed to shine genially on his head; but for the most part his lot was to walk with dark and lowering skies above him.

If he held any preferment, it was to quarrel with his rector, his dean, or his bishop; to be cited before commissions, tried by surrogates, pronounced contumacious, suspended, and Heaven knows what else. He was everlastingly in litigation with churchwardens and parish authorities, discovering rights of which he was defrauded, and privileges of which he was deprived. None like him to ferret out Acts of Edward or Henry, and obsolete bequests of long-buried founders of this, that, or t'other, of which the present guardians were little better than pickpockets. Adverse decisions and penalties pressing on him, he grew libellous, he spoke, wrote, and published all manner of defamatory things, accused every one of peculation, fraud, and falsehood, and, as the spirit of attack strengthened in him by exercise, menaced this man with prosecution, and that with open exposure. Trials by law, and costs accumulated against him, and he was only out of jail here, to enter it again there. From the Courts "above" he soon descended to those "below;" he became dissipated and dissolute, his hireling pen scrupled at nothing, and he assailed anything or any one, to order. Magistrates "had him up" as the author of threatening letters or begging epistles. To-day he was the mock secretary of an imaginary charity; tomorrow he 'd appear as a distressed missionary going out to some island in the Pacific. He was eternally before the world, until the paragraph that spoke of him grew to be headed by the words, "The Reverend Paul Classon again!" or, more briefly, "Paul Classon's last!" His pen, all this while, was his sole subsistence; and what a bold sweep it took!—impeachment of Ministers, accusation of theft, forgery, intimation of even worse crimes against the highest names in the realm, startling announcements of statesmen bribed, ambassadors corrupted, pasquinades against bishops and judges, libellous stories of people in private life, prize fights, prophetic almanacs, mock missionary journals, stanzas to celebrate quack remedies,—even street ballads were amongst his literary efforts; while, personally, he presided at low singing-establishments, and was the president of innumerable societies in localities only known to the police. It was difficult to take up a newspaper without finding him either reported drunk and disorderly in the police-sheet, obstructing the thoroughfare by a crowd assembled to hear him, having refused to pay for his dinner or his bed, assaulted the landlady, or, crime of crimes, used intemperate language to "G 493." At last they got actually tired of trying him for begging, and imprisoning him for battery; the law was wearied out; but the world also had its patience exhausted, and Paul saw that he must conquer a new hemisphere. He came abroad.

What a changeful life was it now that he led,—at one time a tutor, at another a commissionaire for an hotel, a railway porter, a travelling servant, a police spy, the doorkeeper of a circus company, editor of an English journal, veterinary, language master, agent for patent medicines, picture-dealer, and companion to a nervous invalid, which, as Paul said, meant a furious maniac. There is no telling what he went through of debt and difficulty, till the police actually preferred passing him quietly over the frontier to following up with penalty so incurable an offender. In this way had he wandered about Europe for years, the terror of legations, the pestilence of charitable committees. Contributions to enable the Rev. Paul Classon to redeem his clothes, his watch, his divinity library, to send him to England, to the Andes, to Africa, figured everywhere. I dare not say how often he had been rescued out of the lowest pit of despondency, or snatched like a brand from the burning; in fact, he lived in a pit, and was always on fire.

"I am delighted," said Davis, as he replenished his friend's plate,—"I am delighted to see that you have the same good, hearty appetite as of old, Paul."

"Ay, Kit," said he, with a gentle sigh, "the appetite has been more faithful than the dinner; on the same principle, perhaps, that the last people who desert us are our creditors!"

"I suspect you 've had rather a hard time of it," said Davis, compassionately.

"Well, not much to complain of,—not anything that one would call hardships," said Classon, as he pushed his plate from him and proceeded to light a cigar; "we 're all stragglers, Kit, that's the fact of it."

"I suppose it is; but it ain't very disagreeable to be a straggler with ten thousand a year."

"If the having and enjoying were always centred in the same individual," said Classon, slowly, "what you say would be unanswerable; but it's not so, Kit. No, no; the fellows who really enjoy life never have anything. They are, so to say, guests on a visit to this earth, come to pass a few months pleasantly, to put up anywhere, and be content with everything." Grog shook his head dissentingly, and the other went on, "Who knows the truth of what I am saying better than either of us? How many broad acres did your father or mine bequeath us? What debentures, railroad shares, mining scrip, or mortgages? And yet, Kit, if we come to make up the score of pleasant days and glorious nights, do you fancy that any noble lord of them all would dispute the palm with us? Oh," said he, rapturously, "give *me* the unearned enjoyments of life,—pleasures that have never cost me a thought to provide, nor a sixpence to pay for! Pass the wine, Kit,—that bottle is better than the other;" and he smacked his lips, while his eyes closed in a sort of dreamy rapture.

"I 'd like to hear something of your life, Paul," said Davis. "I often saw your name in the 'Times' and the 'Post,' but I 'd like to have your own account of it."

"My dear Kit, I 've had fifty lives. It's the man you should understand,— the fellow that is here;" and he slapped his broad chest as he spoke. "As for mere adventures, what are they? Squalls that never interfere with the voyage,—not even worth entering in the ship's log."

"Where's your wife, Paul?" asked Davis, abruptly, for he was half impatient under the aphorizing tone of his companion.

"When last I heard of her," said Classon, slowly, as he eyed his glass to the light, "she was at Chicago,—if that be the right prosody of it,—lecturing on 'Woman's Rights.' Nobody knew the subject better than Fanny."

"I heard she was a very clever woman," said Davis.

"Very clever," said Classon; "discursive; not always what the French call 'consequent,' but, certainly, clever, and a sweet poetess." There was a racy twinkle in that reverend eye as he said the last words, so full of malicious drollery that Davis could not help remarking it; but all Classon gave for explanation was, "This to her health and happiness!" and he drained off a bumper. "And yours, Kit,—what of her?" asked he.

"Dead these many years. Do you remember her?"

"Of course I do. I wrote the article on her first appearance at the Surrey. What a handsome creature she was then! It was I predicted her great success; it was I that saved her from light comedy parts, and told her to play Lady Teazle!"

"I 'll show you her born image to-morrow,—her daughter," said Davis, with a strange choking sensation that made him cough; "she's taller than her mother,—more style also."

"Very difficult, that,—very difficult, indeed," said Classon, gravely. "There was a native elegance about her I never saw equalled; and then her walk, the carriage of the head, the least gesture, had all a certain grace that was fascination."

"Wait till you see Lizzy," said Davis, proudly; "you 'll see these all revived."

"Do you destine her for the boards, Kit?" asked Classon, carelessly.

"For the stage? No, of course not," replied Davis, rudely.

"And yet these are exactly the requirements would fetch a high price just now. Beauty is not a rare gift in England; nor are form and symmetry; but, except in the highly born, there is a lamentable deficiency in that easy gracefulness of manner, that blended dignity and softness, that form the chief charm of woman. If she be what you say, Kit,—if she be, in short, her mother's daughter,—it is a downright insanity not to bring her out."

"I 'll not hear of it! That girl has cost me very little short of ten thousand pounds,—ay, ten thousand pounds,—schooling, masters, and the rest of it. She 's no fool, so I take it; it ain't thrown away! As regards beauty, I'll stake fifteen to ten, in hundreds, that, taking your stand at the foot of St. James's Street on a drawing-room day, you don't see her equal. I'm ready to put down the money to-morrow, and that's giving three to two against the field! And is that the girl I 'm to throw away on the Haymarket? She's a Derby filly, I tell you, Paul, and will be first favorite one of these days."

"Faustum sit augurium!" said Classon, as he raised his glass in a theatrical manner, and then drained it off. "Still, if I be rightly informed, the stage is often the antechamber to the peerage. The attractions that dazzle thousands form the centre of fascination for some one."

"She may find her way to a coronet without that," said Davis, rudely.

"Ah, indeed!" said Paul, with a slight elevation of the eyebrow; but though his tone invited a confidence, the other made no further advance's.

"And now for yourself, Classon, what have you been at lately?" said Davis, wishing to change the subject.

"Literature and the arts. I have been contributing to a London weekly, as Crimean correspondent, with occasional letters from the gold diggings. I have been painting portraits for a florin the head, till I have exhausted all the celebrities of the three villages near us. My editor has, I believe, run away, however, and supplies have ceased for some time back."

"And what are your plans now?"

"I have some thoughts of going back to divinity. These newly invented water-cure establishments are daily developing grander proportions; some have got German bands, some donkeys, some pleasure-boats, others rely upon lending libraries and laboratories; but the latest dodge is a chaplain."

"But won't they know you, Paul? Have not the newspapers 'blown you'?"

"Ah, Davis, my dear friend," said he, with a benevolent smile, "it's far easier to live down a bad reputation than to live up to a good one. I 'd only ask a week—one week's domestication with the company of these places—to show I was a martyred saint. I have, so to say, a perennial fount of goodness in my nature that has never failed me."

"I remember it at school," said Davis, dryly.

"*You* took the clever line, Kit, 'suum cuique;' it would never have suited *me*. *You* were born to thrive upon men's weaknesses, mine the part to have a vested interest in their virtues."

"If you depend upon their virtues for a subsistence, I 'm not surprised to see you out at elbows," said Davis, roughly.

"Not so, Kit,—not so," said the other, blandly, in rebuke. "There 's a great deal of weak good-nature always floating about life. The world is full of fellows with 'Pray take me in' written upon them."

"I can only vouch for it very few have come in my way," said Davis, with a harsh laugh.

"So much the better for *them*," said Paul, gravely.

A pause of considerable duration now ensued between them, broken, at last, by Davis abruptly saying, "Is it not a strange thing, it was only last night I was saying to myself, 'What the deuce has become of Holy Paul?—the newspapers have seemingly forgotten him. It can't be that he is dead.'"

"Lazarus only sleepeth," said Classon; "and, indeed, my last eleven weeks here seem little other than a disturbed sleep."

Continuing his own train of thought, Davis went on, "If I could chance upon him now, he's just the fellow I want, or, rather, that I may want."

"If it is a lampoon or a satire you 're thinking of, Kit, I 've given them up; I make no more blistering ointments, but turn all my skill to balsams. They give no trouble in compounding, and pay even better. Ah, Davis, my worthy friend, what a mistake it is to suppose that a man must live by his talents, while his real resource is his temperament. For a life of easy enjoyment, that blessed indolence that never knew a care, it is heart, not head, is needed."

"All I can say is, that with the fellows I 've been most with, heart had very little to do with them, and the best head was the one that least trusted his neighbors."

"A narrow view, my dear friend,—a narrow view, take my word for it; as one goes on in life he thinks better of it."

A malicious grin was all the answer Davis made to this remark. At last he turned his eyes full upon the other, and in a low but distinct voice said: "Let us have no more of this, Paul. If we are to play, let us play, as the Yankees say, without the 'items,'—no cheating on either side. Don't try the Grand Benevolence dodge with me,—don't. When I said awhile ago, I might want you, it was no more than I meant. You *may* be able to render me a service,—a great service."

"Say how," said Classon, drawing his chair nearer to him,—"say how, Kit, and you'll not find the terms exorbitant."

"It's time enough to talk about the stakes when we are sure the match will come off," said Davis, cautiously. "All I 'll say for the present is, I may want you."

Classon took out a small and very greasy-looking notebook from his waistcoat-pocket, and with his pencil in hand, said, "About what time are you likely to need me? Don't be particular as to a day or a week, but just in a rough-guessing sort of way say when."

"I should say in less than a month from this time,—perhaps within a fortnight."

"All right," said Classon, closing his book, after making a brief note. "You smile," said he, blandly, "at my methodical habits, but I have been a red-tapist all my life, Kit I don't suppose you 'll find any man's papers, letters, documents, and so forth, in such trim order as mine,—all labelled, dated, and indexed. Ah! there is a great philosophy in this practical equanimity; take my word for it, there is."

"How far are we from Neuwied here?" asked Davis, half pettishly; for every pretension of his reverend friend seemed to jar upon his nerves.

"About sixteen or eighteen miles, I should say?"

"I must go or send over there to-morrow," continued Davis. "The postmaster sends me word that several letters have arrived,—some to my address, some to my care. Could you manage to drive across?"

"Willingly; only remember that once I leave this blessed sanctuary I may find the door closed against my return. They 've a strange legislation here—"

"I know—I 've heard of it," broke in Davis. "I 'll guarantee everything, so that you need have no fears on that score. Start at daybreak, and fetch back all letters you find there for me or for the Honorable Annesley Beecher."

"The Honorable Annesley Beecher!" said Classon, as he wrote the name in his note-book. "Dear me! the last time I heard that name was—let me see—fully twelve years ago. It was after that affair at Brighton. I wrote an article for the 'Heart of Oak,' on the 'Morality of our Aristocracy.' How I lashed their vices! how I stigmatized their lives of profligacy and crime!"

"You infernal old hypocrite!" cried Davis, with a half-angry laugh.

"There was no hypocrisy in that, Kit. If I tell you that a statue is bad in drawing, or incorrect in anatomy, I never assert thereby that I myself have the torso of Hercules or the limbs of Antinous."

"Leave people's vices alone, then; they 're the same as their debts; if you're not going to pay them, you 've no right to talk about them."

"Only on public grounds, Kit Our duty to society, my dear friend, has its own requirements!"

"Fiddlestick!" said Davis, angrily, as he pushed his glass from before him; then, after a moment, went on: "Do you start early, so as to be back here before evening,—my mind is running on it. There's three naps," said he, placing the gold pieces on the table. "You'll not want more."

"Strange magnetism is the touch of gold to one's palm," said Classon, as he surveyed the money in the hollow of his hand. "How marvellous that these bits of stamped metal should appeal so forcibly to my inner consciousness!"

"Don't get drunk with them, that's all," said Davis, with a stern savagery of manner, as he arose from his seat. "There's my passport,—you may have to show it at the office. And now, good-bye, for I have a long letter to write to my daughter."

Classon poured the last of the Burgundy into a tumbler, and drank it off, and hiccuping out, "I'll haste me to the Capitol!" left the room.

CHAPTER VI
IMMINENT TIDINGS

It was a very wearisome day to Davis as he waited for the return of Paul Classon. Grog's was not a mind made for small suspicions or petty distrusts,—he was a wholesale dealer in iniquity, and despised minute rogueries; yet he was not altogether devoid of anxiety as hour, by hour went over, and no sign of Classon. He tried to pass the time in his usual mode. He shot with the pistol, he fenced, he whipped the trout-stream, he went over his "martingale" with the cards, but somehow everything went amiss with him. He only hit the bull's-eye once in three shots; he fenced wide; a pike carried off his tackle; and, worst of all, he detected a flaw in the great "Cabal," that, if not remediable, must render it valueless.

"A genuine Friday, this!" muttered he, as he sauntered up a little eminence, from which a view might be had of the road for above a mile. "And what nonsense it is people saying they 're not superstitions! I suppose I have as little of that kind of humbug about me as my neighbors; yet I would n't play half-crowns at blind-hookey today. I'd not take the favorite even against a chance horse. I'd not back myself to leap that drain yonder; and why? Just because I 'm in what the French call *guignon*. There's no other word for it that ever I heard. These are the days Fortune says to a man, 'Shut up, and don't book a bet!' It's a wise fellow takes the warning. I know it so well that I always prepare for a run against me, and as sure as I am here, I feel that something or other is going wrong elsewhere. Not a sign of him,—not a sign!" said he, with a heavy sigh, as he gazed long and earnestly along the line of road. "He has n't bolted, that I'm sure of; he'd not 'try that on' with *me*. He remembers to this very hour a licking I gave him at school. I know what it is, he's snug in a wine 'Schenke.' He's in for a big drink, the old beast, as if he could n't get blind drunk when he came home. I think I see him holding forth to the boors, and telling them what an honor it is to them to sit in his company; that he took a high class at Oxford, and was all but Bishop of—Eh, is that he? No, it 's going t' other way. Confounded fool!—but worse fool myself for trusting him. That's exactly what people would say: 'He gave Holy Paul three naps, and expected to see him come back sober!' Well, so I did; and just answer me this: Is not all the work of this world done by rogues and vagabonds? It suits them to be honest for a while; they ride to order so long as they like the stable. Not a sign of him!" And with a comfortless sigh he turned back to the house.

"I wish I knew how Lizzy was to-night!" muttered he, as he rested his head on his hand, and sat gazing at her picture. "Ay, that is your own saucy smile, but the world will take that out of you, and put a puckered-up mouth and hard lines in its place, that it will, confound it! And those eyes will have another kind of brightness in them, too, when they begin to read life glibly. My poor darling, I wish you could stay as you are. Where are you now, I wonder? Not thinking of old Kit, I'm certain! And yet, maybe, I wrong her,—maybe she is just dwelling on long—long ago—home, and the rest of it. Ay, darling, that's what the lucky ones have in life, and never so much as know their luck in having it. By Jove! she is handsome!" cried he, as he held up the miniature in ecstasy before him. "'If she's so beautiful, Mr. Ross, why don't she come to the Drawing-room?' say the Court people. Ay, you'll see her there yet, or I'm not Kit Davis! Don't be impatient, ladies; make your running while the course is your own, for there's a clipper coming. I'd like to see where they'll be when Lizzy takes the field."

And now, in his pride, he walked the room, with head erect and arms folded. It was only for a very short space, however, that these illusions withdrew him from his gloomier reveries; for, with a start, he suddenly recurred to all the anxieties of the morning, and once more issued forth upon the high-road to look out for Classon. The setting sun sent a long golden stream of light down the road, on which not a living thing was to be seen. Muttering what were scarcely blessings on the head of his messenger, he strolled listlessly along. Few men could calculate the eventualities of life better or quicker than Davis. Give him the man and the opportunities, and he would speedily tell you what would be the upshot. He knew thoroughly well how far experience and temperament mould the daring spirit, and how the caution that comes of education tames down the wild influences suggested by temptation.

"No," said he to himself, "though he had my passport and three Napoleons besides, he has not levanted. He is far too deep a fellow for that."

At last a low rumbling sound came up from the distance; he stopped and listened. It came and went at intervals, till, at last, he could distinctly mark the noise of wheels, and the voice of a man urging on his horse. Davis quickened his pace, till, in the gray half-light, he descried a little one-horse carriage slowly advancing towards him. He could only see one man in it; but as it came nearer, he saw a heap of clothes, surmounted by what indicated the presence of another in the bottom of the conveyance, and Grog quickly read the incident by the aid of his own anticipation. There, indeed, lay Paul

Classon, forgetful of the world and all its cares, his outstretched arm almost touching the wheel, and the heavy wooden shoe of the peasant grazing his face.

"Has he got the letters? Where are they?" cried Davis, eagerly, to the driver.

"They're in his hat"

Grog snatched it rudely from his head, and found several letters of various sizes and shapes, and with what, even in that dim light, seemed a variety of addresses and superscriptions.

"Are you certain none have fallen out or been lost on the road?" said Davis, as he reckoned them over.

"That I am," said the man; "for at every jolt of the wagon he used to grip his hat and hold it fast, as if it was for very life, till we came to the last village. It was there he finished off with a flask of Laubthaler that completely overcame him."

"So, then, he was sober on leaving Neuwied?"

"He was in the so-called 'bemuzzed' state!" said the man, with a half-apologetic air.

"Take him down to the inn; throw him into the hay-yard—or the river, if you like," said Davis, contemptuously, and turned away.

Once in his own room, the candles lighted, the door locked, Davis sat down to the table on which the letters were thrown. Leisurely he took them up one by one and examined their superscriptions.

"Little news in these," said he, throwing three or four to one side; "the old story,—money-seeking." And he mumbled out, "'Your acceptance being duly presented this day at Messrs. Haggitts and Drudge's, and no provision being made for payment of the same—' It's like the burden of an old song in one's ears. Who is this from? Oh, Billy Peach, with some Doncaster news. I do wonder will the day ever come that will bring me good tidings by the post; I 've paid many a pound in my life for letters, and I never yet chanced upon one that told me my uncle Peter had just died, leaving me all his estates in Jamaica, or that my aunt Susan bequeathed to me all her Mexican stock and the shares in four tin-mines. This is also from Peach, and marked 'Immediate;'" and he broke it open. It contained only these lines: "Dark is the word for a week or two still. On Tuesday your name will appear amongst the passengers for New York by the 'Persia.' Saucy Sal is a dead break-down, and we net seven hundred safe; Pot did it with a knitting-needle while they were plaiting her. What am I to do about the jewels?"

Davis's brow darkened as he crushed the paper in his hand, while he muttered, "I wish these infernal fools had not been taught to write! He ought to know that addressing me Captain Christopher never deceived a 'Detective' yet. And this is for the Honorable Annesley Beecher," said he, reading aloud the address, "'care of Captain Christopher, Coblentz—try Bingen—try Neuwied.' A responsible-looking document this; it looks like a despatch, with its blue-post paper and massive seal; and what is the name here, in the corner? 'Davenport Dunn,' sure enough,—'Davenport Dunn.' And with your leave, sir, we 'll see what you have to say," muttered he, as he broke the seal of the packet. A very brief note first met his eyes; it ran thus:—

> "Dear Sir,—While I was just reading a very alarming account of Lord Lackington's illness in a communication from Messrs. Harmer and Gore, the post brought me the enclosed letter for yourself, which I perceive to be in her Ladyship's hand; I forward it at once to Brussels, in the hope that it may reach you there. Should her Ladyship's tidings be better than I can fain persuade myself to hope, may I presume to suggest that you should lose no time in repairing to Italy. I cannot exaggerate the peril of his Lordship's state; in fact, I am hourly expecting news of his death; and, the peculiar circumstances of the case considered, it is highly important you should possess yourself of every information the exigencies of the event may require. I beg to enclose you a bank post-bill for two-hundred pounds, payable at any banker's on your signature, and have the honor to be, with sincere respect,
>
> "Your humble Servant,
>
> "Davenport Dunn.
>
> "P. S.—I have reason to know that certain claims are now under consideration, and will be preferred erelong, if suitable measures be not adopted to restrain them."

"From which side do you hold your brief, Master Davenport Dunn? I should like to know *that!*" said Davis, as he twice over read aloud this postscript. He looked at Lady Lackington's letter, turned it over, examined the seal and the postmark, and seemed to hesitate about breaking it open. Was it that some scruple of conscience arrested his hand, and some mysterious feeling that it was a sisterly confidence he was about to violate? Who knows! At all events, if there was a struggle it was a brief one, for he now smashed the seal and spread the open letter before him.

With a muttered expression of impatience did he glance over the four closely written pages indited in the very minutest of hands and the faintest possible ink. Like one addressing himself, however, to a severe task, he set steadily to work, and for nigh an hour never rose from the table. We have no right, as little have we the wish, to inflict upon our reader any portion of the labor this process of deciphering cost Davis, so that we will briefly state what formed the substance of the epistle. The letter was evidently begun before Lord Lackington had been taken ill, for it opened with an account of Como and the company at the Villa d'Este, where they had gone to resume the water-cure. Her Ladyship's strictures upon the visitors, their morals, and their manners, were pleasantly and flippantly thrown off. She possessed what would really seem an especial gift of her class,—the most marvellous use of the perceptive faculties,—and could read not alone rank and condition, but character and individuality, by traits of breeding and manner that would have escaped the notice of hundreds of those the world calls shrewd observers. This fragment, for it was such, was followed, after a fortnight, by a hastily written passage, announcing that Lord Lackington had been seized with an attack resembling apoplexy, and for several hours remained in great danger. She had detained the letter to give the latest tidings before the post closed, and ultimately decided on not despatching it till the next day. The following morning's communication was a minute account of medical treatment, the bleedings, the blisterings, the watchings, and the anxieties of a sick-bed, with all the vacillating changes that mark the course of malady, concluding with these words: "The doctors are not without hopes, but confess that their confidence is rather based on the great strength and energy of his constitution than upon any success that has attended their treatment, from which I may say that up to this no benefit has accrued. So well as I can interpret his utterance, he seems very anxious to see you, and made an effort to write something to you, which, of course, he could not accomplish. Come out here, therefore, as quickly as possible; the route by Lucerne is, they tell me, the shortest and speediest. If I were to give my own opinion, it would be that he is better and stronger than yesterday; but I do not perceive the doctors disposed to take this view." After this came a lengthened statement of medical hopes and fears, balanced with all the subtle minuteness known to "the Faculty." They explained to a nicety how if that poor watch were to stop it could not possibly be from any fault of theirs, but either from some vice in its original construction, or some organic change occasioned by time. They demonstrated, in fact, that great as was their art, it was occasionally baffled; but pointed with a proud humility to the onward progress of science, in the calm assurance that, doubtless, we should one day know all these things, and treat them as successfully as we now do—I am afraid to say what. One thing, however, was sufficiently clear,—Lord Lackington's case was as bad as possible, his recovery almost hopeless. On the turn-down of the last page was the following, written in evident haste, if not agitation: "In opening the letters which have arrived since his illness, I am astonished to find many referring to some suit, either meditated or actually instituted, against our right to the title. Surely some deep game of treachery is at work here. He never once alluded to such a possibility to myself, nor had I the slightest suspicion that any pretended claim existed. One of these letters is from Mr. Davenport Dunn, who has, I can see from the tone in which he writes, been long conversant with the transaction, and as evidently inclines to give it a real or feigned importance. Indeed, he refers to a 'compromise' of some sort or other, and strongly impresses the necessity of not letting the affair proceed further. I am actually distracted by such news coming at such a moment. Surely Lackington could never have been weak enough to yield to mere menace, and have thus encouraged the insolent pretensions of this claim? As you pass through London, call at Fordyce's, somewhere in Furnival's Inn, and, just in course of conversation, showing your acquaintance with the subject, learn all you can on the matter. Fordyce has all our papers, and must necessarily know what weight is due to these pretensions. Above all, however, hasten out here; there is no saying what any day—any hour—may produce. I have no one here to give me a word of advice, or even consolation; for, though Lady Grace is with us, she is so wrapped up in her new theological studies—coquetting with Rome as she has been all the summer—that she is perfectly useless.

"Have you any idea who is Terence Driscoll? Some extraordinary notes bearing this signature, ill-written and ill-spelt, have fallen into my hands as I rummaged amongst the papers, and they are all full of this claim. It is but too plain Lackington suffered these people to terrify him, and this Driscoll's tone is a mixture of the meanest subserviency and outrageous impertinence. It is not unlikely Fordyce may know him. Of course, I need not add one word of caution against your mention of this affair, even to those of your friends with whom you are in closest intimacy. It is really essential not a hint of it should get abroad.

"I have little doubt, now, looking back on the past, that anxiety and care about this matter have had a large share in bringing on Lackington's attack. He had been sleepless and uneasy for some time back, showing an eagerness, too, about his letters, and the greatest impatience if any accident delayed the post Although all my maturer thoughts—indeed, my convictions—reject attaching any importance to this claim, I will not attempt to conceal from you how unhappy it has made me, nor how severely it has affected my nerves."

With one more urgent appeal to lose not an hour in hastening over the Alps, the letter concluded; the single word "weaker," apparently written after the letter was sealed, giving a deep meaning to the whole.

Davis was not satisfied with one perusal of the latter portion of this letter, but read it over carefully a second time; after which, taking a sheet of paper, he wrote down the names of Fordyce and Terence Driscoll. He then opened a Directory, and running his eye down a column, came to "Fordyce and Fraude, 7 Furnivats Inn, solicitors." Of Terence Driscolls there were seventeen, but all in trade,—tanners, tinmen, last-makers, wharfingers, and so on; not one upon whom Davis could fix the likelihood of the correspondence with the Viscount. He then walked the room, cigar in mouth, for about an hour, after which he sat down and wrote the note to Beecher which we have given in a former chapter, with directions to call upon Stein, the moneylender, and then hasten away from Aix as speedily as possible. This finished, he addressed another and somewhat longer epistle to Lazarus Stein himself, of which latter document this true history has no record.

We, perhaps, owe an apology to our reader for inverting in our narrative the actual order of these events. It might possibly have been more natural to have preceded the account of Beecher's reception of the letter by the circumstances we have just detailed. We selected the present course, however, to avoid the necessity of that continual change of scene, alike wearisome to him who reads as to him who writes; and as we are about to sojourn in Mr. Davis's company for some time to come, we have deferred the explanation to a time when it should form part of a regular series of events. Nor are we sorry at the opportunity of asking the reader to turn once again to that brief note, and mark its contents. Though Davis was fully impressed with the conviction that Lord Lackington's days were numbered; though he felt that, at any moment, some chance rumor, some flying report might inform Beecher what great change was about to come over his fortunes,—yet this note is written in all the seeming carelessness of a gossiping humor: he gives the latest news of the turf, he alludes to Beecher's new entanglements at home, to, his own newly discovered martingale for the play-table, trusting to the one line about "Benson's people" to make Beecher hasten away from Aix, and from the chance of hearing that his brother was hopelessly ill. While Grog penned these lines, he would have given—if he had it—ten thousand pounds that Beecher was beside him. Ay, willingly had he given it, and more, too, that Beecher might be where no voice could whisper to him the marvellous change that any moment might cause in his destiny. Oh, ye naturalists, who grow poetical over the grub and the butterfly, what is there, I ask ye, in the transformation at all comparable with that when the younger brother, the man of strait and small fortune, springs into the peer, exchanging a life of daily vicissitudes, cheap dinners and duns, dubious companionships and high discounts, for the assured existence, the stately banquets, the proud friendships, the pomp and circumstance of a lord? In a moment he soars out of the troubled atmosphere of debts and disabilities, and floats into the balmy region whose very sorrows never wear an unbecoming mourning.

Grog's note was thus a small specimen of what the great Talleyrand used to call the perfection of despatch writing, "not the best thing that could be said on the subject, but simply that which would produce the effect you desired." Having sent off this to Beecher, he then telegraphed to his man of business, Mr. Peach, to ascertain at Fordyce's the latest accounts of Lord Lackington's health, and answer "by wire."

It was far into the night when Davis betook himself to bed, but not to sleep. The complications of the great game he was playing had for him all the interest of the play-table. The kind of excitement he gloried in was to find himself pitted against others,—wily, subtle, and deep-scheming as himself,—to see some great stake on the board, and to feel that it must be the prize of the best player. With the gambler's superstition, he kept constantly combining events with dates and eras, recalling what of good or ill-luck had marked certain periods of his life. He asked himself if September had usually been a fortunate month; did the 20th imply anything; what influence might Holy Paul exert over his destiny; was he merely unlucky himself, or did he bring evil fortune upon others? If he suffered himself to dwell upon such "vain auguries" as these, they still exerted little other sway over his mind than to nerve it to greater efforts; in fact, he consulted these signs as a physician might investigate certain symptoms which, if not of moment enough to call for special treatment, were yet indicative of hidden mischief.

His gambling experiences had given him the ready tact, by a mere glance around the table, to recognize those with whom the real struggle should be waged; to detect, in a second, the deep head, the crafty intelligence, that marvellous blending of caution with rashness that make the gamester; and in the same spirit be now turned over in thought each of those with whom he was now about to contend, and muttered the name of Davenport Dunn over and over. "Could we only 'hit it off' together, what a game might we not play!" was his last reflection ere he fell off to sleep.

CHAPTER VII
A DISCURSIVE CONVERSATION

Davis was surprised, and something more, as he entered the breakfast-room the next morning to find the Rev. Paul Classon already seated at the table, calmly arranging certain little parallelograms of bread-and-butter and sardines. No signs of discomfiture or shame showed themselves in that calmly benevolent countenance. Indeed, as he arose and extended his hand there was an air of bland protection in the gesture perfectly soothing.

"You came back in a pretty state last night," said Davis, roughly.

"Overtaken, Kit,—overtaken. It was a piece of good news rather than the grape juice did the mischief. As the poet says,—

"'Good tidings flowed upon his heart
Like a sea o'er a barren shore,
And the pleasant waves refreshed the spot
So parched and bleak before.'

"The fact is, Kit, you brought me luck. Just as I reached the Post-Office, I saw a letter addressed to the Rev. Paul Classon, announcing that I had been accepted as Chaplain to the great Hydropathic Institution at Como! and, to commemorate the event, I celebrated in wine the triumphs of water! You got the letters all safely?"

"Little thanks to you if I did; nor am I yet certain how many may have dropped out on the road."

"Stay,—I have a memorandum here," said Paul, opening his little note-book. "Four, with London post-marks, to Captain Christopher; two from Brussels for the same; a large packet for the Hon. Annesley Beecher. That's the whole list."

"I got these!" said Grog, gruffly; "but why, might I ask, could you not have kept sober till you got back here?"

"He who dashes his enthusiasm with caution, waters the liquor of life. How do we soar above the common ills of existence save by yielding to those glorious impulses of the heart, which say, 'Be happy!'"

"Keep the sermon for the cripples at the water-cure," said Davis, savagely. "When are you to be there?"

"By the end of the month. I mentioned the time myself. It would be as soon, I thought, as I could manage to have my divinity library out from England."

The sly drollery of his eye, as he spoke, almost extorted a half-smile from Davis.

"Let me see," muttered Grog, as he arose and lighted his cigar, "we are, to-day, the 21st, I believe. No, you can't be there so early. I shall need you somewhere about the first week in October; it might chance to be earlier. You mustn't remain here, however, in the interval. You'll have to find some place in the neighborhood, about fifteen or twenty miles off."

"There's Höchst, on the Lahn, a pleasant spot, eighteen miles from this."

"Höchst be it; but, mark me, no more of last night's doings."

"I pledge my word," said Paul, solemnly. "Need I say, it is as good as my bond?"

"About the same, I suspect; but I 'll give you *mine* too," said Davis, with a fierce energy. "If by any low dissipation or indiscretion of yours you thwart the plans I am engaged in, I 'll leave you to starve out the rest of your life here."

"'So swear we all as liegemen true, So swear to live and die!'" cried out Paul, with a most theatrical air in voice and gesture.

"You know a little of everything, I fancy," said Davis, in a more good-humored tone. "What do you know of law?"

"Of law?" said Paul, as he helped himself to a dish of smoking cutlets,— "if it be the law of debtor and creditor, false arrest, forcible possession, battery, or fraudulent bankruptcy, I am indifferently well skilled. Nor am I ignorant in divorce cases, separate maintenance, and right of guardianship. Equity, I should say, is my weak point."

"I believe you," said Davis, with a grin, for he but imperfectly understood the speech. "But it is of another kind of law I 'm speaking. What do you know about disputed title to a peerage? Have you any experience in such cases?"

"Yes; I have ransacked registries, rummaged out gravestones in my time. I very nearly burned my fingers, too, with a baptismal certificate that turned out to be—what shall I call it?—unauthentic!"

"You forged it!" said Grog, gruffly.

"They disputed its correctness, and, possibly, with some grounds for their opinion. Indeed," added he, carelessly, "it was the first thing of the kind I had ever done, and it was slovenly—slovenly."

"It would have been transportation!" said Davis, gravely.

"With hard labor," added Classon, sipping his tea.

"At all events, you understand something of these sort of cases?"

"Yes; I have been concerned, one way or another, with five. They are interesting when you take to them; there are so many, so to say, surprises; always something turning up you never looked for,—somebody's father that never had a child, somebody's mother that never was married. Then people die,—say a hundred and fifty years ago,—and no proof of the death can be made out; or you build wonderfully upon an act of Parliament, and only find out at the last hour that it has been repealed. These traits give a great deal of excitement to the suit. I used to enjoy them much when I was younger." And Mr. Classon sighed as if he had been calling up memories of cricket-matches, steeple-chases, or the polka,—pleasures that advancing years had rudely robbed him of.

Davis sat deep in thought for some time. Either he had not fully made up his mind to open an unreserved confidence with his reverend friend, or which is perhaps as likely, he was not in possession of such knowledge as might enable him to state his case.

"These suits, or actions, or whatever you call them," said he, at length, "always drag on for years,—don't they?"

"Of course they do; the lawyers take care of that. There are trials at bar, commissions, special examinations before the Masters, arguments before the peers, appeals against decisions; in fact, it is a question of the purse of the litigants. Like everything else, however, in this world, they 've got economy-struck. I remember the time—it was the Bancroft case—they gave me five guineas a day and travelling expenses to go out to Ravenna and take the deposition of an old Marchess, half-sister of the Dowager, and now, I suppose, they 'd say the service was well paid with one half. Indeed, I may say I had as good as accepted a sort of engagement to go out to the Crimea and examine a young fellow whom they fancy has a claim to a peerage, and for a mere trifle,—fifteen shillings a day and expenses. But they had got my passport stopped here, and I could n't get away."

"What was the name of the claimant?"

"Here it is," said he, opening his note-book. "Charles Conway, formerly in the 11th Hussars, supposed to be serving as orderly on the staff of General

La Marmora. I have a long letter of instructions Froode forwarded me, and I suspect it is a strong case got up to intimidate."

"What is the peerage sought for?" asked Davis, with an assumed indifference.

"I can tell you in five minutes if you have any curiosity on the subject," said Paul, rising. "The papers are all in my writing-desk."

"Fetch them," said Davis, as he walked to the window and looked out.

Classon soon re-entered the room with a large open letter in his hand.

"There's the map of the country!" said he, throwing it down on the table. "What would you call the fair odds in such a case, Kit,—a private soldier's chance of a peerage that has been undisturbed since Edward the Third?"

"About ten thousand to one, I 'd call it."

"I agree with you, particularly since Froode is in it. He only takes up these cases to make a compromise. They 're always 'settled.' He's a wonderful fellow to sink the chambers and charge the mine, but he never explodes,—never!"

"So that Froode can always be squared, eh?" asked Davis.

"Always." Classon now ran his eyes over the letter, and, mumbling the lines half aloud, said, "In which case the Conways of Abergeldy, deriving from the second son, would take precedence of the Beecher branch.' The case is this," added he, aloud: "Viscompt Lackington's peerage was united to the estates by an act of Edward; a motion for a repeal of this was made in Elizabeth's time, and lost—some aver the reverse; now the claimant, Conway, relies upon the original act, since in pursuit of the estates he invalidates the title. It's a case to extort money, and a good round sum too. I 'd say Lord Lack-ington might give twenty thousand to have all papers and documents of the claim surrendered into his hands."

"A heavy sum, twenty thousand," muttered Davis, slowly.

"So it is, Kit; but when you come to tot up suits at Nisi Prius, suits in Equity, searches at the Herald's office, and hearings before the Lords, you 'll see it is a downright saving."

"But could Lackington afford this? What is he worth?"

"They call the English property twelve thousand a year, and he has a small estate in Ireland besides. In fact, it is out of that part of the property the mischief has come. This Conway's claim was discovered in some old country-house there, and Froode is only partially instructed in it."

"And now, Paul," said Davis, slowly, "if you got a commission to square this here affair and make all comfortable, how would you go about it?"

"Acting for which party, do you mean?" asked Paul.

"I mean for the Lackingtons."

"Well, there are two ways. I 'd send for Froode, and say, 'What's the lowest figure for the whole?' or I'd despatch a trusty fellow to the Crimea to watch Conway, and see what approaches they are making to him. Of course they'll send a man out there, and it ought n't to be hard to get hold of him, or, if not himself, of all his papers and instructions."

"That looks business-like," said Grog, encouragingly.

"After all, Kit, these things, in ninety-nine cases out of the hundred, are only snaps of the percussion-cap. There 's scarcely a peerage in England is not menaced with an attempt of the kind; but such is the intermarriage— such the close tie of affinity between them—they stand manfully to the fellow in possession. They know in their hearts, if once they let the world begin to pick out a stone here or there, the whole wall may come tumbling down, and so they say, 'Here 's one of us since Henry II.'s time going to be displaced for some upstart fellow none of us ever heard of.' What signifies legitimacy that dates seven centuries back, in favor of one probably a shoemaker or a house-painter? They won't stand that, Kit, and reasonably enough, too. I suppose you've heard all about this case from Beecher?"

"Well, I *have* heard something about it," said Grog, in confusion, for the suddenness of the question disconcerted him; "but *he* don't care about it."

"Very likely not. If Lackington were to have a son, it would n't concern him much."

"Not alone that, but he does n't attach any importance to the claim; he says it's all got up to extort money."

"What of that? When a highwayman stops you with the same errand, does n't the refusal occasionally provoke him to use force? I know very few things so hard to deal with as menaces to extort money. Life is, after all, very like the game the Americans call 'Poker,' where the grand secret is, never to 'brag' too far on a bad hand. What was *your* part in this business, Kit?" asked he, after a brief silence.

"How do you mean by *my* part?" rejoined Davis, gruffly.

"I mean, how were you interested? Do you hold any of Lackington's paper?—have you got any claims on the reversion?—in a word, does it in any way concern you which king reigns in Israel?"

"It might, or it might not," said Grog, dryly. "Now for a question to *you.* Could you manage to get employed in the affair,—to be sent out after this Conway,—or is it too late?"

"It might, or it might not," said Classon, with a significant imitation of the other's tone and manner. Davis understood the sarcasm in a moment, and in a voice of some irritation said,—

"Don't you try to come the whip-hand over me, Holy Paul. If there be anything to do in this matter, it is I, and not *you*, will be paymaster; so much for this, so much for that,—there's the terms!"

"It is such dealings I like best," said Classon, blandly "Men would have benefited largely in this world had probity been parcelled out as task-work instead of being made daily labor."

"I suspect that neither you nor I would have had much employment either way," said Davis, with a bitter laugh. "But come, you must be stirring. You 'll have to be off out of this before the afternoon. The Rhine steamer touches at Neuwied at three, and I expect my daughter by this boat. I don't want her to see you just yet awhile, Paul. You 'll start for Höchst, put up at the inn there, and communicate with me at once, so that I may be able to reckon upon you when needed. It were as well, too, that you'd write a line to Froode, and say that on second thoughts that expedition to the Crimea might suit; explore the way, in fact, and let me know the tidings. As to terms," said Grog,—for the other's blank look expressed hesitation,—"if *I* say, 'Go,' *you* shall say 'For what?'"

"I do love these frank and open dealings," said Paul, warmly.

"Look here!" said Davis, as the other was about to leave the room; "old Joe Morris, of Mincing Lane, made his fortune by buying up all the forged bills of exchange he could lay hands on, well knowing that the fellows he could hang or transport any day would be trusty allies. Now, I have all my life committed every critical thing to somebody or other that no other living man would trust with a sixpence. They stood to *me* as I stood to *them*, and they knew why. Need I tell you that why?"

"No necessity in the world to do so," said Paul, blandly.

"That 's enough," said Davis. "Come to me when you're ready, and I'll have some cash for you."

CHAPTER VIII
A FAMILY MEETING

Along a road pleasantly shaded by linden-trees, Davis strolled leisurely that afternoon to meet his daughter. It was a mellow autumnal day,—calm, silent, and half sombre,—one of those days in which the tranquil aspect of nature has an influence of sad but soothing import, and even the least meditative minds are led to reflection. Down the deep valley, where the clear trout-stream eddied along, while the leafy chestnut-trees threw their shadows over the water; over the rich pasture-lands, where the spotted cattle roamed; high up the blue mountains, whose snowy summits mingled with the clouds,—Davis wandered with his eyes, and felt, he knew not why or how, a something of calming, subduing effect upon a brain racked with many a scheme, wearied with many a plot.

As he gazed down upon that fair scene where form and color and odor were blended into one beauteous whole, a struggling effort of fancy sent through his mind the question, "Is this, after all, the real prize of life? Is this peaceful existence worth all the triumphs that we strive and fight for?" And then came the thought, "Could this be lasting, what would a nature like mine become, thus left in rust and disuse? Could I live? or should I enjoy life without that eternal hand-to-hand conflict with my fellow-men, on which skill and ready wit are exercised?" He pondered long over this notion, nor could he satisfy himself with any conclusion.

He thought he could remember a time when he would thoroughly have liked all this,—when he could have taken leave of the busy world without one regret, and made the great race of life a mere "walk over," but now that he had tasted the poisonous fascination of that combat, where man is pitted against man, and where even the lust of gain is less stimulating than a deadly sense of jealous rivalry, it was too late—too late! How strange, too, did it seem to him, as he looked back upon his wild and stormy life, with all its perils and all its vicissitudes, to think that an existence so calm, so uneventful, and so safe, could yet be had,—that a region existed where craft could find no exercise, where subtlety might be in disuse! It was to him like a haven that he was rejoiced to know,—a harbor whose refuge, some one day or other, he would search out; but there was yet one voyage to make,—one grand venture,—which, if successful, would be the crowning fortune of his life!

The sharp crack, crack of a postilion's whip started him from his musings, and, looking up, he saw a post-carriage approaching at full speed. He waved his hat as the carriage came near for the men to draw up, and the next moment Lizzy Davis was in her father's arms. He kissed her twice, and then, holding her back, gazed with proud delight at her beautiful features, never more striking than in that moment of joyful meeting.

"How well you are looking, Lizzy!" said he, with a thick utterance.

"And you too, dear papa," said she, caressingly. "This quiet rural life seems to have agreed wonderfully with you. I declare you look five years younger for it, does he not, Mr. Beecher?"

"Ah, Beecher, how are you?" cried Davis, warmly shaking the other's hand. "This *is* jolly, to be all together again," said he, as, drawing his daughter's arm within his own, and taking Beecher on the other side, he told the postilions to move forward, while they would find their way on foot.

"How did you ever hit upon this spot?" asked Beecher; "we could n't find it on the map."

"I came through here some four-and-twenty years ago, and I never forget a place nor a countenance. I thought at the time it might suit me, some one day or other, to remember, and you see I was right. You are grown fatter, Lizzy; at least I fancy so. But come, tell me about your life at Aix,— was it pleasant? was the place gay?"

"It was charming, papa!" cried she, in ecstasy; "had you only been with us, I could not have come away. Such delightful rides and drives, beautiful environs, and then the Cursaal of an evening, with all its odd people,—not that my guardian, here, fancied so much my laughing at them."

"Well, you did n't place much restraint upon yourself, I must say."

"I was reserved even to prudery; I was the caricature of Anglo-Saxon propriety," said she, with affected austerity.

"And what did they think of you, eh?" asked Davis trying to subdue the pride that would, in spite of him, twinkle in his eye.

"I was the belle of the season. I assure you it is perfectly true!"

"Come, come, Lizzy—"

"Well, ask Mr. Beecher. Be honest now, and confess frankly, were you not sulky at driving out with me the way the people stared? Didn't you complain that you never expected to come home from the play without a duel or something of the kind on your hands? Did you not induce me to ruin my toilette just to escape what you so delicately called 'our notoriety'? Oh, wretched man! what triumphs did I not relinquish out of compliance to your taste for obscurity!"

"By Jove! we divided public attention with Ferouk Khan and his wives. I don't see that my taste for obscurity obtained any brilliant success."

"I never heard of such black ingratitude!" cried she, in mock indignation. "I assure you, pa, I was a martyr to his English notions, which, to me, seem to have had their origin in Constantinople."

"Poor Beecher!" said Davis, laughingly.

"Poor Beecher, no, but happy Beecher, envied by thousands. Not indeed," added she, with a smile, "that his appearance at this moment suggests any triumphant satisfaction. Oh, papa, you should have seen him when the Russian Prince Ezerboffsky asked me to dance, or when the Archduke Albrecht offered me his horses; or, better still, the evening the Margrave lighted up his conservatory just to let me see it."

"Your guardianship had its anxieties, I perceive," said Davis, dryly.

"I think it had," said Beecher, sighing. "There were times I'd have given five thousand, if I had it, that she had been safe under your own charge."

"My dear fellow, I'd have given fifty," said Davis, "if I did n't know she was just in as good hands as my own." There was a racy heartiness in this speech that thrilled through Beecher's heart, and he could scarcely credit his ears that it was Grog spoke it. "Ay, Beecher," added he, as he drew the other's arm closer to his side, "there was just one man—one single man in Europe—I 'd have trusted with the charge."

"Really, gentlemen," said Lizzy, with a malicious sparkle of the eye, "I am lost in my conjectures whether I am to regard myself as a sort of human Koh-i-noor—a priceless treasure—or something so very difficult to guard, so perilous to protect, as can scarcely be accounted a flattery. Say, I entreat of you, to which category do I belong?"

"A little to each, I should say,—ch, Beecher?" cried Grog, laughingly.

"Oh, don't appeal to *him*, papa. *He* only wants to vaunt his heroism the higher, because the fortress he guarded was so easy of assault!"

Beecher was ill-fitted to engage in such an encounter, and stammered out some commonplace apology for his own seeming want of gallantry.

"She's too much for us, Beecher,—too much for us. It's a pace we can't keep up," muttered Grog in the other's ear. And Beecher nodded a ready assent to the speech.

"Well," said Lizzy, gayly, "now that your anxieties are well over, I do entreat of you to unbend a little, and let us see the lively, light-hearted Mr. Annesley Beecher, of whose pleasant ways I have heard so much."

"I used to be light-hearted enough once, eh, Davis?" said Beecher, with a sigh. "When you saw me first at the Derby—of, let me see, I don't remember the year, but it was when Danby's mare Petrilla won,—with eighteen to one 'given and taken' against her, the day of the race,—Brown Davy, the favorite, coming in a bad third,—he died the same night."

"Was he 'nobbled'?" asked Lizzy, dryly.

"What do you mean?" cried Grog, gruffly. "Where did you learn that word?"

"Oh, I'm quite strong in your choice vocabulary," said she, laughingly; "and you are not to fancy that in the dissipations of Aix I have forgotten the cares of my education. My guardian there set me a task every morning,—a page of Burke's Peerage and a column of the 'Racing Calendar;' and for the ninth Baron of Fitzfoodle, or the fifteenth winner of the Diddlesworth, you may call on me at a moment."

The angry shadow on Davis's brow gradually faded away, and he laughed a real, honest, and good-humored laugh.

"What do you say to the Count, Lizzy?" asked he next. "There was a fine gentleman, wasn't he?"

"There was the ease and the self-possession of good breeding without the manners. He was amusing from his own self-content, and a sort of latent impression that he was taking you in, and when one got tired of that, he became downright stupid."

"True as a book, every word of it!" cried Beecher, in hearty gratitude, for he detested the man, and was envious of his small accomplishments.

"His little caressing ways, too, ceased to be flatteries, when you saw that, like the cheap bonbons scattered at a carnival, they were made for the million."

"Hit him again, he hasn't got no friends!" said Beecher, with an assumed slang in his tone.

"But worst of all was that mockery of good nature,—a false air of kindliness about him. It was a spurious coinage, so cleverly devised that you looked at every good guinea afterwards with distrust."

"How she knows him,—how she reads him!" cried Davis, in delight.

"He was very large print, papa," said she, smiling.

"Confound me!" cried Beecher, "if I didn't think you liked him, you used to receive him so graciously; and I'll wager he thinks himself a prime favorite with you."

"So he may, if it give him any pleasure," said she, with a careless laugh.

Davis marked the expression of Beecher's face as she said these words; he saw how that distrustful nature was alarmed, and he hastened to repair the mischief.

"I am sure you never affected to feel any regard for him, Lizzy?" said Davis.

"Regard for him!" said she, haughtily; "I should think not! Such people as he are like the hired horses that every one uses, and only asks that they should serve for the day they have taken them."

"There, Beecher," said Davis, with a laugh. "I sincerely hope she's not going to discuss *your* character or *mine*."

"By Jove! I hope not." And in the tone in which Beecher uttered this there was an earnestness that made the other laugh heartily.

"Well, here we are. This is your home for the present," said Davis, as he welcomed them to the little inn, whose household were all marshalled to receive them with fitting deference.

The arrangements within doors were even better than the picturesque exterior promised; and when Lizzy came down to dinner, she was in raptures about her room, its neatness even to elegance, and the glorious views that opened before the windows.

"I'm splendidly lodged too," said Beecher; "and they have given me a dressing-room, with a little winding-stair to the river, and a bath in the natural rock. It is downright luxury, all this."

Davis smiled contentedly as he listened. For days past had he been busied with these preparations, determined to make the spot appear in all its most favorable colors. Let us do him justice to own that his cares met a full success. Flowers abounded in all the rooms; and the perfumed air, made to seem tremulous by the sounds of falling water, was inexpressibly calming after the journey. The dinner, too, would have done honor to a more pretentious "hostel;" and the Steinberger, a cabinet wine, that the host would not part with except for "love as well as money," was perfection. Better than all these,—better than the fresh trout with its gold and azure speckles,—

better than the delicate Rehbraten with its luscious sauce,—better than the red partridges in their bed of truffles, and a dessert whose grapes rivalled those of Fontainebleau,—better, I say, than all, was the happy temper of the hour! Never were three people more disposed for enjoyment. To Lizzy, it was the oft dreamed-of home, the quiet repose of a spot surrounded with all the charm of scenery, coming, too, just as the dissipations of gayety had begun to weary and pall upon her. To Beeeher, it was the first moment of all his life in which he tasted peace. Here were neither duns nor bailiffs. It was a Paradise where no writ had ever wandered, nor the word "outlawry" had ever been uttered. As for Davis, if he had not actually won his game, he held in his hand the trump card that he knew must gain it. What signified, now, a day or even a week more or less; the labor of his long ambition was all but completed, and he saw the goal reached that he had striven for years to attain.

Nor were they less pleased with each other. Never had Lizzy seemed to Beecher's eyes more fascinating than now. In all the blaze of full dress she never looked more beautiful than in that simple muslin, with the sky-blue ribbon in her glossy hair, and the boquet of moss roses coquettishly placed above her ear, for—I mention it out of accuracy—she wore her hair drawn back, as was the mode about a century ago, and was somewhat ingenious in her imitation of that mock-shepherdess *coiffure* so popular with fine ladies of that time. She would have ventured on a "patch" if it were not out of fear for her father; not, indeed, that the delicate fairness of her skin, or the dazzling brilliancy of her eyes, needed the slightest aid from art. Was it with some eye to keeping a toilette that she wore a profusion of rings, many of great price and beauty? I know not her secret; if I did, I should assuredly tell it, for I suspect none of her coquetries were without their significance. To complete Beecher's satisfaction, Davis was in a mood of good humor, such as he had never seen before.

Not a word of contradiction, not one syllable of disparagement fell from his lips, that Beecher usually watched with an utmost childish terror, dreading reproof at every moment, and not being over certain when his opinions would pass without a censure. Instead of this, Grog was conciliating even to gentleness, constantly referred to Beecher what he thought of this or that, and even deferred to his better judgment on points whereon he might have been supposed to be more conversant. Much valued reader, has it ever been your fortune in life to have had your opinions on law blandly approved of by an ex-Chancellor, your notions of medicine courteously confirmed by a great physician, or your naval tactics endorsed by an admiral of the fleet? If so, you can fully appreciate the ecstasy of Annesley Beecher as he found all his experiences of the sporting world corroborated by the "Court above." This was the gold medal he had set his heart on for years,—this the great prize of all his life; and now he had won it, and he was really a "sharp fellow." There is an intense delight in the thought of having realized a dream of ambition, of which, while our own hearts gave us the assurance of success, the world at large only scoffed at our attempting. To be able to say, "Yes, here I am, despite all your forebodings and all your predictions,—I knew it was 'in me'!" is a very proud thing, and such a moment of vaingloriousness is pardonable enough.

How enjoyable at such a moment of triumph was it to hear Lizzy sing and play, making that miserable old piano discourse in a guise it had never dreamed of! She was in one of those moods wherein she blended the wildest flights of fancy with dashes of quaint humor, now breathing forth a melody of Spohr's in accents of thrilling pathos, now hitting off in improvised doggerel a description of Aix and its company, with mimicries of their voice and manner irresistibly droll. In these imitations the Count, and even Beecher himself, figured, till Grog, fairly worn out with laughter, had to entreat her to desist.

As for Beecher, he was a good-tempered fellow, and the little raillery at himself took nothing from the pleasure of the description, and he laughed in ready acknowledgment of many a little trait of his own manner that he never suspected could have been detected by another.

"Ain't she wonderful,—ain't she wonderful?" exclaimed Grog, as she strolled out into the garden, and left them alone together.

"What I can't make out is, she has no blank days," said Beecher. "She was just as you saw her there, the whole time we were at Aix; and while she's rattling away at the piano, and going on with all manner of fun, just ask her a serious question,—I don't care about what,——and she'll answer you as if she had been thinking of nothing else for the whole day before."

"Had she been born in *your* rank of life, Beecher, where would she be be now,—tell me that?" said Davis; and there was an almost fierce energy in the words as he spoke them.

"I can tell you one thing," cried Beecher, in a transport of delight,— "there's no rank too high for her this minute."

"Well said, boy,—well said," exclaimed Davis, warmly; "and here's to her health."

"That generous toast and cheer must have been in honor of myself," said Lizzy, peeping in at the window, "and in acknowledgment I beg to invite you both to tea."

CHAPTER IX
A SAUNTER BY MOONLIGHT

Lizzy Davis had retired to her room somewhat weary after the day's journey, not altogether unexcited by her meeting with her father. How was it that there was a gentleness, almost a tenderness, in his manner she had never known before? The short, stern address, the abrupt question, the stare piercing and defiant of one who seemed ever to distrust what he heard, were all replaced by a tone of quiet and easy confidence, and a look that bespoke perfect trustfulness.

"Have I only seen him hitherto in moments of trial and excitement; are these the real traits of his nature; is it the hard conflict of life calls forth the sterner features of his character; and might he, in happier circumstances, be ever kind and confiding, as I see him now?" What a thrill of ecstasy did the thought impart! What a realization of the home she had often dreamed of! "He mistakes me, too," said she, aloud, "if he fancies that my heart is set upon some high ambition. A life of quiet obscurity, in some spot peaceful and unknown as this, would suffice for all my wishes. I want no triumphs,—I covet no rivalries." A glance at herself in the glass at this moment sent the deep color to her cheek, and she blushed deeply. Was it that those bright, flashing eyes, that fair and haughty brow, and those lips tremulous with proud significance gave a denial to these words? Indeed, it seemed as much, for she quickly added, "Not that I would fly the field, or ingloriously escape the struggle—Who's there?" cried she, quickly, as a low tap came to the door.

"It is I, Lizzy. I heard you still moving about, and I thought I'd propose half an hour's stroll in the moonlight before bed. What do you say to it?"

"I should like it of all things, papa," cried she, opening the door at once.

"Throw a shawl across your shoulders, child," said he; "the air is not always free from moisture. We'll go along by the river-side."

A bright moon in a sky without a cloud lit up the landscape, and by the strongly marked contrast of light and shadow imparted a most striking effect to a scene wild, broken, and irregular. Fantastically shaped rocks broke the current of the stream; at every moment gnarled and twisted roots straggled along the shelving banks, and in the uncertain light assumed goblin shapes and forms, the plashing stream, as it rushed by, appearing to give motion to the objects around. Nor was the semblance all unreal, for here and there a pliant branch rose and fell on the surging water like the arm of some drowning swimmer.

The father and daughter walked along for some time in utter silence, and the thoughts of each filled with the scene before them. Lizzy fancied it was a conflict of river gods,—some great Titanic war, where angry giants were the combatants; or again, as fairer forms succeeded, they seemed a group of nymphs bathing in the soft moonlight. As for Grog, it reminded him of a row at Ascot, where the swell-mob smashed the police; and so strikingly did it call up the memory of the event that he laughed aloud and heartily.

"Do tell me what you are laughing at, papa," said she, entreatingly.

"It was something that I saw long ago,—something I was reminded of by those trees yonder, bobbing up and down with the current."

"But what was it?" asked she, more eagerly; for even yet the memory kept him laughing.

"Nothing that could interest you, girl," said he, bluntly; and then, as if ashamed of the rudeness of his speech, he added, "Though I have seen a good deal of life, Lizzy, there's but little of it I could recall for either your benefit or instruction."

Lizzy was silent; she wished him to speak on, but did not choose to question him. Strangely enough, too, though be shunned the theme, he had been glad if she had led him on to talk of it.

After a long pause he sighed heavily, and said: "I suppose every one, if truth were told, would have rather a sad tale to tell of the world when he comes to my age. It don't improve upon acquaintance, I promise you. Not that I want to discourage *you* about it, my girl. You 'll come to my way of thinking one of these days, and it will be quite soon enough."

"And have you really found men so false and worthless as you say?"

"I'll tell you in one word the whole story, Lizzy. The fellows that are born to a good station and good property are all fair and honest, if they like it; the rest of the world must be rogues, whether they like it or not."

"This is a very disenchanting picture you put before me." "Here 's how it is, girl," said he, warming with his subject. "Every man in the world is a gambler; let him rail against dice, racing, cards, or billiards, he has a game of his own in his heart, and he's playing for a seat in the Cabinet, a place in the colonies, a bishopric, or the command of a regiment. The difference is, merely, that your regular play-man admits chance into his calculations, the other fellows don't; they pit pure skill against the table, and trust to their knowledge of the game."

She sighed deeply, but did not speak.

"And the women are the same," resumed he: "some scheming to get their husbands high office, some intriguing for honors or Court favor; all of them ready to do a sharp thing,—to make a hit on the Stock Exchange."

"And are there none above these mean and petty subterfuges?" cried she, indignantly.

"Yes; the few I have told you,—they who come into the world to claim the stakes. They can afford to be high-minded, and generous, and noble-hearted, as much as they please. They are booked 'all right,' and need never trouble their heads about the race; and that is the real reason, girl, why these men have an ascendancy over all others. They are not driven to scramble for a place; they have no struggles to encounter; the crowd makes way for them as they want to pass; and if they have anything good, ay, or even good-looking, about them, what credit don't they get for it!"

"But surely there must be many a lowly walk where a man with contentment can maintain himself honorably and even proudly?"

"I don't know of them, if there be," said Davis, sulkily. "Lawyers, parsons, merchants, are all, I fancy, pretty much alike,—all on 'the dodge.'"

"And Beecher,—poor Beecher?" broke in Lizzy. And there was a blended pity and tenderness in the tone that made it very difficult to say what her question really implied.

"Why do you call him poor Beecher?" asked he, quickly. "He ain't so poor in one sense of the word."

"It was in no allusion to his fortune I spoke. I was thinking of him solely with reference to his character."

"And he is poor Beecher, is he, then?" asked Davis, half sternly.

If she did not reply, it was rather in the fear of offending her father, whose manner, so suddenly changing, apprised her of an interest in the subject she had never suspected.

"Look here, Lizzy," said he, drawing her arm more closely to his side, while he bespoke her attention; "men born in Beecher's class don't need to be clever; they have no necessity for the wiles and schemes and subtleties that—that fellows like myself, in short, must practise. What they want is good address, pleasing manners,—all the better if they be good-looking. It don't require genius to write a check on one's banker; there is no great talent needed to say 'Yes,' or 'No,' in the House of Lords. The world—I mean their own world—likes them all the more if they have n't got great abilities. Now Beecher is just the fellow to suit them."

"He is not a peer, surely?" asked she, hastily.

"No, he ain't yet, but he may be one any day. He is as sure of the peerage as—I am not! and then, poor Beecher—as you called him awhile ago—becomes the Lord Viscount Lackington, with twelve or fourteen thousand a year! I tell you, girl, that of all the trades men follow, the very best, to enjoy life, is to be an English lord with a good fortune."

"And is it true, as I have read," asked Lizzy, "that this high station, so fenced around by privileges, is a prize open to all who have talent or ability to deserve it,—that men of humble origin, if they be gifted with high qualities, and devote them ardently to their country's service, are adopted, from time to time, into that noble brotherhood?"

"All rubbish; don't believe a word of it. It's a flam and a humbug,—a fiction like the old story about an Englishman's house being his castle, or that balderdash, 'No man need criminate himself.' They 're always inventing 'wise saws' like these in England, and they get abroad, and are believed, at last, just by dint of repeating. Here 's the true state of the case," said he, coming suddenly to a halt, and speaking with greater emphasis. "Here I stand, Christopher Davis, with as much wit under the crown of my hat as any noble lord on the woolsack, and I might just as well try to turn myself into a horse and be first favorite for the Oaks, as attempt to become a peer of Great Britain. It ain't to be done, girl,—it ain't to be done!"

"But, surely, I have heard of men suddenly raised to rank and title for the services—"

"So you do. They want a clever lawyer, now and then, to help them on with a peerage case; or, if the country grows forgetful of them, they attract some notice by asking a lucky general to join them; and even then they do it the way a set of old ladies would offer a seat in the coach to a stout-looking fellow on a road beset with robbers,—they hope he 'll fight for 'em; but, after all, it takes about three generations before one of these new hands gets regularly recognized by the rest."

"What haughty pride!" exclaimed she; but nothing in her tone implied reprobation.

"Ain't it haughty pride?" cried he; "but if you only knew how it is nurtured in them, how they are worshipped! They walk down St. James's Street, and the policeman elbows me out of the way to make room for them; they stroll into Tattersall's, and the very horses cock their tails and step higher as they trot past; they go into church, and the parson clears his throat and speaks up in a fine round voice for them. It's only because the blessed sun is not an English institution, or he'd keep all his warmth and light for the peerage!"

"And have they, who render all this homage, no shame for their self-abasement?"

"Shame! why, the very approach to them is an honor. When a lord in the ring at Newmarket nods his head to me and says, 'How d'ye do, Davis?' my pals—my acquaintances, I mean—are twice as respectful to me for the rest of the day. Not that *I* care for that," added he, sternly; "I know *them* a deuced sight better than they fancy!—far better than *they* know *me!*"

Lizzy fell into a revery; her thoughts went back to a conversation she had once held with Beecher about the habits of the great world, and all the difficulties to its approach.

"I wish I could dare to put a question to you, papa," said she, at last.

"Do so, girl. I'll do my best to answer it"

"And not be angry at my presumption,—not be offended with me?"

"Not a bit. Be frank with me, and you'll find me just as candid."

"What I would ask, then, is this,—and mind, papa, it is in no mere curiosity, no idle indulgence of a passing whim I would ask it, but for sake of self-guidance and direction,—who are we?—what are we?"

The blood rose to Davis's face and temples till he became crimson; his nostrils dilated, and his eyes flashed with a wild lustre. Had the bitterest insult of an enemy been hurled at his face before the open world, his countenance could not have betrayed an expression of more intense passion.

"By heaven!" said he, with a long-drawn breath, "I did n't think there was one in Europe would have asked me that much to my face. There's no denying it, girl, you have my own pluck in you."

"If I ever thought it would have moved you so—"

"Only to make me love you the more, girl,—to make me know you for my own child in heart and soul," cried he, pressing her warmly to him.

"But I would not have cost you this emotion, dearest pa—"

"It's over now; I am as cool as yourself. There 's my hand,—there 's not much show of nervousness there. 'Who are we?'" exclaimed he, fiercely, echoing her question. "I 'd like to know how many of that eight-and-twenty millions they say we are in England could answer such a question? There's a short thick book or two tells about the peerage and baronetage, and says who are they; but as for the rest of us—" A wave of the hand finished the sentence. "My own answer would be that of many another: I 'm the son of a man who bore the same name, and who, if alive, would tell the same story. As to what we are, that's another question," added he, shrewdly; "though, to be sure, English life and habits have established a very easy way of treating the matter. Everybody with no visible means of support, and who does nothing for his own subsistence, is either a gentleman or a vagrant. If he be positively and utterly unable to do anything for himself, he 's a gentleman; if he can do a stroke of work in some line or other, he 's only a vagrant."

"And you, papa?" asked she, with an accent as calm and unconcerned as might be.

"I?—I am a little of both, perhaps," said he, after a pause.

A silence ensued, long enough to be painful to each; Lizzy did not dare to repeat her question, although it still remained unanswered, and Davis knew well that he had not met it frankly, as he promised. What a severe struggle was that his mind now endured! The hoarded secret of his whole life,—the great mystery to which he had sacrificed all the happiness of a home, for which he had consented to estrange himself from his child, training her up amidst associations and habits every one of which increased the distance between them,—there it was now on his lip; a word might reveal it, and by its utterance might be blasted all the fondest hopes his heart had ever cherished. To make Lizzy a lady, to surround her not only with all the wants and requirements of station, but to imbue her mind with sentiments and modes of thought such as befit that condition, had been the devoted labor of his life. For this he had toiled and struggled, contrived, plotted, and schemed for years long. What terrible scenes had he not encountered, with what desperate characters not associated! In the fearful commerce of the play-table there was not a dark passion of the human heart he had not explored,—to know men in their worst aspects, in their insolence of triumph, the meanness of their defeat, in their moments of avarice, in their waste; to read their natures so that every start or sigh, a motion of the finger, a quivering of the lip should have its significance; to perceive, as by an instinct, wherein the craft or subtlety of each lay, and by the same rapid intuition to know his weak point also! Men have won high collegiate honors with less intensity of study than he gave to this dark pursuit; men have come out of battle with less peril to life than he faced every day of his existence, and all for one object,—all that his daughter might breathe an atmosphere from which he must live excluded, and know a world whose threshold he should never pass. Such was the terrible conflict that now raged within him as he reviewed the past, and saw to what a narrow issue he had reduced his one chance of happiness. "There she stands now," thought he, "all that my fondest hopes had ever fashioned her; and who is to say what one word—one single word uttered by my lips—may not make of that noble nature, pure and spotless as it is? How will she bear to hear that her station is a deception, her whole life a lie,—that she is the daughter of Grog Davis, the leg?" Heaven knows with what dexterous artifices he had often met this difficulty as it used to present itself to his mind, how he had seen in what way he could extricate himself, how reconcile his own shortcomings with her high-soaring tastes and habits! Whatever such devices he had ever conceived, none came to his aid now; not one offered him the slightest assistance.

Then came another thought,—"How long is this deception to be carried on? Am I to wait?" said he, "and if so, for what? Ay, there's the question, for what? Is it that some other may break the news to her, and tell her whose daughter she is?" In that world he knew best he could well imagine with what especial malice such a tale would be revealed. Not that slander need call imagination to its aid. Alas! his life had incidents enough for malignity to gloat over!

His stout arm shook, and his strong frame trembled with a sort of convulsive shudder as these thoughts flashed across his mind.

"Are you cold, dearest pa? Are you ill?" asked she, eagerly.

"No. Why do you ask?" said he, sternly.

"You trembled all over; I was afraid you were not well."

"I 'm never ill," said he, in the same tone. "There 's a bullet in me somewhere about the hip—they can't make out exactly where—gives me a twinge of pain now and then. Except that, I never knew what ailment means."

"In what battle?"

"It was n't a battle," broke he in; "it was a duel. It's an old story now, and not worth remembering. There, you need not shudder, girl; the fellow who shot me is alive, though, I must say, he has n't a very graceful way of walking. Do you ever read the newspapers,—did they allow you ever to read them at school?"

"No; but occasionally I used to catchy a glance at them in the drawing-room. It was a kind of reading fascinated me intensely, it was so real. But why do you ask me?"

"I don't know why I asked the question," muttered he, half moodily, and hung his head down. "Yes, I do," cried he, after a pause. "I wanted to know if you ever saw *my* name—our name—in the public prints."

"Once,—only once, and very long ago, I did, and I asked the governess if the name were common in England, and she said, 'Yes.' I remember the paragraph that attracted me to this very hour. It was the case of a young man—I forget the name—who shot himself in despair, after some losses at play, and the narrative was headed, 'More of Grog Davis!'"

Davis started back, and, in a voice thick and hoarse with passion, cried out,—

"And then? What next?" The words were uttered in a voice so fearfully wild that Lizzy stood in a sort of stupefied terror, and unable to reply. "Don't you hear me, girl?" cried he. "I asked you what came next."

"There was an account of an inquest,—some investigation as to how the poor fellow had met his death. I remember little about that. I was only curious to learn who this Grog Davis might be—"

"And they could n't tell you, it seems!"

"No; they had never heard of him."

"Then I 'll tell you, girl. Here he stands before you."

"You! papa—you—dearest pa! Oh, no, no!" cried she, imploringly, as she threw herself on his neck and sobbed bitterly,—"oh no! I 'll not believe it."

"And why not believe it? What was there in that same story that should prejudice *me*? There, there, girl, if you give way thus, it will offend me,—ay, Lizzy, offend me."

She raised her head from his shoulder, dried her eyes, and stood calm and unmoved before him. Her pale face, paler in the bright moonlight, now showed not a trace of passion or emotion.

Davis would have given his right hand at that moment that she had been led into some burst of excitement, some outbreak of passionate feeling, which, in rebuking, might have carried him away from all thoughts about himself; but she was cold and still and silent, like one who has heard some terrible tidings, but yet has summoned up courage for the trial. There was that in her calm, impassive stare that cut him to the very heart; nor could any words have reproached him so bitterly as that steadfast look.

"If you don't know who we are, you know what we are, girl. Is that not so?" cried he, in a thick and passionate tone. "I meant to have told it you fifty times. There was n't a week in the last two years that I did n't, at least, begin a letter to you about it I did more: I cut all the things out of the newspapers and made a collection of them, and intended, some day or other, you should read them. Indeed, it was only because you seemed so happy there, I spared you. I felt the day must come, though. Know it you must, sooner or later, and better from me than another I mean better for the other; for, by heaven! I 'd have shot him who told you. Why don't you speak to me, girl? What's passing in your mind?"

"I scarcely know," said she, in a hollow voice. "I don't quite feel sure I am awake!"

"Yes!" cried he, with a terrible oath, "you *are* awake; it was the past was the dream! When you were the Princess, and every post brought you some fresh means of extravagance,—*that* was the dream! The world went well with myself in those days. Luck stood to me in whatever I touched. In all I ventured I was sure to come right, as if I had made my bargain with Fortune. But the jade threw me over at last, that she did. From the hour I went in against Hope's stables at Rickworth,—that's two years and eleven days to-day,—I never won a bet! The greenest youngsters from Oxford beat me at my own weapons. I went on selling,—now a farm, now a house, now a brood mare. I sent the money all to you, girl, every guinea of it. What I did myself I did on tick till the September settling at Cottiswoode, and then it was all up. I was ruined!"

"Ruined!" echoed she, while she grasped his arm and drew him closer to her side; "you surely had made friends—"

"Friends are capital things when the world goes well with you, but friends are fond of a good cook and iced champagne, and they don't fancy broken boots and a bad hat. Besides, what credit is to the merchant, luck is to one of us. Let the word get abroad luck is against you; let them begin to say, 'There 's that poor devil Davis in for it again; he's so unlucky!'— once they say that, you are shunned like a fellow with the plague; none will associate with you, none give you a helping hand or a word of counsel. Why, the grooms wouldn't gallop if I was on the ground, for fear my bad luck might strain a sinew and slip a ligament! And they were right too! Smile if you like, girl,—I am not a very superstitious fellow,—but nobody shall persuade me there ain't such a thing as luck. Be that as it may, *mine* turned,—I was ruined!"

"And were there none to come to your aid? You must surely have lent a helping hand to many—"

"Look here, girl," said he; "now that we are on this subject, you may as well understand it aright. If a gentleman born—a fellow like Beecher, there—comes to grief, there's always plenty of others ready to serve him; some for the sake of his family, some for his name, some because there's always the chance that he may pay one day or other. Snobs, too, would help him, because he's the Honorable Annesley Beecher; but it's vastly different when it's Grog Davis is in case. Every one rejoices when a leg breaks down."

"A leg is the slang for—for—"

"For a betting man," interposed Davis. "When a fellow takes up the turf as a profession, they call him 'a leg,'—not that they'd exactly say it to his face!" added he, with a smile of intense sarcasm.

"Go on," said she, faintly, after a slight pause.

"Go on with what?" cried he, rudely. "I've told you everything. You wanted to know what I was, and how I made my living. Well, you know it all now. To be sure, the newspapers, if you read them, could give you more precise details; but there's one thing, girl, they could n't blink,—there's not one of them could say that what my head planned overnight my hand was not ready to defend in the morning! I can't always throw a main, but I 'll hit my man,—and at five-and-thirty paces, if he don't like to stand closer."

"And what led you to this life, papa? Was it choice?"

"I have told you enough already; too much, mayhap," said he, doggedly. "Question me no more!"

Had Davis but seen the face of her at his side, what a terrible shock it would have given him, hard and stern as he was! She was pale as marble,—even the lips were colorless; while along her cheeks a heavy tear stole slowly along. It was the only one she shed, but it cost an agony.

"And this is the awaking from that glorious dream I have long been lost in?—this the explanation of that life of costly extravagance, where every wish was answered, every taste pampered. This is the reverse of that medal which represented me as noble by birth and high in station!" If these were the first bitter thoughts that crossed her mind, her next were to ask herself why it was that the tidings had not humiliated her more deeply. "How is it that while I see and hear all this," cried she, "I listen in a spirit of defiance, not defeat? Is it that in my heart I dare to arraign the decrees the world has adopted for its guidance? Do I presume to believe that I can play the rebel successfully against the haughtiest aristocracy of Europe?—There is yet one question, papa," said she, slowly and deliberately, "that I would wish to ask you. It is the last I will ever put, leaving to your own discretion to answer it or not. Why was it—I mean, with what object did you place me where by habit and education I should contract ideas of life so widely different from those I was born to?"

"Can't you guess?" said he, rudely.

"Mayhap I do guess the reason," said she, in a low but unbroken voice. "I remember your saying one night to Mr. Beecher, 'When a colt has a turn of speed, he 's always worth the training.'"

Davis grew crimson; his very ears tingled as the blood mounted to his head. Was it shame, was it anger, was it a strange pride to see the traits of his own heart thus reflected on his child, or was it a blending of all three together? At all events, he never uttered a word, but walked slowly along at her side.

A low faint sigh from Lizzy suddenly aroused him, and he said, "Are you ill,—are you tired, girl?"

"I 'd like to go back to the house," said she, calmly but weakly. He turned without a word, and they walked on towards the inn.

"When I proposed this walk, Lizzy, I never meant it to have been so sad a one."

"Nor yours the fault if it is so," said she, drearily.

"I could, it is true, have kept you longer in the dark. I might have maintained this deception a week or two longer."

"Oh, that were useless; the mistake was in not—No matter—it was never a question wherein I could have a voice. Has n't the night grown colder?"

"No; it's just what it was when we came out," said he, gruffly. "Now that you know all this affair," resumed he, after a lapse of some minutes, "there 's another matter I 'd like to talk over; it touches yourself, too, and we may as well have it now as later. What about Beecher; he has been paying you attentions, hasn't he?"

"None beyond what I may reasonably expect from one in his position towards me."

"Yes, but he has, though. I sent over Lienstahl to report to me, and he says that Beecher's manner implied attachment, and yours showed no repugnance to him. Is this true?"

"It may be, for aught I know," said she, indifferently. "Mr. Beecher probably knows what he meant. I certainly can answer for myself, and will say that whatever my manner might imply, my heart—if that be the name for it—gave no concurrence to what the Count attributed to me."

"Do you dislike him?"

"Dislike? No; certainly not; he is too gentle, too obliging, too conciliating in manner, too well bred to create dislike. He is not very brilliant—"

"He'll be a peer," broke in Davis.

"I suspect that all his views of life are deeply tinged with prejudice?"

"He'll be a peer," continued Davis.

"He has been utterly neglected in education."

"He don't want it."

"I mean that to suit the station he fills—"

"He has got the station; he's sure of it; he can't be stripped of it. In one word, girl, he has, by right and birth, rank and fortune, such as ten generations of men like myself, laboring hard every hour of their lives, could never win. He'll be a peer of England, and I know of no title means so much."

"But of all his failings," said Lizzy, who seemed to take little heed of her father's interruptions, while steadily following out her own thoughts,—"of all his failings, he has none greater or more pernicious than the belief that it is a mark of intelligence to outwit one's neighbor; that cunning is a high quality, and craft means genius."

"These might be poor qualities to gain a living with," said Davis, "but I tell you, once for all, he does n't need to be brilliant, or witty, or any other nonsense of that kind. He'll have the right to go where all the cleverness of the world couldn't place him, to live in a set where, if he could Write plays like Shakspeare, build bridges like Brunel, or train a horse like John Scott, it would n't avail him a brass farthing; and if you only knew, child, what these people think of each other, and what the world thinks of *them*, you'd see it's the best stake ever was run for."

Lizzy never replied a word; every syllable of her father's speech was, as it were, "filtering down" into her mind, and she brooded long over the thoughts thus suggested. Thus, walking along in silence, side by side, they drew nigh the house. They had now gained the little garden before the door, and were standing in the broad full moonlight, face to face, Davis saw that her eyes were red and her cheeks marked by tears; but an impassive calm, and a demeanor subdued even to coldness, seemed to have succeeded to this emotion. "Oh, my poor girl," broke he out, in a voice of deepest feeling, "if I did n't know the world so well, — if I did n't know how little one gains by indulging affection, — if I did n't know, besides, how you yourself will think of all this some ten or twelve years hence, I could n't have the heart for it."

"And — must — it — be?" faltered she out, in a broken accent.

Davis threw his arm around her, and, pressing her to him, sobbed bitterly. "There, there," cried he, "go in, — go in, child; go to bed, and get some sleep." And with this he turned quickly away and left her.

CHAPTER X
A RIDE TO NEUWIED

Long before Lizzy had composed herself to sleep—for her heart was torn by a first sorrow, and she lay restless and fevered—her father, mounted on a post-horse, was riding away towards the Rhine. He had desired that the reply to his telegraphic message should be addressed to him at the post-office of Neuwied, and thither he was now bent. It is a strange thing, that when the affections of men of this stamp are deeply moved,—when their sensibilities, long dulled and hardened by the rubs of life, are once evoked,—the feelings excited are less those of gentleness and tenderness than an almost savage desire for some personal conflict. Urging his horse to full speed, Davis spared neither whip nor spur. Alone upon that solitary road, he asked himself aloud if he were less alone in the broad, bleak world? "Is not the 'field' against me wherever I go? I never heard of the fellow that had not some 'moorings'—some anchorage—except myself." But a brief hour ago and there was one who loved him with all her heart,—who saw, or fancied she saw, a rich mine of generous qualities in his rough manners and blunt address,—who pictured to her mind what such a nature might have been under happier circumstances and with better culture. "And now," cried he, aloud,—"now she knows me for what I am, how will she bear this? Will she sink under it, will it crush her, or has she enough of my own blood in her veins to meet it courageously? Oh! if she only knew the world as I do,—what a mean coward it is, how it bullies the weak and truckles to the strong, how it frowns down the timid and simpers to the sturdy! Every man—ay, and every woman—can sell his life dearly; and strange it is, one only learns the value of this secret too late. Let a fellow start with it, and see what it does for him. *I* went at them single-handed; *I* went down all alone into the ring, and have they beaten *me*? I had no honorable or right honorable friends to pick *me* out of a scrape. It would be hard to find three men, with good hats on them, would bail me to the amount of ten pounds; and here I am to-day just as ready to face them all as ever."

What canting nonsense do we occasionally read in certain quarters to disparage mere personal courage,—"mere personal courage"! We are reminded that the ignoble quality is held in common with the bull-dog, and that in this essential he is our master; we are reminded that it is a low and vulgar attribute that neither elevates nor enlightens, that the meanest creatures are often gifted with it, and the noblest natures void of it. To all this we give a loud and firm denial; and we affirm as steadfastly, that without it there is neither truth nor manliness. The self-reliance that makes a man maintain his word, be faithful to his friendships, and honorable in his dealings, has no root in a heart that shakes with craven fear. The life of a coward is the voyage of a ship with a leak,—eternal contrivance, never-ceasing emergency. All thoughts dashed with a perpetual fear of death, what room is there for one generous emotion, one great or high-hearted ambition?

What a quality must that be, I would ask, that gives even to such a nature as this man's a sort of rugged dignity? Yes, with all his failings and short-comings, and I am not going to hide one of them, his personal courage lifted him out of that category of contempt to which his life assigned him. How well the world understands such men to be the *feræ naturæ* of humanity! It may shun, deprecate, disparage, but it never despises them. If then of such value be a gift that makes even the bad appear tolerable, there is this evil in the quality, that it disposes men like Davis to be ever on the attack. Their whole policy of life is aggressive.

It was about eight o'clock, on a mellow autumnal morning, as Grog reached Neuwied, and rode down the main street, already becoming thronged with the peasantry for the market: Guiding his horse carefully through the booths of flaunting wares, gay stalls of rural finery, and stands of fruit, he reached the little inn where he meant to breakfast.

The post was not to open for an hour, so that he ordered his meal to be at once got ready, and looked also to the comfort of his beast, somewhat blown by a long stage. His breakfast had been laid in the public room, in which two travellers were seated, whose appearance, even before he heard them speak, proclaimed them to be English. They were both young, fresh-looking, and well favored; that stamp of half-modesty, half-boldness, so essentially British, was on them, and, notwithstanding the entrance of a stranger, they talked away in their native language with all the fearless security your genuine John Bull feels that no confounded foreigner can understand him. It is but fair to admit that Grog's beard and moustaches, his frogged and braided grass-green coat, and his blue spectacles made him resemble anything on earth rather than a subject of Queen Victoria.

In the mere glance Grog bestowed upon them as he passed, he saw the class to which they pertained,—young Oxford or Cambridge men, "out" for their vacation,—an order for which he ever entertained a supreme contempt. He despised their mock shrewdness, their assumed craft, and that affectation of being "fast men," which in reality never soared above running up a bill at the pastrycook's, thrashing a townsman, and giving a stunning wine-party at their rooms. To what benefit could such miniature vices be turned? It was only "punting" with the Evil One, and Grog thought so and avoided them.

Deep in the "mysterious gutturals" of the "Cologne Gazette," or busily discussing his carbonadoed beefsteak, Davis gave no heed to the bald, disjointed chat of his neighbors; broken phrases reached him at intervals about proctors and the "little go," the stroke oar of Brazennose, or some new celebrity of the ballet, when suddenly the name of Annesley Beecher startled him. He now listened attentively, and heard one of them relating to the other that while waiting for his arrival at Aix la-Chapelle, he had devoted himself to watching Beecher and "the stunning girl" that was with him. It appeared from what he said that all Aix was wildly excited by curiosity on her account. That she was neither wife, sister, nor mistress, none disputed. Who was she, then? or what could be the explanation of that mysterious companionship? "You should have seen her at the rooms," continued the narrator; "she used to make her appearance about eleven—rarely before—dressed with a magnificence that threw all the little German royalties into the shade,—such lace and ornaments! They said, of course, it was all false; I can only tell you that old Lady Bamouth got beside her one night just to examine her scarf, and she proclaimed it real Brussels, and worth I can't say how much; and for the recovery of an opal that fell out of her bracelet one night Beecher gave six hundred francs next morning."

"Then it was the money was false," broke in the other; "Beecher is ruined, he hasn't sixpence,—at least I've always heard him mentioned as a fellow regularly cleaned out years ago."

"He was before my day," resumed the first; "but I heard the same story you did. But what's the meaning of calling a fellow ruined that can go about the world stopping at first-rate hotels, having carriages, horses, opera-boxes? Why, the waiter at Aix told me that he paid above five hundred florins for flowers. This girl, whoever she was, was wild about moss-roses and pink hyacinths, and they fetched them from Rotterdam for her. Pretty well that for a ruined man!"

"Perhaps it was she herself had the money," suggested the other, half carelessly.

"That's possible, too; I know that whenever she came down to the wells and took a glass of the waters, she always gave a gold piece to the girl that served her."

"Then she was not a lady by birth; that trait is quite sufficient to decide the point."

Davis started as if he had been stung; here, from the lips of these raw youths, was he to receive a lesson in life, and be told that all the cost and splendor by which he purposed to smooth over the difficult approaches to society were fatal blunders and no more,—that the very extravagance so imposing in one of acknowledged station becomes "suspect" in those of dubious rank. Like all men of quick resentments, he soon turned the blame from himself to others. It was Lizzy's fault. What right had she to draw upon herself all the censorious tongues of a watering-place? Why should she have attracted this foolish notoriety? After all, she was new to life and the world, and might be pardoned; but Beecher,—it was just the one solitary thing he *did* know,—Beecher ought to have warned her against this peril; he ought to have guarded against it himself. Why should such a girl be exposed to the insolent comments of fellows like these? and he measured them deliberately, and thought over in his mind how little trouble it would cost him to put two families into mourning,—mayhap, to throw a life-long misery into some happy home, and change the whole destinies of many he had never seen,—never should see! There was, however, this difficulty, that in doing so he drew a greater publicity upon her,—all whose interests required secrecy and caution. "'Till she have the right to another name than mine, she must not be the talk of newspapers," said he to himself; and, like many a prudent reflection, it had its sting of pain.

These meditations were rudely cut short by the sound of his own name. It was the elder of the two young men who was discussing the duel at Brussels, and detailing, with all the influence of his superior experience, the various reasons "why no man was called upon to meet such a fellow as Davis." "I talked it over with Stan worth and Ellis, and they both agreed with me."

"But what is to be done?" asked the younger.

"You hand him over to the police, or you thrash him right well with a horsewhip, pay five pounds penalty for the assault, and there's an end on't."

"And is 'Grog' as they call him, the man to put up with that mode of treatment?"

"What can he do? Notoriety must ruin him. The moment it gets abroad that a wolf has been seen near a village, all turn out for the pursuit."

Had he who uttered this sentiment only cast his eyes towards the stranger at the table in the corner, he would have seen, by the expression of the features, that his simile was not a bad one. Davis shook with passion, and his self-control, to sit still and listen, was almost like a fit.

"All the more ungenerous, then, would be the conduct," said the younger, "to resent a personal wrong by calling in others to your aid."

"Don't you see, George," broke in the other, "that men have their beasts of prey like other animals, and agree to hunt them down, out of common security, for the mischief he causes, and the misery he spreads through the world? One of these fellows in his lair is worse than any tiger that ever crouched in a jungle. And as to dealing with him, as Ellis says, do you ever talk of giving a tiger fair play,—do you make a duel of it, with equal weapons; or do you just shoot him down when you can and how you can?"

Davis arose and drew himself up, and there was a moment of irresolution in his mind, of which, could the two travellers-have read the secret, they would almost as soon have smoked their cigars in the den of a wild beast. And yet there they sat, puffing indolently away the blue cloud, scarcely deigning a passing glance at Grog, as he proceeded to leave the room.

Anatomists assure us that if we but knew the delicate tissues by which the machinery of our life is carried on, how slight the fibres, how complex the functions on which vitality depends, we should not have courage to move, or even speak, lest we should destroy an organization so delicate and sensitive. In like manner, did we but know in life the perils over which we daily pass, the charged mines over which we walk, the volcanoes that are actually throbbing beneath our feet, what terrors would it give to mere existence! It was on the turn of a straw how Davis decided,—a word the more, a look from one of them, a laugh, might have cost a life. With a long-drawn breath, the sigh of a pent-up emotion, Grog found himself in the open air; there was a vague feeling in his mind of having escaped a peril, but what or where or how he could n't remember.

He sat down in the little porch under the clustering vines; the picturesque street, with its carved gables and tasteful balconies, sloped gently down to the Rhine, which ran in swift eddies beneath. It was a fair and pleasant scene, nor was its influence all lost upon him. He was already calmed. The gay dresses and cheerful faces of the peasants, as they passed and repassed, their merry voices, their hearty recognitions and pleasant greetings, gave a happier channel to his thoughts. He thought of Lizzy,—how *she* would like it, how enjoy it! and then a sudden pang shot through his heart, and he remembered that she, too, was no longer the same. The illusion that had made her life a fairy tale was gone,—dissipated forever. The spell that gave the charm to her existence was broken! What was all the cultivation of mind,—what the fascinations by which she moved the hearts of all around her, — what the accomplishments by which she adorned society, if they only marked the width of that chasm that separated her from the well-born and the wealthy? To be more than their equal in grace, beauty, and genius, less than their inferior in station, was a sad lesson to learn, and this the last night had taught her.

"Ay," muttered he, below his breath, "she knows who she is now, but she has yet to learn all that others think of her." How bitterly, at that instant, did he reproach himself for having revealed his secret! A thousand times better to have relinquished all ambition, and preserved the warm and confiding love she bore him. "We might have gone to America, — to Australia. In some far-away country I could easily earn subsistence, and no trace of my former life follow me. She, at least, would not have been lost to me, — her affection would have clung to me through every trial. Mere reverse of fortune — for such and no more had it seemed — would never have chilled the generous glow of her woman's heart, and I need not have shocked her self-love, nor insulted her dignity, by telling her that she was the gambler's daughter."

As he was thus musing, the two travellers came out and seated themselves in the porch; the elder one, needing a light for his cigar, touched his hat to Davis, and muttered some broken words of German, to request permission to light it from him. Grog bowed a stiff acquiescence; and the younger said, "Not over-courteous, — a red Jew, I take it!"

"A travelling jeweller, I fancy," said the other; "twig the smart watch-chain."

Oh, young gentlemen, how gingerly had you trod there if you only knew how thin was the ice under your feet, and how cold the depth beneath it! Davis arose and walked down the street. The mellow notes of a bugle announced the arrival of the post, and the office must now open in a few minutes. Forcing his way through the throng to the open window, he asked if there were any letters for Captain Christopher? None. Any for Captain Davis? None. Any for the Hon. Annesley Beecher? The same reply. He was turning away in disappointment, when a voice called out, "Wait! here's a message just come in from the Telegraph-office. Please to sign the receipt for it." He wrote the name C. Christopher boldly, and pushed his way through the crowd once more.

If his heart throbbed painfully with the intensity of anxiety, his fingers never trembled as he broke the seal of the despatch. Three brief lines were all that were there; but three brief lines can carry the tidings of a whole destiny. We give it as it stood: —

"William Peach to Christopher, Neuwied, in Nassau.

"The Viscount died yesterday, at four p. m. Lawyers want A. B.'s address immediately.

"Proceedings already begun."

Davis devoured the lines four—five times over, and then muttered between his teeth, "Safe enough now,—the match as good as over!"

"I say, George," said one of the young travellers to his companion, "our friend in the green frock must have got news of a prize in the lottery. Did you ever see anything like his eyes? They actually lit up the blue spectacles."

"Clap the saddle on that black horse," cried Grog, as he passed into the stable; "give him a glass of Kirsch-wasser and bring him round to the door."

"He knows how to treat an old poster," said the ostler; "it's not the first ride he has taken on a courier's saddle."

CHAPTER XI
HOW GROG DAVIS DISCOURSED, AND ANNESLEY BEECHER LISTENED

When Davis reached the little inn at evening, he was surprised to learn that Annesley Beecher had passed the day alone. Lizzy complained of headache, and kept her room. Grog listened to this with a grave, almost stern look; he partly guessed that the ailment was a mere pretext; he knew better to what to attribute her absence. They dined tête-à-tête; but there was a constraint over each, and there was little of that festive enjoyment that graced the table on the day before. Beecher was revolving in his mind all the confessions that burdened his conscience about Stein and the mystical volume he had bought from him; the large sums he had drawn for were also grievous loads upon his heart, and he knew not in what temper or spirit Davis would hear of them. Grog, too, had many things in his head; not, indeed, that he meant to reveal them, but they were like secret instructions to his own heart, to be referred to for guidance and direction.

They sipped their wine under the trellised vines, and smoked their cigars in an atmosphere fragrant with the jessamine and the rose, the crystal river eddying along at their feet, and the purple mountain glowing in the last tints of declining day. "We want Lizzy to enliven us," said Davis, after a long silence on both sides. "We 're dull and heavy without her."

"By Jove! it does make a precious difference whether she's here or not," said Beecher, earnestly.

"There's a light-heartedness about that girl does one good," said Davis, as he puffed his cigar. "And she's no fool, either."

"I should think she's not," muttered Beecher, half indignantly.

"It could n't be supposed she should know life like you or me, for instance; she hasn't seen the thing,—never mixed with it; but let the time come that she shall take her part in the comedy, you 'll see whether she 'll not act it cleverly."

"She has head for anything!" chimed in Beecher.

"Ay, and what they call tact too. I don't care what company you place her in; take her among your duchesses to-morrow, and see if she'll not keep her own place,—and that a good one."

Beecher sighed, but it was not in any despondency.

And now a long silence ensued; not a sound heard save the light noise of the bottle as it passed between them, and the long-drawn puffs of smoke that issued from their lips.

"What did you do with Stein? Did he give you the money?" asked Davis, at last.

"Oh yes, he gave it—he gave it freely enough; in fact, he bled so easily that, as the doctors say, I took a good dash from him. You mentioned two thousand florins, but I thought, as I was about it, a little more would do us no harm, and so I said, 'Lazarus, old fellow, what if we make this for ten thousand—"

"Ten thousand!" said Davis, removing his cigar from his lips and staring earnestly, but yet not angrily, at the other.

"Don't you see that as I have the money with me," began Beecher, in a tone of apology and terror, "and as the old fellow didn't put 'the screw on' as to discount—"

"No, he's fair enough about that; indeed, so far as my own experience goes, all Jews are. It's your high-class Christian I'm afraid of; but you took the cash?"

"Yes!" said Beecher, timidly, for he was n't sure he was yet out of danger.

"It was well done,—well thought of," said Grog, blandly. "We 'll want a good round sum to try this new martingale of mine. Opening with five naps, we must be able to bear a run of four hundred and eighty, which, according to the rule of chances, might occur once in seventeen thousand three hundred and forty times."

"Oh, as to that," broke in Beecher, "I have hedged famously. I bought old Stein's conjuring-book; what he calls his 'Kleinod,' showing how every game is to be played, when to lay on, when to draw off. Here it is," said he, producing the volume from his breast-pocket. "I have been over it all day. I tried three problems with the cards myself, but I couldn't make them come up right."

"How did you get him to part with this?" asked Davis, as he examined the volume carefully.

"Well, I gave him a fancy price,—that is, I am to give it, which makes all the difference," said Beecher, laughing. "In short, I gave him a bit of stiff, at three months, for one thousand—"

"Florins?"

"No, pounds,—pounds sterling," said Beecher, with a half-choking effort.

"It *was* a fancy price," said Grog, slowly, not the slightest sign of displeasure manifesting itself on his face as he spoke.

"You don't think, then, that it was too much?" faltered out Beecher.

"Perhaps not, *under* the circumstances," said Davis, keenly.

"What do you mean by 'under the circumstances'?"

Davis threw his cigar into the stream, pushed bottle and glasses away from him,—far enough to permit him to rest both his arms on the table,—and then, steadfastly fixing his eyes on the other, with a look of intense but not angry significance, said, "How often have I told you, Beecher, that it was no use to try a 'double' with me? Why, man, I know every card in your hand."

"I give you my sacred word of honor, Grog—"

"To be renewed at three months, I suppose?" said Davis, sneeringly. "No, no, my boy, it takes an earlier rise to get to the blind side of Kit Davis. I 'm not angry with you for trying it,—not a bit, lad; there 's nothing wrong in it but the waste of time."

"May I be hanged, drawn, and quartered, if I know what you are at, Grog!" exclaimed the other, piteously.

"Well, all I can say is I read *you* easier than *you* read *me*. *You* gave old Lazarus a thousand pounds for that book after reading that paragraph in the 'Times.'"

"What paragraph?"

"I mean that about your brother's title not being legal."

"I never saw it,—never heard of it," cried Beecher, in undisguised terror.

"Well, I suppose I 'm to believe you," said Davis, half reluctantly. "It was in a letter from the Crimea, stating that so confident are the friends of a certain claimant to the title and estates now enjoyed by Lord Lackington, that they have offered the young soldier who represents the claim any amount of money he pleases to purchase promotion in the service."

"I repeat to you my word of honor, I never saw nor heard of it"

"Of course, then, I believe you," said Grog.

Again and again did Beecher reiterate assurances of his good faith; he declared that during all his stay at Aix he had never looked into a newspaper, nor had he received one single letter, except from Davis himself; and Davis believed him, from the simple fact that such a paragraph as he quoted had no existence,—never was in print, never uttered till Grog's own lips had fashioned it.

"But, surely, Grog, it is not a flying rumor—the invention of some penny-a-liner—would find any credence with *you?*"

"I don't know," said Davis, slowly; "I won't say I 'd swear to it all, but just as little would I reject it as a fable. At all events, I gave you credit for having trimmed your sails by the tidings; and if you did n't, why, there's no harm done, only you 're not so shrewd a fellow as I thought you."

Beecher's face grew scarlet; how near, how very near, he was of being "gazetted" the sharp fellow he had been striving for years to become, and now, by his own stupid admission, had he invalidated his claim to that high degree.

"And this is old Stein's celebrated book? I 've heard of it these five-and-thirty years, though I never saw it till now. Well, I won't say you made a bad bargain—"

"Indeed, Grog,—indeed, by George! I 'm as glad as if I won five hundred to hear you say so. To tell you the truth, I was half afraid to own myself the purchaser. I said to myself, 'Davis will chaff me so about this book, he 'll call me all the blockheads in Europe—'"

"No, no, Beecher, you ain't a blockhead, nor will I suffer any one to call you such. There are things—there are people, too, Just as there are games—that you don't know, but before long you 'll be the match of any fellow going. I can put you up to them, and I will. There's my hand on it."

Beecher grasped the proffered hand, and squeezed it with a warmth there was no denying. What wonderful change had come over Grog he could not guess. Whence this marvellous alteration in his manner towards him? No longer scoffing at his mistaken notions of people, or disparaging his abilities, Davis condescended now to talk and take counsel with him as an equal.

"That 's the king of wines," said Davis, as he pushed a fresh bottle across the table. "When you can get Marcobrunner like that, where's the Burgundy ever equalled it? Fill up your glass, and drink a bumper to our next venture, whatever it be!"

"'Our next venture, whatever it be!'" echoed Beecher, as he laid the empty glass on the table.

"Another toast," said Davis, replenishing the glasses. "'May all of our successes be in company.'"

"I drink it with all my heart, old fellow. You 've always stood like a man to me, and I 'll never desert you," cried Beecher, whose head was never proof against the united force of wine and excitement.

"There never were two fellows on this earth so made to run in double harness," said Davis, "as you and myself. Let us only lay our heads together, and there's nothing can resist us."

Grog now launched forth into one of those descriptions which he could throw off with a master's hand, sketching life as a great hunting-ground, and themselves as the hunters. What zest and vigor could he impart to such a picture!—how artfully, too, could he make Beecher the foreground figure, he himself only shadowed forth as an accessory! Listening with eagerness to all he said, Beecher continued to drink deeply; the starry night, the perfumed air, the rippling sounds of the river, all combining with the wine and the converse to make up a dreamland of fascination. Nor was the enchantment less perfect that the objects described passed before him like a series of dissolving views. They represented, all of them, a life of pleasure and enjoyment,—means inexhaustible, means for every extravagance, and, what he relished fully as much, the undisputed recognition by the world to the claim of being a "sharp fellow,"—a character to which Grog's aid was so dexterously contributed as to escape all detection.

Perhaps our reader might not have patience with us were we to follow Davis through all the devious turns and windings of this tortuous discourse. Perhaps, too, we should fail signally were we to attempt to convey in our cold narrative what came from his lips with all the marvellous power of a good story-teller, whose voice could command many an inflection, and whose crafty nature appreciated the temper of the metal beneath his beat If we could master all these, another and a greater difficulty would still remain; for how could we convey, as Davis contrived to do, that through all these gorgeous scenes of worldly success, in the splendor of a life of magnificence, amidst triumphs and conquests, one figure should ever pass before the mind's eye, now participating in the success, now urging its completion, now, as it were, shedding a calm and chastened light over all,—a kind of angelic influence that heightened every enjoyment of the good, and averted every approach of evil?

Do not fancy, I beseech you, that this was a stroke of high art far above the pencil of Grog Davis. Amongst the accidents of his early life the "stage" had figured, and Grog had displayed very considerable talents for the career. It was only at the call of what he considered a higher ambition he had given up "the boards" for "the ring." Besides this, he was inspired by the Marcobrunner, which had in an equal degree affected the brain of him who listened. If Grog were eloquent, Beecher was ductile. Indeed, so eagerly did he devour all that the other said, that when a moment of pause occurred, he called out, "Go on, old fellow,—go on! I could listen to you forever!"

Nor was it altogether surprising that he should like to hear words of praise and commendation from lips that once only opened in sarcasm and ridicule of him. How pleasant to know, at last, that he was really and truly a great partner in the house of Davis and Co., and not a mere commission agent, and that this partnership—how that idea came to strike him we cannot determine—was to be binding forever. How exalting, too, the sentiment that it was just at the moment when all his future looked gloomiest this friendship was ratified. The Lackington peerage might go, but there was Grog Davis, stanch and true,—the ancient estates be torn from his house, but there was the precious volume of old Lazarus, with wealth untold within its pages. Thus threading his way through these tortuous passages of thought, stumbling, falling, and blundering at every step, that poor brain lost all power of coherency and all guidance, and he wavered between a reckless defiance of the world and a sort of slavish fear of its censure.

"And Lackington, Grog,—Lackington," cried he, at length,—"he's as proud as Lucifer; what will he say?"

"Not so much as you think!" remarked Grog, dryly. "Lackington will take it easier than you suspect."

"No, no, you don't know him,—don't know him at all. I wouldn't stand face to face with him this minute for a round sum!"

"I 'd not like it over-much myself!" muttered Davis, with a grim smile.

"It's all from pride of birth and blood, and he 'd say, 'Debts, if you like; go ahead with Jews and the fifty per centers, but, hang it, don't tie a stone round your throat, don't put a double ditch between you and your own rank! Look where I am,' he 'd say,—'look where I am!'"

"Well, I hope he finds it comfortable!" muttered Grog, with a dry malice.

"Look where I am!" resumed Beecher, trying to imitate the pretentious tones of his brother's voice. "And where is it, after all?"

"Where we 'll all be, one day or other," growled out Grog, who could not help answering his own reflections.

"'And are you sure of where you are?'—that's what I 'd ask him, eh, Grog?—'are you sure of where you are?'"

"That *would* be a poser, I suspect," said Davis, who laughed heartily; and the contagion catching Beecher, he laughed till the tears came.

"I might ask him, besides, 'Are you quite sure how long you are to remain where you are?' eh, Grog? What would he say to that?"

"The chances are, he 'd not answer at all," said Davis, dryly.

"No, no! you mistake him, he's always ready with a reason; and then he sets out by reminding you that he's the head of the house,—a fact that a younger brother does n't need to have recalled to his memory. Oh, Grog, old fellow, if I were the Viscount,—not that I wish any ill to Lack-ington,—not that I 'd really enjoy the thing at any cost to *him*,—but if I were—"

"Well, let's hear. What then?" cried Davis, as he filled the other's glass to the top,—"what then?"

"Would n't I trot the coach along at a very different pace. It's not poking about Italy, dining with smoke-dried cardinals and snuffy old 'marchesas,' I 'd be; but I 'd have such a stable, old fellow, with Jem Bates to ride and Tom Ward to train them, and yourself, too, to counsel me. Would n't we give Binsleigh and Hawksworth and the rest of them a cold bath, eh?"

"That ain't the style of thing at all, Beecher," said Grog, deprecatingly; "you ought to go in for the 'grand British nobleman dodge,'—county interests, influence with a party, and a vote in the Lords. If you were to try it, you 'd make a right good speech. It wouldn't be one of those flowery things the Irish fellows do, but a manly, straightforward, genuine English discourse."

"Do you really think so, Grog?" asked he, eagerly.

"I 'm sure of it I never mistook pace in my life; and I know what's in you as well as if I saw it. The real fact is, you have a turn of speed that you yourself have no notion of, but it will come out one of these days if you 're attacked,—if they say anything about your life on the turf, your former companions, or a word about the betting-ring."

The charm of this flattery was far more intoxicating than even the copious goblets of Marcobrunner, and Beecher's flushed cheeks and flashing eyes betrayed how it overpowered him. Davis went on:—

"You are one of those fellows that never show 'the stuff they 're made of' till some injustice is done them,—eh?"

"True as a book!" chimed in Beecher.

"Take you fairly, and a child might lead you; but try it on to deny you what you justly have a right to,—let them attempt to dictate to you, and say, 'Do this, and don't do the other,'—little they know on what back they 've put the saddle. You 'll give them such a hoist in the air as they never expected!"

"How you read every line of me!" exclaimed Beecher, in ecstasy.

"And I 'll tell you more; there's not another man breathing knows you but myself. They 've always seen you in petty scrapes and little difficulties, pulling the devil by the last joint of his tail, as Jack Bush says; but let them wait till you come out for a cup race,—the Two Thousand Guinea Stakes,— then I'm not Kit Davis if you won't be one of the first men in England."

"I hope you 're right, Davis. I almost feel as if you were," said Beecher, earnestly.

"When did you find me in the wrong, so far as judgment went? Show me one single mistake I ever made in a matter of opinion? Who was it foretold that Bramston would bolt after the Cotteswold if Rugby didn't win? Who told the whole yard at Tattersall's that Grimsby would sell Holt's stable? Who saw that Rickman Turner was a coward, and would n't fight?—and I said it, the very day they gave him 'the Bath' for his services in China! I don't know much about books, nor do I pretend to; but as to men and women—men best—I 'll back myself against all England and the Channel Islands."

"And I 'll take as much as you 'll spare me out of your book, Grog," said Beecher, enthusiastically, while he filled his glass and drained it.

"You see," said Davis, in a low, confidential tone, as if imparting a great secret, "I've always remarked that the way they smash a fellow in Parliament—I don't care in which House—is always by raking up something or other he did years before. If he wrote a play, or a novel, or a book of poems, they 're down on him at once, about his imagination and his fancy,—that means, he never told a word of truth in his life. If he was unfortunate in business, they 're sure to refer to him about some change in the Law of Bankruptcy, and say, 'There's my honorable friend yonder ought to be able to help us by his experiences!' Then, if a fellow has only his wits about him, how he floors them! You see there's a great deal of capital to be made out of one of these attacks. You rise to reply, without any anger or passion; only dignity,—nothing but dignity! You appeal to the House if the assault of the right honorable baronet opposite was strictly in good taste,— whatever that means. You ask why you are signalled out to be the mark of his eloquence, or his wit, or whatever it be; and then you come out with a fine account of yourself, and all the honorable motives that nobody ever suspected you of. That's the moment to praise everything you ever did, or meant to do, or couldn't do; that's the time to show them what a man they have amongst them."

"Capital, glorious, excellent!" cried Beecher, in delight "Well, suppose now," said Davis, "there 's a bill about marriages,—they 're always changing the law about them; it's evidently a contract does n't work quite smoothly for all parties,—well, there's sure to be many a spicy remark and impertinent allusion in the debate; it's a sore subject, and every one has a 'raw' on it; and, at last, somebody says something about unequal matches, alliances with an inferior class, 'noble lords that have not scrupled to mingle the ancient blood of their race with the—the thin and washy current that flows in plebeian veins.' I 'm the Lord Chancellor, now," said Grog, boldly, "and I immediately turn round and fix my eyes upon *you*. Up you get at once, and say, 'I accept, my Lords,—I accept for myself, and my own case, every word the noble Duke or Marquis has just uttered. It never would have occurred to me to make my personal history the subject of your Lordships' attention; but when thus rudely brought before you,—rudely and gratuitously introduced—'Here you 'd frown at the last speaker, as much as to say, 'You 'll hear more about this outside—'"

"Go on,—go on!" cried Beecher, with impatience.

"'I rise in this place,'—that has always a great impression, to say 'this place,'—'I rise in this place to say that I am prouder in the choice that shares with me the honors of my coronet, than in all the dignity and privilege that same coronet confers.' What a cheer, what a regular hurrah follows that, for they have seen her,—ay, that have they! They have beheld her sweeping down the gilded drawing-room,—the handsomest woman in England! Where's the Duchess with her eyes, her skin, her dignity, and her grace? Does n't she look 'thoroughbred in every vein of her neck'? Where did she get that graceful sweep, that easy-swimming gait, if she had n't it in her very nature'?"

"By Heaven, it's true, every syllable of it!" cried out Beecher, in all the wild ecstasy of delight.

"Where is the man—I don't care what his rank might be—who would n't envy you after you 'd made that speech? You 'd walk down Westminster the proudest man in England after it."

Beecher's features glowed with a delight that showed he had already anticipated the sense of his popularity.

"And then how the newspapers will praise you! It will be as if you built a bridge over the gulf that separates two distinct classes of people. You 'll be a sort of noble reformer. What was the wisest thing Louis Napoleon ever did? His marriage. Do you mark that he was always following his uncle's footsteps in all his other policy; he saw that the only great mistake he ever made was looking out for a high match, and, like a shrewd fellow, he said, 'I have station, rank, power, and money enough for two. It 's not to win the good favor of a wrinkled old Archduchess or a deaf old Princess, I 'm going to marry. I 'll go in for the whole field. I 'll take the girl that, if I was n't an Emperor, I 'd be proud to call my own.' And signs on 't, they all cried out, 'See if he has n't his heart in the right place; there's an honest drop there! Let him be as ambitious as you like, he married just as you or I would.' Ain't it a fine thing," exclaimed Grog, enthusiastically, "when one has all the middle classes in one's favor,—the respectable ruck that's always running, but seldom showing a winner? Get these fellows with you, and it's like Baring's name on the back of your bill. And now, Beecher," said Davis, grasping the other's hand, and speaking with a deep earnestness,—"and now that I 've said what you might have done, I 'll tell you what I *will do*. I have just been sketching out this line of country to see how you 'd take your fences, nothing more. You 've shown me that you 're the right sort, and I 'm not the man to forget it. If I had seen the shadow of a shade of a dodge about you,—if I 'd have detected one line in your face, or one shake in your voice, like treachery,—so help me! I 'd have thrown you over like winking! You fancied yourself a great man, and was stanch and true to your old friends; and now it's my turn to tell you that I would n't give that empty flask yonder for all your brother Lackington's lease of his peerage! Hear me out I have it from his own lawyers,—from the fellows in Furnival's Inn,— it's up with him; the others are perfectly sure of their verdict There's how it is! And now, Annesley Beecher, you were willing to marry Kit Davis's daughter when you thought you could make her a peeress; now I say, that when you 've nothing, nor haven't a sixpence to bless yourself with, it's Kit himself will give her to you, and say, there's not the other man breathing he'd as soon see the husband of this same Lizzy Davis!"

The burst of emotion with which Beecher met this speech was, indeed, the result of very conflicting feelings. Shock at the terrible tidings of his brother's downfall, and the insult to his house and name, mingled with a burst of gratitude to Davis for his fidelity; but stronger and deeper than these was another sentiment,—for, smile if you will, most sceptical reader, the man was in love, after *his* fashion. I do not ask of you to believe that he felt as you or I might or ought to feel the tender passion. I do not seek to persuade you that the object of his affection, mingled with all his thoughts, swayed them and etherealized them; that she was the theme of many a heart-woven story, the heroine of many an ecstatic dream: still she was one who could elicit from that nature, in all its selfishness, little traits of generous feeling, little bursts of honest sentiment, that made him appear better to his own heart. And so far has the adage truth with it, virtue is its own reward, in the conscious sense of well doing, in the peaceful calm of an unrepining spirit, and, not least of all, in that sympathy which good men so readily bestow upon even faint efforts to win their suffrage.

And so he sobbed out something that meant grief and gratitude; hope, fear, and uncertainty—worse than fear—all agitating and distracting him by turns.

Very little time did Grog give himself for calmer reflection; away he went at full speed to sketch out their future life. They were to make the tour of Europe, winning all before them. All the joyous part, all the splendor of equipage, retinue, mode of life, and outlay being dictated by Beecher; all the more business detail, the play and the money-getting, devolving upon Davis. Baden, Ems, Wiesbaden, Hamburg, and Aix,—all glowed in the descriptions like fields of foretold glory. How they were to outshine Princes in magnificence and Royal Highnesses in display; the envy of Beecher, of his unvarying luck; the splendor of all his belongings; Lizzy's beauty, too! What a page would he fill in the great gossip calendar of Europe!

Well Davis knew how to feed the craving vanity of that weak nature, whose most ardent desire was to be deemed cunning and sharp, the cautious reserve of prudent men in his company being a tribute to his acuteness, the dearest his heart could covet Oh, if he longed for anything as success, it was for a time when his coming would spread a degree of terror at a play-table, and men would rise rather than risk their fortune against *his!* Should such a moment ever be his? Was that great triumph ever to befall him? And all this as the husband of Lizzy Davis!

"Ay!" said Grog, as he read and traced each succeeding emotion in that transparent nature,—"ay! that's what may be called life; and when we 've done Europe, smashed every bank on the Continent, we 'll cross the Atlantic, and give Jonathan a 'touch of our quality.' I know all their games well, and I 've had my 'three bullets and a poker' before now on a Mississippi steamer! Your Yankee likes faro, and I've a new cabal to teach him; in short, my boy, there's a roving commission of fun before us, and if it don't pay, *my* name ain't Davis!"

"Was this your scheme, then, Grog," asked Beecher, "when you told me at Brussels that you could make a man of me?"

"It was, my boy," cried Davis, eagerly. "You 've guessed it. There was only one obstacle to the success of the plan at that time, and this exists no longer."

"What was the obstacle you speak of?"

"Simply, that so long as you fancied yourself next in succession to a peerage, you 'd never lay yourself down regularly to your work; you'd say, 'Lackington can't live forever; he's almost twenty years my senior. I must be the Viscount yet. Why should I, therefore, cumber myself with cares that I have no need of, and involve myself amongst people I'll have to cut one of these days? No, I'll just make a waiting race of it, and be patient.' Now, however, that you can't count upon this prospect,—now that to-morrow or next day will declare to the world that Henry Hastings Beecher is just Henry Hastings Beecher, and not Viscount Lackington, and that the Honorable Annesley is just Annesley, and no more,—now, I say, that you see this clearly with your own eyes, you 'll buckle to, and do your work manfully. And there was another thing—" And here Davis paused, and seemed to meditate.

"What was that, Grog? Be candid, old fellow, and tell me all."

"So I will, then," resumed Davis. "That other thing was this. So long as you were the great man in prospective, and might some fine day be a Lord, you could always persuade yourself—or some one else could persuade you—that Kit Davis was hanging on you just for your rank; that he wanted the intimacy of a man in your station, and so on. Now, if you ever came to believe this, there would have been an end of all confidence between us; and without confidence, what can a fellow do for his pal? This was, therefore, the obstacle; and even if you could have got over it, *I* couldn't. No, hang me if I could! I was always saying to myself, 'It's all very nice and smooth now, Kit, between you and Beecher,—you eat, drink, and sleep together,—but wait till he turns the corner, old fellow, and see if he won't give you the cold shoulder."

"You could n't believe—"

"Yes, but I could, and did too; and many's the time I said to myself, 'If Beecher was n't a top-sawyer, what a trump he 'd be! He has head for anything, and address for anything.' And do you know,"—here Grog dropped his-voice to a whisper, and spoke as if under great emotion,—"and do you know that I could n't be the same man to you myself just because of your rank? That was the reason I used to be so sulky, so suspicious, and so—ay, actually cruel with you, telling you, as I did, what could n't I do with certain acceptances? Now, look here, Beecher—Light that taper beside you; there's a match in that box at your elbow."

Unsteady enough was Beecher's hand; indeed, it was not wine alone now made him tremble. An intense agitation shook his frame, and he shivered like one in an ague fit. He couldn't tell what was coming; the theme alone was enough to arrest all process of reasoning on his part. It was like the force of a blow that stunned and stupefied at once.

"There, that will do," said Grog, as he drew a long pocket-book from his breast-pocket, and searched for some time amongst its contents. "Ay, here they are; two—three—four of them,—insignificant-looking scraps of paper they look; and yet there's a terrible exposure in open court, a dreary sea-voyage over the ocean, and a whole life of a felon's suffering in those few lines."

"For the love of mercy, Davis, if you have a spark of pity in your heart,—if you have a heart at all,—don't speak in this way to me!" cried Beecher, in a voice almost choked with sobs.

"It is for the last time in my life you'll ever hear such words," said Grog, calmly. "Read them over carefully; examine them well. Yes, I wish and require it."

"Oh, I know them well!" said Beecher, with a heavy sigh. "Many's the sleepless night the thought of them has cost me."

"Go over every line of them; satisfy yourself that they 're the same,—that the words 'Johnstone Howard' are in your own hand."

Beecher bent over the papers; but, with his dimmed eyes and trembling fingers, it was some time ere he could decipher them. A sigh from the very bottom of his heart was all the reply he could make.

"They'll never cost you another sleepless night, old fellow!" said Davis, as he held them over the flame of the taper. "There's the end of 'em now!"

CHAPTER XII
REFLECTIONS OF ANNESLEY BEECHER

A wiser head than that of Annesley Beecher might have felt some confusion on awaking the morning after the events we have just related. Indeed, his first sensations were those of actual bewilderment as he opened his eyes, and beheld the pine-clad mountains rising in endless succession; the deep glens; the gushing streams, crossed by rude bridges of a single tree; the rustic saw-mills all dripping with spray. And trembling with the force of their own machinery. Where was he? What strange land was this? How came he there? Was this in reality the "new world beyond the seas" Davis had so often described to him? By a slow, laborious process, like filtering, stray memories dropped, one by one, through his clouded faculties; and, at length, he remembered the scene of the preceding night, and all that had passed between Davis and himself. Yet, withal, there was much of doubt and uncertainty mixed up, nor could he, by any effort, satisfy himself how much was fact, how much mere speculation. Was it true that Lackington was to lose his peerage? Was it possible such a dreadful blow was to fall on their house? If so, what portion of the estates would follow the title? Would a great part—would all the property be transferred to the new claimant? What length of time, too, might the suit occupy?—such things often lasted for years upon years. Was it too late for a compromise? Could not some arrangement be come to "some way"? Grog was surely the man to decree a plan for this; at all events, he could protract and spin out proceedings. "It's not p.p.; the match may never come off," muttered Beecher, "and I'll back old Grog to 'square it' *somehow*."

And then the bills, the forged acceptances,—they were actually burned before his face! It was well-nigh incredible; but he had seen them, held them in his own hand, and watched them as the night wind wafted away their blackened embers never more to rise in judgment against him,—never to cost him another night of sleepless terror! Who would have believed Davis capable of such magnanimity? Of all men living, he had deemed him the last to forego any hold over another; and then the act was his own spontaneous doing, without reservation, without condition.

Beecher's heart swelled proudly as he thought over this trait of his friend. Was it that he felt a sense of joy in believing better of mankind? Was it that it awoke within his breast more hopeful thoughts of his fellow-men? Did it appeal to him like a voice, saying, "Despair of no man; there are touches of kindliness in natures the very roughest, that redeem whole lives of harshness"? No, my good reader, it would be unfair and unjust to you were I to say that such sentiments as these swayed him. Annesley Beecher's thoughts flowed in another and very different channel. The words he whispered to his heart were somewhat in this wise: "What a wonderful fellow must you be, Beecher, to acquire such influence over a man like Davis; what marvellous gifts must you not be endowed with! Is it any wonder that Grog predicts a brilliant future to him who can curb to his will the most stubborn of natures, and elicit traits of sacrifice out of the most selfish of men? Who but yourself could work this miracle?" Mean and ignoble as such a mode of arguing may seem, take my word for it, most patient reader, it is not unfrequent in this world of ours, nor is Annesley Beecher the only one who has ascribed all his good fortune to his own deservings.

"Shrewd fellow, that Davis! He always saw what stuff was in *me; he* recognized the real metal, while others were only sneering at the dross,—just as he knows this moment, that if I start fresh without name, fortune, or title, that I 'm sure to be at the top of the tree at last. Give me his daughter! I should think he would! It's not all up with Lackington yet, dark as it looks; we 're in possession, and there is a 'good line of country' between the Honorable Annesley Beecher, next Viscount in succession, and Kit Davis, commonly called Grog of that ilk! Not that the girl isn't equal to any station,—there's no denying *that!* Call her a Greville, a Stanley, or a Seymour, and she's a match for the finest man in England! Make her a Countess to-morrow, and she 'll look it!"

It is but fair to acknowledge that Beecher was not bewildered without some due cause; for if Davis had at one time spoken to him as one who no longer possessed claim to rank and station, but was a mere adventurer like himself, at another moment he had addressed him as the future Viscount, and pictured him as hurling a proud defiance to the world in the choice he had made of his wife. This was no blunder on Grog's part. That acute individual had, in the course of his legal experiences, remarked that learned counsel are wont to insert pleas which are occasionally even contradictory, alleging at times that "there was no debt," and then, that "if there had been, it was already paid." In the same spirit did Davis embrace each contingency of fortune, showing that, whether Peer or Commoner, Annesley Beecher "stood to win" in making Lizzy his wife. "Scratch the pedigree, and she 'll be a stunning peeress; and if the suit goes against us, show me the girl like her to meet the world!" This was the sum of the reflections that cost him a whole morning's intellectual labor, and more of actual mental fatigue than befalls a great parliamentary leader after a stormy debate.

That Davis had no intention to intimidate him was clearly shown by his destroying the acceptances: had he wished to lean on coercion, here was the means. Take your choice between matrimony and a felony, was a short and easy piece of argumentation, such as would well have suited Grog's summary notions; and yet he had, of his own accord, freely and forever relinquished this vantage ground. Beecher was now free. For the first time for many a long year of life he arose from his bed without a fear of the law and its emissaries. The horrible nightmare that had scared him so often, dashing the wildest moments of dissipation with sudden fear, deepening the depths of despondency with greater gloom, had all fled, and he awoke to feel that there was no terror in a "Beak's" eye, nothing to daunt him in the shrewd glances of a detective. They who have lived years long of insecurity, tortured by the incessant sense of an impending peril, to befall them to-day, tomorrow, or next day, become at length so imbued with fear that when the hour of their emancipation arrives, they are not able for a considerable time to assure themselves of their safety. The captive dreams of his chains through many a night after he has gained his liberty; the shipwrecked sailor can never forget the raft and the lone ocean on which he tossed; nor was it altogether easy for Beecher to convince himself that he could walk the world with his head high, and bid defiance to Crown prosecutors and juries!

"I 'm out of *your* debt, Master Grog," said he, with a pleasant laugh to himself; "catch me if you can running up another score in *your* books. Wait till you see me slipping my neck into a noose held by *your* fingers. You made me feel the curb pretty sharp for many a long day, and might still, if you had n't taken off the bridle with your own hands; but I 'm free now, and won't I show you a fair pair of heels! Who could blame me, I 'd like to know? When a fellow gets out of jail, does he take lodgings next door to the prison? *I* never asked him to burn those bills. It was all his own doing. I conclude that a fellow as shrewd as he knew what he was about. Mayhap he said to himself, 'Beecher's the downiest cove going. It will be a deuced sight better to have him as my friend and pal than to send him to break stones in Australia. I can stand to win a good thing on him, and why should I send him over seas just out of spite? I'll come the grand magnanimous dodge over him, — destroy the papers before his face, and say, "Now, old fellow, what do you say to that for a touch of generosity?"'

"'Well, I'll tell you what I say, Master Davis,'" said he, drawing himself up, and speaking boldly out. "'I say that you're a regular trump, and no mistake; but you 're not the sharp fellow I took you for. No, no, old gent, you 're no match for A. B.! He's been running in bandages all this time past; and now that his back sinews are all right, you'll see if he hasn't a turn of speed in him.' And what is more, I 'd say to him, 'Look here, Grog, we've jogged along these ten or twelve years or so without much profit to either of us,—what say you if we dissolve the partnership and let each do a little business on his own account? If I should turn out anything very brilliant, you 'll be proud of me, just as England says she is when a young colony takes a great spring of success, and say, "Ay, he was one of my rearing!"' Of course all dictation, all that bullying intolerance is at an end now, and time it was! Wasn't I well weary of it! wasn't I actually sick of life with it! I couldn't turn to anything, could n't think of anything, with that eternal fear before me, always asking myself, 'Is he going to do it now?' It is very hard to believe it's all over." And he heaved a deep sigh as though disburdening his heart of its last load of sorrow.

"Davis is very wide awake," continued he; "he 'll soon see how to trim his sails to this new wind; he 'll know that he can't bully, can't terrorize."

A sharp quick report of a pistol, with a clanging crash, and then a faint tinkle of a bell, cut short his musings, and Beecher hastened to the window and looked out. It was Davis in the vine alley practising with the pistol; he had just sent a ball through the target, the bell giving warning that the shot had pierced the very centre. Beecher watched him as he levelled again; he thought he saw a faint tremor of the hand, a slight unsteadiness of the wrist; vain illusion,—bang went the weapon, and again the little bell gave forth the token of success.

"Give me the word—one—two," cried out Davis to the man who loaded and handed him the pistols. "One—two," called out the other; and the same instant rang out the bell, and the ball was true to its mark.

"What a shot,—what a *deadly* shot!" muttered Beecher, as a cold shudder came over him.

As quickly as he could take the weapons, Davis now fired; four—five—six balls went in succession through the tiny circle, the bell tinkling on and never ceasing, so rapidly did shot follow upon shot, till, as if sated with success, he turned away, saying, "I' ll try to-morrow blindfold!"

"I'm certain," muttered Beecher, "no man is bound to go out with a fellow like that. A duel is meant to be a hazard, not a dead certainty! To stand before him at twenty—ay, forty paces, is a suicide, neither more nor less; he must kill you. I'd insist on his fighting across a handkerchief. I 'd say, 'Let us stand foot to foot!'" No, Beecher, not a bit of it; you 'd say nothing of the kind, nor, if you did, would it avail you! Your craven heart could not beat were those stern gray eyes fixed upon you, looking death into you from a yard off. He 'd shoot you down as pitilessly, too, at one distance as at the other.

Was it in the fulness of a conviction that his faltering lips tried to deny, that he threw himself back upon a chair, while a cold, clammy sweat covered his face and forehead, a sickness like death crept over him, objects grew dim to his eyes, and the room seemed to turn and swim before him? Where was his high daring now? Where the boastful spirit in which he had declared himself free, no more the slave of Grog's insolent domination, nor basely cowering before his frown? Oh, the ineffable bitterness. Of that thought, coming, too, in revulsion to all his late self-gratulations! Where was the glorious emancipation he had dreamed of, now? He could not throw him into prison, it is true, but he could lay him in a grave.

"But I 'd not meet him," whispered he to himself. "One is not bound to meet a man of this sort."

There is something marvellously accommodating and elastic in the phrase, "One is not bound" to do this, that, and t' other. As the said bond is a contract between oneself and an imaginary world, its provisions are rarely onerous or exacting. Life is full of things "one is not bound to do." You are "not bound," for instance, to pay your father's debts, though, it might be, they were contracted in your behalf and for your benefit. You are not bound to marry the girl whose affections have been your own for years if you can do better in another quarter, and she has nothing in your handwriting to establish a contract. You are not bound, — good swimmer though you be, — to rescue a man from drowning, lest he should clutch too eagerly and peril your safety. You are not bound to risk the chance of a typhus by visiting a poor friend on his sick-bed. You are not bound to aid charities you but half approve, — to assist people who have been improvident, — to associate with many who are uninteresting to you. But why go on with this expurgatorial catalogue? It is quite clear the only things "one *is* bound" to do are those the world will enforce at his hands; and let our selfishness be ever so inveterate, and ever so crafty, the majority will beat us, and the Ayes have it at last!

Now, few men had a longer list of the things they were "not bound to do" than Annesley Beecher; in reality, if the balance were to be struck between them and those he acknowledged to be obligatory, it would have been like Falstaff's sack to the miserable morsel of bread. Men of his stamp fancy themselves very wise in their generation. They are not easy-natured, open, trustful, and free-handed, like that Pharisee! Take my word for it, the system works not so well as it looks, and they pass their existence in a narrow prison-ward of their own selfish instincts,—their fears their fetters, their cowardly natures heavy as any chains!

Beecher reasoned somewhat in this wise. Grog was "not bound" to destroy the acceptances. He might have held them in terrorism over him for a long life, and used them, at last, if occasion served. At all events, they were valuable securities, which it was pure and wanton waste to burn. Still, the act being done, Beecher was "bound" in the heaviest recognizances to his own heart to profit by the motion; and the great question with him was, what was the best and shortest road to that desirable object? Supposing Lackington all right,—no disputed claim to the title, no litigation of the estate,—Beecher's best course had possibly been to slip his cable, make all sail, and part company with Davis forever. One grave difficulty, however, opposed itself to this scheme. How was it possible for any man walking the earth to get out of reach of Grog Davis? Had there been a planet allotted for the special use of peers,—were there some bright star above to which they could betake themselves and demand admission by showing their patent, and from which all of inferior birth were excluded, Beecher would assuredly have availed himself of his privilege; but, alas! whatever inequalities pervade life, there is but one earth to bear us living, and cover us when dead! Now, the portion of that earth which constitutes the continent of Europe Davis knew like a detective. A more hopeless undertaking could not be imagined than to try to escape him. Great as was his craft, it was nothing to his courage,—a courage that gave him a sort of affinity to a wild animal, so headlong, reckless, and desperate did it seem. Provoke him, he was ever ready for the conflict; outrage him, and only your life's blood could be the expiation. And what an outrage had it been if Beecher had taken this moment,—the first, perhaps the only one in all his life, in which Davis had accomplished a noble and generous action,—to desert him! How he could picture to his mind Grog, when the tidings were told him!—not overwhelmed by astonishment, not stunned by surprise, not irresolute even for a second, but starting up like a wounded tiger, and eager for pursuit, his fierce eyeballs glaring, and his sinewy hands closed with a convulsive grip. It was clear, therefore, that escape was impossible. What, then, was the alternative that remained? To abide,—sign a lifelong partnership with Grog, and marry Lizzy. "A stiff line of country,—a very stiff line of country, Annesley, my boy," said he, addressing himself: "many a dangerous rasper, many a smashing fence there,—have you nerve for it?" Now Beecher knew life well enough to see that such an existence was, in reality, little else than a steeple-chase, and he questioned himself gravely whether he possessed head or hand for the effort. Grog, to be sure, was a marvellous trainer, and Lizzy,—what might not Lizzy achieve of success, with her beauty, her gracefulness, and her genius! It was not till after a long course of reflection that her image came up before him; but when once it did come, it was master of the scene. How he recalled all her winning ways, her siren voice, her ready wit, her easy, graceful motion, her playful manner, that gave to her beauty so many new phases of attraction! What a fascination was it that in her company he never remembered a sorrow,—nay, to think of her was the best solace he had ever found against the pain of gloomy reveries. She was never out of humour, never out of spirits,—always brilliant, sparkling, and happy-minded.

What a glorious thing to obtain a share of such a nature,—the very next best thing to having it oneself! "But all this was not Love," breaks in my impatient reader. Very true; I admit it in all humility. It was not what you, nor perhaps I, would call by that name; but yet it was all that Annesley Beecher had to offer in that regard.

Have you never remarked the strange and curious efforts made by men who have long lived on narrow fortunes to acquit themselves respectably on succeeding to larger means? They know well enough that they need not pinch and screw and squeeze any longer,—that fortune has enlarged her boundaries, and that they can enter into wider, richer, and pleasanter pasturage,—and yet, for the life of them, they cannot make the venture! or if they do, it is with a sort of convulsive, spasmodic effort far more painful than pleasurable. Their old instincts press heavily upon them, and bear down all the promptings of their present prosperity; they really do not want all these bounties of fate,—they are half crashed by the shower of blessings. So is it precisely with your selfish man in his endeavors to expand into affection, and so was it with Beecher when he tried to be a lover.

Some moralists tell us that, even in the best natures, love is essentially a selfish passion. What amount of egotism, then, does it not include in those who are far—very far—from being "the best"? With all this, let us be just to poor Beecher. Whatever there was of heart about him, she *had* touched; whatever of good or kind or gentle in his neglected being existed, she had found the way to it. If he were capable of being anything better, she alone could have aided the reformation. If he were not to sink still lower and lower, it was to her helping hand his rescue would be owing. And somehow— though I cannot explain how—he felt and knew this to be the case. He could hear generous sentiments from *her*, and not deem them hypocrisy. He could listen to words of trust and hopefulness, and yet not smile at her credulity. *She* had gained that amount of ascendancy over his mind which subjugated all his own prejudices to her influence, and, like all weak natures, he was never so happy as in slavery. Last of all, what a prize it would be to be the husband of the most beautiful woman in Europe! There was a notoriety in that, far above the fame of winning "Derbys" or breaking Roulette Banks; and he pictured to himself how they would journey through the Continent, admired, worshipped, and envied,—for already he had invested himself with the qualities of his future wife, and gloried in the triumphs she was so sure to win.

"By Jove! I'll do it," cried he, at last, as he slapped his hand on the table. "I don't care what they'll say, I *will* do it; and if there's any fellow dares to scoff or sneer at it, Grog shall shoot him. I'll make that bargain with him; and he 'll like it, for he loves fighting." He summed up his resolution by imagining that the judgment of the world would run somehow in this fashion: "Wonderful fellow, that Annesley Beecher! It's not above a year since his brother lost the title, and there he is now, married to the most splendid woman in all Europe, living like a prince,—denying himself nothing, no matter what it cost,—and all by his own wits! Show me his equal anywhere! Lackington used to call him a 'flat.' I wonder what he 'd say now!"

CHAPTER XIII
A DARK CONFIDENCE

What a wound would it inflict upon our self-love were we occasionally to know that the concessions we have extorted from our own hearts by long effort and persuasion would be deemed matters of very doubtful acceptance by those in whose favor they were made. With what astonishment should we learn that there was nothing so very noble in our forgiveness, nothing so very splendid in our generosity! I have been led to this reflection by thinking over Annesley Beecher's late resolve, and wondering what effect it might have had on him could he have overheard what passed in the very chamber next his own.

Though Lizzy Davis was dressed and ready to come down to breakfast, she felt so ill and depressed that she lay down again on her bed, telling the maid to close the shutters and leave her to herself.

"What's this, Lizzy? What's the matter, girl?" said Davis, entering, and taking a seat at her bedside. "Your hand is on fire."

"I slept badly,—scarcely at all," said she, faintly, "and my head feels as if it would split with pain."

"Poor child!" said he, as he kissed her burning forehead; "I was the cause of all this. Yes, Lizzy, I know it, but I had been staving off this hour for many and many a year. I felt in my heart that you were the only one in all the world who could console or cheer me, and yet I was satisfied to forego it all—to deny myself what I yearned after—just to spare you."

The words came with a slow and faltering utterance from him, and his lips quivered when he had done speaking.

"I'm not quite sure the plan was a good one," said she, in a low voice.

"Nor am I now," said he, sternly; "but I did it for the best."

She heaved a heavy sigh, and was silent.

"Mayhap I thought, too," said he, after a pause, "that when you looked back at all the sacrifices I had made for you, how I toiled and labored,—not as other men toil and labor, for *my* handicraft was always exercised with a convict ship in the offing—There, you needn't shudder now; I'm here beside you safe. Well, I thought you 'd say, 'After all, he gave me every advantage in his power. If he could n't bestow on me station and riches, he made me equal to their enjoyment if they ever befell me. He didn't bring me down to his own level, nor to feel the heartburnings of his own daily life, but he made me, in thought and feeling, as good as any lady in the land.'"

"And for what—to what end?" said she, wildly.

"That you might be such, one day, girl," said he, passionately. "Do you think I have not known every hour, for the last thirty-odd years, what I might have been, had I been trained, and schooled, and taught the things that others know? Have I not felt that I had pluck, daring, energy, and persistence that only wanted knowledge to beat them all, and leave them nowhere? Have I not said to myself, 'She has every one of these, and she has good looks to boot; and why shouldn't she go in and carry away the cup?' And do you think, when I said that, that I was n't striking a docket of bankruptcy against my own heart forever? for to make *you* great was to make *me* childless!"

Lizzy covered her face with her hands, but never uttered a word.

"I did n't need any one to tell me," resumed he, fiercely, "that training you up in luxury and refinement was n't the way to make you satisfied with poverty, or proud of such a father as myself. I knew deuced well what I was preparing for myself there. 'But no matter,' I said, 'come what will, *she* shall have a fair start of it. Show me the fellow will try a balk,—show me the man will cross the course while she's running.'"

Startled by the thick and guttural utterance of his words, Lizzy removed her hands from her face, and stared eagerly at him. Strongly shaken by passion as he was, every line and lineament tense with emotion, there was a marvellous resemblance between her beautiful features and the almost demoniac savagery of his. Had he not been at her side, the expression was only that of intense pain on a face of surpassing beauty, but, seen through the baneful interpretation of his look, she seemed the type of a haughty nature spirited by the very wildest ambition.

"Ay, girl," said he, with a sigh, "you 've cost me more than money or money's worth; and if I ever come to have what they call a 'conscience,' I 'll have an ugly score to settle on your account."

"Oh, dearest father!" cried she, bitterly, "do not wring my heart by such words as these."

"There, you shall hear no more of it," said he, withdrawing his hand from her grasp and crossing his arm on his breast.

"Nay," said she, fondly, "you shall tell me all and everything. It has cost you heavily to make this confidence to me. Let us try if it cannot requite us both. I know the worst. No?" cried she, in terror, as he shook his head; "why, what is there remains behind?"

"How shall I tell you what remains behind?" broke he in, sternly; "how shall I teach you to know the world as I know it,—to feel that every look bent on me is insult,—every word uttered as I pass a sarcasm,—that fellows rise from the table when I sit down at it? and though, now and then, I'm lucky enough to catch one who goes too far, and make him a warning to others, they can do enough to spite me, and yet never come within twelve paces of me. I went over to Neuwied yesterday to fetch my letters from the post. You 'd fancy that in a little village on this untravelled bank of the Rhine I might have rested an hour to bait my horse and eat my breakfast unmolested and without insult. You 'd say that in a secluded spot like that I would be safe. Not a bit of it. Scandal has its hue and cry, and every man that walks the earth is its agent. Two young fellows fresh from England—by their dress, their manner, and their bad French, I judged them to be young students from Oxford or Cambridge—breakfasted in the same room with me, and deeming me a foreigner, and therefore—for it is a right English conclusion—unable to understand them, talked most freely of events and people before me. I paid little attention to their vapid talk till my ear caught the name of Beecher. They were discussing him and a lady who had been seen in his company at Aix-la-Chapelle. Yes, they had seen her repeatedly in her rides and drives, followed her to the Cursaal, and stared at her at the opera. They were quite enthusiastic about her beauty, and only puzzled to know who this mysterious creature might be that looked like a queen and dressed like a queen. One averred she was not Beecher's sister,—the peerage told them that; as little was she his wife. Then came the other and last alternative. And I had to sit still and listen to every *pro* and *con* of this stupid converse,—their miserable efforts to reason, or their still more contemptible attempts to jest, and dare not stand up before them and say, 'Hold your slanderous tongues, for she is my daughter,' because, to the first question they would put to me, I must say, 'My name is Davis—Christopher Davis'—ay, 'Grog Davis,' if they would have it so. No, no, girl, all your beauty, all your grace, all your fascinations would not support such a name,—the best horse that ever won the Derby will break down if you overweight him; and so I had to leave my breakfast uneaten and come away how I could. For one brief moment I was irresolute. I felt that if I let them off so easily I 'd pine and fret over it after, and maybe give way to passion some other time with less excuse; but my thoughts came back to you, Lizzy, and I said, 'What signifies about me? I have no object, no goal in life, but her. She must not be talked of, nor made matter for newspaper gossip. She will one day or other hold a place at which slander and malevolence only talk in whispers, and even these must be uttered with secrecy!' I could n't help laughing as I left the room. One of them declined to eat salad because it was unwholesome. Little he knew on what a tiny chance it depended whether that was to be his last breakfast. The devilish pleasure of turning back and telling him so almost overcame my resolution."

"There was, then, an impropriety in my living at Aix as I did?" asked Lizzy, calmly.

"The impropriety, as you call it, need not have been notorious," said he, in angry confusion. "If people will attract notice by an ostentatious display,—horses, equipage, costly dressing, and so on,—the world will talk of them. You could n't know this, but Beecher did. It was his unthinking folly drew these bad tongues on you. It is a score he 'll have to settle with me yet."

"But, dearest papa, let me bear the blame that is my due. It was I—I myself—who encouraged, suggested these extravagances. I fancied myself possessed of boundless wealth; he never undeceived me; nay, he would not even answer my importunate questions as to my family, my connections, whence we came, and of what county."

"If he had," muttered Grog, "I 'd be curious to have heard his narrative."

"I saw, at last, that there was a secret, and then I pressed him no more."

"And you did well. Had you importuned, and had he yielded, it had been worse for *him.*"

"Just as little did I suspect," continued she, rapidly, "that any reproach could attach to my living in his society; he was your friend; it was at your desire he accepted this brief guardianship; he never, by a word, a look, transgressed the bounds of respectful courtesy; and I felt all the unconstrained freedom of old friendship in our intercourse."

"All his reserve and all your delicacy won't silence evil tongues, girl. I intended you to have stayed a day or two, at most, at Aix. You passed weeks there. Whose fault that, you say? Mine,—of course, mine, and no one else's. But what but my fault every step in your whole life? Why was n't I satisfied to bring you up in my own station, with rogues and swindlers for daily associates? Then I might have had a daughter who would not be ashamed to own me."

"Oh, that I am not; that I will never be," cried she, throwing her arm around his neck. "What has your whole life been but a sacrifice to me? It may be that you rate too highly these great prizes of life; that you attach to the station you covet for me a value I cannot concur in. Still, I feel that it was your love for me prompted this hope, and that while *you* trod the world darkly and painfully, you purchased a path of light and pleasantness for *me*."

"You have paid me for it all by these words," said he, drawing his hand across his eyes. "I 'd work as a daily laborer on the road, I'd be a sailor before the mast, I'd take my turn with the chain-gang and eat Norfolk Island biscuit, if it could help to place you where I seek to see you."

"And what is this rank to which you aspire so eagerly?"

"I want you to be a peeress, girl. I want you to be one of the proudest guild the world ever yet saw or heard of; to have a station so accredited that every word you speak, every act you do, goes forth with its own authority."

"But stay!" broke she in, "men's memories will surely carry them back to who I was."

"Let them, girl. Are you the stuff to be chilled by that? Have I made you what you are, that you cannot play their equal? There are not many of them better looking; are there any cleverer or better informed? Even those Oxford boys said you looked like an empress. If insult will crush you, girl, you 've got little of *my* blood in you."

Lizzy's face flushed scarlet, and her eyes glittered wildly, as they seemed to say, "Have no fears on that score." Then, suddenly changing to an ashy pallor, and in a voice trembling with intense feeling, she said: "But why seek out an existence of struggle and conflict? It is for me and my welfare that all your anxieties are exercised. Is it not possible that these can be promoted without the dangerous risk of this ambition? You know life well; tell me, then, are there not some paths a woman may tread for independence, and yet cause no blush to those who love her best? Of the acquirements you have bestowed upon me, are there not some which could be turned to this account? I could be a governess."

"Do you know what a governess is, girl?—a servant in the garb of a lady; one whose mind has been cultivated, not to form resources for herself, but to be drained and drawn on by others. They used to kill a serf, in the middle ages, that a noble might warm his feet in the hot entrails; our modern civilization is satisfied by driving many a poor girl crazy, to cram some stupid numbskull with a semblance of knowledge. You shall not be a governess."

"There is the stage, then," cried she. "I'm vain enough to imagine I should succeed there."

"I'll not hear of it," broke in Davis, passionately. "If I was certain you could act like Siddons herself, you should not walk the boards. *I* know what a theatre is. I know the life of coarse familiarity it leads to. The corps is a family gathered together like what jockeys call 'a scratch team,'—a wheeler here, and a leader there, with just smartness enough to soar above the level of a dull audience, crammed with the light jest of low comedy, and steered by no higher ambition than a crowded benefit, or a junketing at Greenwich. How would *you* consort with these people?"

"Still, if I achieved success—"

"I won't have it,—that's enough. I tell you, girl, that there is but one course for *you*. You must be declared winner at the stand-house before you have been seen on the ground. If you have to run the gauntlet through all the slanders and stories they will rake up of *me*,—if, before you reach the goal, you have to fight all the lost battles of *my* life over again,—you 'll never see the winning-post."

"And is it not better to confront the storm, and risk one's chances with the elements, than suffer shipwreck at once? I tell you, father," cried she, eagerly, "I 'll face all the perils you speak of, boldly; I'll brave insolence, neglect, sarcasm,—what they will,—only let me feel one honest spot in my heart, and be able to say to myself, 'You have toiled lowly, and fared ill; you have dared a conflict and been worsted; but you have not made traffic of your affections, nor bought success by that which makes it valueless.'"

"These are the wild romances of a girl's fancy," said Davis. "Before a twelvemonth was over, you could n't say, on your oath, whether you had married for love or interest, except that poverty might remind you of the one, and affluence suggest the other. Do you imagine that the years stop short with spring, and that one is always in the season of expectancy? No, no; months roll along, and after summer comes autumn, and then winter, and the light dress you fancied that you never need change would make but scanty clothing."

"But if I am not able to bring myself to this?"

"Are you certain you will be able to bring *me* to worse?" said he, solemnly. "Do you feel, Lizzy, as if you could repay my long life of sacrifice and struggle by what would undo them all? Do you feel strong enough to say, 'My old father was a fool to want to make *me* better than himself; I can descend to the set he is ashamed of; and, more still, I can summon courage to meet taunts and insults on him, which, had I station to repel them from, had never been uttered'?"

"Oh, do not tempt me this way!" cried she, bitterly.

"But I will, girl; I will leave nothing unsaid that may induce you to save yourself from misery, and *me* from disgrace. I tell you, girl, if I face the world again, it must be with such security as only you can give me,—you, a lady high in rank and position, can then save *me*. My enemies will know that their best game will not be to ruin me."

"And are you sure it would save you?" said she, sternly and coldly.

"I am," said he, in a voice like her own.

"Will you take a solemn oath to me that you see no other road out of these difficulties, whatever they are, than by my doing this?"

"I will swear it as solemnly as ever words were sworn. I believe—before Heaven I say it—that there's not another chance in life by which your future lot can be secured."

"Do not speak of mine; think solely of your fortunes, and say if this alone can save them."

"Just as firmly do I say, then, that once in the position I mean, you can rescue me out of every peril. You will be rich enough to pay some, powerful enough to promote others, great enough to sway and influence all."

"Good God! what have you done, then, that it is only by sacrificing all my hopes of happiness that you can be ransomed?" cried she, with a burst of irrepressible passion.

"You want a confession, then," said Davis, in a tone of most savage energy; "you 'd like to hear my own indictment of myself. Well, there are plenty of counts in it."

"Stand forward, Kit Davis. You are charged with various acts of swindling and cheating,—light offences, all of them,—committed in the best of company, and in concert with honorable and even noble colleagues. By the virtue of your oath, Captain Davis, how many horses have you poisoned, how many jockeys have you drugged, what number of men have you hocussed at play, what sums have you won from others in a state of utter insensibility? Can you state any case where you enforced a false demand by intimidation? Can you charge your memory with any instance of shooting a man who accused you of foul play? What names besides your own have you been in the habit of signing to bills? Have you any revelations to make about stock transferred under forgery? Will you kiss the book, and say that nineteen out of twenty at the hulks have not done a fiftieth part of what you have done? Will you solemnly take oath that there are not ten, fifteen, twenty charges, which might be prosecuted against you, to transportation for life? and are there not two—or, certainly, is there not one—with a heavier forfeiture on it? Are there not descriptions of you in almost every police bureau in Europe, and photographic likenesses, too, on frontier passport-offices of little German States, that Hesse and Cassel and Coburgh should not be ravaged by the wolf called Grog Davis?"

"And if this be so, to what end do I sacrifice myself?" cried she, in bitter anguish. "Were it not better to seek out some far-away land where we cannot be traced? Let us go to America, to Australia,—I don't care how remote it be,—the country that will shelter us—"

"Not a step. I'll not budge out of Europe; win or lose, here I stay! Do as I tell you, girl, and the game is our own. It has been my safety this many a year that I could compromise so many in my own fall. Well, time has thinned the number marvellously. Many have died. The Cholera, the Crimea, the Marshalsea, broken hearts, and what not, have done their work; and of the few remaining, some have grown indifferent to exposure, others have dropped out of view, and now it would be as much as I could do to place four or five men of good names in the dock beside me. That ain't enough. I must have connections.

"I want those relations that can't afford disgrace. Let me only have *them*, they 'll take care of their own reputations. You don't know, but I know, what great folk can do in England. There 's not a line in the Ten Commandments they could n't legalize with an Act of Parliament. They can marry and unmarry, bind and loosen, legitimize or illegitimize, by a vote 'of the House;' and by a vote of society they can do just as much: make a swindling railroad contractor the first man in London, and, if they liked it, and saw it suited their book, they could make Kit Davis a member of White's, or the Carlton; and once they did it, girl, they 'd think twice before they 'd try to undo it again. All I say is, give me a Viscount for a son-in-law, and see if I don't 'work the oracle.' Let me have just so much backing as secures a fair fight, and my head be on't if they don't give in before I do! They 're very plucky with one another, girl, because they keep within the law; but mark how they tremble before the fellow that does n't mind the law,—that goes through it, at one side of it, or clean over it. That's the pull *I* have over them. The man that don't mind a wetting can always drag another into the water; do you see that?"

Davis had now so worked upon himself that he walked the room with hasty steps, his cheeks burning, and his eyes wildly, fiercely glaring. Amongst the traits which characterize men of lawless and depraved lives, none is more remarkable than the boastful hardihood with which they will at times deploy all the resources of their iniquity, even exaggerating the amount of the wrongs they have inflicted on society. There is something actually satanic in their exultation over a world they have cheated, bullied, injured, and insulted, so that, in their infernal code, honesty and trustfulness seem only worthy of contempt, and he alone possessed of true courage who dares and defies the laws that bind his fellow-men.

Davis was not prone to impulsiveness; very few men were less the slaves of rash or intemperate humors. He had been reared in too stern a school to let mere temper master him; but his long practised self-restraint deserted him here. In his eagerness to carry his point, he was borne away beyond all his prudence, and once launched into the sea of his confessions, he wandered without chart or compass. Besides this, there was that strange, morbid sense of vanity which is experienced in giving a shock to the fears and sensibilities of another. The deeper the tints of his own criminality, the more terrible the course he had run in life, so much the more was he to be feared and dreaded. If he should fail to work upon her affections, he might still hope to extract something from her terror; for who could say of what a man like him was not capable? And last of all, he had thrown off the mask, and he did not care to retain a single rag of the disguise he so long had worn; thus was it, then, that he stood before her in all the strong light of his iniquities,—a criminal, whose forfeitures would have furnished Guilt for fifty.

"Shall I go on?" said he, in a voice of thick and labored utterance, "or is this enough?"

"Oh, is it not enough?" cried she, bitterly.

"You asked me to tell you all,—everything,—and now that you 've only caught a passing glimpse of what I could reveal, you start back affrighted. Be it so; there are, at least, no concealments between us now; and harsh as my lesson has been, it is not a whit harsher than if the world had given it I 've only one word more to say, girl," said he, as he drew nigh the door and held his hand on the lock; "if it be your firm resolve to reject this fortune, the sooner you let me know it the better. I have said all that I need say; the rest is within your own hands; only remember that if such be your determination, give me the earliest notice, for I, too, must take my measures for the future."

If there was nothing of violence in the manner he uttered these words, there was a stern, impassive serenity that made them still more impressive; and Lizzy, without a word of reply, buried her face between her hands and wept.

Davis stood irresolute; for a moment it seemed as if his affection had triumphed, for he made a gesture as though he would approach her; then, suddenly correcting himself with a start, he muttered, below his breath, "It is done now," and left the room.

CHAPTER XIV
SOME DAYS AT GLENGARIFF

The little Hermitage of Glengariff, with its wooded park, its winding river, its deep solitudes fragrant with wild-rose and honeysuckle, is familiar to my reader. He has lingered there with me, strolling through leafy glades, over smooth turf, catching glimpses of blue sea through the dark foliage, and feeling all the intense ecstasy of a spot that seemed especially created for peaceful enjoyment. What a charm was in those tangled pathways, overhung with jessamine and arbutus, or now flanked by moss-clad rock, through whose fissures small crystal rivulets trickled slowly down into little basins beneath. How loaded the air with delicious perfume; what a voluptuous sense of estrangement from all passing care crept over one as he stole noiselessly along over the smooth sward, and drank in the mellow blackbird's note, blended with the distant murmur of the rippling river! And where is it all now? The park is now traversed in every direction with wide, unfinished roads; great open spaces appear at intervals, covered with building materials; yawning sand-quarries swarming with men; great brick-fields smoking in all the reeking oppression of that filthy manufacture; lime-kilns spreading their hateful breath on every side; vast cliffs of slate and granite-rock, making the air resound with their discordant crash, with all the vulgar tumult of a busy herd. If you turn seaward, the same ungraceful change is there: ugly and misshapen wharfs have replaced the picturesque huts of the fishermen; casks and hogsheads and bales and hampers litter the little beach where once the festooned net was wont to hang, and groups of half-drunken sailors riot and dispute where once the merry laugh of sportive childhood was all that woke the echoes. If the lover of the picturesque could weep tears of bitter sorrow over these changes, to the man of speculation and progress they were but signs of a glorious prosperity. The Grand Glengariff Villa Allotment and Marine Residence Company was a splendid scheme, whose shares were eagerly sought after at a high premium. Mr. Dunn must assuredly have lent all his energies to the enterprise, for descriptions of the spot were to be found throughout every corner of the three kingdoms. Colored lithographs and stereoscopes depicted its most seductive scenes through the pages of popular "weeklies," and a dropping fire of interesting paragraphs continued to keep up the project before the public through the columns of the daily press. An "Illustrated News" of one week presented its subscribers with an extra engraving of the "Yachts entering Glengariff harbor after the regatta;" the next, it was a finished print of the "Lady Augusta Arden laying the foundation-stone of the Davenport Obelisk." At one moment the conflict between wild nature and ingenious art would be shown by a view of a clearing in Glengariff forest, where the solid foundations of some proud edifice were seen rising amidst prostrate pines and fallen oak-trees, prosaic announcements in advertising columns giving to these pictorial devices all the solemn stability of fact, so that such localities as "Arden Terrace," "Lackington Avenue," "Glengariff Crescent," and "Davenport Heights" became common and familiar to the public ear.

The imaginative literature of speculation—industrial fiction it might be called—has reached a very high development in our day. Not content with enlisting all the graces of fancy in the cause of enterprise, heightening the charms of scenery and aiding the interests of romance by historic association, it actually allies itself with the slighter infirmities of our social creed, and exalts the merits of certain favored spots by the blessed assurance that they are patronized by our betters. Amongst the many advantages fortune bestowed upon the grand Glengariff scheme was conspicuously one,—Dukes had approved, and Earls admired it "We are happy to learn," said the "Post," "that the Marquis of Duckington has intrusted the construction of his marine villa at Glengariff to the exquisite skill and taste of Sir Jeffrey Blocksley, who is, at present, engaged in preparing Noodleton Hall for his Grace the Duke of Rowood, at the same charming locality." In the "Herald" we find: "The Earl of Hanaper is said to have paid no less than twelve thousand guineas for the small plot of land in which his bathing-lodge at Glengariff is to stand. It is only right to mention that the view from his windows will include the entire bay, from the Davenport Obelisk to Dunn Lighthouse,—a prospect unequalled, we venture to assert, in Europe." And, greater than these, the "Chronicle" assures us, the arrival of a Treasury Lord, accompanied by the Chairman of the Board of Works, on Monday last, at Glengariff, proclaimed the gracious intention of her Majesty to honor this favored spot by selecting it for a future residence. "'Queen's Cot,' as it will be styled, will stand exactly on the site formerly occupied by the late residence of Lord Glengariff, well known as the Hermitage, and be framed and galleried in wood in the style so frequently seen in the Tyrol."

Where is the born Briton would not feel the air balmier and the breeze more zephyr-like if he could see that it waved a royal standard? Where the Anglo-Saxon who would not think the sea more salubrious that helped to salt a duke? Where the alley that was not cooler if a marquis walked beneath its shadow? It is not that honest John Bull seeks the intimacy or acquaintance of these great folk; he has no such weakness or ambition,— he neither aspires to know or be known of them; the limit of his desire is to breathe the same mountain air, to walk the same chain pier, to be fed by their poulterer and butcher, and, maybe, buried by their undertaker. Were it the acquaintanceship he coveted, were it some participation in the habits of refined and elegant intercourse, far be it from us to say one word in disparagement of such ambition, satisfied, as we are, that in all that concerns the enjoyment of society, for the charms of a conversation where fewest prejudices prevail, where least exaggerations are found, where good feeling is rarely, good taste never, violated, the highest in rank are invariably the most conspicuous. But, unhappily, these are not the prizes sought after; the grand object being attained if the Joneses and Simpkinses can spend their autumn in the same locality with titled visitors, bathe in the same tides, and take their airings at the same hours. What an unspeakable happiness might it yield them to know they had been "bored" by the same monotony, and exhausted by the same *ennuis!*

They who were curious in such literature fancied they could detect the fine round hand of Mr. Hankes in the glowing descriptions of Glengariff. Brought up at the feet of that Gamaliel of appraisers, George Robins, he really did credit to his teachings. Nor was it alone the present delights of the spot he dwelled upon, but expatiated on the admirable features of an investment certain to realize, eventually, two or three hundred per cent It was, in fact, like buying uncleared land in the Bush, upon which, within a few years, streets and squares were to be found, purchasing for a mere nominal sum whole territories that to-morrow or next day were to be sold as building lots and valued by the foot.

As in a storm the tiniest creeks and most secluded coves feel in their little bays the wild influence that prevails without, and see their quiet waters ruffled and wave-tossed, so, too, prosperity follows the same law, and spreads its genial sunshine in a wide circle around the spot it brightens. For miles and miles along the shore the grand Glengariff scheme diffused the golden glory of its success. Little fishing-villages, solitary cottages in sequestered glens, lonely creeks, whose yellow strands had seldom seen a foot-track,—all felt it. The patient habits of humble industry seemed contemptible to those who came back to their quiet homesteads after seeing the wondrous doings at Glengariff; and marvellous, indeed, were the narratives of sudden fortunes. One had sold his little "shebeen" for more gold than he knew how to count; another had become rich by the price of the garden before his door; the shingly beach seemed paved with precious stones, the rocks appeared to have grown into bullion. How mean and despicable seemed daily toil; the weary labor of the field, the precarious life of the fisherman, in presence of such easy prosperity, were ignoble drudgery. It savored of superior intelligence to exchange the toil of the hands for the exercise of speculative talents, and each began to compute what some affluent purchaser might not pay for this barren plot, what that bleak promontory might not bring in this market of fanciful bidders.

Let us note the fact that the peasant was not a little amused by the absurd value which the rich man attached to objects long familiar and unprized by himself. The picturesque and the beautiful were elements so totally removed from all his estimate of worth, that he readily ascribed to something very like insanity the great man's fondness for them. That a group of stone pines on a jutting cliff, a lone and rocky island, a ruined wall, an ancient well canopied by a bower of honeysuckle, should be deemed objects of price, appeared to be the most capricious of all tastes; and, in his ignorance as to what imparted this value, he glutted the market with everything that occurred to him. Spots of ground the least attractive, tenements occupying the most ill-chosen sites, ugly and misshapen remains of cottages long deserted, were all vaunted as fully as good or better than their neighbors had sold for thousands. It must be owned, the market price of any article seemed the veriest lottery imaginable. One man could actually find no purchaser for four acres of the finest potato-garden in the county; another got a hundred guineas for his good-will of a bit of stony land that wouldn't feed a goat; here was a slated house no one would look at, there was a mud hovel a Lord and two Members of Parliament were outbidding each other over these three weeks. Could anything be more arbitrary or inexplicable than this? In fact, it almost seemed as if the old, the ruinous, the neglected, and the unprofitable had now usurped the place of all that was neat, orderly, or beneficial.

If we have suffered ourselves to be led into these remarks, they are not altogether digressionary. The Hermitage, we have said, was doomed. Common report alleged that the Queen had selected the spot for her future residence, and of a truth it was even worthy of such a destiny. Whether in reality royalty had made the choice, or that merely it was yet a speculation in hope of such an event, we cannot say, but an accomplished architect had already begun the work of reconstruction, and more than two-thirds of the former building were now demolished. The fragment that still remained was about the oldest part of the cottage, and not the least picturesque. It was a little wing with three gables to the front, the ancient framework, of black oak, quaintly ornamented with many a tasteful device and grim decoration. A little portico, whose columns were entirely concealed by the rich foliage of a rhododendron, stood before the windows, whose diamond panes told of an era when glass bore a very different value; a gorgeous flower-plat, one rich expanse of rare tulips and ranunculi, sloped from the portico to the river, over which a single plank formed a bridge. The stream, which was here deep and rock-bottomed, could be barely seen between the deep hanging branches of the weeping-ash; but its presence might be recognized by the occasional plash of a leaping trout, or the still louder stroke of a swan's wing as he sailed in solemn majesty over his silent domain. So straggling and wide-spreading had been the ancient building, that, although a part of the condemned structure, the clank of the mason's trowel and the turmoil of the falling materials could scarcely be heard in this quiet, sequestered spot. Here Sybella Kellett still lived,—left behind by her great protectors,—half in forgetfulness. Soon after the triumph of the Ossory Bank they had removed to Dublin, thence to London, where they now awaited the passage of a special bill to make the Glen-gariff allotment scheme a chartered company. Although the great turn in the fortunes of Glengariff had transmitted to other hands the direction and guidance of events there, her zeal, energy, and, above all, her knowledge of the people, especially marked her out as one whose services were most valuable. English officials, new to Ireland and its ways, quickly discovered the vast superiority she possessed over them in all dealings with the peasantry, whose prejudices she understood, and whose modes of thought were familiar to her. By none were her qualities more appreciated than by Mr. Hankes. There was a promptitude and decision in all she did, a ready-witted intelligence to encounter whatever difficulty arose, and a bold, purpose-like activity of character about her that amazed and delighted that astute gentleman.

"She's worth us all, sir," he would say to Sir Elkanah Paston, the great English engineer,—"worth us all. Her suggestions are priceless; see how she detected the cause of those shifting sands in the harbor, and supplied the remedy at once; mark how she struck out that line of road from the quarries; think of her transplanting those pinasters five-and-thirty feet high, and not a failure,—not one failure amongst them; and there's the promontory, now the most picturesque feature of the bay: and as to those terraced gardens that she laid out last week, I vow and declare Sir Joseph himself couldn't have done it better. And then, after a day of labor—riding, perhaps, five-and-twenty or thirty miles—she'll sit down to her desk and write away half the night."

If it had not been for one trait, Mr. Hankes would have pronounced her perfection; there was, however, a flaw, which the more he thought over the more did it puzzle him. She was eminently quick-sighted, keen to read motives and appreciate character, and yet with all this she invariably spoiled every bargain made with the people. Instead of taking advantage of their ignorance and inexperience, she was continually on the watch over *their* interests; instead of endeavoring to overreach them, she was mindful of their advantage, cautiously abstaining from everything that might affect their rights.

"We might have bought up half the county for a song, sir, if it were not for that girl," Mr. Hankes would say; "she has risen the market on us everywhere. 'Let us be just,' she says. I want to be just, Miss Kellett, but just to ourselves."

A pleasant phrase is that same one "just to ourselves;" but Mr. Hankes employed it like many other people, and never saw its absurdity.

Now, Sybella Kellett fancied that justice had a twofold obligation, and found herself very often the advocate of the poor man, patiently sustaining his rights, and demanding their recognition. Confidence, we are told by a great authority, is a plant of slow growth, and yet she acquired it in the end. The peasantry submitted to her claims the most complex and involved; they brought their quaint old contracts, half illegible by time and neglect; they recited, and confirmed by oral testimony, the strangest possible of tenures; they recounted long narratives of how they succeeded to this holding, and what claims they could prefer to that; histories that would have worn out almost any human patience to hear, and especially trying to one whose apprehension was of the quickest. And yet she would listen to the very end, make herself master of the case, and give it a deep and full consideration. This done, she decided; and to that decision none ever objected. Whatever her decree, it was accepted as just and fair, and even if a single disappointed or discontented suitor could have been found, he would have shrunk from avowing himself the opponent of public opinion.

It was, however, by the magic of her sympathy, by the secret charm of understanding their natures, and participating in every joy and sorrow of their hearts, that she gained her true ascendancy over them. There was nothing feigned or factitious in her feeling for them; it was not begotten of that courtly tact which knows names by heart, remembers little family traits, and treasures up an anecdote; it was true, heart-felt, honest interest in their welfare. She had watched them long and closely; she knew that the least amiable trait in their natures was also that which oftenest marred their fortunes,—distrust; and she set herself vigorously to work to uproot this vile, pernicious weed, the most noxious that ever poisoned the soil of a human heart. By her own truthful dealings with them she inspired truth, by *her* fairness she exacted fairness, and by the straightforward honesty of her words and actions they grew to learn how far easier and pleasanter could be the business of life where none sought to overreach his neighbor.

To such an extent had her influence spread that it became at last well-nigh impossible to conclude any bargain for land without her co-operation. Unless her award had decided, the peasant could not bring himself to believe that his claim had met a just or equitable consideration; but whatever Miss Bella decreed was final and irrevocable. From an early hour each morning the suitors to her court began to arrive. Under a large damson-tree was placed a table, at which she sat, busily writing away, and listening all the while to their long-drawn-out narratives. It was her rule never to engage in any purchase when she had not herself made a visit to the spot in question, ascertained in person all its advantages and disadvantages, and speculated how far its future value should influence its present price. In this way she had travelled far and near over the surrounding country, visiting localities the wildest and least known, and venturing into districts where a timid traveller had not dared to set foot. It required all her especial acuteness, often-times, to find out—from garbled and incoherent descriptions—the strange and out-of-the-way places no map had ever indicated. In fact, the wild and untravelled country was pathless as a sea, and nothing short of her ready-witted tact had been able to navigate it.

She was, as usual, busied one morning with her peasant levee when Mr. Hankes arrived. He brought a number of letters from the post, and was full of the importance so natural to him who has the earliest intelligence.

"Great news, Miss Bella," said he, gayly,—"very great news. One of the French Princes announces his intention to build a villa here. He requires a small park of some forty or fifty acres, access to the sea, and a good anchorage for his yacht. This note here will give all particulars. Here is an application from Sir Craven Tollemache; he wants us to build him a house on any picturesque site near the shore, and contracts to take it on lease. Here is a demand for one hundred shares, fifty to be exchanged for shares in the Boquantilla Cobalt and Zinc Mines, now at a premium. Kelsal and Waterline wish to know what facilities we would afford them to establish yacht-building in Crooke's Harbor. If liberally dealt with, they propose to expend fifty thousand on permanent improvements. Lord Drellington is anxious for a house in Lackington Crescent. I believe he is too late. There are also seven applications for 'Arden House,' which, I fancy, has been promised to Sir Peter Parkeswith. Founde's Cliff, too, is eagerly run after; that sketch you made of it has been a great success. We must extend our territories, Miss Bella,—we must widen our frontier; never was there such a hit. It is the grandest operation of Mr. Dunn's life. Seven hundred and twenty-three thousand pounds,—one-fourth already paid, the remainder available at short calls. Those Welsh people, Plimnon and Price, are eager about our lead-mine, and we can run up the shares there to sixty-five or seventy whenever we please. Here, too, are the plans for the new Casino and Baths. This is the sketch of a Hydropathic Establishment, — a pet scheme of Lord Glengariffs; we must let him have it. And here is Truevane's report about the marble. It will serve admirably for every purpose but statuary. Our slate slabs are pronounced the finest ever imported. We mean to flag the entire terrace along the sea with them. This is from Dunn himself; it is very short, and hurriedly written: 'Chevass will move the second reading of our bill on Tuesday. I have spoken to the Chancellor, and it is all right. Before it goes to the Lords we must have a new issue of shares. I want, at least, two hundred and fifty thousand by the end of the year.' He says nothing about politics; indeed, he is so occupied with gayeties and fine company, he has little time for business. He only mentions that 'till we have done with this stupid war we cannot hope for any real extension to our great enterprise.'"

"And does he put our miserable plottings here in competition with the noble struggle of our glorious soldiers in the Crimea?" cried she, now breaking silence for the first time.

Mr. Hankes actually started with the energy of her manner, and for a moment could scarcely collect himself to reply.

"Well, you know, Miss Bella," said he, faltering at every word, "we are men of peace, — we are people engaged in the quiet arts of trade, — we cannot be supposed indifferent to the interests our lives are passed in forwarding."

"But you are Englishmen, besides, sir; not to say you *are* brothers and kinsmen of the gallant men who are fighting our enemies."

"Very true, Miss Bella, — very true; they have their profession and we have ours. We rejoice in their success as we participate in all the enthusiasm of their gallantry. I give you my word of honor, I could n't help filling out an extra glass of sherry yesterday to the health of that fine fellow who dashed at the Russian staff and carried off a colonel prisoner. You saw it, I suppose, in the papers?"

"No. Pray let me hear it," said she, eagerly.

"Well, it was an observation — a 'reconnaissance' I think they called it — the Russians were making of the Sardinian lines, and they came so near that a young soldier — an orderly of General La Marmora's — heard one of them say, 'Yes, I have the whole position in my head.' Determining that so dangerous a fellow should not get back to head-quarters, he watched him closely, till he knew he could not be mistaken in him, and then setting off at speed, — for he was mounted, — he crossed the Tchernaya a mile or so further up, and, waiting for them, he lay concealed in a small copse. His plan was to sell his own life for this officer's; but whether he relinquished that notion, or that chance decided the event, there's no knowing. In he dashed, into the midst of them, cut this colonel's bridle-arm across at the wrist, and, taking his horse's reins, rode for it with all speed towards his own lines. He got a start of thirty or forty strides before they could rally in pursuit, which they did actually up to the very range of the rifle-pits, and only retired at last when three fell dead or wounded."

"But *he* escaped?" cried she.

"That he did, and carried his prisoner safe into the lines, and presented him to the General, modestly remarking, 'He is safer here than over yonder,'—pointing to Sebastopol; and, strangest part of the whole thing, he turns out to be an Englishman."

"An Englishman?"

"Yes. He was serving, by some strange accident, on General La Marmora's staff, as a simple orderly, though evidently a man of some education and position,—one of those wild young bloods, doubtless, that had gone too fast at home, but who really do us no discredit when it comes to a question of pluck and daring."

"Do us no discredit!" cried she; "and have you nothing more generous to say of one who has asserted the honor of England so nobly in the face of an entire army? Do us no discredit! Why, one such feat as this adds more glory to the nation than all the schemes of all the jobbers who deal in things like these." And she threw contemptuously from her the colored plans and pictures that littered the table.

"Dear me, Miss Kellett, here's a whole ink-bottle spilled over the Davenport Obelisk."

"Do us no discredit!" burst out she again. "Are we really the nation of shopkeepers that France calls us? Have we no pride save in successful bargaining, no glory save in growing rich? Is money-getting so close at the nation's heart that whatever retards or delays its hoardings savors of misfortune? When you were telling me that anecdote, how I envied the land that owned such a hero; and when you said he was our own,—our countryman; my heart felt bursting with gratitude. Tell me his name."

"His name,—his name,—how strange that I should have forgotten it; for, as I told you, I toasted his health only yesterday."

"Yes, you remember the sherry!" said she, bitterly.

Mr. Hankes's cheek tingled and grew crimson. It was a mood of passionate excitement he had never witnessed in her before, and he was astounded at the change in one usually so calm and self-possessed. It was then in no small confusion that he turned over the letter before him to find something which might change the topic in discussion.

"Ah, here is a matter," said he, referring once more to Dunn's letter. "He says: 'Beg of Miss Kellett to see a small holding called "Kilmaganagh;" I cannot exactly say where, but it lies to the north of Bantry Bay. I suspect that it possesses few recommendations such as would entitle it to a place in the "scheme;" but, if to be had on reasonable terms, I would be well pleased to obtain it. Driscoll had effected a part purchase, but, having failed to pay up the instalment due last March, his claim lapses. By the way, can you ascertain for me where this same Driscoll has gone to? It is now above four months since I have heard of him. Trace him, if possible. As to Kilmaganagh, tell Miss K. that she may indulge that generosity she is not indisposed to gratify, and be on this occasion a liberal purchaser.' He fancies you lean a little to the country-people, Miss Bella," said Hankes, as he stole a cautious glance at her now heightened color. "I will even consent to what is called a fancy price for the tenement, and certainly not lose it for a hundred or two above its actual value. Look to this, and look to Driscoll. There's a riddle here, Miss Bella, if we knew how to read it," said Hankes, as he looked over the few lines once more.

"I have but scant wits to read riddles, Mr. Hankes. Let us see where this place lies." And she turned to a large map on the table, the paths and cross-paths of which had been marked in different colored inks by her own hand. "I remember the name. There was an old tower called Kilmaganagh Fort, which used to be visible from the bay. Yes, here it is,—a strange, wild spot, too, and, as Mr. Dunn opines, scarcely available for his great scheme."

"But he has so many great schemes," said Hankes, with a sly and sidelong glance towards her.

Sybella, however, paid no attention to the remark, but, leaning over the map, continued to trace out the line of route to the spot in question. "By crossing Bantry Bay at Gortalassy, one might save above thirty miles of way. I have been over the road before, and remember it well."

"And you really mean to undertake the journey?" asked Hankes, in some astonishment.

"Of course I do. I ask nothing better than to be fully occupied, and am well pleased when in so doing I can exchange the desk for the saddle, or, almost better, the stern-sheets of a Bantry Hooker. You are not a woman, and you cannot feel, therefore, the sense of pride inspired by mere utility."

"I wish I might ask you a favor, Miss Kellett," said he, after a moment's thought.

"A favor of *me!*" said she, laughing, as though the idea amused her.

"Yes," said he, resuming. "I would beg to be permitted to accompany you on this same journey. I have never been any of these wild, untravelled tracts, and it would be a great additional charm to visit them in your company."

"So far as I am concerned, I grant you the permission freely; but it were well for you to remember that you must not only be well mounted, but prepared to ride over some rough country. I go, usually, as the crow flies, and, as nearly as I can, the same pace too. Now, between this and Loughbeg, there are, at least, three trying fences: one a wall with a deep drop beyond it, and another a steep bank, where I remember that somebody narrowly escaped having an ugly fall; there's a small estuary, too, to cross, near Gortalassy. But I am ashamed to enumerate these petty obstacles; such as they are, they are the only ones,—there are none on my part."

"When do you mean to set out?" asked Hankes, in a tone far less eager than his former question.

"There's a full moon to-morrow night, so that, leaving this about midnight, we might reach the bay by six or seven o'clock, and then, if we should be fortunate with the wind, arrive at Kilmaganagh by about four o'clock. Taking there three or four hours to see the place, we could start again about eight, or even nine—"

"Good heavens! that gives nothing for repose,—no time to recruit."

"You forget there are fully five hours on board the boat. I 'll not be the least offended if you sleep the entire time. If there 's not wind enough to take in a reef, I 'll give the tiller to old Mark Spillane, and take a sleep myself."

"It is really like a Tartar journey," said the terrified Hankes.

"I have told you the worst of it, I must own," said she, laughing, "for I feel I have no right to obtain your escort on false pretences."

"And you would go alone over this long distance,—land and sea?"

"Land and sea are very grand words, Mr. Hankes, for some five-and-twenty miles of heather and a few hours in an open boat; but such as they are, I would go them alone."

Mr. Hankes would like to have said something complimentary, something flattering, but it did not exactly occur to him how he was to do it. To have exalted her heroism would be like a confession of his own poltroonery; to have seen any surprising evidence of boldness in her daring might possibly reflect upon her delicacy. He felt—none could have felt more thoroughly—that she was very courageous and very full of energy; but, somehow, these were humble aid to propagate that notion,—I had almost said that fallacy. "Only hear me out," said she, as he tried to interrupt "I began my duties in the most sanguine of all moods. Heaven knows not what dreams I had of a land of abundance and content. Well, I have seen the abundance,—the wealth has really poured in; every one is richer, better fed, clothed, housed, and cared for, and almost in an equal ratio are they grown more covetous, grasping, envious, and malevolent—You won't let me finish," cried she, as he showed an increasing impatience. "Well, perhaps, as we stroll along the cliffs to-morrow, you will be more disposed to listen; that is, if I have not already terrified you from accepting the companionship."

"Oh, no! by no means; but how are we to go,—do we drive?"

"Drive! why, my dear Mr. Hankes, it is only a Kerry pony has either legs or head for the path we must follow. Cast your eye along this coast-line; Jagged and fanciful as it looks, it conveys no notion of its rugged surface of rock, and its wild and darksome precipices. Take my word for it, you have as much to learn of the scenery as of the temperament of the land."

"But I'd like to go," repeated he, his accent being marvellously little in accordance with the sentiment.

"Nothing easier, sir. I'll give orders to have a pony—a most reliable pony—ready for you here to-morrow evening, when I shall expect you at tea."

Mr. Hankes bowed his grateful acknowledgments.

"I suspect, sir," said she, playfully, "that I have guessed your reason for this journey."

"My reason, my dear Miss Kellett," said he, in confusion,—"my reason is simply the pleasure and honor of *your* company, and the opportunity of visiting an interesting scene with—with   with—"

"No matter for the compliment; but I began really to imagine that you wished to learn my secret of bargaining with the people; that you wanted to witness one of these contracts you have heard so much of. Well, sir, you shall have it: our sole secret is, we trust each other."

CHAPTER XV
A BRIDLE-PATH

Sybella Kellett was less than just when she said that the country which lay between the Hermitage and Bantry Bay had few claims to the picturesque. It may possibly have been that she spoke with reference to what she fancied might have been Mr. Hankes's judgment of such a scene. There was, indeed, little to please an English eye,—no rich and waving woods, no smiling corn-fields, no expanse of swelling lawn or upland of deep meadow; but there was a wild and grand desolation, a waving surface fissured with deep clefts opening on the sea, which boomed in many a cavern far beneath. There were cliffs upright as a wall, hundreds of feet in height, on whose bare summits some rude remains were still traceable,—the fragment of a church, or shrine, or some lone cross, symbol of a faith that dated from centuries back. Heaths of many a gorgeous hue—purple, golden, and azure—clad a surface ever changing, and ferns that would have overtopped a tall horseman mingled their sprayey leaves with the wild myrtle and the arbutus. The moon was at her full as Sybella, accompanied by Mr. Hankes, and followed by an old and faithful groom,—a servant of her father's in times past,—took her way across this solitary tract.

If my reader is astonished that Mr. Hankes should have offered himself for such an expedition, it is but fair to state that the surprise was honestly shared in by that same gentleman. Was it that he made the offer in some moment of rash enthusiasm; had any impulse of wild chivalry mastered his calmer reason; was it that curious tendency which occasionally seems to sway Cockney natures to ascend mountains, cross dangerous ledges, or peep into volcanic craters? I really cannot aver that any of these was his actual motive, while I have my suspicion that a softer, a gentler, though a deeper sentiment influenced him on this occasion. Mr. Hankes—to use a favorite phrase of his own—"had frequent occasion to remark" Miss Kellett's various qualities of mind and intelligence; he had noticed in her the most remarkable aptitude for "business." She wrote and answered letters with a facility quite marvellous; details, however complicated, became by her treatment simple and easy; no difficulties seemed to deter her; and she possessed a gift—one of the rarest and most valuable of all—never to waste a moment on the impracticable, but to address herself, with a sort of intuition, at once, to only such means as could be rendered available.

Now, whether it was that Mr. Hankes anticipated a time when Mr. Dunn, in his greatness, might soar above the meaner cares of a business life,—when, lifted into the Elysian atmosphere of the nobility, he would look down with contemptuous apathy at the straggles and cares of enterprise,—or whether Mr. Hankes, from sources of knowledge available peculiarly to himself, knew that the fortunes of that great man were not built upon an eternal foundation, but shared in that sad lot which threatens all things human with vicissitude; whether stern facts and sterner figures taught him that all that splendid reputation, all that boundless influence, all that immense riches, might chance, one day or other, to be less real, less actual, and less positive than the world now believed them to be; whether, in a word, Mr. Hankes felt that Fortune, having smiled so long and so blandly on her favorite, might not, with that capriciousness so generally ascribed to her, assume another and very different aspect,—whatever the reason, in short, he deemed the dawn of his own day was approaching, and that, if only true to himself, Mr. Hankes was sure to be the man of the "situation,"—the next great star in the wide hemisphere that stretches from the Stock Exchange to—the Marshalsea, and includes all from Belgravia to Boulogne-sur-Mer.

Miss Kellett's abilities, her knowledge, her readiness, her tact, a certain lightness of hand in the management of affairs that none but a woman ever possesses, and scarcely one woman in ten thousand combines with the more male attributes of hard common-sense, pointed her out to Mr. Hankes as one eminently suited to aid his ambition. Now, men married for money every day in the week; and why not marry for what secured not alone money, but fame, station, and influence? Mr. Hankes was a widower; his own experience of married life had not been fortunate. The late Mrs. Hankes was a genius, and had the infirmities of that unsocial class; she despised her husband, quarrelled with him, lampooned him in a book, and ran off with the editor of a small weekly review that eulogized her novel. It was supposed she died in Australia,—at least, she never came back again; and as the first lieutenant gravely confirms the sun's altitude when he mutters, "Make it noon," so Mr. Hankes, by as simple a fiat, said, "Make her dead," and none disputed him. At all events, he was a widower by brevet, and eligible to be gazetted a husband at any moment.

Miss Kellett possessed many personal attractions, nor was he altogether insensible to them; but he regarded them, after all, pretty much as the intended purchaser of an estate might have regarded an ornamental fish-pond or a flower-garden on the property,—something, in short, which increased the attraction, but never augmented the value. He was glad they were there, though they by no means would have decided him to the purchase. He knew, besides, that the world set a high price on these things, and he was not sorry to possess what represented value of any kind. It was always scrip, shares, securities, even, although one could not well say how, when, or where the dividend was to be paid.

There was another consideration, too, weighed materially with him. The next best thing, in Mr. Hankes's estimation, to marrying into a good connection, was to have none at all,—no brothers, no sisters-in-law, no cousins-german or otherwise, no uncles, aunts, or any good friends of parental degree. Now, except a brother in the Crimea,—with an excellent chance of being killed,—Sybella had none belonging to her. In the happy phrase of advertisements, she had no encumbrances. There was no one to insist upon this or that settlement; none to stipulate for anything in her favor; and these were, to his thinking, vast advantages. Out of these various considerations our reader is now to fashion some of the reasons which induced Mr. Hankes to undertake an excursion alike foreign to his taste and uncongenial to his habits; but as a placeman would not decline the disagreeables of a sea-voyage as the preliminary to reaching the colony he was to govern, so this gentleman consoled himself by thinking that it was the sole penalty attached to a very remunerative ambition.

If Sybella was not without some astonishment at his proposal to accompany her, she never gave herself the slightest trouble to explain the motive. She acceded to his wish from natural courtesy and the desire to oblige, and that was all. He had been uniformly polite and civil in all their intercourse; beyond that, he was not a person whose companionship she would have sought or cared for, and so they rode along, chatting indifferently of whatever came uppermost,—the scene, the road, the season, the condition of the few people who formed the inhabitants of this wild region, and how their condition might possibly be affected by the great changes then in progress near them.

Guarded and cautious as he was in all he said, Mr. Hankes could not entirely conceal how completely he separated, in his own mind, the success of the great scheme and the advantage that might accrue to the people; nor was she slow to detect this reservation. She took too true and just a view of her companion's temper and tone to approach this theme with the scruples that agitated herself, but at once said,—

"Let us suppose this scheme to be as prosperous as its best friends can wish it, Mr. Hankes; that you all—I mean you great folk, who are directors, chairmen, secretaries, and so forth—become as rich and powerful as you desire, see your shares daily increasing in value, your speculations more and more lucrative, what becomes of the people—the poor man—all this while?"

"Why, of course he participates in all these successes; he grows rich too; he sells what he has to sell at a better market, obtains higher wages for his labor, and shares all our prosperity."

"Granted. But who is to teach him the best use of this newly acquired prosperity? You, and others like you, have your tastes already formed; the channels are already made in which your affluence is to run: not so with him; abundance may—nay, it will—suggest waste, which will beget worse. Who are to be his guides,—who his examples?"

"Oh, as to that, his increase of fortune will suggest its own appropriate increase of wants. He will be elevated by the requirements of his own advancing condition, and even if he were not, it is not exactly any affair of ours; we do our part when we afford him the means of a higher civilization."

"I don't think so. I suspect that not alone do you neglect a duty, but that you inflict a wrong. But come, I will take another alternative; I will suggest—what some are already predicting—that the project will not prove a success."

"Who says that?" cried Hankes, hastily, and in his haste forgetting his habitual caution of manner.

"Many have said it. Some of those whose opinions I am accustomed to place trust in, have told myself that the speculation is too vast,—disproportioned to the country, undertaken on a scale which nothing short of imperial resources could warrant—"

"But surely you do not credit such forebodings?" broke he in.

"It is of little consequence how far I credit them. I am as nothing in the event. I only would ask, What if all were to fail?—what if ruin were to fall upon the whole undertaking, what is to become of all those who have invested their entire fortunes in the scheme? The great and affluent have many ventures,—they trust not their wealth to one argosy; but how will it be with those who have embarked their all in one vessel?"

Mr. Hankes paused, as if to reflect over his reply, and she continued: "It is a question I have already dared to address to Mr. Dunn himself. I wrote to him twice on the subject. The first time I asked what guarantee could be given to small shareholders,—those, for instance, who had involved their whole wealth in the enterprise. He gave me no answer. To my second application came the dry rejoinder that I had possibly forgotten in whose service I was retained; that I drew my resources from the Earl of Glengariff, and not from the peasantry, whose advocate I had constituted myself."

"Well?" cried Hankes, curious to hear what turn the correspondence took.

"Well," said she, smiling gently, "I wrote again. I said it was true I had forgotten the fact of which he reminded me, but I pleaded in excuse that neither the Earl nor her Ladyship had refreshed my memory on the circumstance by any replies to eight, or, I believe, nine letters I sent them. I mentioned, too, that though I could endure the slight of this neglect for myself, I could not put up with it for the sake of those whose interest I watched over. Hear me out," said she, perceiving that he was about to interrupt. "It had become known in Glengariff that all the little fortune I was possessed of—the few hundred pounds Mr. Dunn had rescued for me out of the wreck of our property—was invested in this scheme. Mr. Dunn counselled this employment of the money, and I consented to it. Now, this trustfulness on my part induced many others to imitate what they deemed my example."

"And you really did make this investment?" said Hankes, whose eagerness could not brook longer delay.

"Yes," said she, with a quiet smile, "though, evidently, had I consulted Mr. Hankes, he would never have counselled the step." After a moment, she resumed, "I have half a mind to tell you how it happened."

"I pray you let me hear it."

"Well, it was in this way: Shortly after that affair of the Ossory Bank,— the run for gold, I mean,—I received a few hurried lines from Mr. Dunn, urging me to greater exertion on the score of the Glengariff scheme, and calling upon me to answer certain newspaper insinuations against its solvency, and so forth. Before replying to these attacks, I was, of course, bound to read them; and, shall I confess it, such was the singular force of the arguments they employed, so reasonable did their inferences appear, and so terrible the consequences should the plan prove a failure, that I for the first time perceived that it was by no means impossible the vast superstructure we were raising might be actually on the brink of a volcano. I did not like exactly to tell Mr. Dunn these misgivings; in fact, though I attempted two or three letters to that effect, I could not, without great risk of offending, convey my meaning, and so I reflected and pondered over the matter several days, working my brain to find some extrication from the difficulty. At last, I bethought me of this: Mr. Dunn was my guardian; by his efforts was the small fragment of property that fell to me rescued and saved. What if I were to request him to invest the whole of it in this scheme? Were its solvency but certain, where could the employment of the money be safer or more profitable? If he consented, I might fairly suppose my fears were vain, and my misgivings unfounded. If, however, he showed any reluctance, even backwardness, to the project, the very phrase he might employ to dissuade me would have its especial significance, and I could at once have something to reason upon. Well, I wrote to him, and he answered by the next post: 'I fully coincide with your suggestion, and, acting on it, you are now the possessor of fifty-four shares in the allotment. As the moment for buying in is favorable, it is a thousand pities you could not make an equally profitable investment for your brother, whose twelve hundred pounds is yielding the very inglorious interest of the bank.'"

"And so you took the shares?" said Hankes, sighing; then added, "But let me see,—at what rate did you buy?"

"I am ashamed to confess, I forget; but I know the shares were high?"

"After the Ossory run," muttered he,—"that was about September. Shares were then something like one hundred and twenty-seven and a quarter; higher afterwards; higher the whole month of November; shaky towards the end of the year; very shaky, indeed, in January. No, no," said he to himself, "Dunn ought not to have done it."

"I perceive," said she, half smiling, "Mr. Hankes opines that the money had been better in the bank."

"After all," continued he, not heeding her remark, "Dunn could n't do anything else. You own, yourself, that if he had attempted to dissuade you, you would immediately have taken alarm; you 'd have said, 'This is all a sham. All these people will find themselves "let in" some fine morning;' and as Dunn could very readily make good your few hundred pounds, why, he was perfectly justified in the advice he gave."

"Not when his counsel had the effect of influencing mine," said she, quickly; "not when it served to make me a perfidious example to others. No, no, Mr. Hankes; if this scheme be not an honest and an upright one, I accept no partnership in its details."

"I am only putting a case, remember," said Hankes, hurriedly,—"a possible, but most improbable case. I am supposing that a scheme with the fincst prospectus, the best list of directors, the most respectable referees in the empire, to be—what shall I say?—to be sickly,—yes, sickly,—in want of a little tonic treatment, generous diet, and so forth."

"You 'll have to follow me here, Mr. Hankes," broke in Sybella; "the pathway round this cliff only admits one at a time. Keep close to the rock, and if your head be not steady, don't look down."

"Good heavens! we are not going round that precipice!" cried Hankes, in a voice of the wildest terror.

"My servant will lead your horse, if you prefer it," said she, without answering his question; "and mind your footing, for the moss is often slippery with the spray."

Sybella made a signal with her whip to the groom, who was now close behind, and then, without awaiting for more, moved on. Hankes watched her as she descended the little slope to the base of a large rock, around which the path wound itself on the very verge of an immense precipice. Even from where he now stood the sea could be seen surging and booming hundreds of feet below; and although the night was calm and still, the ever-restless waves beat heavily against the rocks, and sent masses of froth and foam high into the air. He saw her till she turned the angle of the path, and then she was lost to his view.

"I don't think I have head for it. I 'm not used to this kind of thing," said Hankes, in a voice of helpless despondency to the old groom, who now stood awaiting him to dismount "Is there much danger? Is it as bad as it looks?"

"'Tis worse when you get round the rock there," said the groom, "for it's always going down you are, steeper than the roof of a house, with a shingle footing, and sloping outwards."

"I'll not go a step; I 'll not venture," broke in Hankes.

"Indeed, I wouldn't advise your honor," said the man, in a tone too sincere to be deemed sarcastic.

"I know my head could n't bear it," said he, with the imploring accents of one who entreated a contradiction. But the old groom, too fully convinced of the sentiment to utter a word against it, was now only thinking of following his mistress.

"Wait a moment," cried Hankes, with an immense effort. "If I were once across this"—he was going to add an epithet, but restrained himself—"this place, is there nothing more of the same kind afterwards?"

"Is n't there, faith!" cried the man. "Isn't there the Clunk, where the beast has to step over gullies five-and-thirty or forty feet deep? Isn't there Tim's Island, a little spot where you must turn your horse round with the sea four hundred feet under you? Is n't there the Devil's Nose—"

"There, there, you need n't go on, my good fellow; I 'll turn back."

"Look where she is now," said the man, pointing with his whip to a rocky ledge hundreds of feet down, along which a figure on horseback might be seen creeping slowly along. "'Tis there, where she's stealing along now, you need the good head and the quick hand. May I never!" exclaimed he, in terror, "if them isn't goats that's coming up to meet her! Merciful Joseph! what'll she do? There, they are under the horse's legs, forcing their way through! Look how the devils are rushing all round and about her! If the beast moves an inch—" A wild cry broke from the old man here, for a fragment of rock, displaced by the rushing herd, had just come thundering down the cliff, and splashed into the sea beneath. "The heavens be praised! she's safe," muttered he, piously crossing himself; and then, without a word more, and as if angry at his own delay, he pressed his horse forward to follow her.

It was in vain Hankes cried to him to wait,—to stop for only an instant,—that he, too, was ready to go,—not to leave him and desert him there,—that he knew not where to turn him, nor could ever retrace his way,—already the man was lost to view and hearing, and all the vain entreaties were uttered to the winds. As for Sybella, her perilous pathway gave her quite enough to do not to bestow a thought upon her companion; nor, indeed, had she much recollection of him till the old groom overtook her on the sandy beach, and recounted to her, not without a certain touch of humor, Mr. Hankes's terror and despair.

"It was cruel to leave him, Ned," said she, trying to repress a smile at the old man's narrative. "I think you must go back, and leave me to pursue my way alone."

"Sorra one o' me will go back to the likes of him. 'T is for your own self, and ne'er another, I'd be riskin' my neck in the same spot," said he, resolutely.

"But what's to become of him, Ned? He knows nothing of the country; he 'll not find his way back to Glengariff."

"Let him alone; devil a harm he 'll come to. 'T is chaps like that never comes to mischief. He 'll wander about there till day breaks, and maybe find his way to Duffs Mill, or, at all events, the boy with the letter-bag from Caherclough is sure to see him."

Even had this last assurance failed to satisfy Sybella, it was so utterly hopeless a task to overrule old Ned's resolve that she said no more, but rode on in silence. Not so Ned; the theme afforded him an opportunity for reflecting on English character and habits which was not to be lost.

"I'd like to see your brother John turn back and leave a young lady that way," said he, recurring to the youth whose earliest years he had watched over.

No matter how impatiently, even angrily, Bella replied to the old man's bigoted preference of his countrymen, Ned persisted in deploring the unhappy accident by which fate had subjected the finer and more gifted race to the control and dominion of an inferior people. To withdraw him effectually from a subject which to an Irish peasant has special attraction, she began to tell him of the war in the East and of her brother Jack, the old man listening with eager delight to the achievements of one he had carried about in his arms as a child. Her mind filled with the wondrous stories of private letters,—the intrepid daring of this one, the noble chivalry of that,—she soon succeeded in winning all his attention. It was singular, however, that of all the traits she recorded, none made such a powerful appeal to the old man's heart as the generous self-devotion of those women who, leaving home, friends, country, and all, gave themselves up to the care of the sick and wounded. He never wearied of hearing how they braved death in its most appalling shape amidst the pestilential airs of the hospital, in the midst of such horrors as no pen can picture, taking on them the most painful duties, accepting fatigue, exhaustion, and peril as the common incidents of life, braving scenes of agony such as in very recital sickened the heart, descending to all that was menial in their solicitude for some poor sufferer, and all this with a benevolence and a kindness that made them seem less human beings than ministering angels from heaven.

"Oh, Holy Joseph! is n't it yourself ought to be there?" cried the old man, enthusiastically. "Was there ever your like to give hope to a sick heart? Who ever could equal you to cheer up the sinking spirit, and even make misery bearable? Miss Bella, darling, did you never think of going out?"

"Ay, Ned, a hundred times," said she, sighing drearily. "I often, too, said to myself, There's not one of these ladies—for they are ladies born and bred—who has n't a mother, father, sisters, and brothers dear to her, and to whom she is herself dear. She leaves a home where she is loved, and where her vacant place is daily looked at with sorrow; and yet here am I, who have none to care for, none to miss me, who would carry over the sea with me no sorrows from those I was leaving, for I am friendless,—surely I am well fitted for such a task—"

"Well," said he, eagerly, as she seemed to hesitate, "well, and why—"

"It was not fear held me back," resumed she. "It was not that I shrank from the sights and sounds of agony that must have been more terrible than any death; it was simply a hope—a wish, perhaps, more than a hope—that

I might be doing service to those at home here, who, if I were to leave them, would not have one on their side. Perhaps I overrated what I did, or could do; perhaps I deemed my help of more value than it really was; but every day seemed to show me that the people needed some one to counsel and to guide them,—to show them where their true interests lay, and by what little sacrifices they could oftentimes secure a future benefit."

"That's thrue, every word of it. Your name is in every cabin, with a blessing tacked to it. There's not a child does n't say a prayer for you before he goes to sleep; and there's many a grown man never thought of praying at all till he axed a blessing for yourself!"

"With that, too," resumed she, "was coupled power, for my Lord left much to my management. I was able to help the deserving, to assist the honest and industrious; now I aided this one to emigrate, now I could contribute a little assistance of capital. In fact, Ned, I felt they wanted me, and I knew I liked *them*. There was one good reason for not going away. Then there were other reasons," said she, falteringly. "It is not a good example to give to others to leave, no matter how humble, the spot where we have a duty, to seek out a higher destiny. I speak as a woman."

"And is it thrue, Miss Bella, that it's Mister Dunn has it all here under his own hand,—that the Lord owns nothing only what Dunn allows him, and that the whole place down to Kenmare River is Dunn's?"

"It is quite true, Ned, that the control and direction of all the great works here are with Mr. Dunn. All the quarries and mines, the roads, harbors, quays, 'bridges, docks, houses, are all in his hands."

"Blessed hour! and where does he get the money to do it all?" cried he, in amazement.

Now, natural as was the question, and easy of reply as it seemed, Sybella heard it with something almost like a shock. Had the thought not occurred to her hundreds of times? And, if so, how had she answered it? Of course there could be no difficulty in the reply; of course such immense speculations, such gigantic projects as Mr. Dunn engaged in, supplied wealth to any amount. But equally true was it, that they demanded great means; they were costly achievements,—these great lines of railroad, these vast harbors. Nor were they always successful; Mr. Hankes himself had dropped hints about certain "mistakes" that were very significant. The splendid word "Credit" would explain it all, doubtless, but how interpret credit to the mind of the poor peasant? She tried to illustrate it by the lock of a canal, in which the water is momentarily utilized for a particular purpose, and then restored, unimpaired, to the general circulation; but Ned unhappily damaged the imagery by remarking, "But what's to be done if there's no water?" Fortunately for her logic, the road became once more only wide enough for one to proceed at a time, and Sybella was again left to her own musings.

Scarcely conscious of the perilous path by which she advanced, she continued to meditate over the old man's words, and wonder within herself how it was that he, the poor, unlettered peasant, should have conceived that high notion of what her mission ought to be,—when and how her energies should be employed. She had been schooling herself for years to feel that true heroism consisted in devoting oneself to some humble, unobtrusive career, whose best rewards were the good done to others, where self-denial was a daily lesson, and humility a daily creed; but, do what she could, there was within her heart the embers of the fire that burned there in childhood. The first article of that faith taught her that without danger there is no greatness,—that in the hazardous conflicts where life is ventured, high qualities only are developed. What but such noble excitement could make heroes of those men, many of whom, without such stimulus, had dropped down the stream of life unnoticed and undistinguished? "And shall I," cried she, aloud, "go on forever thus, living the small life of petty cares and interests, confronting no dangers beyond a dark December day, encountering no other hazards than the flippant rebuke of my employer?" "There's the yawl, Miss Bella; she's tacking about, waiting for us," said Ned, as he pointed to a small sailboat like a speck in the blue sea beneath; and at the same instant a little rag of scarlet bunting was run up to the peak, to show that the travellers had been seen from the water.

CHAPTER XVI
THE DISCOVERY

It is possible that my reader might not unwillingly accompany Sybella as she stepped into the little boat, and, tripping lightly over the "thwarts," seated herself in the stern-sheets. The day was bright and breezy, the sea scarcely ruffled, for the wind was off the land; the craft, although but a fishing-boat, was sharp and clean built, the canvas sat well on her, and, last of all, she who held the tiller was a very pretty girl, whose cheek, flushed with exercise, and loosely waving hair, gave to her beauty the heightened expression of which care occasionally robbed it. The broad bay, with its mountain background and its wide sea-reach, studded with tall three-masters, was a fine and glorious object; and as the light boat heeled over to the breeze, and the white foam came rustling over the prow, Sybella swept her fair hand through the water, and bathed her brow with the action of one who dismissed all painful thought, and gave herself to the full enjoyment of the hour. Yes, my dear reader, the companionship of such a girl on such a day, in such a scene, was worth having; and so even those rude fishermen thought it, as, stretched at full length on the shingle ballast, they gazed half bashfully at her, and then exchanged more meaning looks with each other as she talked with them.

Just possible it is, too, that some curiosity may exist as to what became of Mr. Hankes. Did that great projector of industrial enterprise succeed in retracing his steps with safety? Did he fall in with some one able to guide him back to Glengariff? Did he regain the Hermitage after fatigue and peril, and much self-reproach for an undertaking so foreign to his ways and habits; and did he vow to his own heart that this was to be the last of such excursions on his part? Had he his misgivings, too, that his conduct had not been perfectly heroic; and did he experience a sense of shame in retiring before a peril braved by a young and delicate girl? Admitted to a certain share of that gentleman's confidence, we are obliged to declare that his chief sorrows were occasioned by the loss of time, the amount of inconvenience, and the degree of fatigue the expedition had caused him. It was not till late in the afternoon of the day that he chanced upon a fisherman on his way to Bantry to sell his fish. The poor peasant could not speak nor understand English, and after a vain attempt at explanation on either side, the colloquy ended by Hankes joining company with the man, and proceeding along with him, whither he knew not.

If we have not traced the steps of Sybella's wanderings, we are little disposed to linger along with those of Mr. Hankes, though, if his own account were to be accepted, his journey was a succession of adventures and escapes. Enough if we say that he at last abandoned his horse amid the fissured cliffs of the coast, and, as best he might, clambered over rock and precipice, through tall mazes of wet fern and deep moss, along shingly shores and sandy beaches, till he reached the little inn at Bantry, the weariest and most worn-out of men, his clothes in rags, his shoes in tatters, and he himself scarcely conscious, and utterly indifferent as to what became of him.

A night's sound sleep and a good breakfast were already contributing much to efface the memory of past sufferings, when Sybella Kellett entered his room. She had been over to the cottage, had visited the whole locality, transacted all the business she had come for, and only diverged from her homeward route on hearing that Mr. Hankes had just arrived at Bantry. Rather apologizing for having left *him* than accusing him of deserting *her*, she rapidly proceeded to sketch out her own journey. She did not dwell upon any incidents of the way,—had they been really new or strange she would not have recalled them,—she only adverted to what had constituted the object of her coming,—the purchase of the small townland which she had completed.

"It is a dear old place," said she, "of a fashion one so rarely sees in Ireland, the house being built after that taste known as Elizabethan, and by tradition said to have once been inhabited by the poet Spenser. It is very small, and so hidden by a dense beech-wood, that you might pass within fifty yards of the door and never see it. This rude drawing may give you some idea of it."

"And does the sea come up so close as this?" asked Hankes, eagerly.

"The little fishing-boat ran into the cove you see there; her mainsail dropped over the new-mown hay."

"Why, it 's the very thing Lord Lockewood is looking for, He is positively wild about a spot in some remote out-of-the-way region; and then, what you tell me of its being a poet's house will complete the charm. You said Shakspeare—"

"No, Spenser, the poet of the 'Faërie Queene,'" broke she in, with a smile.

"It's all the same; he 'll give it a fanciful name, and the association with its once owner will afford him unceasing amusement."

"I hope he is not destined to enjoy the pleasure you describe."

"No?—why not, pray?"

"I hope and trust that the place may not pass into his hands; in a word, I intend to ask Mr. Dunn to allow me to be the purchaser. I find that the sum is almost exactly the amount I have invested in the Allotment scheme,— these same shares we spoke of,—and I mean to beg as a great favor,—a very great favor,—to be permitted to make this exchange. I want no land,— nothing but the little plot around the cottage."

"The cottage formerly inhabited by the poet Spenser, built in the purest Elizabethan style, and situated in a glen,—you said a glen, I think, Miss Kellett?" said Hankes,—"in a glen, whose wild enclosure, bosomed amongst deep woods, and washed by the Atlantic—"

"Are you devising an advertisement, sir?"

"The very thing I was doing, Miss Kellett. I was just sketching out a rough outline of a short paragraph for the 'Post.'"

"But remember, sir, I want to possess this spot. I wish to be its owner—"

"To dispose of, of course, hereafter,—to make a clear three, four, or five thousand by the bargain, eh?"

"Nothing of the kind, Mr. Hankes. I mean to acquire enough—some one day or other—to go back and dwell there. I desire to have what I shall always, to myself at least, call mine—my home. It will be as a goal to win, the time I can come back and live there. It will be a resting-place for poor Jack when he returns to England."

Mr. Hankes paused. It was the first time Miss Kellett had referred to her own fortunes in such a way as permitted him to take advantage of the circumstance, and he deliberated with himself whether he ought not to profit by the accident. How would she receive a word of advice from him? Would it be well taken? Might it possibly lead to something more? Would she be disposed to lean on his counsels; and, if so, what then? Ay, Mr. Hankes, it was the "what then?" was the puzzle. It was true his late conduct presented but a sorry emblem of that life-long fidelity he thought of pledging; but if she were the clear-sighted, calm-reasoning intelligence he believed, she would lay little stress upon what, after all, was a mere trait of a man's temperament. Very rapidly, indeed, did these reflections pass through his mind; and then he stole a glance at her as she sat quietly sipping her tea, looking a very ideal of calm tranquillity. "This cottage," thought he, "has evidently taken a hold of her fancy. Let me see if I cannot turn the theme to my purpose." And with this intention he again brought her back to speak of the spot, which she did with all the eagerness of true interest.

"As to the association with the gifted spirit of song," said Mr. Hankes, soaring proudly into the style he loved, "I conclude that to be somewhat doubtful of proof, eh?"

"Not at all, sir. Spenser lived at a place called Kilcoleman, from which he removed for two or three years, and returned. It was in this interval he inhabited the cottage. Curiously enough, some manuscript in his writing — part of a correspondence with the Lord-Deputy — was discovered yesterday when I was there. It was contained in a small oak casket with a variety of other papers, some in quaint French, some in Latin. The box was built in so as to form a portion of a curiously carved chimney-piece, and chance alone led to its discovery."

"I hope you secured the documents?" cried Hankes, eagerly.

"Yes, sir; here they are, box and all. The Rector advised me to carry them away for security' sake." And so saying, she laid upon the table a massively bound and strong-built box, of about a foot in length.

It was with no inexperienced hand that Mr. Hankes proceeded to investigate the contents. His well-practised eye rapidly caught the meaning of each paper as he lifted it up, and he continued to mutter to himself his comments upon them. "This document is an ancient grant of the lands of Cloughrennin to the monks of the Abbey of Castlerosse, and bears date 1104. It speaks of certain rights reserved to the Baron Hugh Pritchard Conway. Conway—Conway," mumbled he, twice or thrice; "that's the very name I tried and could not remember yesterday, Miss Kellett. You asked me about a certain soldier whose daring capture of a Russian officer was going the round of the papers. The young fellow had but one arm too; now I remember, his name was Conway."

"Charles Conway! Was it Charles Conway?" cried she, eagerly; "but it could be no other,—he had lost his right arm."

"I 'm not sure which, but he had only one, and he was called an orderly on the staff of the Piedmontese General."

"Oh, the noble fellow! I could have sworn he would distinguish himself. Tell me it all again, sir; where did it happen, and how, and when?"

Mr. Hankes's memory was now to be submitted to a very searching test, and he was called on to furnish details which might have puzzled "Our own Correspondent." Had Charles Conway been rewarded for his gallantry? What notice had his bravery elicited? Was he promoted, and to what rank? Had he been decorated, and with what order? Were his wounds, as reported, only trifling? Where was he now?—was he in hospital or on service? She grew impatient at how little he knew,—how little the incident seemed to have impressed him. "Was it possible," she asked, "that heroism like this was so rife that a meagre paragraph was deemed enough to record it,—a paragraph, too, that forgot to state what had become of its hero?"

"Why, my dear Miss Kellett," interposed he, at length, "one reads a dozen such achievements every week."

"I deny it, sir," cried she, angrily. "Our soldiers are the bravest in the world; they possess a courage that asks no aid from the promptings of self-interest, nor the urgings of vanity; they are very lions in combat; but it needs the chivalrous ardor of the gentleman, the man of blood and lineage to conceive a feat like this. It was only a noble patriotism could suggest the thought of such an achievement."

"I must say," said Hankes, in confusion, "the young fellow acquitted himself admirably; but I would also beg to observe that there is nothing in the newspaper to lead to the conclusion you are disposed to draw. There's not a word of his being a gentleman."

"But I know it, sir,—the fact is known to *me*. Charles Conway is a man of family; he was once a man of fortune: he had served as an officer in a Lancer regiment; he had been extravagant, wild, wasteful, if you will."

"Why, it can't be the Smasher you're talking of?—the great swell that used to drive the four chestnuts in the Park, and made the wager he'd go in at one window of Stagg and Mantle's and out at t'other?"

"I don't care to hear of such follies, sir, when there are better things to be remembered. Besides, he is my brother's dearest friend, and I will not hear him spoken of but with respect. Take *my* word for it, sir, I am but asking what you had done, without a hint, were he only present."

"I believe you,—by Jove, I believe you!" cried Hankes, with an honesty in the tone of his voice that actually made her smile. "And so this is Conway the Smasher!"

"Pray, Mr. Hankes, recall him by some other association. It is only fair to remember that he has given us the fitting occasion."

"Ay, very true,—what you say is perfectly just; and, as you say, he is your brother's friend. Who would have thought it!—who would have thought it!".

Without puzzling ourselves to inquire what it was that thus excited Mr. Hankes's astonishment, let us observe that gentleman, as he turns over, one by one, the papers in the box, muttering his comments meanwhile to himself: "Old title-deeds,—very old indeed,—all the ancient contracts are recited. Sir Gwellem Conway must have been a man of mark and note in those days. Here we find him holding 'in capite' from the king, twelve thousand acres, with the condition that he builds a strong castle and a 'bawn.' And these are, apparently, Sir Gwellem's own letters. Ah! and here we have him or his descendant called Baron of Ackroyd and Bedgellert, and claimant to the title of Lackington, in which he seems successful. This is the writ of summons calling him to the Lords as Viscount Lackington. Very curious and important these papers are,—more curious, perhaps, than important,—for in all likelihood there have been at least half a dozen confiscations of these lands since this time."

Mr. Hankes's observations were not well attended to, for Sybella was already deep in the perusal of a curious old letter from a certain Dame Marian Conway to her brother, then Sheriff of Cardigan, in which some very strange traits of Irish chieftain life were detailed.

"I have an antiquarian friend who'd set great store by these old documents, Miss Kellett," said Hankes, with a sort of easy indifference. "They have no value save for such collectors; they serve to throw a passing light over a dark period of history, and perhaps explain a bygone custom or an obsolete usage. What do you mean to do with them?"

"Keep them. If I succeed in my plans about the cottage, these letters of Spenser to Sir Lawrence Esmond are in themselves a title. Of course, if I fail in my request, I mean to give them to Mr. Dunn."

"These were Welsh settlers, it would seem," cried Hankes, still bending over the papers. "They came originally from Abergedley."

"Abergedley!" repeated Sybella, three or four times over. "How strange!"

"What is strange, Miss Kellett?" asked Hankes, whose curiosity was eagerly excited by the expression of her features.

Instead of reply, however, she had taken a small notebook from her pocket, and sat with her eyes fixed upon a few words written in her own hand: "The Conways of Abergedley—of what family—if settled at any time in Ireland, and where?" These few words, and the day of the year when they were written, recalled to her mind a conversation she had once held with Terry Driscoll.

"What is puzzling you, Miss Kellett?" broke in Hankes; "I wish I could be of any assistance to its unravelment."

"I am thinking of 'long ago;' something that occurred years back. Didn't you mention," asked she, suddenly, "that Mr. Driscoll had been the former proprietor of thia cottage?"

"Yes, in so far as having paid part of the purchase-money. Does his name recall anything to interest you, Miss Kellett?"

If she heard she did not heed his question, but sat deep sunk in her own musings.

If there was any mood of the human mind that had an especial fascination for Mr. Hankes, it was that frame of thought which indicated the possession of some mysterious subject,—some deep and secret theme which the possessor retained for himself alone,—a measure of which none were to know the amount, to which none were to have the key. It would be ignoble to call this passion curiosity, for, in reality, it was less exercised by any desire to fathom the mystery than it was prompted by an intense jealousy of him who thus held in his own hands the solution of some portentous difficulty. To know on what schemes other men were bent, what hopes and fears filled them, by what subtle trains of reasoning they came to this conclusion or to that, were the daily exercises of his intelligence. He was eternally, as the phrase is, putting things together, comparing events, confronting this circumstance with that, and drawing inferences from every chance and accident of life. Now, it was clear to him Miss Kellett had a secret; or, at least, had the clew to one. Driscoll was "in it," and this cottage was "in it," and, not impossibly too, some of these Conway s were "in it." There was something in that note-book; how was he to obtain sight of it? The vaguest line—-a word—would be enough for him. Mr. Hankes remembered how he had once committed himself and his health to the care of an unskilful physician simply because the man knew a fact which he wanted, and did worm out of him during his attendance. He had, at another time, undertaken a short voyage in a most unsafe craft, with a drunken captain, because the stewardess was possessed of a secret of which, even in his sea-sickness, he obtained the key. Over and over again had he assumed modes of life he detested, dissipation the most distasteful to him, to gain the confidence of men that were only assailable in these modes; and now he bethought him that if he only had a glimmering of his present suspicion, the precipice and the narrow path and the booming sea below had all been braved, and he would have followed her unflinchingly through every peril with this goal before him. Was it too late to reinstate himself in her esteem? He thought not; indeed, she did not seem to retain any memory of his defection. At all events, there was little semblance of it having influenced her in her manner towards him.

"We shall meet at Glengariff, Mr. Hankes," said Sybella, rising, and replacing the papers in the box. "I mean to return by the coast road, and will not ask you to accompany me."

"It is precisely what I was about to beg as a favor. I was poorly yesterday,—a nervous headache, an affection I am subject to; in short, I felt unequal to any exertion, or even excitement."

"Pray let me counsel you to spare yourself a journey of much fatigue with little to reward it. Frequency and long habit have deprived the mountain tract of all terror for me, but I own that to a stranger it is not without peril. The spot where we parted yesterday is the least dangerous of the difficulties, and so I would say be advised, and keep to the high-road."

Now, there was not the slightest trace of sarcasm in what she said; it was uttered in all sincerity and good faith, and yet Mr. Hankes could not help suspecting a covert mockery throughout.

"I 'm determined she shall see I am a man of courage," muttered he to himself; and then added, aloud, "You must permit me to disobey you, Miss Kellett. I am resolved to bear you company."

There was a dash of decision in his tone that made Sybella turn to look at him, and, to her astonishment, she saw a degree of purpose and determination in his face very unlike its former expression. If she did not possess the craft and subtlety which long years had polished to a high perfection in him, she had that far finer and more delicate tact by which a woman's nature reads man's coarser temperament. She watched his eye, too, and saw how it rested on the oaken box, and, even while awaiting her answer, never turned from that object.

"Yes," said she to herself, "there is a game to be played out between us, and yonder is the stake."

Did Mr. Hankes divine what was passing in her mind? I know not. All he said was,—

"May I order the horses, Miss Kellett?"

"Yes, I am ready."

"And this box, what is to be done with it? Best to leave it here in the possession of the innkeeper. I suppose it will be safe?" asked he, half timidly.

"Perfectly safe; it would be inconvenient to carry with us. Will you kindly tell the landlord to come here?"

No sooner had Mr. Hankes left the room on his errand, than Sybella unlocked the box, and taking out the three papers in which the name of Conway appeared, relocked it. The papers she as quickly consigned to a small bag, which, as a sort of sabretasche, formed part of her riding-costume.

Mr. Hankes was somewhat longer on his mission than appeared necessary, and when he did return there was an air of some bustle and confusion about him, while between him and the landlord an amount of intimacy had grown up—a sort of confidence was established—that Bella's keen glance rapidly read.

"An old-fashioned lock, and doubtless worth nothing, Miss Kellett," said Hankes, as with a contemptuous smile he regarded the curiously carved ornament of the keyhole. "You have the key, I think?"

"Yes; it required some ingenuity to withdraw it from where, I suppose, it has been rusting many a year."

"It strikes me I might as well put a band over the lock and affix my seal. It will convey the notion of something very precious inside," added he, laughing, "and our friend here, Mr. Rorke, will feel an increased importance in the guardianship of such a treasure."

"I 'll guard it like goold, sir; that you may depend on," chimed in the landlord.

Why was it that, as Bella's quick glance was bent upon him, he turned so hastily away, as if to avoid the scrutiny?

Do not imagine, valued reader, that while this young girl scanned the two faces before her, and tried to discover what secret understanding subsisted between these two men,—strangers but an hour ago,—that she herself was calm and self-possessed. Far from it; as little was she self-acquitted. It was under the influence of a sudden suspicion flashing across her mind—whence or how she knew not—that some treachery was being planned, that she withdrew these documents from the box. The expression of Hankes's look, as it rested on the casket, was full of significance. It meant much, but of what nature she could not read. The sudden way he had questioned her about Driscoll imparted a link of connection between that man and the contents of the box, or part of them; and what part could that be except what concerned the name of Conway? If these were her impulses, they were more easily carried out than forgiven, and in her secret heart she was ashamed of her own distrust, and of what it led her to do.

"It would be a curious question at law," said Hankes, as he affixed the third and last seal,—"a very curious question, who owns that box. Not that its contents would pay for the litigation," added he, with a mocking laugh; "but the property being sold this morning, with an unsettled claim of Driscoll's over it, and the purchaser being still undeclared,—for I suppose you bought it in for the Earl, or for Mr. Dunn, perhaps—"

"No, sir, in my own name, and for myself, waiting Mr. Dunn's good pleasure to confirm the sale in the way I have told you."

"Indeed!" exclaimed he, looking with an unfeigned admiration at a young girl capable of such rapid and decisive action, "so that you really may consider yourself its owner."

"I do consider myself its owner," was her calm reply.

"Then pray excuse my officiousness in this sealing up. I hope you will pardon my indiscreet zeal."

She smiled without answering, and the blood mounted to Mr. Hankes's face and forehead till they were crimson. He, too, felt that there was a game between them, and was beginning to distrust his "hand."

"Are we to be travelling-companions, Mr. Hankes?" asked she. And though nothing was said in actual words, there was that in the voice and manner of the speaker that made the question run thus: "Are we, after what we have just seen of each other, to journey together?"

"Well, if you really wish me to confess the truth, Miss Kellett, I must own I am rather afraid of my head along these mountain paths,—a sort of faintness, a rushing of blood to the brain, and a confusion; in short, Nature never meant me for a chamois-hunter, and I should bring no credit on your training of me."

"Your resolve is all the wiser, sir, and so to our next meeting." She waved him a half-familiar, half-cold farewell, and left the room.

Mr. Hankes saw her leave the town, and he loitered about the street till he could mark two mounted figures ascending the mountain. He then ordered a chaise to the door with all speed.

"Will you take it now, sir, or send for it, as you said at first?" asked the innkeeper, as he stood with the oak box in his hands.

"Keep it till I write,—keep it till you hear from me; or, no, put it in the chaise,—that's better."

CHAPTER XVII
THE DOUBLE BLUNDER

Short as had been Sybella's absence from the Hermitage, a vast number of letters had arrived for her in the mean while. The prospect of a peace, so confidently entertained at one moment, was now rudely destroyed by the abrupt termination of the Vienna conferences, and the result was a panic in the money-market.

The panic of an army rushing madly on to victory; the panic on shipboard when the great vessel has struck, and after three or four convulsive throes the mighty masts have snapped, and the blue water, surging and bounding, has riven the hatchways and flooded the deck; the panic of a mob as the charge of cavalry is sounded, and the flash of a thousand sabres is seen through the long vista of a street; the panic of a city stricken by plague or cholera,—are all dreadful and appalling things, and have their scenes of horror full of the most picturesque terror; still are there incidents of an almost equal power when that dread moment has arrived which is called a "Panic on 'Change."

It was but yesterday, and the world went well and flourishingly, mills were at work, foundries thundered with their thousand hammers, vessels sailed forth from every port, and white-sailed argosies were freighted with wealth from distant colonies. None had to ask twice for means to carry out his speculations, for every enterprise there was capital; and now scarcely twenty-four hours have passed, and all is changed. A despatch has been received in the night; a messenger has arrived at Downing Street; the Minister has been aroused from his sleep to hear that we have met some great reverse; a terrible disaster has befallen us; two line-of-battle ships, whose draught of water was too great, have grounded under an enemy's fire; in despite of the most heroic resistance, they have been captured; the union-jacks are on their way to Moscow. Mayhap the discomfiture, less afflicting to national pride, is the blunder of a cavalry officer or the obstinacy of an envoy. Little matter for the cause, we have met a check. Down goes credit, and up go the discounts; the mighty men of millions have drawn their purse-strings, and not a guinea is to be had; the city is full of sad-visaged men in black, presaging every manner of misfortune. More troops are wanted; more ships; we are going to have an increase of the income-tax,—a loan,—a renewal of war burdens in fifty shapes! Each fancies some luxury of which he must deprive himself, some expense to be curtailed; and all are taking the dreariest view of a future whose chief feature is to be privation.

So was it now. Amidst a mass of letters was one from Davenport Dunn, written with brevity and in haste. By a mistake, easily made In the hurry and confusion of such correspondence, it was, though intended for Mr. Hankes, addressed to Miss Kellett; the words "Strictly private and confidential" occupying a conspicuous place across the envelope, while lower down was written "Immediate."

It was a very rare event, latterly, for Mr. Dunn to write to Miss Kellett, nor had she, in all their intercourse, once received from him a letter announced thus "confidential."

It was, then, in some surprise, and not without a certain anxiety, that she broke the seal. It was dated "Wednesday, Irish Office," and began thus: "Dear S."—she started,—he had never called her Sybella in his life; he had been most punctiliously careful ever to address her as Miss Kellett. She turned at once to the envelope, and read the address, "Miss Kellett, the Hermitage, Glengariff." And yet there could be no mistake. It opened, "Dear S." "He has forgotten a word," thought she; "he meant in his mood of confidence to call me Miss Sybella, and has omitted the title." The letter ran thus: "We have failed at Vienna, as we do everywhere and in everything. The war is to continue; consequently, we are in a terrible mess. Glumthal telegraphs this morning that he will not go on; the Frankfort people will, of course, follow his lead, so that Mount Cenis will be 'nowhere' by the end of the week. I am, however, more anxious about Glengariff, which must be upheld, *for the moment*, at any cost To-day I can manage to keep up the shares; perhaps, also, to-morrow.. The old Earl is more infatuated about the scheme than ever, though the accounts he receives from that girl"—"That girl," muttered she; "who can he mean?"—"from that girl occasionally alarm him. She evidently has her own suspicions, though I don't clearly see by what they have been suggested. The sooner, therefore, you can possess yourself of the correspondence, the better. I have written to her by this post with a proposition she will most probably accept; advise it, by all means."—"This is scarcely intelligible," said she, once more reverting to the direction of the letter.—"Should the Ministry be beaten on Monday, they mean to dissolve Parliament. Now, they cannot go to the country, in Ireland, without me, and my terms I have already fixed. They *must* give us aid,—material, substantial aid; I will not be put off with office or honors,—it is no time for either. Meanwhile, I want all the dividend warrants, and a brief sketch of our next statement; for we meet on Saturday. Come what will, the Allotment must be sustained till the new election be announced. I hope Lackington's check was duly presented, for I find that his death was known here on the 4th. Where the new Viscount is, no one seems even to guess. Get rid of the girl, and believe me, yours ever,—D. D."

"Surely, there is some strange mystification here," said she, as she sat pondering over this letter. "There are allusions which, had they not been addressed to me, I might have fancied were intended for myself. This girl, whose accounts have terrified Lord Glengariff, and who herself suspects that all is not right, may mean *me*; but yet it is to me he writes, confidentially and secretly. I cannot complain that the letter lacks candor; it is frank enough; every word forebodes coming disaster, the great scheme is threatened with ruin, nothing can save it but Government assistance,—an infamous compact, if I read it aright. And if all this be so, in what a game have I played a part! This great venture is a swindling enterprise! All these poor people whose hard-earned gains have been invested in it will be ruined; my own small pittance, too, is gone. Good heavens! to what a terrible network of intrigue and deception have I lent myself! How have I come to betray those whose confidence I strove so hard to gain! This girl,—this girl,—who is she, and of whom does he speak?" exclaimed she, as, in an outburst of emotion, she walked the room, her whole frame trembling, and her eyes glaring in all the wildness of high excitement.

"May I come in?" whispered a soft voice, as a low tap was heard at the door; and without waiting for leave, Mr. Hankes entered. Nothing could be silkier nor softer than his courteous approach; his smile was the blandest, his step the smoothest, his bow the nicest blending of homage and regard; and, as he took Miss Kellett's hand, it was with the air of a courtier dashed with the devotion of an admirer. Cruel is the confession that she noticed none—not one—of these traits. Her mind was so engrossed by the letter, that, had Mr. Hankes made his entry in a suit of chain armor, and with a mace in his hand, she would not have minded it.

"I am come to entreat forgiveness,—to sue your pardon, Miss Kellett, for a very great offence, of which, however, I am the guiltless offender. The letter which I hold here, and which, as you see, is addressed S. Hankes, Esq.,' was certainty intended for you, and not me."

"What—how—misdirected—a mistake in the address?" cried she, eagerly.

"Just so; placed in a wrong enclosure," resumed he, in a tone of well-graduated calm. "A blunder which occurs over and over in life, but I am fain to hope has never happened with less serious results."

"In short," said she, hastily, "my letter, or the letter meant for me, came directed to *you*?"

"Precisely. I have only to plead, as regards myself, that immediately on discovery—and I very soon discovered that it could not have been destined for my perusal—I refolded the epistle and hastened to deliver it to your own hands."

"More discreet and more fortunate than I," said she, with a very peculiar smile, "since this letter which I hold here, and which bore my address, I now perceive was for you, and this I have not read merely once or twice, but fully a dozen times; in truth, I believe I could repeat it, word for word, if the task were required of me."

What has become of Mr. Hankes's soft and gentle manner? Where are his bland looks, his air of courtesy and kindness, his voice so full of sweetness and deference? Why, the man seems transfixed, his eyeballs are staring wildly, and he actually clutches, not takes, the letter from her hands.

"Why, the first words might have undeceived you," cried he, rudely. "Your name is not Simpson Hankes."

"No, sir; but it is Sybella, and the writer begins 'Dear S.,'—a liberty, I own, I felt it, but one which I fancied my position was supposed to permit. Pray read on, sir, and you will see that there was matter enough to puzzle finer faculties than mine."

Perhaps the tone in which she spoke these words was intentionally triumphant; perhaps Mr. Hankes attributed this significance to them causelessly; at all events, he started and stared at her for above a minute steadfastly, he then addressed himself suddenly to the letter.

"Gracious heavens! what a terrible blunder!" exclaimed he, when he had finished the reading.

"A great mistake, certainly, sir," said she, calmly.

"But still one of which you are incapable to take advantage, Miss Kellett," said he, with eagerness.

"Is it to the girl who is to be got rid of, sir, you address this speech? Is it to her whose trustfulness has been made the instrument to deceive others and lure them to their ruin? Nay, Mr. Hankes, your estimate of my forbearance is, indeed, too high."

"But what would you do, young lady?"

"Do, sir! I scarcely know what I would not do," burst she in, passionately. "This letter was addressed to *me*. I know nothing of the mistake of its direction; here is the envelope with my name upon it. It is, consequently, mine,—mine, therefore, to publish, to declare to the world, through its words, that the whole of this grand enterprise is a cheat; that its great designer is a man of nothing, living the precarious life of a gambling speculator, trading on the rich man's horde and the poor man's pittance, making market of all, even to his patriotism. I would print this worthy document with no other comment than the words, 'Received by me, Sybella Kellett, this day of September, and sworn to as the handwriting of him whose initials it bears, Davenport Dunn.' I would publish it in such type that men might read it as they went, that all should take warning and put no faith in these unprincipled tricksters. Ay, sir, and I would cling, as my hope of safety from the world's scorn, to that insulting mention of myself, and claim as my vindication that I am the girl to be 'got rid of.' None shall dare to call me complice, since the little I once called my own is lost. But I would do more, sir. The world I have unwittingly aided to deceive has a full right to an expiation at my hands. I would make public the entire correspondence I have for months back been engaged in. You seem to say 'No' to this. Is it my right you dispute, or my courage to assert the right?"

"You must be aware, Miss Kellett," said he, deprecatingly, "that you became possessed of this letter by a mistake; that you had no right to the intelligence it contains, and, consequently, have none to avail yourself of that knowledge. It may be perfectly true that you can employ it to our detriment. It would, I have little doubt, serve to shake our credit for a day or two; but do you know what misery, what utter ruin, your rashness will have caused meanwhile? By the fall of our securities you will beggar hundreds. All whose necessities may require them to sell out on the day of your disclosures will be irretrievably ruined. You meditate a vengeance upon Mr. Dunn, and your blow falls on some poor struggling creatures that you never so much as heard of. I do not speak," continued he, more boldly, as he saw the deep effect his words produced,—"I do not speak of the destitution and misery you will spread here,—all works stopped, all enterprise suspended, thousands thrown out of employment. These are the certain, the inevitable evils of what you propose to do. And now, let me ask, What are to be the benefits? You would depose from his station of power and influence the only man in the kingdom who has a brain to conceive, or a courage to carry out these gigantic enterprises,—the only man of influence sufficient to treat with the Government, and make his own terms. You would dethrone him, to install in his place some inferior intelligence,—some mere creature of profit and loss, without genius or patriotism; and all for what?—for a mere phrase, and that, too, in a letter which was never intended for your eyes."

Mr. Hankes saw that he was listened to, and he continued. Artfully contriving to take the case out of its real issue, he made it appear to Miss Kellett that she was solely impelled by personal motives, and had no other object in view than a vengeance on the man who had insulted her. "And now just throw your eyes over the letter intended for yourself. I only glanced at it, but it seemed to me written in a tone of sincerest well-wishing."

It was so. It contained the offer of a most advantageous position. A new Governor-General of India desired a suitable companion for his daughters, who had lost their mother. He was a nobleman of highest rank and influence. The station was one which secured great advantages, and Dunn had obtained the promise of it in her behalf by considerable exertion on his part Nay, more. Knowing that her fortune was engaged in the "Allotment scheme," he volunteered to take her shares at the highest rate they had ever borne, as she would, probably, require immediate means to procure an Indian outfit. The whole wound up with a deeply expressed regret at the loss Glengariff would sustain by her departure; "but all my selfishness," added he, "could not blind me to the injustice of detaining in obscurity one whose destiny so certainly points her out for a station lofty and distinguished."

She smiled at the words, and, showing them to Hankes, said, "It is most unfortunate, sir, that I should have seen the other letter. I could so readily have yielded myself up to all this flattery, which, even in its hollowness, has a certain charm."

"I am certain Miss Kellett has too much good sense—too much knowledge of life—too much generosity, besides—"

"Pray, sir, let me stop you, or the catalogue of my perfections may become puzzling, not to say that I need all the good gifts with which you would endow me to aid me to a right judgment here. I wish I knew what to do."

"Can you doubt it?"

"If the road be so clear, will you not point it out?"

"Write to Mr. Dunn. Well, let *me* write to him. I will inform him how this mischance occurred. I will tell him that you had read and re-read his letter before discovering the mistake of the address; that, consequently, you are now—so far as this great enterprise is concerned—one of ourselves; that, although you scorn to take advantage of a circumstance thus accidentally revealed, yet that, as chance has put you in possession of certain facts, that—-that, in short—"

"That, in short, I ought to profit by my good fortune," said she, calmly, finishing the phrase for him.

"Unquestionably," chimed in Hankes, quickly; "and, what's more, demand very high terms too. Dunn is a practical man," added he, in a lower and more confidential tone; "nobody knows better when liberality is the best policy."

"So that this is a case for a high price?" asked she, in the same calm tone.

"I'd make it so if I were in your place. I'd certainly say a 'high figure,' Miss Keliett."

"Shall I confess, sir, that, in so far as knowing how to profit by it, I am really unworthy of this piece of fortune? Is Mr. Hankes enough my friend to enlighten me?"

There was a smile that accompanied this speech which went far—very far—to influence Mr. Hankes. Once again did his personal fortunes rise before him; once again did he bethink him that this was an alliance that might lead to much.

"I can give you a case in point, Miss Keliett,—I mean as to the value of a secret. It was when Sir Robert Peel meditated his change in the Corn-laws. One of the council—it does not matter to say his name—accidentally divulged the secret intention, and a great journal gave no less than ten thousand pounds for the intelligence,—ten thousand pounds sterling!"

She seemed to pause over this story, and reflect upon it.

"Now," resumed Hankes, "it is just as likely he'd say, 'Money is scarce just now; your demand comes at an inconvenient moment' This would be true,—there's no gainsaying it; and I'd reply, 'Let me have it in shares,—some of the new preference scrip just issued.'"

"How it does allay difficulties to deal with persons of great practical intelligence,—men of purpose-like mind!" said Sybella, gravely.

"Ah, Miss Kellett, if I could only believe that this was a favorable moment to appeal to you in their behalf,—at least, in so far as regards one of their number,—one who has long admired your great qualities in silence, and said to himself, 'What might she not be if allied to one well versed in life, trained to all its chances and changes—'"

"It never occurred to me to fancy I had inspired all this interest, sir," said she, calmly.

"Probably because your thoughts never dwelt on *me*," said Hankes, with a most entreating look; "but I assure you," added he, warmly, "the indifference was not reciprocal. I have been long—very long attracted by those shining abilities you display. Another might dwell upon your personal attractions, and say the impression your beauty had made upon him; but beauty is a flower,—a perishable hot-house flower. Not," added he, hastily, "that I pretend to be insensible to its fascinations; no, Miss Kellett, I have my weaknesses like the rest."

Sybella scarcely heard his words. It was but a day before, and a poor unlettered peasant, an humble creature unread in life and human nature, told her that he deemed her one fit for high and devoted enterprise, and that her rightful place was amidst the wounded and the dying in the Crimea. Had he construed her, then, more truly? At all events, the career was a noble one. She did not dare to contrast it any longer with her late life, so odious now did it seem to her, with all its schemes for wealth, its wily plot-tings and intrigues.

"I am afraid, sir, I have been inattentive,—I fear that my thoughts were away from what you have been saying," said she, hastily.

"Shall I just throw my ideas on paper, Miss Kellett, and wait your answer—say to-morrow?"

"My answer to what, sir?"

"I have been presumptuous enough to make you an offer of my hand, Miss Kellett," said he, with a half-offended dignity. "There are, of course, a number of minor considerations—I call them minor, as they relate to money matters—to be discussed after; for instance, with regard to these shares—"

"It will save us both a world of trouble, sir, when I thank you deeply for the honor you would destine me, and decline to accept it."

"I know there is a discrepancy in point of years—"

"Pray, sir, let us not continue the theme. I have given my answer, and my only one."

"Or if it be that any meddling individual should have mentioned the late Mrs. H.," said he, bristling up,— "for she is the late, that I can satisfy you upon,—I have abundant evidence to show how that woman behaved—"

"You are confiding to me more than I have the right or wish to hear, sir."

"Only in vindication,—only in vindication. I am aware how her atrocious book has libelled me. It made me a perfect martyr for the season after it came out; but it is out of print,—not a copy to be had for fifty pounds, if it were offered."

"But really, sir—"

"And then, Miss Kellett," added he, in a sort of thrilling whisper, "she drank; at first sherry,—brown sherry—but afterwards brandy,—ay, ma'am, brandy neat and a matter of a bottle daily. If you only knew what I went through with her,—the scenes in the streets, in the playhouses, in coffee-rooms,—ay, and police-offices,—I give you my sacred word of honor Simpson Hankes was rapidly becoming as great a public scandal as the Rev. Paul Classon himself!"

"Cannot you perceive, sir, that these details are less than uninteresting to me?"

"Don't say that, Miss Kellett,—don't, I beg you, or else you 'll make me fear that you 'll not read the little pamphlet I published, entitled 'A Brief Statement by Simpson Hankes,'—a brochure that I am proud to believe decided the world in my favor."

"Once for all, Mr. Hankes, I decline to hear more of these matters. If I have not more plainly told you how little they claim to interest me, it is because my own selfish cares fill up my thoughts. I will try to hand you the correspondence Mr. Dunn desires to see in your keeping by to-morrow morning. There are many circumstances will require special explanation in it. However I will do my best to be ready."

"And my offer, Miss Kellett?"

"I have declined it, sir."

"But really, young lady, are you well aware of what it is you refuse?" asked he, angrily.

"I will not discuss the question, sir," said she, haughtily. "Give me that letter I showed you."

"The letter, I opine, is mine, Miss Kellett. The address alone pertains to you."

"Do you mean, then, to retain possession of the letter?" asked she, hurriedly.

"I protest, I think it is better—better for all of us—that I should do so. You will pardon me if I observe that you are now under the influence of excited feelings,—you are irritated. Any line of action, under such circumstances, will necessarily be deficient in that calm, matured judgment which is mainly your characteristic."

"It needed but this, sir, to fill up the measure!" ex-claimed she, passionately.

"I don't perfectly apprehend you, Miss Kellett."

"I mean, sir, that this last trait of yours was alone wanting to complete the utter contempt I now feel for my late life and its associates. Mr. Dunn's letter, with all its disgraceful disclosures,—your own crafty counsels how best to profit by the accidental knowledge,—and now this refusal to restore the letter,—this mean distrust based on a breach of confidence—"

"By no means, madam. In withholding this letter, I maintain it to be my own. I have already explained to you that the address is all you can lay claim to; a recent legal decision is in my favor. It was tried last Hilary term before Justice Whitecroff. The case was Barnes *versus* Barnes."

"If my anger prompt me to rasher acts than my calmer reason might have counselled," broke in Sybella, "remember, sir, it is to yourself you owe it. At least upon one point you may rely. Whatever I decide to do in this affair, it will not be swayed by any—the slightest—regard for your friends or their interests. I will think of others alone,—never once of *them*. Your smile seems to pay, 'The war between us is an unequal one.' I know it. I am a woman, poor, friendless, unprotected; you and yours are rich, and well thought of; and yet, with all this odds, if I accept the conflict I do not despair of victory."

As she left the room and the door closed after her, Mr. Hankes wiped the perspiration from his forehead, and sat down, the perfect picture of dismay.

"What *is* she up to?" cried he, three or four times to himself. "If she resolves to make a public scandal of it, there's an end of us! The shares would be down—down to nothing—in four-and-twenty hours! I'll telegraph to Dunn at once!" said he, rising, and taking his hat. "The mischance was his own doing; let him find the remedy himself."

With all that perfection of laconic style which practice confers, Mr. Hankes communicated to Davenport Dunn the unhappy mistake which had just befallen. Under the safeguard of a cipher used between them, he expressed his deepest fears for the result, and asked for immediate counsel and guidance.

This despatch, forwarded by telegraph, he followed by a long letter, entering fully into all the details of the mischance, and reporting with—it must be acknowledged—a most scrupulous accuracy an account of the stormy scene between Miss Kellett and himself. He impressed upon his chief that no terms which should secure her silence would be too high, and gently insinuated that a prompt and generous offer on Dunn's part might not impossibly decide the writer to seal his devotion to the cause, by making the lady Mrs. Hankes. "Only remember," added he, "it must be in cash or approved bills."

Partly to illustrate the difficulty of the negotiation he was engaged in, partly to magnify the amount of the sacrifice he proposed to make, he depicted Sybella in colors somewhat less flattering than ardent love usually employs. "It is clear to me now," wrote he, "from what I witnessed to-day, that neither you nor I ever understood this girl aright. She has a temper of her own, and an obstinacy perfectly invincible. Acting on the dictate of what she fancies to be her conscience, she is quite capable of going to any extreme, and I have the strongest doubt that she is one to be moved by affection or deterred by fear." After a little more of this eulogistic strain, he wound up by repeating his former generous proposal He adroitly pointed out that it was in the interest of only such a patron he could ever dream of so great a sacrifice; and then in that half-jocular way in which he often attained to all the real and businesslike elements of a project, he added, "Say ten thousand, and the 'match' will come off,—a very moderate stake, if you only remember the 'forfeit.'"

In a brief postscript he mentioned the discovery of the ancient document found at the cottage, with, as he said, "some curious papers about the Conway family. These I have duly sealed up in the box, and retain in my possession, although Miss K. has evidently an eye upon them.

"Write fully and explicitly whatever you mean to do; should you, however, fully agree to what I propose, telegraph back to

"Yours, ever faithfully,

"Simpson Hankes.

"They have come to tell me she is packing up her things and has sent a twenty-pound note to be changed."

CHAPTER XVIII
DOWNING STREET

If our story had a hero—which it has not—that hero would be Mr. Davenport Dunn himself, and we might, consequently, feel certain compunctious scruples as to the length of time that has elapsed since we last saw him. When we parted, however, we took care to remind our reader that we left him in good company, and surely such a fact ought to allay all apprehensions on his behalf.

Months have rolled over; the London season has passed; Parliament has but a few days to run; the wearied speakers are longing to loiter along green lanes, or be touring or water-curing it in Germany; cities are all but deserted, and town-houses have that dusty, ill-cared-for air that reminds one of an estate in Chancery, or a half-pay lieutenant. Why is it, then, that Mr. Dunn's residence in Merrion Square wears a look of unusual trimness? Fresh paint—that hypocrisy of architecture—has done its utmost; the hall door is a marvel of mock oak, as are the columns of spurious marble; the Venetian blinds are of an emerald green, and the plate-glass windows mirror the parched trees in the square, and reflect back the almost equally picturesque jaunting-cars as they drive past; the balcony, too, throughout its whole length, is covered with rich flowers and flowery shrubs. In a word, there is a look of preparation that bespeaks a coming event. What can it be?

Various rumors are afloat as to the reason of these changes, some averring that Mr. Dunn is about to take a high official position, and be raised to a distinguished rank; others opine that he is about to retire from the cares of a business life, and marry. What may he not be? Whom may he not aspire to? Surely the world has gone well with this roan. What a great general is to an army in the field,—what a great leader to a party in the "House," was he to every industrial enterprise. His name was a guarantee for all that was accurate in discipline and perfect in organization. The Board over which he presided as Chairman was sure to meet with regularity and act with energy. The officials who served under him, even to the very humblest, seemed to typify the wise principles by which he had himself been guided in life. They appeared as though imbued with the same patient industry; the same untiring application, the same grave demeanor marked them. "I served under Mr. Davenport Dunn," "Mr. Dunn knows me," "Mr. Dunn will speak for me," were characters that had the force of a diploma, since they vouched not alone for capacity, but for conduct.

It is a very high eminence to attain when a man's integrity and ability throw such a light about him that they illumine not alone the path he treads in life, but shine brightly on those who follow his track, making an atmosphere in which all around participate. To this height had Dunn arrived, and he stood the confessed representative of those virtues Englishmen like to honor, and that character they boast to believe national,—the man of successful industry. The fewer the adventitious advantages he derived from fortune, the greater and more worthy did he appear. He was no aristocrat, propped and bolstered by grand relatives. He had no Most Noble or Right Honorable connections to push him. He was not even gifted with those qualities that win popular favor,—he had none of those graces of easy cordiality that others possess,—he was not insinuating in address, nor ready of speech. They who described him called him an awkward, bashful man, always struggling against his own ignorance of society, and only sustained by a proud consciousness that whispered the "sterling stuff that was inside,"— qualities which appeal to large audiences, and are intelligible to the many. Ay, there was indeed his grand secret. Genius wounds deeply, talent and ability offend widely, but the man of mere commonplace faculties, using common gifts with common opportunities, trading rather upon negative than positive properties, succeeding because he is not this, that, and t' other, plodding along the causeway of life steadily and unobtrusively, seen by all, patched and noticed in every successive stage of his upward progress, so that each may say, "I remember him a barefooted boy, running errands in the street,—a poor clerk at forty pounds a year,—I knew him when he lived in such an alley, up so many pair of stairs!" Strange enough, the world likes all this; there is a smack of self-gratulation in it that seems to say, "If I liked it, I could have done as well as he." Success in life won, these men rise into another atmosphere, and acquire another appreciation. They are then used to point the moral of that pleasant fallacy we are all so fond of repeating to each other, when we assert, amongst the blessings of our glorious Constitution, that there is no dignity too great, no station too high, for the Englishman who combines industry and integrity with zeal and perseverance. Shame on us, that we dare to call fallacy that which great Lord Chancellors and Chief Justices have verified from their own confessions; nay, we have even heard a Lord Mayor declare that he was, once upon a time, like that "poor" publican! The moral of it all is that with regard to the Davenport Dunns of this world, we pity them in their first struggles, we are proud of them in their last successes, and we are about as much right in the one sentiment as in the other.

The world—the great wide world of man—is marvellously identical with the small ingredient of humanity of whose aggregate it consists. It has its moods of generosity, distrust, liberality, narrowness, candor, and suspicion,—its fevers of noble impulse, and its cold fits of petty meanness,—its high moments of self-devotion, and its dark hours of persecution and hate. Men are judged differently in different ages, just as in every-day life we hear a different opinion from the same individual, when crossed by the cares of the morning and seated in all the voluptuous repose of an after-dinner *abandonnement*.

Now it chanced that Mr. Dunn's lot in life had thrown him into a fortunate conjuncture of the world's temper. The prosperity of a long peace had impressed us with an exaggerated estimate of all the arts that amass wealth; riches became less the reward than the test of ability; success and merit had grown to be convertible terms; clever speakers and eloquent writers assured us that wars pertained only to ages of barbarism,—that a higher civilization would repudiate them,—that men, now bent upon a high and noble philanthropy, would alone strive to diffuse the benefits of abundance and refinement amongst their fellows, and that we were about to witness an elysian age of plenty, order, and happiness. The same men who stigmatized the glory of war as the hypocrisy of carnage, invented another hypocrisy infinitely meaner and more ignoble, and placed upon the high altars of our worship the golden image of Gain.

As the incarnation of this passion Davenport Dunn stood out before the world; nor was there a tribute of its flattery that was not laid at his feet. Even they who had neither wish nor necessity to benefit by his peculiar influence did not withhold their homage, but joined in the general acclamation that pronounced him the great man of our time; and at his Sunday dinners were met the most distinguished in rank,—all that the country boasted of great in station, illustrious by services or capacity. His splendid house in Piccadilly—rented for the season for a fabulous sum—was beset all the morning by visitors, somewhat unlike, it must be owned, the class who frequented his Dublin levees. Here they were not deputations or bank directors, railway chairmen or drainage commissioners; they were all that fashion claims as her own,—proud duchesses of princely fortune, great countesses high in courtly favor, noble ladies whose smile of recognition was a firman to the highest places. They met there, by one of those curious compacts the grand world occasionally makes with itself, to do something, in a sort of half imitation of that inferior race of mortals who live and marry and die in the spheres beneath them. In fact, Dunn's house was a sort of bourse, where shares were trafficked in, and securities bought and sold, with an eagerness none the less that the fingers that held them wore gloves fastened with rubies and emeralds.

In those gorgeous drawing-rooms, filled with objects of high art, statues stolen from the Vatican, gems obtained by Heaven knows what stratagems from Italian or Spanish convents, none deigned to notice by even a passing look the treasures that surrounded them. In vain the heavenly beauty of Raphael beamed from the walls, — in vain the seductive glances of Greuze in all their languishing voluptuousness, — in vain the haughty nobility of Van Dyck claimed the homage of a passing look. All were eagerly bent upon lists of stocks and shares, and no words were heard save such as told of rise or fall, — the alternations of that chance which makes or mars humanity.

It was while in the midst of that distinguished company Mr. Dunn received the telegram we have mentioned in our last chapter as despatched by Mr. Hankes. His was a nature long inured to the ups and downs of fortune; his great self-teaching had been principally directed to the very point of how best to meet emergencies; and yet, as he read over these brief lines, for a moment his courage seemed to have deserted him.

"Chimbarago Artesian Well and Water Company," lisped out a very pale, sickly-looking Countess. "Shares are rising, Mr. Dunn; may I venture upon them?"

"Here's the Marquesas Harbor of Refuge scheme going to smash, Dunn!" whispered an old gentleman, with a double eye-glass, his hand trembling as it held the share-list. "Eh, what do you say to that?"

"Glengariff 's going steadily up, — steadily up," muttered Lord Glengariff, in Dunn's ear. Then, struck by the sudden pallor of his face, he added, "Are you ill? — are you faint?"

"A mere nothing," said Dunn, carelessly. "By the way, what hour is it? Near one, and I have an appointment with the Chancellor of the Exchequer. Yes, Lady Massingberd, perfectly safe; not a splendid investment, but quite sure. Cagliari Cobalts are first-rate, Sir George; take all you can get of them. The Dalmatian line *is* guaranteed 'by the Austrian Government, my Lord. I saw the Ambassador yesterday. Pray excuse a hasty leave-taking."

His carriage was quickly ordered, but before he set out he despatched a short telegraphic message to Hankes. It ran thus: "Detain her; suffer no letters from her to reach the post." This being duly sent off, he drove to Downing Street. That dingy old temple of intrigue was well known to him. His familiar steps had mounted that gloomy old stair some scores of times; but now, for the first — the very first time in his life, instead of being at once ushered into the presence of the Minister, he was asked to "wait for a few moments." What a shock did the intimation give him! Was the news already abroad,—had the fell tidings escaped? A second's consideration showed this was impossible; and yet what meant this reserve?

"Is the Council sitting, Mr. Bagwell?" asked he, of a very well-dressed young gentleman, with a glass fixed in his eye, who acted as Private Secretary to the Minister.

"No; they're chatting, I fancy," lisped out the other. "The Council was up half an hour ago."

"Have you mentioned my name, sir?" asked Dunn, with a formidable emphasis on the pronoun.

"Yes," said he, arranging his hair before the glass; "I sent in your card."

"Well, and the answer?"

"There was no answer, which, I take it, means 'wait,'" replied he, in the same light and graceful tone of voice.

Dunn took his hat hastily from the table; and with a stern stare, intended to mean "I shall remember your face again," said,—

"You may inform Lord Jedburg that I came by appointment; that I was here punctually at one o'clock; that I waited full fifteen minutes; that—"

What more Mr. Dunn was about to say was cut short by the opening of a-door, and the issuing forth of some five or six gentlemen, all laughing and talking together.

"How d'ye do, Mr. Dunn?" "How d'ye do, Dunn?" "How are you, Dunn?" said some three or four, familiarly, as they passed through the room. And ere he could acknowledge the salutations, Lord Jedburg himself appeared at the door, and made a sign for him to enter. Never before had Davenport Dunn crossed those precincts with so nervous a heart. If his reason assured him that there was no cause of fear, his instincts and his conscience spoke a different language. He bent one quick penetrating glance on the Minister ere he sat down, as though to read there what he might of the future; but there was nothing to awaken anxiety or distrust in that face. His Lordship was far advanced in life, his hair more white than gray, his brow wrinkled and deep-furrowed; and yet, if, instead of the cares of a mighty empire, his concern had been the passing events of a life of society and country habits, nothing could have more suited the easy expression, the graceful smile, and the pleasant *bonhomie* of that countenance. Resuming the cigar he had been smoking as Dunn came in, he lounged back indolently in his deep chair, and said,—

"What can I do for you at the Isle of Wight, Dunn? I fancy we shall have a trip to Osborne to-morrow morning."

"Indeed, my Lord?" asked he, anxiously; "are you going out?"

"So they say," replied the other, carelessly. "Do you smoke? You 'll find those Cubans very mild. So they say, Dunn. Monksley assures us that we shall be in a minority to-night of fifteen or sixteen. Drake thinks five-and-twenty."

"From your Lordship's easy mode of taking it, I conclude that there is either a remedy for the disaster, or that—"

"It is no disaster at all," chimed in his Lordship, gayly. "Well, the Carlton Club are evidently of that mind, and some of the evening papers too."

"I perceive, my Lord," said Dunn, with a peculiar smile, "the misfortune *is* not irremediable."

"You are right, Dunn," said the other, promptly. "We have decided to accept a defeat, which, as our adversaries have never anticipated, will find them perfectly unprepared how to profit by it They will beat us, but, when called upon to form a Government, will be utterly unable. The rest is easy enough: a new Parliament, and ourselves stronger than ever."

"A very clever countryman of mine once told me, my Lord, that he made a ruinous coach-line turn out a most lucrative speculation by simply running an opposition and breaking it; so true are the world in their attachment to success."

A hearty laugh from the Minister acknowledged the parallel, and he added carelessly,—

"Sir George Bosely has a story of a fellow who once established a run on his own bank just to get up his credit. A hit above even you, Master Dunn,—eh?"

If Dunn laughed, it was with a face of deepest crimson, though he saw, the while, his secret was safe. Indeed, the honest frankness of his Lordship's laugh guaranteed that all was well.

"The fellow ought to have been a Cabinet Minister, Dunn. He had the true governing element in him, which is a strong sense of human gullibility."

"A little more is needed, my Lord,—how to turn that flame tendency to profit."

"Of course,—of course. By the way, Dunn, though not *apropos*," said he, laughingly, "what of the great Glengariff scheme? Is it prospering?"

"The shares stand at one hundred and seventy-seven and an eighth, my Lord," said Dunn, calmly. "I can only wish your Lordship's party as favorable a fortune."

"Well, we are rather below par just now," said the Minister, laughing, while he busied himself to select another cigar from the heap before him.

"It was just about that very enterprise I came to speak to your Lordship this morning," said Dunn, drawing his chair closer. "I need not tell you how far the assurance of Government support has aided our success. The report of the Parliamentary Committee as to the Harbor of Refuge, the almost certain promise of her Majesty's marine residence, the flattering reception your Lordship gave to the deputation in the matter of the American packet-station, have all done us good and efficient service. But we want more, my Lord, — we want more!"

"The deuce you do! Why, my good friend, these marks of our preference for your scheme have cost us some hundred angry addresses and recriminations from all parts of the kingdom, where, we are told, there is more picturesque scenery, more salubrious air, deeper water, and better anchorage. If you built a villa for every member of the Cabinet, and settled it on us in freehold there, it would not repay us for all we have suffered in your cause."

"We should be both proud and happy to accommodate your Lordship's colleagues on Jedburg Crescent," said Dunn, bowing with a well-assumed seriousness.

"But what do you want us to do?" said his Lordship, peevishly; for he had the dislike great men generally feel to have their joke capped. It is for them to be smart, if they please, but not for the Mr. Davenport Dunns of this world to take up the clew of the facetiousness.

Mr. Dunn seemed somewhat posed by the abrupt directness of this question. Lord Jedburg went on: —

"You surely never supposed that we could send you material assistance. You are far too conversant with the working of our institutions to expect such. These things are possible in France, but they won't do here. No, Dunn; perfectly impossible here."

"And yet, my Lord, it is precisely in France that they ought to be impossible. Ministers in that country have no responsibility except towards their sovereign. If they become suddenly enriched, one sees at once how they have abused the confidence of their master."

"I'll not enter upon that question," said his Lordship, smartly. "Tell me, rather, something about Ireland; how shall we fare there in a general election?"

"With proper exertions you may be able to hold your own," was the dry rejoinder.

"Not more? Not any more than this?"

"Certainly not, my Lord, nor do I see how you could expect it. What you are in the habit of calling concessions to Irish interests have been little other than apologies for the blunders of your colleagues. You remove some burden imposed by yourselves, or express sorrow for some piece of legislation your own hands have inflicted—"

"Come, come, Mr. Dunn, the only course of lectures I attend are delivered in the House of Commons; besides, I have no time for these things." There was a tone of prompt decision in the way he uttered this that satisfied Dunn he had gone fully as far as was safe. "Now as to Ireland, we shall look for at least sixty, or perhaps seventy, sure votes. Come, where's your list, Dunn? Out with it, man! We are rather rich in patronage just now. We can make a Bishop, a Puisne Judge, three Assistant Barristers, a Poor Law Commissioner, not to say that there are some fifty smaller things in the Revenue. Which will you have?"

"All, my Lord," said Dunn, coolly,—"all, and some colonial appointments besides, for such of our friends as find living at home inexpedient."

His Lordship lay back in his chair, and laughed pleasantly. "There's Jamaica just vacant; would that suit you?"

"The Governorship? The very thing I want, and for a very old supporter of your Lordship's party."

"Who is he?"

"The Earl of Glengariff, my Lord, a nobleman who has never received the slightest acknowledgment for a political adherence of fifty-odd years."

"Why, the man must be in second childhood. If I remember aright, he was—"

"He is exactly four years your Lordship's senior; he says you fagged for him his last half at Eton."

"Pooh, pooh! he mistakes; it was of my father he was thinking. But to the point: what can he do for us?"

"I was alluding to what he had done, my Lord," said Dunn, pointedly.

"Ah, Dunn, we are not rich enough for gratitude. That is the last luxury of a 'millionnaire;' besides, you are aware how many claimants there will be for so good a thing as this."

"Which of them all, my Lord, can promise you ten votes in the Houses?"

"Well, is the bargain finished? Is all paid?"

"Not yet, my Lord; not yet You are averse to affording us any support to the Glengariff scheme, and, for the present, I will not hamper you with the consideration; you can, however, serve us in another way. Glumthal is very anxious about the Jew Bill; he wishes, Heaven knows why, to see his brother in the House. May I promise him that the next session will see it law? Let me just have your Lordship's word to that effect, so that I may telegraph to him when I leave this."

His Lordship shook his head dubiously, and said, "You forget that I have colleagues, Dunn."

"I remember it well, my Lord, and I only asked for your own individual pledge. The fact is, my Lord, the Jews throughout the world have attached an immense importance to this question; and if Glumthal—confidentially, of course—be made the depositary of the secret, it will raise him vastly in the estimation of his co-religionists."

"Let us see if the thing can be done. Is it practicable, and how?" "Oh, as to that, my Lord, modern legislation is carried on pretty much like a mercantile concern; you advertise your want, and it is supplied at once. Ask the newspapers. 'How are we to admit the Jews?' and you 'll get your answer as regularly as though it were a question of sport addressed to 'Bell's Life.'"

"Candor being the order of the day, what does Mr. Davenport Dunn want for himself?"

"I am coming to him, my Lord, but not just yet."

"Why, really, Dunn, except that we turn Colonel Blood in your behalf, and steal the crown for you, I don't see what more we can do."

"It is a mere trifle in point of patronage, my Lord, though, in my ignorance of such matters, it may be, possibly, not without difficulty," said Dunn; and, for the first time, his manner betrayed a sign of embarrassment "The Earl of Glengariff has an only unmarried daughter, a lady of great personal attractions, and remarkably gifted in point of ability; one of those persons, in short, on whom Nature has set the stamp of high birth, and fitted to be the ornament of a Court."

"But we are all married in the Cabinet. Even the Treasury Lords have got wives," said Lord Jedburg, laughing, and enjoying the discomfiture of Dunn's face even more than his own jest.

"I am aware of it, my Lord," replied Dunn, with inflexible gravity; "my ambitious hopes did not aspire so highly. What I was about to entreat was your Lordship's assistance to have the lady I have mentioned appointed to a situation in the household,—one of her Majesty's ladies—"

"Impossible! perfectly impossible, Dunn!" said the Minister, flinging away his cigar in impatient anger; "really, you seem to have neither measure nor moderation in your demands. Such an interference on my part, if I were mad enough to attempt it, would meet a prompt rebuke."

"If your Lordship's patience had permitted me to finish, you would have heard that what I proposed was nothing beyond the barren honor of a 'Gazette.' On the day week that her Ladyship's name had so appeared she would be married."

"It does not alter the matter in the least. It is not in my province to make such a recommendation, and I refuse it flatly."

"I am sorry for it, my Lord. Your Lordship's refusal may inflict great evils upon the country,—the rule of an incompetent and ungenial Government,—the accession to power of men the most unscrupulous and reckless.". "Cannot you see, sir," said the Minister, sharply, "that I am in a position to comprehend what my office admits of, and where its limits are laid? I have told you that these appointments are not in our hands."

"Sir Robert Peel did not say so, my Lord; he insisted—actually insisted—on his right to surround the throne with political partisans."

"The Cabinet is not an Equity Court, to be ruled by precedents; and I tell you once more, Dunn, I should fail if I attempted it."

"The Viscountess might obtain this favor," said Dunn, with an obdurate persistence that was not to be resisted; "and even if unsuccessful, it would inflict no rebuff on your Lordship. Indeed, it would come more gracefully as a proposition from her Ladyship, who could also mention Lady Augusta's approaching marriage."

"I almost think I might leave you to finish the discussion with my wife," said his Lordship, laughing; "I half suspect it would be the best penalty on your temerity. Are you engaged for Sunday?—well, then, dine with us. And now, that bill being adjourned," said he, with a weary sigh, "what next?"

"I am now coming to myself,—to my own case, my Lord," said Dunn, with the very slightest tremor in his voice. "Need I say that I wish it were in the hands of any other advocacy? I am so far fortunate, however, that I address one fully conversant with my claims on his party. For five-and-twenty years I have been the careful guardian of their interests in a country where, except in mere name, they never possessed any real popularity. Your Lordship smiles a dissent; may I enter upon the question?"

"Heaven forbid!" broke in the Minister, smiling good-humoredly.

"Well, my Lord, were I to reduce my services to a mere monetary estimate, and furnish you with a bill of costs, for what a goodly sum should I stand in the estimates. I have mainly sustained the charge of seven county elections, hardly contested. I have paid the entire charges on twenty-two borough contests. I have subsidized the provincial press in your favor at a cost of several thousand pounds out of my own pocket I have compromised three grave actions about to be brought against the Government. Of the vast sums I have contributed to local charities, schools, nunneries, societies of various denominations, all in the interest of your party, I take no account I have spent in these and like objects a princely fortune, and yet these hundreds of thousands of pounds are as nothing—mere nothing to the actual personal services I have rendered to your party. In the great revolution effected by the sale of encumbered estates, I have so watchfully guarded your interests that I have replaced the old rampant Toryism of the land by a gentry at once manageable and practicable,—men intent less upon party than personal objects, consequently available to the Minister, always accessible by an offer of direct advantage. I have, with all this, so thrown a Whig light over the rising prosperity of the country, that it might seem the result of your wise rule that stimulated men to the higher civilization they have attained to, and that a more forbearing charity and a more liberal spirit went hand in hand with improved agriculture and higher farming. To identify a party with the great march of this prosperity, to make of your policy a cause of these noble results, was the grand conception which, for a quarter of a century, I have carried out. When Mr. O'Connell kept your predecessors in power, his price was the bit-by-bit surrender of what in your hearts you believed to be bulwarks of the constitution. In return for my support what have I got? Some patronage—be it so—for my own dependants and followers, no doubt! Show me one man of my name, one man of my convictions, holding place under the Crown. No, my Lord, my power to serve your party was based on this sure foundation, that I was open to no imputation; I was the distributor of your patronage to the men best worthy to receive it,—no more."

"Four o'clock, Dunn; time's up," said his Lordship. "I must go down to the House."

"I am sorry to have detained your Lordship with so ungracious a theme."

"Well, I do think you might have spared me some of it I know well my colleagues all know your invaluable services,—an admirable member of the party, active and able, but not quite neglected, either, eh, Dunn?—not entirely left in oblivion?"

While he spoke, he busied himself in the search for a paper amidst the heap of those before him, and could not, therefore, notice the mortification so palpably expressed on Dunn's face.

"I can't find it," muttered he; "I should like, however, to show you the memorandum itself, in which your name stands recommended to her Majesty for a baronetcy."

Dunn's sudden start made the speaker look up; and as he turned his eyes on him, there was no mistaking the look of determined anger on his features.

"A baronetcy, my Lord," said he, with a slow, thick utterance, "has become the recognized reward of a popular writer, or a fashionable physician, whose wives acquire a sort of Brummagem rank in calling themselves 'My Lady;' but men like myself,—men who have sustained a party,—men who, wielding many arms of strength, have devoted them all to the one task of maintaining in power a certain administration, which, whatever their gifts, assuredly did not possess the art of conciliating—"

"Come, it is a peerage you want?" broke in his Lordship, whose manner betrayed a temper pushed to its last limits.

"If I am to trust your Lordship's tone, the pretension would seem scarcely credible," said Dunn, calmly.

"I believe I can understand how it would appear to others. I can, without great difficulty, imagine the light in which it would be viewed."

"As to that, my Lord, any advancement to a man like me will evoke plenty of animadversion. I have done too-much for your party not to have made many enemies. The same objection would apply were I to accept the paltry acknowledgment you so graciously contemplated for me, and which I warn you not to offer me."

Was it the naked insolence of this speech, or was it that in uttering it the proud pretension of the man summoned a degree of dignity to his manner; but certainly the Minister now looked at him with a sort of respect, he had not deigned hitherto to bestow.

"You know well, Dunn," he began, in a tone of conciliation, "that fitness for the elevation is only one of the requirements in such a case. There are a mass of other considerations,—the ostensible claims; I mean such as can be-avowed and declared openly,—of the pretending party,—the services he has rendered to the country at large,—the merits he can show for some great public recognition. The press, whatever be its faults nowadays, has no defects on the score of frankness, and we shall have the question put in twenty different quarters, 'What brilliant campaign has Mr. Dunn concluded?' 'What difficult negotiation carried to successful issue?' 'Where have been his great achievements in the law courts?' To be sure, it might be said that we honor the industrial spirit of our country in ennobling one who has acquired a colossal fortune by his own unaided abilities; but Manchester and Birmingham have also their 'millionnaires.'"

"Your Lordship's time is far too valuable to be passed in such discussion; even mine might be more profitably spent than in listening to it, My demand is now before you; in some three weeks hence it is not impossible it may await the consideration of your Lordship's successors. In one word, if I leave this room without your distinct pledge on the subject, you will no longer reckon me amongst the followers of your party."

"Half-past four, I protest," said Lord Jedburg, taking up his gloves. "I shall be too late at the House. Let us conclude this to-morrow morning. Come down here at eleven."

"Excuse me, my Lord. I leave town to-night I am going over to Ireland."

"Yes, you ought to be there; I forgot. Well, you must leave this affair in my hands. I 'll speak to Croydon and Locksley about it,—both stanch friends of yours. I can make no pledge, you know,—no actual promise—"

"Nor I either, my Lord," said Dunn, rising. "Let me, however, ask you to accept of my excuses for Sunday at dinner."

"I regret much that we are not to have the pleasure of your company," said his Lordship, with a formal courtesy.

"These appointments," said Dunn, laying down a list he had made on the table, "are, of course, in your Lordship's hands."

"I conclude so," was the dry reply, as the Minister but-toned his coat.

"I wish your Lordship a very good morning. Good-bye, my Lord." And the words had their peculiar utterance.

"Good-bye, Mr. Dunn," said the Minister, shortly, and rang for his carriage.

Dunn had but reached the foot of the stairs, when he heard a rapid tread behind him. "I beg pardon, Mr. Dunn," cried Bagwell, the private secretary; "his Lordship sent me to overtake you, and say that the matter you are desirous about shall be done. His Lordship also hopes you can dine with him on Sunday."

"Oh, very well; say 'Yes, with much pleasure.' Has his Lordship gone?"

"Yes, by the private door. He was in a great hurry, and will, I fear, be late, after all."

"There's a good thing to be done just now in potash, Bagwell, at Pesaro. If you have a spare hundred or two, give me a call to-morrow morning." And with a gesture to imply secrecy, Dunn moved away, leaving Bagwell in a dream of gold-getting.

CHAPTER XIX
THE COTTAGE NEAR SNOWDON

At an early portion of this true story, our reader was incidentally told that Charles Conway had a mother, and that she lived in Wales. Her home was a little cottage near the village of Bedgellert, a neighborhood wherein her ancestors had once possessed large estates, but of which not an acre now acknowledged her as owner. Here, on a mere pittance, she had lived for years a life of unbroken solitude. The few charities to the poor her humble means permitted had served to make her loved and respected; while her gentle manners and kind address gave her that sort of eminence which such qualities are sure to attain in remote and simple circles.

All her thoughts in life, all her wishes and ambitions, were centred in her son; and although it was to the wild and reckless extravagance of his early life that she owed the penury which now pressed her, although but for his wasteful excesses she had still been in affluence and comfort, she never attached to him the slightest blame, nor did her lips ever utter one syllable of reproach. Strong in the conviction that so long as the wild excesses of youth stamp nothing of dishonor on the character, the true nature within has sustained no permanent injury, she waited patiently for the time when, this season of self-indulgence over, the higher dictates of manly reason would assert their influence, and that Charley, having sown his wild oats, would come forth rather chastened and sobered than stained by his intercourse with the world.

If this theory of hers has its advocates, there are many—and wise people, too—who condemn it, and who deem those alone safe who have been carefully guarded from the way of temptation, and have been kept estranged from the seductions of pleasure. To ourselves the whole question resolves itself into the nature of the individual, at the same time that we had far rather repose our confidence in one who had borne his share in life's passages, gaining his experience, mayhap, with cost, but coming honorably through the trial, than on him who, standing apart, had but looked out over the troubled ocean of human passion, nor risked himself on the sea of man's temptations.

The former was Conway's case: he had led a life of boundless extravagance; without any thought of the cost, he had launched out into every expensive pursuit. What we often hear applied to others figuratively, was strictly applicable to him; he never knew the value of money; he never knew that anything one desired could be overpaid for. The end came at last. With a yacht ready stored and fitted out for a Mediterranean cruise, with three horses heavily engaged at Doncaster, with a shooting-lodge filled with distinguished company in the Highlands, with negotiations all but completed for the Hooksley hounds, with speculations rife as to whether the Duchess of This or the Countess of That had secured him for a daughter or a niece, there came, one morning, the startling information from his solicitor that a large loan he had contemplated raising was rendered impossible by some casualty of the money-market Recourse must be had to the Jews; heavy liabilities incurred at Newmarket must be met at once and at any cost. A week of disaster fell exactly at this conjuncture; he lost largely at the Portland, largely on the turf; a brother officer, for whom he had given surety, levanted immensely in debt; while a local bank, in which a considerable sum of his was vested, failed. The men of sixty per cent saved him from shipwreck; but they took the craft for the salvage, and Conway was ruined.

Amidst the papers which Conway had sent to his solicitor as securities for the loan, a number of family documents had got mingled, old deeds and titles to estates of which the young man had not so much as heard, claims against property of whose existence he knew nothing. When questioned about them by the man of law, he referred him coolly to his mother, saying, frankly, "it was a matter on which he had never troubled his head."' Mrs. Conway herself scarcely knew more. She had heard that there was a claim in the family to a peerage; her husband used to allude to it in his own dreamy, indolent fashion, and say that it ought to be looked after, and that was all.

Had the information come to the mind of an active or enterprising man of business, it might have fared differently. The solicitor to the family was, however, himself a lethargic, lazy sort of person, and he sent back the papers to Mrs. Conway, stating that he was not sure "something might not be made of them;" that is, added he, "if he had five or six thousand pounds to expend upon searches, and knew where to prosecute them."

This was but sorry comfort, but it did not fall upon a heart high in hope or strong in expectation. Mrs. Conway had never lent herself to the impression that the claim had much foundation, and she heard the tidings with calm; and all that was remembered of the whole transaction was when some jocular allusion would be made by Charles to the time when he should succeed to his peerage, or some as light-hearted jest of the old lady as to whether she herself was to enjoy a title or not The more stirring incidents of a great campaign had latterly, however, so absorbed all the young soldier's interest that he seemed totally to have forgotten the oft-recurring subject of joke between them. Strange enough was it, yet, that in the very letter which conveyed to his mother an account of his Tchernaya achievement, a brief postscript had the following words:—

> *"Since I have been confined to hospital, a person connected with the newspapers, I believe, has been here to learn the exact story of my adventure, and, curiously enough, has been pumping me about our family history. Can it be that 'our peerage' is looking up again? This last sabre-cut on my skull makes me rather anxious to exchange a chako for a coronet. Can you send me anything hopeful in this direction?"*

It was on an answer to this letter the old lady was occupied, seated at an open window, as the sun was just setting on a calm and mellow evening in late autumn. Well understanding the temperament of him she addressed, she adverted little to the danger of his late achievement, and simply seemed to concur in his own remark when recounting it, that he who has made his name notorious from folly has, more than others, the obligation to achieve a higher and better reputation; and added, at the same time: "Charley, what I liked best in your feat was its patriotism. The sense of rendering a good and efficient service to the cause of your country was a nobler prompting than any desire for personal distinction." From this she turned to tell him about what she well knew he loved best to hear of,—her home and her daily life, with its little round of uneventful cares, the little Welsh pony "Crw," and his old spaniel "Belle," and the tulips he had taken such pains about, and the well he had sunk in the native rock. She had good tidings, too, that the railroad—the dreadful railroad—was not to take the line of their happy valley, but to go off in some more "favored" direction. Of the cottage itself she had succeeded in obtaining a renewed lease,—a piece of news well calculated to delight him, "if," as she said, "grand dreams of the peerage might not have impaired his relish for the small hut at the foot of Snowdon." She had just reached so far when a little chaise, drawn by a mountain pony, drew up before the door, and a lady in a sort of half-mourning dress got out and rang the bell. As the old lady rose to admit her visitor,—for her only servant was at work in the garden,—she felt no small astonishment. She was known to none but the peasant neighborhood about her; she had not a single acquaintance in the country with its gentry; and although the present arrival came with little display, in her one glance at the figure of the stranger she saw her to be distinctly of a certain condition in life.

It will conduce equally to brevity and to the interests of our story if we give what followed in the words wherein Mrs. Conway conveyed it to her son:—

"Little, I thought, my dear Charley, that I should have to cross this already long letter,—little suspected that its real and only interest was to have been suggested as I drew to its close; and here, if I had the heart for it, were the place to scold you for a pretty piece of mystification you once practised upon me, when you induced me to offer the hospitality of this poor cottage to an humble gentlewoman, whose poverty would not deem even my life an existence of privation,—the sister of a fellow-soldier you called her, and made me to believe—whose the fault I am not sure—that she was some not very young or very attractive person, but one whose claim lay in her friendless lot and forlorn condition. Say what you will, such was my impression, and it could have no other source than your description. "Yes, Charley, my mind-picture was of a thin-faced, somewhat sandy-haired lady, of some six or eight and thirty years, bony, angular, and awkward, greatly depressed, and naturally averse to intercourse with those who had not known her or her better fortunes; shall I add that I assisted my portrait by adding coarse hands, and filled up my anticipation by suspecting a very decided Irish brogue? Of course this flattering outline could not have been revealed in a vision, and must have come from your hands, deny it whenever and however you may! And now for the reality,—the very prettiest girl I ever saw, since I left off seeing pretty people, when I was young and had pretensions myself: even then I do not remember any one handsomer, and with a winning grace of manner equal, if not superior, to her beauty. You know me as a very difficult critic on the subject of breeding and maintien. I feel that I am so, even to injustice, because I look for the reserved courtesy of one era as well as the easy frankness of another. She has both; and she is a court lady who could adorn a cottage. Of my own atrocious sketch there was nothing about her. Stay, there was. She had the Irish accent, but by some witchery of her

own I got to like it,—fancied it was musical and breathed of the sweet south; but if I go on with her perfections, I shall never come to the important question, for which you care more to hear besides, as to how I know all these things. And now, to my horror, I find how little space is left me to tell you. Well, in three words you shall have it. She has been here to see me on her way somewhere, her visit being prompted by the wish to place in my hands some very curious and very old family records, found by a singular accident in an Irish country-house. They relate to the claim of some ancestor of yours to certain lands in Ireland, and the right is asserted in the name of Baron Conway, and afterwards the Lord Viscount Lackington. I saw no further; indeed, except that they all relate to our dear peerage, they seem to possess no very peculiar interest. If it were not that she would introduce your name, push me with interminable questions as to what it was you had really done, what rewards you had or were about to reap, where you were, and, above all, how, I should have called her visit the most disinterested piece of kindness I ever heard of. Still she showed a sincere and ardent desire to serve us, and said that she would be ready to make any delay in London to communicate with our lawyer, and acquaint him fully with the circumstances of this discovery.

"I unceasingly entreated her to be my guest, were it only for a few days. I even affected to believe that I would send for our lawyer to come down and learn the curious details of the finding of the papers; but she pleaded the absolute necessity of her presence in London so strongly—she betrayed, besides, something like a deep anxiety for some coming event—that I was obliged to abandon my attempt, and limit our acquaintance by the short two hours we had passed together.

"It will take some time, and another long letter, to tell you of the many topics we talked over; for, our first greeting over, we felt towards each other like old friends. At last she arose to leave me, and never since the evening you bade me good-bye did the same loneliness steal over my heart as when I saw her little carriage drive away from the door.

"One distressing recollection alone clouds the memory of our meeting: I suffered her to leave me without a promise to return. I could not, without infringing delicacy, have pressed her more to tell me of herself and her plans for the future, and yet even now I regret that, at any hazard, I did not risk the issue. The only pledge I could obtain was that she would write to me. I am now at the end of my paper, but not of my theme, of which you shall hear more in my next. Meanwhile, if you are not in love with her, I am.

"Your affectionate mother,

"Marian Conway."

We have ourselves nothing to add to the narrative of this letter save the remark that Mrs. Conway felt far more deeply than she expressed the disappointment of not being admitted to Sybella's full confidence. The graceful captivation of the young girl's manner, heightened in interest by her friendless and lone condition,—the perilous path in life that must be trodden by one so beautiful and unprotected,—had made a deep impression on the old lady's heart, and she was sincere in self-reproach that she had suffered her to leave her.

She tried again and again, by recalling all that passed between them, to catch some clew to what Sybella's future pointed; but so guardedly had the young girl shrouded every detail of her own destiny, that the effort was in vain. Sybella had given an address in town, where Mrs. Conway's lawyer might meet her if necessary, and with a last hope the old lady had written a note to that place, entreating, as the greatest favor, that she would come down and pass some days with her at the cottage; but her letter came back to her own hands. Miss Kellett was gone.

CHAPTER XX
A SUPPER

In long-measured sweep the waves flowed smoothly in upon the low shore at Baldoyle of a rich evening in autumn, as a very old man tottered feebly down to the strand and seated himself on a rock. Leaning his crossed arms on his stout stick, he gazed steadily and calmly on the broad expanse before him. Was it that they mirrored to him the wider expanse of that world to which he was so rapidly tending; was it in that measured beat he recognized the march of time, the long flow of years he could count, and which still swept on, smooth but relentless; or was it that the unbroken surface soothed by its very sameness a brain long wearied by its world conflict? Whatever the cause, old Matthew Dunn came here every evening of his life, and, seated on the self-same spot, gazed wistfully over the sea before him.

Although his hair was snow-white and the wrinkles that furrowed his cheeks betrayed great age, his eyes yet preserved a singular brightness, and in their vivid glances showed that the strong spirit that reigned within was still unquenched. The look of defiance they wore was the very essence of the man,—one who accepted any challenge that fortune flung him, and, whether victor or vanquished, only prepared for fresh conflict.

There was none of the weariness so often observable in advanced age about his features, nothing of that expression that seems to crave rest and peace, still as little was there anything of that irritable activity which seems at times to' counterfeit past energy of temperament; no, he was calm, stern, and self-possessed, the man who had fought this way from boyhood, and who asked neither grace nor favor of fortune as he drew nigh the end of the journey!

"I knew I'd find you here," said a deep voice close to his ear. "How are you?"

The old man looked up, and the next moment his son was in his arms. "Davy, my own boy—Davy, I was just thinking of you; was it Friday or Saturday you said you 'd come."

"I thought I could have been here Saturday, father, but Lord Jedburg made a point of my dining with him yesterday; and it was a great occasion, — three Cabinet Ministers present, a new Governor-General of India too, — I felt it was better to remain."

"Right, Davy, — always right, — them's the men to keep company with!"

"And how are you, sir? Are you hale and stout and hearty as ever?" said Dunn, as he threw his head back, the better to look at the old man.

"As you see me, boy: a little shaky about the knees, somewhat tardy about getting up of a morning; but once launched, the old craft can keep her timbers together. But tell me the news, lad, — tell me the news, and never mind *me*."

"Well, sir, last week was a very threatening one for us. No money to be had on any terms, discounts all suspended, shares failing everywhere, good houses crashing on all sides, nothing but disasters with every post; but we 've worked through it, sir. Glumthal behaved well, though at the very last minute; and Lord Glengariff, too, deposited all his title-deeds at Hanbridge's for a loan of thirty-six thousand; and then, as Downing Street also stood to us, we weathered the gale; but it was close work, father, — so close at one moment I telegraphed to Liverpool to secure a berth in the 'Arctic.'"

A sudden start from the old man stopped him, but he quickly resumed: "Don't be alarmed, sir; my message excited no suspicion, for I sent a fellow to New York by the packet, and now all is clear again, and we have good weather before us."

"The shares fell mighty low in the allotment, Davy; how was that?"

"Partly from the cause I have mentioned, father, the tightness in the money market; partly that I suspect we had an enemy in the camp, that daughter of Kellett's—"

"Did n't I say so? Did n't I warn you about her? Did n't I tell you that it was the brood of the serpent that stung us first?" cried out the old man, with a wild energy; "and with all that you would put her there with the Lord and his family, where she 'd know all that was doing, see the letters, and maybe write the answers to them! Where was the sense and prudence of that, Davy?"

"She was an enthusiast, father, and I hoped that she'd have been content to revel in that realm, but I was mistaken."

There was a tone of dejection in the way he spoke the last words that made the old man fix his eyes steadfastly on him. "Well, Davy, go on," said he.

"I have no more to say, sir," said he, in the same sad voice. "The Earl has dismissed her, and she has gone away."

"That's right, that's right,—better late than never. Neither luck nor grace could come of Paul Kellett's stock. I hope that's the last we 'll hear of them; and now, Davy, how is the great world doing? How is the Queen?"

Dunn could scarcely suppress a smile as he answered this question, asked as it was in real and earnest anxiety; and for some time the old man continued to press him with eager inquiries as to the truth of various newspaper reports about royal marriages and illustrious visitors, of which it was strange how he preserved the recollection.

"You have not asked me about myself, father," said Dunn at last, "and I think *my* fortunes might have had the first place in your interest."

"Sure you told me this minute that you didn't see the Queen," said the old man, peevishly.

"Very true, sir, I did not, but I saw her Minister. I placed before him the services I had done his party, my long sacrifices of time, labor, and money in their cause; I showed him that I was a man who had established the strongest claim upon the Government."

"And wouldn't be refused,—wouldn't be denied, eh, Davy?"

"Just so, sir. I intimated that also, so far as it was prudent to do so."

"The stronger the better, Davy; weak words show a faint heart. 'Tis knowing the cost of your enmity will make men your friends."

"I believe, sir, that in such dealings my own tact is my safest guide. It is not to-day or yesterday that I have made acquaintance with men of this order. For upwards of two-and-twenty years I have treated Ministers as my equals."

The old man heard this proud speech with an expression of almost ecstasy on his features, and grasped his son's hand in a delight too great for words.

"Ay, father, I have made our name a cognate number in this kingdom's arithmetic. Men talk of Davenport Dunn as one recognized in the land."

"'Tis true; 'tis true as the Bible!" muttered the old man.

"And what is more," continued the other, warming with his theme, "what I have done I have done for all time. I have laid the foundations deep, that the edifice might endure. A man of inferior ambition would have been satisfied with wealth, and the enjoyments it secures; he might have held a seat in Parliament, sat on the benches beside the Minister, mayhap have held some Lordship of This or Under-Secretaryship of that, selling his influence ere it matured, as poor farmers sell their crops standing,—but I preferred the' patient path. I made a waiting race of it, father, and see what the prize is to be. Your son is to be a peer of Great Britain!"

The old man's mouth opened wide, and his eyes glared with an almost unnatural brightness, as, catching his son with both arms, he tried to embrace him.

"There, dear father,—there!" said Dunn, calmly; "you must not over-excite yourself."

"It's too much, Davy,—it's too much; I'll never live to see it."

"That you will, sir,—for a time, indeed, I was half disposed to stipulate that the title should be conferred upon yourself. It would have thus acquired another generation in date, but I remembered how indisposed you might feel to all the worry and care the mere forms of assuming it might cost you. You would not like to leave this old spot, besides—"

"No, on no account," said the old man, pensively.

"And then I thought that your great pride, after all, would be to hear of me, your own Davy, as Lord Castle-dunn."

"I thought it would be plain Dunn,—Lord Dunn," said the old man, quickly.

"If the name admitted of it, I 'd have preferred it so."

"And what is there against the name?" asked he angrily.

"Nothing, father; none have ever presumed to say a word against it. In talking the matter over, however, with some members of the Cabinet, one or two suggested Dunnscourt, but the majority inclined to Castledunn."

"And what did your Lordship say?" asked the old man, with a gleeful cackle. "Oh, Davy! I never thought the day would come that I 'd call you by any name I 'd love so well as that you bore when a child; but see, now, it makes my old eyes run over to speak to you as 'my Lord.'"

"It is a fair and honest pride, father," said Dunn, caressingly. "We stormed the breach ourselves, with none to help, none to cheer us on."

"Oh, Davy, but it does me good to call you 'my Lord.'"

"Well, sir, you are only anticipating a week or two. Parliament will assemble after the elections, and then be prorogued; immediately afterwards there will be four elevations to the peerage,—mine one of them."

"Yes, my Lord," mumbled the old man, submissively.

"But this is not all, father; the same week that sees me gazetted a peer will announce my marriage with an Earl's daughter."

"Davy, Davy, this luck is coming too quick! Take care, my son, that there's no pit before you."

"I know what I am doing, sir, and so does the Lady Augusta Arden. You remember the Earl of Glengariffs name?"

"Where you were once a tutor, is it?"

"The same, sir."

"It was they that used to be so cruel to you, Davy, wasn't it?"

"I was a foolish boy, ignorant of the world and its ways at the time. I fancied fifty things to mean offence which never were intended to wound me."

"Ay, they made you eat in the servants' hall, I think."

"Never, sir,—never; they placed me at a side table once or twice when pressed for room."

"Well, it was the room you had somewhere in a hayloft, eh?"

"Nothing of the kind, sir. Your memory is all astray. My chamber was small,—for the cottage had not much accommodation,—but I was well and suitably lodged."

"Well, what was it they did?" muttered he to himself. "I know it was something that made you cry the whole night after you came home."

"Father, father! these are unprofitable memories," said Dunn, sternly. "Were one to treasure up the score of all the petty slights he may have received in life, so that in some day of power he might acquit the debt, success would be anything but desirable."

"I'm not so sure of that, Davy. I never forgot an injury."

"I am more charitable, sir," said Dunn, calmly.

"No, you 're not, Davy,—no, you 're not," replied the old man, eagerly, "but you think it's wiser to be never-minding; and so it would, boy, if the man that injured you was to forget it too. Ay, Davy, that's the rub. But *he* won't; he 'll remember to his dying day that there's a score between you."

"I tell you, father, that these maxims do not apply to persons of condition, all whose instincts and modes of thought are unlike those of the inferior classes."

"They are men and women, Davy,—they are men and women."

Dunn arose impatiently, observing that the night was growing chilly, and it were better to return to the house.

"I mean to sup with you," said he, gayly, "if you have anything to give me."

"A rasher and eggs, and a bladebone of cold mutton is all I have," muttered the old man, gloomily. "I would not let them buy a chicken this week, when I saw the shares falling. Give me your arm, Davy, I've a slight weakness in the knees; it always took me at this season since I was a boy." And mumbling how strange it was that one did not throw off childish ailments as one grew older, he crept slowly along towards the house.

As they entered the kitchen, Dunn remarked with astonishment how little there remained of the abundance and plenty which had so characterized it of old. No hams, no flitches hung from the rafters; no sturdy barrels of butter stood against the walls; the chicken-coop was empty; and even to the good fire that graced the hearth there was a change, for a few half-sodden turf-sods were all that lingered in the place. Several baskets and hampers, carefully corded and sealed, were ranged beside the dresser, in which Dunn recognized presents of wine, choice cordials and liqueurs, that he had himself addressed to the old man.

"Why, father, how is this?" asked he, half angrily. "I had hoped for better treatment at your hands. You have apparently not so much as tasted any of the things I sent you."

"There they are, indeed, Davy, Just as they came for 'Matthew Dunn, Esq., with care,' written on them, and not a string cut!"

"And why should this be so, sir, may I ask?"

"Well, the truth is, Davy," said he, with a sigh, "I often longed to open them, and uncork a bottle of ale, or brandy, or, maybe, sherry, and sore tempted I felt to do it when I was drinking my buttermilk of a night; but then I'd say to myself, 'Ain't you well and hearty? keep cordials for the time when you are old, and feeble, and need support; don't be giving yourself bad habits, that maybe some fifteen or twenty years hence you'll be sorry for.' There's the reason, now, and I see by your face you don't agree with me."

Dunn made no answer, but taking up a knife he speedily cut the cordage of a large hamper, and as speedily covered a table with a variety of bottles.

"We'll drink this to the Queen's health, father," said he, holding up a flask of rare hock; "and this to the 'House of Lords,' for which estimable body I mean to return thanks; and then, father, I'll give 'Prosperity to the landed interest and the gentry of Ireland,' for which you shall speak."

Dunn went gayly along in this jesting fashion while he emptied the hamper of its contents, displaying along the dresser a goodly line of bottles, whose shape and corkage guaranteed their excellence. Meanwhile an old servant-woman had prepared the table, and was busily engaged with the materials of the meal.

"If I only thought we were going to have a feast, Davy, I 'd have made her light a fire in the parlor," said the old man, apologetically.

"We're better here, sir; it's cosier and homelier, and I know you think so. Keep your own corner, father, and I 'll sit here."

With appetites sharpened by the sea air and a long fast, they seated themselves at table and eat heartily. If their eyes met, a smile of pleasant recognition was exchanged; for while the old man gazed almost rapturously on his illustrious son, Dunn bent a look of scarcely inferior admiration on that patriarchal face, whereon time seemed but to mellow the traits that marked its wisdom.

"And what name do they give this, Davy?" said he, as he held up his glass to the light.

"Burgundy, father,—the king of wines. The wine-merchant names this Chambertin, which was the favorite drinking of the great Napoleon."

"I wonder at that, now," said the old man, sententiously.

"Wonder at it! And why so, father?—is it not admirable wine?"

"It's just for that reason, Davy; every sup I swallow sets me a-dreaming of wonderful notions,—things I know the next minute is quite impossible,—but I feel when the wine is on my lips as if they were all easy and practicable."

"After all, father, just remember that you cannot imagine anything one half so strange as the change in our own actual condition. There you sit, with your own clear head, to remind you of when and how you began life, and here am I!—for I am, as sure as if I held my patent in my hand, the Right Honorable Lord Castledunn."

"To your Lordship's good health and long life," said the old man, fervently.

"And now to a worthier toast, father,—Lady Castledunn that is to be."

"With all my heart. Lady Castledunn, whoever she is."

"I said, 'that is to be,' father; and I have given you her name,—the Lady Augusta Arden."

"I never heard of her," muttered the old man, dreamily.

"An Earl's daughter, sir; the ninth Earl of Glengariff," said Dunn, pompously.

"What 's her fortune, Davy? She ought to bring you a good fortune."

"Say rather, sir, it is I that should make a splendid settlement,—so proud a connection should meet its suitable acknowledgment."

"I understand little about them things, Davy; but there's one thing I do know, there never was the woman born I 'd make independent of me if she was my wife. It is n't in nature, and it isn't in reason."

"I can only say, sir, that with *your* principles you would not marry into the peerage."

"Maybe I 'd find one would suit me as well elsewhere."

"That is very possible, sir," was the dry reply.

"And if she cost less, maybe she'd wear as well," said the old man, peevishly; "but I suppose your Lordship knows best what suits your Lordship's station."

"That also is possible, sir," said Dunn, coldly.

The old man's brow darkened, he pushed his glass from him, and looked offended and displeased.

Dunn quickly saw the change that had passed over him, and cutting the wire of a champagne flask, he filled out a foaming tumbler of the generous wine, saying, "Drink this to your own good health, father,—to the man whose wise teachings and prudent maxims have made his son a foremost figure in the age, and who has no higher pride than to own where he got his earliest lessons."

"Is it true, Davy,—are them words true?" asked the old man, trembling with eagerness.

"As true as that I sit here." And Dunn drained his glass as he spoke.

The old man, partly wearied by the late sitting, partly confused by all the strange tidings he had heard, drooped his head upon his chest and breathed heavily, muttering indistinctly a few broken and incoherent words. Lost in his own reveries, Dunn had not noticed this drowsy stupor, when suddenly the old man said,—

"Davy,—are you here, Davy?"

"Yes, father, here beside you."

"What a wonderful dream I had, Davy!" he continued; "I dreamed you were made a lord, and that the Queen sent for you, and I was looking everywhere, up and down, for the fine cloak with the ermine all over it that you had to wear before her Majesty; sorra a one of me could find it at all; at last I put my hand on it, and was going to put it on your shoulders, when what should it turn out but a shroud!—ay, a shroud!"

"You are tired, father; these late hours are bad for you. Finish that glass of wine, and I'll say good-night."

"I wonder what sign a shroud is, Davy?" mumbled the old man, pertinaciously adhering to the dream. "A coffin, they say, is a wedding."

"It is not a vigorous mind like yours, father, that lends faith to such miserable superstitions."

"That is just what they are not. Dreams is dreams, Davy."

"Just so, sir; and, being dreams, have neither meaning nor consistency."

"How do you know that more than me? Who told you they were miserable superstitions? I call them warnings,—warnings that come out of our own hearts; and they come to us in our sleep just because that's the time our minds is not full of cares and troubles, but is just taking up whatever chances to cross them. What made Luke Davis dream of a paycock's feather the night his son was lost at sea? Answer me that if you can."

"These are unprofitable themes, father; we only puzzle ourselves when we discuss them. Difficult as they are to believe, they are still harder to explain."

"I don't want to explain them," said the old man, sternly, for he deemed that the very thought of such inquiry had in it something presumptuous.

"Well, father," said Dunn, rising, "I sincerely trust you will sleep soundly now, and be disturbed by none of these fancies. I must hasten away. I leave for Belfast by the early train, and have a mass of letters to answer before that."

"When am I to see you again, Davy?" asked the old man, eagerly.

"Very soon, I hope, sir; as soon as I can, of that you may be certain," said he, cordially.

"Let it be soon, then, Davy, for the meeting does me good. I feel to-night ten years younger than before you came, and it isn't the wine either; 'tis the sight of your face and the touch of your hand. Good-night, and my blessing be with you!" And a tear coursed down his seared cheek as he spoke.

CHAPTER XXI
A SHOCK

It was past midnight when Davenport Donn reached his own house. His return was unexpected, and it was some time before he gained admission. The delay, however, did not excite his impatience; his head was so deeply occupied with cares and thoughts for the future that he was scarcely conscious of the time he had been kept waiting.

Mr. Clowes, hurriedly summoned from his bed, came up full of apologies and excuses.

"We did not expect you till to-morrow, sir, by the late packet," said he, in some confusion. Dunn made no answer, and the other went on: "Mr. Hankes, too, thought it not improbable you would not be here before Wednesday."

"When was he here?"

"To-day sir; he left that oak box here this morning, and those letters, sir."

While Dunn carelessly turned over the superscriptions, among which he found none to interest him, Clowes repeatedly pressed his master to take some supper, or at least a biscuit and a glass of dry sherry.

"Send for Mr. Hankes," said Dunn, at last, not condescending to notice the entreaties of his butler. "Let him wait for me here when he comes." And so saying, he took a candle and passed upstairs.

Mr. Clowes was too well acquainted with his master's temper to obtrude unseasonably upon him, so that he glided noiselessly away till such time as he might be wanted.

When Dunn entered the drawing-room, he lighted the candles of the candelabra over the chimney and some of those which occupied the branches along the walls, and then, turning the key in the door, sat down to contemplate the new and splendid decorations of the apartment.

The task had been confided to skilful hands, and no more attempted than rooms of moderate size and recent architecture permitted. The walls, of a very pale green, displayed to advantage a few choice pictures,—Italian scenes by Turner, a Cuyp or two, and a Mieris,—all of them of a kind to interest those who had no connoisseurship to be gratified. A clever statuette of the French Emperor, a present graciously bestowed by himself, stood on a console of malachite, and two busts of Whig statesmen occupied brackets at either side of a vast mirror. Except these, there was little ornament, and the furniture seemed rather selected for the indulgence of ease and comfort than for show or display. A few bronzes, some curious carvings in ivory, an enamelled miniature, and some illuminated missals were scattered about amongst illustrated books and aquarelles, but in no great profusion; nor was there that indiscriminate litter which too frequently imparts to the salon the character of a curiosity-shop. The rooms, in short, were eminently habitable.

Over the chimney in the back drawing-room was a clever sketch, by Thorburn, of Lady Augusta Arden. She was in a riding-habit, and standing with one hand on the mane of an Arab pony,—a beautiful creature presented to her by Dunn. While he stood admiring the admirable likeness, and revolving in his mind the strange traits of that thoughtfulness which had supplied the picture,—for it was all Sybella Kellett's doing, every detail of the decorations, the color of the walls, the paintings, even to the places they occupied, had all been supplied by her,—Dunn started, and a sudden sickness crept over him. On a little table beside the fireplace stood a small gold salver, carved by Cellini, and which served to hold a few objects, such as coins and rings and antique gems. What could it be, then, amidst these century-old relics, which now overcame and so unmanned him that he actually grew pale as death, and sank at last, trembling, into a seat, cold perspiration on his face, and his very lips livid?

Mixed up amid the articles of *virtù* on that salver was an old-fashioned penknife with a massive handle of bloodstone, to which a slip of paper was attached, containing two or three words in Miss Kellett's hand. Now, the sight of this article in that place so overcame Dunn that it was some minutes ere he could reach out his hand to take the knife. When giving to Miss Kellett the charge of several rare and valuable objects, he had intrusted her with keys to certain drawers, leaving to her own judgment the task of selection. He had totally forgotten that this knife was amongst these; but even had he remembered the circumstance, it would not have caused alarm, naturally supposing how little worthy of notice such an object would seem amidst others of price and rarity. And yet there it was, and, by the slip of paper fastened to it, attesting a special notice.

With an effort almost convulsive he at last seized the knife, and reads the words. They were simply these: "A penknife, of which Mr. Dunn can probably supply the history." He dropped it as he read, and lay back, with a sense of fainting sickness.

The men of action and energy can face the positive present perils of life with a far bolder heart than they can summon to confront the terrors of conscience-stricken imagination. In the one case danger assumes a shape and a limit; in the other it looms out of distance, vast, boundless, and full of mystery. She knew, then, the story of his boyish shame; she had held the tale secretly in her heart through all their intercourse, reading his nature, mayhap, through the clew of that incident, and tracing out his path in life by the light it afforded; doubtless, too, she knew of his last scene with her father, — that terrible interview, wherein the dying man uttered a prediction that was almost a curse: she had treasured up these memories, and accepted his aid with seeming frankness, and yet, all the while that she played the grateful, trusting dependant, she had been slowly pursuing a vengeance. If Paul Kellett had confided to her the story of this childish transgression, he had doubtless revealed to her how heavily it had been avenged — how, with a persistent, persecuting hate, Dunn had tracked him, through difficulty and debt, to utter ruin. She had therefore read him in his real character, and had devoted herself to a revenge deeper than his own. Ay, he was countermined!

Such was the turn of his thoughts, as he sat there wiping the cold sweat that broke from his forehead, and cursing the blindness that had so long deceived him; and he, whose deep craft had carried him triumphant through all the hardest trials of the world, the man who had encountered the most subtle intellects, the great adventurer in a whole ocean of schemes, was to be the dupe and sport of a girl!

And now, amid his self-accusings, there rose up that strange attempt at compromise the baffled heart so often clings to, that he had, at times, half suspected this deep and secret treachery, — that she had not been either so secret or so crafty as she fancied herself. "If my mind," so reasoned he, "had not been charged with far weightier themes, I should have detected her at once; all her pretended gratitude, all her assumed thankfulness, had never deceived *me*; her insignificance was her safeguard. And yet withal, I sometimes felt, she is too deeply in our confidence, — she sees too much of the secret machinery of our plans. While I exulted over the ignoble dependence she was doomed to, — while I saw, with a savage joy, how our lots in life were reversed, — was I self-deceived?"

So impressed was he with the idea of a game in which he had been defeated, that he went over in his mind every circumstance he could recall of his intercourse with her. Passages the simplest, words of little significance, incidents the most trivial, he now charged with deepest meaning. Amidst these, there was one for which he could find no solution, — why had she so desired to be the owner of the cottage near Bantry? It was there that

Driscoll had discovered the Conway papers. Was it possible—the thought flashed like lightning on him—that there was any concert between the girl and this man? This suspicion no sooner occurred to him than it took firm hold of his mind. None knew better than Dunn the stuff Driscoll was made of, and knowing, besides, how he had, by his own seeming luke-warmness, affronted that crafty schemer, it was by no means improbable that such an alliance as this existed. And this last discovery of documents,—how fortunate was it that Hankes had secured them! The papers might or might not be important; at all events, the new Lord Lackington might be brought to terms by their means; he would have come to his peerage so unexpectedly that all the circumstances of the contested claim would be strange to him. This was a point to be looked at; and as he reasoned thus, again did he go back to Sybella Kellett, and what the nature of her game might be, and how it should first display itself.

A tap at the door startled him. "Mr. Hankes is below, sir," said Clowes.

"I will be with him in a moment," replied Dunn; and again relapsed into his musings.

CHAPTER XXII
A MASTER AND MAN

"Is she gone?—where to?" cried Dunn, without answering Mr. Hankes's profuse salutations and welcomes.

"Yes, sir; she sailed yesterday."

"Sailed, and for where?"

"For Malta, sir, in the Euxine steamer. Gone to her brother in the Crimea. One of the people saw her go on board at Southampton."

"Was she alone?"

"Quite alone, sir. My man was present when she paid the boatman. She had very little luggage, but they demanded half a guinea—"

"What of Driscoll? Have you traced him?" asked Dunn, impatient at the minuteness of this detail.

"He left London for Havre on the 12th of last month, sir, with a passport for Italy. He carried one of Hart-well's circulars for three hundred pounds, and was to have taken a courier at Paris, but did not."

"And where is he now?" asked Dunn, abruptly.

"I am unable to say, sir," said Hankes, almost abjectly, for he felt self-rebuked in the acknowledgment. "My last tidings of him came from Como,—a new Hydropathic Institution there."

"Expecting to find the Viscount Lackington," said Dunn, with a sardonic laugh. "Death was before you, Master Driscoll; you did not arrive in time for even the funeral. I say, Hankes," added he, quickly, "what of the new Viscount? Has he answered our letters?"

"Not directly, sir; but there came a short note signed 'C. Christopher,' stating that his Lordship had been very ill, and was detained at Ems, and desiring to have a bank post-bill for two hundred forwarded to him by return."

"You sent it?"

"Of course, sir; the letter had some details which proved it to be authentic."

"And the sum a trifle," broke in Dunn. "She is scarcely at Malta by this, Hankes. What am I thinking of? She 'll not reach it before next Friday or Saturday. Do you remember young Kellett's regiment?"

"No, sir."

"Well, find it out. I'll write to the Horse Guards tomorrow to have him promoted,—to give him an Ensigncy in some regiment serving in India. Whom do you know at Malta, Hankes?"

"I know several, sir; Edmond Grant, in the Storekeeper's Department; James Hocksley, Second Harbor-Master; Paul Wesley, in the Under-Secretary's Office."

"Any of them will do. Telegraph to detain her; that her brother is coming home; she must not go to the Crimea." There was a stern fixity of purpose declared in the way these last words were spoken, which at the same time warned Hankes from asking any explanation of them. "And now for business. What news from Arigua,—any ore?"

"Plenty, sir; the new shaft has turned out admirably. It is yielding upwards of twenty-eight per cent, and Holmes offers thirty pounds a ton for the raw cobalt."

"I don't care for that, sir. I asked how were shares," said Dunn, peevishly.

"Not so well as might be expected, sir. The shake at Glengariff was felt widely."

"What do you mean? The shares fell, but they rose again; they suffered one of those fluctuations that attend on all commercial or industrial enterprises; but they rallied even more quickly than they went down. When I left town yesterday, they were at one hundred and forty-three."

"I know it, sir. I received your telegram, and I showed it to Bayle and Childers, but they only smiled, and said, 'So much the better for the holders.'"

"I defy any man—I don't care what may be his abilities or what his zeal—to benefit this country!" exclaimed Dunn, passionately. "There is amongst Irishmen, towards each other, such an amount of narrow jealousy— mean, miserable, envious rivalry—as would swamp the best intentions, and destroy the wisest plans that ever were conceived. May my fate prove a warning to whoever is fool enough to follow me!"

Was it that when Dunn thus spoke he hoped to persuade Mr. Hankes that he was a noble-hearted patriot, sorrowing over the errors of an ungrateful country? Did he fancy that his subtle lieutenant, the associate of all his deep intrigues, the confidant of his darkest schemes, was suddenly to see in him nothing but magnanimity of soul and single-hearted devotedness? No, I cannot presume to say that he indulged in any such delusion. He uttered the words just to please himself,—to flatter himself! as some men drink off a cordial to give them Dutch courage. There are others that enunciate grand sentiments, high sounding and magniloquent, the very music and resonance of their words imparting a warm glow within them.

It is a common error to imagine that such "stage thunder" is confined to that after-dinner eloquence in whose benefit the canons of truth-telling are all repealed. Far from it. The practice enters into every hour of every-day life, and the greatest knave that ever rogued never cheated the world half as often as he cheated himself!

As though it had been a glass of brown sherry that he swallowed, Mr. Dunn felt "better" after he had uttered these fine words. He experienced a proud satisfaction in thinking what a generous heart beat within his own waistcoat; and thus reassured, he thought well of the world at large.

"And Ossory, Mr. Hankes,—how is Ossory?"

"A hundred and fourteen, with a look upwards," responded Mr. Hankes. "Since the day of 'the run' deposits have largely increased. Indeed, I may say we are now the great country gentry bank of the midland. We discount freely, too, and we lend generously."

"I shall want some ready money soon, Hankes," said Dunn, as he paced the room with his hands behind his back, and his head bent forward. "You 'll have to sell out some of those Harbor shares."

"Bantry's, sir? Glumthal's have them as securities!"

"So they have; I forgot. Well, St Columbs, or the Patent Fuel, or that humbug discovery of Patterson's,—the Irish Asphalt There's an American fellow, by the way, wants that."

"They're very low,—very low, all these, sir," said Hankes, lugubriously. "They sank so obstinately that I just withdrew our name quietly, so that we can say any day we have long ceased any connection with these enterprises."

"She 'll scarcely make any delay in Malta, Hankes. Your message ought to be there by Thursday at latest" And then, as if ashamed of showing where his thoughts were straying, he said, "All kinds of things—odds and ends of every sort—are jostling each other in my brain to-night."

"You want rest, sir; you want nine or ten hours of sound sleep."

"Do I look fatigued or harassed?" asked Dunn, with an eagerness that almost startled the other.

"A little tired, sir; not more than that," cautiously answered Hankes.

"But I don't *feel* tired. I am not conscious of any weariness," said he, pettishly. "I suspect that you are not a very acute physiognomist, Hankes. I have told you," added he, hastily, "I shall want some twelve or fifteen thousand pounds soon. Look out, too, for any handsome country-seat—in the South, I should prefer it—that may be in the market I 'll not carry out my intentions about Kellett's Court. It is a tumble-down old concern, and would cost us more in repairs than a handsome house fit to inhabit."

"Am I to have the honor of offering my felicitations, sir?" said Hankes, obsequiously; "are the reports of the newspapers as to a certain happy event to be relied on?"

"You mean as to my marriage? Yes, perfectly true. I might, in a mere worldly point of view, have looked higher,—not higher, certainly not,—but I might have contracted what many would have called a more advantageous connection; in fact, I might have had any amount of money I could care for, but I determined for what I deemed the wiser course. You are probably not aware that this is a very long attachment. Lady Augusta and myself have been as good as engaged to each other for—for a number of years. She was very young when we met first,—just emerging from early girlhood; but the sentiment of her youthful choice has never varied, and, on *my* part, the attachment has been as constant."

"Indeed, sir!" said Hankes, sorely puzzled what to make of this declaration.

"I know," said Dunn, returning rapidly to the theme, "that nothing will seem less credible to the world at large than a man of *my* stamp marrying for love! The habit is to represent us as a sort of human monster, a creature of wily, money-getting faculties, shrewd, over-reaching, and successful. They won't give us feelings, Hankes. They won't let us understand the ties of affection and the charms of a home. Well," said he, after a long pause, "there probably never lived a man more mistaken, more misconceived by the world than myself."

Hankes heaved a heavy sigh; it was, he felt, the safest thing he could do, for he did not dare to trust himself with a single word. The sigh, however, was a most profound one, and, plainly as words, declared the compassionate contempt he entertained for a world so short-sighted and so meanly minded.

"After all," resumed Dunn, "it is the penalty every man must pay for eminence. The poor little nibblers at the rind of fortune satisfy their unsuccess when they say, 'Look at him with all his money!'"

Another and deeper sigh here broke from Hankes, who was really losing all clew to the speaker's reflections.

"I'm certain, Hankes, you have heard observations of this kind five hundred times."

"Ay, have I, sir," answered he, in hurried confusion, — "five thousand!"

"Well, and what was your reply, sir? How did you meet such remarks?" said Dunn, sternly.

"Put them down, sir, — put them down at once; that is, I acknowledged that there was a sort of fair ground; I agreed in thinking that, everything considered, and looking to what we saw every day around us in life — and Heaven knows it is a strange world, and the more one sees of it the less he knows—"

"I 'm curious to hear," said Dunn, with a stern fixedness of manner, "in what quarter you heard these comments on my character."

Hankes trembled from head to foot. He was in the witness-box, and felt that one syllable might place him in the dock.

"You never heard one word of the kind in your life, sir, and you *know* it," said Dunn, with a savage energy of tone that made the other sick with fear. "If ever there was a man whose daily life refuted such a calumny, it was myself."

Dunn's emotions were powerful, and he walked the room from end to end with long and determined strides. Suddenly halting at last, he looked Hankes steadily in the face, and said, —

"It was the Kellett girl dared thus to speak of me, was it not? The truth, sir, — the truth; I *will* have it out of you!"

"Well, I must own you are right. It was Miss Kellett."

Heaven forgive you, Mr. Hankes, for the lie, inasmuch as you never intended to tell it till it was suggested to you.

"Can you recall the circumstance which elicited this remark? I mean," said he, with an affected carelessness of manner, "how did it occur? You were chatting together, — discussing people and events, eh?"

"Yes, sir; just so."

"And she observed — Do you chance to remember the phrase she used?"

"I give you my word of honor I do not, sir," said Hankes, with a sincere earnestness.

"People who fancy themselves clever—and Miss Kellett is one of that number—have a trick of eliminating every trait of a man's character from some little bias,—some accidental bend given to his youthful mind. I am almost certain—nay, I feel persuaded—it was by some such light that young lady read me. She had heard I was remarkable as a schoolboy for this, that, or t' other,—I saved my pocket-money, or lent it out at interest. Come, was it not with the aid of an ingenious explanation of this kind she interpreted me?"

Mr. Hankes shook his head, and looked blankly disconsolate.

"Not that I value such people's estimate of me," said Dunn, angrily. "Calumniate, vilify, depreciate as they will, here I stand, with my foot on the first step of the peerage. Ay, Hankes, I have made my own terms; the first 'Gazette' after the new elections will announce Mr. Davenport Dunn as Lord Castledunn."

Hankes actually bounded on his chair. Had he been the faithful servant of some learned alchemist, watching patiently for years the wondrous manipulations and subtle combinations of his master, following him from crucible to crucible and from alembic to alembic, till the glorious moment when, out of smoke and vapor, the yellow glow of the long-sought metal gleamed before his eyes, he could not have regarded his chief with a more devoted homage.

Dunn read "worship" in every lineament of the other's face. It was as honest veneration as his nature could compass, and, sooth to say, the great man liked it, and sniffed his incense with the-air of Jove himself.

"I mean to take care of you, Hankes," said he, with a bland protectiveness. "I do not readily forget the men who have served me faithfully. Of course we must draw out of all our enterprises here. I intend at once to realize— yes, Hankes—to realize a certain comfortable sum and withdraw."

These were not very explicit nor very determinate expressions, but they were amply intelligible to him who heard them.

"To wind up, sir, in short," said Hankes, significantly.

"Yes, Hankes, 'to wind up.'"

"A difficult matter,—a very difficult matter, sir."

"Difficulties have never deterred me from anything, Mr. Hankes. The only real difficulty I acknowledge in life is to choose which of them I will adopt; that done, the rest is matter of mere detail." Mr. Dunn now seated himself at a table, and in the calm and quiet tone with which he treated every business question, he explained to Hankes his views on each of the great interests he was concerned in. Shares in home speculations were to be first exchanged for foreign scrip, and these afterwards sold. Of the vast securities of private individuals pledged for loans, or given as guarantees, only such were to be redeemed as belonged to persons over whom Dunn had no control. Depositary as he was of family secrets, charged with the mysterious knowledge of facts whose publication would bring ruin and disgrace on many, this knowledge was to have its price and its reward; and as he ran his finger down the list of names so compromised, Hankes could mark the savage exultation of his look while he muttered unintelligibly to himself.

Dunn stopped at the name of the Viscount Lackington, and, leaning his head on his hand, said, "Don't let us forget that message to Malta."

"A heavy charge that, sir," said Hankes. "The Ossory has got all his Lordship's titles; and we have set them down, too, for twenty-one thousand seven hundred above their value."

"Do you know who is the Viscount Lackington?" asked Dunn, with a strange significance.

"No, sir."

"Neither do I," said Dunn, hurriedly following him. "Mayhap it may cost some thousands of pounds and some tiresome talk to decide that question; at all events, it will cost you or me nothing."

"The Earl of Glengariff's claim must, I suppose, be satisfied, sir?"

"Of course, it must, and the very first of all! But I am not going to enter minutely into these things now, Hankes. I need a little of that rest you were just recommending me to take. Be here to-morrow at twelve; do not mention my arrival to any one, but come over with the Ossory statement and the two or three other most important returns."

Mr. Hankes rose to withdraw; and as he moved towards the door, his eye caught the oaken box, with three large seals placed by his own hand.

"You have scarcely had time to think about these papers, sir; but they will have their importance when that peerage case comes to be discussed. The Lackingtons were Conways—"

"Let me have a look at them," said Dunn, rapidly.

Hankes broke open the paper bands, and unlocked the box. For some time he searched through the documents as they lay, and then emptying them all upon the table, he went over them more carefully, one by one. "Good heavens!" cried he, "how can this be?"

"What do you mean?" exclaimed Dunn; "you do not pretend that they are missing?"

"They are gone,—they are not here!" said the other, almost fainting from agitation.

"But these are the seals you yourself fastened on the box."

"I know it,—I see it; and I can make nothing of it."

"Mr. Hankes, Mr. Hankes, this is serious," said Dunn, as he bent upon the affrighted man a look of heart-searching significance.

"I swear before Heaven—I take my most solemn oath—"

"Never mind swearing; how could they have been extricated? That is the question to be solved."

Hankes examined the seals minutely; they were his own. He scrutinized the box on every side to see if any other mode of opening it existed; but there was none. He again went through the papers,—opening, shaking, sifting them, one by one; and then, with a low, faint sigh, he sank down upon a chair, the very image of misery and dismay. "Except it was the devil himself—"

"The devil has plenty of far more profitable work on hand, sir," said Dunn, sternly; and then, in a calmer tone, added, "Is it perfectly certain that you ever saw the documents you allude to? and when?"

"Saw them? Why, I held them in my hands for several minutes. It was myself replaced them in the box before sealing it."

"And what interval of time occurred between your reading them and sealing them up?"

"A minute,—half a minute, perhaps; stay," cried he, suddenly, "I remember now that I left the room to call the landlord. Miss Kellett remained behind."

With a dreadful imprecation Dunn struck his forehead with his hand, and sank into his seat. "What cursed folly," cried he, bitterly, "and what misfortune and ruin may it beget!"

"It was then that she took them,—that was the very moment," muttered Hankes, as he followed on his own dreary thoughts.

"My father was right," said Dunn, below his breath; "that girl will bring sorrow on us yet."

"But, after all, what value could they have in her eyes? She knows nothing about the questions they refer to; she could not decipher the very titles of the documents."

"I ought to have known,—I ought to have foreseen it," cried Dunn, passionately. "What has my whole life been but a struggle against the blunders, the follies, and the faults of those who should have served me! Other men are fortunate in their agents. It was reserved for me to have nothing but incapables, or worse."

"If you mean to include *me* in either of these categories, sir, will you please to say which?" said Hankes, reddening with anger.

"Take your choice,—either, or both!" said Dunn, savagely.

"A man must be very strong in honesty that can afford to speak in this fashion of others," said Hankes, his voice tremulous with rage. "At all events, the world shall declare whether he be right or not."

"How do you mean, 'the world shall declare'? Is it that what has passed between us here can be made matter for public notoriety? Would you dare—"

"Oh, I would dare a great deal, sir, if I was pushed to it," said Hankes, scoffingly. "I would dare, for instance, to let the world we are speaking of into some of the mysteries of modern banking. I have a vast amount of information to give as to the formation of new companies,—how shares are issued, cancelled, and reissued. I could tell some amusing anecdotes about title-deeds of estates that never were transferred—"

Why is it that Mr. Hankes, now in the full flood of his sarcasm, stops so suddenly? What has arrested his progress; and why does he move so hurriedly towards the door, which Dunn has, however, already reached before him and locked? Was it something in the expression of Dunn's features that alarmed him?—truly, there was in his look what might have appalled a stouter heart,—or was it that Dunn had suddenly taken something, he could not discern what, from a drawer, and hastily hidden it in his pocket?

"Merciful heavens!" cried Hankes, trembling all over, "you would not dare—"

"Like yourself, sir, I would dare much if pushed to it," said Dunn, in a voice that now had recovered all its wonted composure. "But come, Hankes, it is not a hasty word or an ungenerous speech is to break up the ties of a long friendship. I was wrong; I was unjust; I ask your pardon for it. You have served me too faithfully and too well to be requited thus. Give me your hand, and say you forgive me."

"Indeed, sir, I must own I scarcely expected—that is, I never imagined—"

"Come, come, do not do it grudgingly; tell me, frankly, all is forgiven."

Hankes took the outstretched hand, and muttered some broken, unintelligible words.

"There, now, sit down and think no more of this folly." He opened a large pocket-book as he spoke, and searching for some time amongst its contents, at last took forth a small slip of paper. "Ay, here it is," said he: "'Sale of West Indian estates; resident commissionership; two thousand per annum, with allowance for house,' &c. Sir Hepton Wallis was to have it. Would this suit you, Hankes? The climate agrees with many constitutions."

"Oh, as to the climate," said Hankes, trembling with eagerness and delight, "I 'd not fear it."

"And then with ample leave of absence from time to time, and a retiring allowance, after six years' service, of—if I remember aright—twelve hundred a year. What say you? It must be filled up soon. Shall I write your name instead of Sir Hepton's?"

"Oh, sir, this is, indeed, generosity!"

"No, Hankes, mere justice; nothing more. The only merit I can lay claim to in the matter is the sacrifice I make in separating myself from a well-tried and trusted adherent."

"These reports shall be ready immediately, sir," said Hankes. "I 'll not go to bed to-night—"

"We have ample time for everything, Hankes; don't fatigue yourself, and be here at twelve to-morrow."

CHAPTER XXIII
ANNESLEY BEECHER IN A NEW PART

About five weeks have elapsed since we last sojourned with Grog Davis and his party at the little village of Holbach. Five weeks are a short period in human life, but often enough has it sufficed to include great events, and to make marvellous changes in a man's fortunes! Now, the life they all led here might seem well suited to exclude such calculations. Nothing seemed less likely to elicit vicissitudes. It was a calm, tame monotony; each day so precisely like its predecessor that it was often hard to remember how the week stole on. The same landscape, with almost the same effects of sun and shadow, stretched daily before their eyes; the same gushing water foamed and fretted; the same weeds bent their heads to the flood; the self-same throbbing sounds of busy mills mingled with the rushing streams; the very clouds, as they dragged themselves lazily up the mountain side, and then broke into fragments on the summit, seemed the same; and yet in that little world of three people there was the endless conflict of hope and fear, and all the warring interests which distract great masses of men filled their hearts and engaged their minds.

At first Beecher chafed and fretted at the delay; Lizzy appeared but rarely; and when she did it was with a strange reserve, almost amounting to constraint, that he could not comprehend. She did not seem angry or offended with him, simply more distant. Her high spirits, too, were gone; no more the light-hearted, gay, and playful creature he remembered, she was calm even to seriousness. A look of thoughtful preoccupation marked her as she sat silently gazing on the landscape, or watching the eddies of the circling river. There was nothing—save a slight increase of paleness—to denote sorrow in her appearance; her features were placid, and her expression tranquil. If her voice had lost its ringing music, it had acquired a tone of deep and melting softness that seemed to leave an echo in the heart that heard it. To this change, which at first chilled and repelled Beecher, he grew day by day to accustom himself. If her mood was one less calculated to enliven and to cheer him, it was yet better adapted to make his confidence. He could talk to her more freely of himself than heretofore. No longer did he stand in dread of the sharp and witty epigrams with which she used to quiz his opinions and ridicule his notions of life. She would listen to him now with patience, if not with interest, and she would hear him with attention as he talked for hours on the one sole theme he loved,—himself. And, oh, young ladies,—not that you need any counsels of mine in such matters; but if, perchance, my words of advice should have any weight with you,—let me impress this lesson on your hearts: that for the man who is not actually in love with you, but only "spooney," there is no such birdlime as the indulgence of his selfishness. Let him talk away about his dogs and his horses, his exploits in China or the Crimea, his fishings in Norway, his yachtings in the Levant; let him discourse about his own affairs, of business as well as pleasure; how briefs are pouring in or patients multiply; hear him as he tells you of his sermon before the bishop, or his examination at Burlington House,—trust me, no theme will make *him* so eloquent nor *you* so interesting. Of all "serials,"—as the phrase is,—there is none can be carried out to so many "numbers" as Egotism; and though the snowball grows daily bigger, it rolls along even more easily.

I am not going to say that Lizzy Davis did this of "prepense;" I am even candid enough to acknowledge to you that I am not quite sure I can understand her. She had ways of acting and thinking peculiarly her own. She was not always what the French call *conséquente*, but she was marvellously quick to discover she was astray, and "try back." She was one of those people who have more difficulty in dealing with themselves than with others. She had an instinctive appreciation of those whose natures she came in contact with, joined to a strong desire to please; and, lastly, there was scarcely a human temperament with which she could not sympathize somewhere. She let Beecher talk on, because it pleased *him*, and pleasing *him* became, at last, a pleasure to herself. When he recalled little traits of generosity, the kind things he had done here, the good-natured acts he had done there, she led him on to feel a more manly pride in himself than when recounting tales of his sharp practices on the turf and his keen exploits in the ring.

Beecher saw this leaning on her part, and ascribed it all to her "ignorance of the world," and firmly believed that when she saw more of life she would think more highly of his intellect than even of his heart. Poor fellow! they were beautifully balanced, and phrenology for once would have its triumph in showing the mental and the moral qualities in equilibrium. After the first week they were always together, for Davis was continually on the road,—now to Neuwied, now to Höchst. The letters and telegrams that he despatched and received were incredible in number; and when jested with on the amount of his correspondence by Beecher, his only answer was, "It's all *your* business, my boy,—the whole concerns *you*." Now, Annesley Beecher was far too much of a philosopher to trouble his head about anything which could be avoided, and to find somebody who devoted himself to his interests, opened and read the dunning appeals of creditors, answered their demands by "renewals," or cajoled them by promises, was one of the highest luxuries he could imagine. Indeed, if Grog would only fight for him and go to jail for him, he 'd have deemed his happiness complete. "And who knows," thought he, "but it may come to that yet? I seem to have thrown a sort of fascination over the old fellow that may lead him any lengths."

Meanwhile there was extending over himself another web of fascination not the less complete that he never perceived it His first waking thought was of Lizzy. As he came down to breakfast, his dress showed how studiously he cultivated appearance. The breakfast over, he sat down to his German lesson beside her with a patient perseverance that amazed him. There he was, with addled head and delighted heart, conjugating "Ich liebe," and longing for the day when he should reach the imperative mood; and then they walked long country walks into the dark beech woods, along grassy alleys where no footfall sounded, or they strayed beside some river's bank, half fancying that none had ever strolled over the same sward before. And how odd it was to see the Honorable Annesley Beecher, the great lion of the Guards' Club, the once celebrity of the Coventry, carrying a little basket on his arm, like a stage peasant in a comic opera, with the luncheon, or, mayhap, bearing a massive stone in his arms to bridge a stream for Lizzy to cross. Poor fellow! he did these things with a good will, and even in his awkwardness there was that air of "gentleman" which never left him; and then he would laugh so heartily at his own inaptitude, and join in' Lizzy's mirth at the mischances that befell him. And was it not delightful, through all these charming scenes, on the high mountain-aide, in the deep heather, or deep in some tangled glen, with dog-roses and honeysuckle around them, he could still talk of himself, and she could listen?

For the life of him he could not explain how it was that the time slipped over so pleasantly. As he himself said, "there was not much to see, and nothing to do," and yet, somehow, the day was always too short for either. He wanted to write to his brother, to his sister-in-law, to Dunn, to his man of business,—meaning the Jew who raised money for him,—but never could find time. He was so puzzled by the problem that he actually asked Lizzy to explain it; but she only laughed.

Now and then, when he chanced to be all alone, a sudden thought would strike him that he was leading a life of inglorious idleness. He would count up how many weeks it was since he had seen a "Bell's Life," and try to calculate what races were coming off that very same day; then he would draw a mind-picture of Tattersall's on a settling day, and wonder who were the defaulters, and who were getting passports for the Continent; and he would wind up his astonishment by thinking that Grog was exactly leading the game indolent existence, "although we have that 'grand book with the martingale,' and might be smashing the bank at Baden every night."

That a man should have the cap of Fortunatus, and yet never try it on, even just for the experiment's sake, was downright incredible. You might not want money,—not that he had ever met the man in that predicament yet,—you might, perhaps, have no very strong desire for this, that, or t' other; yet, somehow, "the power was such a jolly thing!" The fact that you could go in and win whenever you pleased was a marvellously fine consideration. As for himself,—so he reasoned,—he did not exactly know why, but he thought his present life a very happy one. He never was less beset with cares: he had no duns; there was not a tailor in Bond Street knew his address; the very Jews had not traced him; he was as free as air. Like most men accustomed to eat and drink of the best, the simple fare of an humble inn pleased him. Grog, whenever he saw him, was good-humored and gay; and as for Lizzy, "of all the girls he had ever met, she was the only one ever understood him."

As Annesley Beecher comprehended his own phrase, being "understood" was no such bad thing. It meant, in the first place, a generous appreciation of all motives for good, even though they never went beyond motives; a hopeful trust in some unseen, unmanifested excellence of character; a broadcast belief that, making a due allowance for temptations, human frailties, and the doctrine of chances,—this latter most of all,—the balance would always be found in favor of good *versus* evil; and, secondly, that all the imputed faults and vices of such natures as *his* were little else than the ordinary weaknesses of "the best of us." Such is being "understood," good reader; and, however it may chance with others, I hope that "you and I may."

But Lizzy Davis understood him even better and deeper than all this. She knew him, if not better than I do myself, at least, better than I am able to depict to you. Apart, then, from the little "distractions" I have mentioned, Beecher was very happy. It had been many a long day since he felt himself so light-hearted and so kindly-minded to the world at large. He neither wished any misfortune to befall Holt's "stable" or Shipman's "three-year old;" he did not drop off to sleep hoping that Beverley might break down or "Nightcap" spring a back sinew; and, stranger than all, he actually could awake of a morning and not wish himself the Viscount Lackington. Accustomed as he was to tell Lizzy everything, to ask her advice about all that arose, and her explanation for all that puzzled him, he could not help communicating this new phenomenon of his temperament, frankly acknowledging that it was a mystery he could not fathom.

"Nothing seems ever to puzzle you, Lizzy,"—he had learned to call her Lizzy some time back,—"so just tell me what can you make of it? Ain't it strange?"

"It *is* strange," said she, with a faint smile, in which a sort of sad meaning mingled.

"So strange," resumed he, "that had any one said to me, 'Beecher, you 'll spend a couple of months in a little German inn, with nothing to do, nothing to see, and, what's more, it will not bore you,' I 'd have answered, 'Take you fifty to one in hundreds on the double event,—thousands if you like it better,'—and see, hang me if I should n't have lost!"

"Perhaps not. If you had a heavy wager on the matter, it is likely you would not have come."

"Who knows! Everything is Fate in this world. Ah, you may laugh; but it is, though. What else, I ask you—what brings you here just now?—why am I walking along the river with you beside me?"

"Partly, because, I hope, you find it pleasant," said she, with a droll gravity, while something in her eyes seemed to betoken that her own thoughts amused her.

"There must be more than that," said he, thoughtfully, for he felt the question a knotty one, and rather liked to show that he did not skulk the encounter with such difficulties.

"Partly, perhaps, because it pleases *me*," said she, in the same quiet tone.

He shook his head doubtingly; he had asked for an explanation, and neither of these supplied that want. "At all events, Lizzy, there is one thing you will admit,—if it is Fate, one can't help it,—eh?"

"If you mean by that that you must walk along here at my side, whether you will or not, just try, for experiment's sake, if you could not cross over the stream and leave me to go back alone."

"Leave *you* to go back alone!" cried he, upon whom the last words were ever the most emphatic. "But why so, Lizzy; are you angry with me?—are you weary of me?"

"No, I 'm not angry with you," said she, gently.

"Wearied, then—tired of me—bored?"

"Must I pay you compliments on your agreeability, Mr. Beecher?"

"There it is again," broke he in, pettishly. "It was only yesterday you consented to call me Annesley, and you have gone back from it already,— forgotten it all!"

"No, I forget very seldom—unfortunately." This last word was uttered to herself and for herself.

"You will call me Annesley, then?" asked he, eagerly.

"Yes, if you wish it,—Annesley." There was a pause before she spoke the last word; and when she did utter it, her accent faltered slightly, and a faint blush tinged her cheek.

As for Beecher, his heart swelled high and proudly; he felt at that moment a strange warm glow within him that counterfeited courage; for an instant he thought he would have liked something perilous to confront,— something in encountering which he might stand forth before Lizzy as a Paladin. Was it that some mysterious voice within him whispered, "She loves you; her heart is yours"? and, oh, if so, what a glorious sentiment must there be in that passion, if love can move a nature like this, and mould it to one great or generous ambition!

"Lizzy, I want to talk to you seriously," said he, drawing her arm within his own. "I have long wanted to tell you something; and if you can hear it without displeasure, I swear to you I 'd not change with Lackington to-morrow! Not that it's such good fun being a younger son,—few men know that better than myself; still, I repeat, that if you only say 'yes' to me, I pledge you my oath I 'd rather hear it than be sure I was to win the Oaks,—ay, by Heaven! Oaks and Derby, too! You know now what I mean, dearest Lizzy, and do not, I beseech you, keep me longer in suspense."

She made no answer; her cheek became very pale, and a convulsive shudder passed over her; but she was calm and unmoved the next instant.

"If you love another, Lizzy," said he, and his lips trembled violently, "say so frankly. It's only like all my other luck in life, though nothing was ever as heavy as this."

There was an honesty, a sincerity in the tone, of these words that seemed to touch her; for she stole a side look at his face, and the expression of her glance was of kindly pity.

"Is it true, then, that you *do* love another, Lizzy?" repeated he, with even deeper emotion.

"No!" said she, with a slow utterance.

"Will you not tell me, dearest Lizzy, if—if—I am to have any hope? I know well enough that you need n't take a poor beggar of a younger son. I know where a girl of your beauty may choose. Far better than you do I know that you might have title, rank, fortune; and as for me, all I have is a miserable annuity Lackington allows me, just enough to starve on,—not that I mean to go on, however, as I have been doing; no, no, by Jove! I 'm round the corner now, and I intend to make play, and 'take up my running.' Your father and I understand what we're about."

What a look was that Lizzy gave him! What a piercing significance must the glance have had that sent the blood so suddenly to his face and forehead, and made him falter, and then stop.

"One thing I 'll swear to you, Lizzy,—swear it by all that is most solemn," cried he, at last: "if you consent to share fortunes with me, I 'll never engage in anything—no matter how sure or how safe—without your full concurrence. I have been buying experience this many a year, and pretty sharply has it cost me. They make a gentleman pay his footing, I promise you; but I *do* know a thing or two at last; I *have* had my eyes opened!"

Oh, Annesley Beecher, can you not see how you are damaging your own cause? You have but to look at that averted head, or, bending round, to catch a glimpse of those fair features, and mark the haughty scorn upon them, to feel that you are pleading against yourself.

"And what may be this knowledge of which you are so proud?" said she, coldly.

"Oh, as to that," said he, in some confusion at the tone she had assumed, "it concerns many a thing you never heard of. The turf, and the men that live by it, make a little world of their own; they don't bother their heads about parties or politics,—don't care a farthing who 's 'in' or who 's 'out.' They keep their wits—and pretty sharp wits they are—for what goes on in Scott's stable, and how Holt stands for the St. Léger. They 'd rather hear how Velocipede eat his corn, than hear all the Cabinet secrets of Europe; and for that matter, so would I."

"I do not blame you for not caring for State secrets,—it is very possible they would interest you little; but surely you might imagine some more fitting career than what, after all, is a mere trading on the weakness of others. To make of an amusement a matter of profit is, in my eyes, mean; it is contemptible."

"That's not the way to look on it at all. The first men in England have race-horses."

"And precisely in the fact of their great wealth do they soar above all the ignoble associations the turf obliges to those who live by it."

"Well, I 'll give it up; there's my word on't I 'll never put my foot in Tattersall's yard again. I 'll take my name off the Turf Club,—is that enough?"

She could not help smiling at the honest zeal of this sacrifice; but the smile had none of the scorn her features displayed before.

"Oh, Lizzy!" cried he, enthusiastically, "if I was sure we could just live on here as we are doing,—never leave this little valley, nor see more of the world than we do daily,—I'd not exchange the life for a duke's fortune—"

"And Holt's stable," added she, laughing. "Come, you must not omit the real bribe."

He laughed heartily at this sally, and owned it was the grand temptation.

"You are certainly very good-tempered, Annesley," said she, after a pause.

"I don't think I am," said he, half piqued, for he thought the remark contained a sort of disparagement of that sharpness on which he chiefly prided himself. "I am very hot at times."

"I meant that you bore with great good-humor from me what you might, if so disposed, have fairly enough resented as an impertinence. What do I, what could I, know of that play-world of which you spoke? How gentlemen and men of fashion regard these things must needs be mysteries to me; I only wished to imply that you might make some better use of your faculties, and that knowledge of life you possess, than in conning over a betting-book or the 'Racing Calendar.'"

"So I mean to do. That's exactly what I 'm planning."

"Here's the soup cooling and the sherry getting hot," cried Grog, as he shouted from the window of the little inn, and waved his napkin to attract their notice.

"There's papa making a signal to us," said Lizzy; "did you suspect it was so late?"

"Seven o'clock, by Jove!" cried Beecher, as he gave her his hand to cross the stepping-stones. "What a fuss he 'll make about our keeping the dinner back!"

"I have eaten all the caviare and the pickles, and nearly finished a bottle of Madeira, waiting for you," said Grog; "so, no dressing, but come in at once."

"Oh, dearest Lizzy!" cried Beecher, as they gained the porch, "just one word,—only one word,—to make me the happiest fellow in the world or the most miserable." But Lizzy sprang up the stairs, and was in her room almost ere his words were uttered.

"If I had bad but another moment," muttered Beecher to himself, "just one moment more, I'd have shown her that I meant to turn over a new leaf,—that I was n't going to lead the life I have done. I 'd have told her—though, I suppose, old Grog would murder me if he knew it—of our grand martingale, and how we mean to smash the bank at Baden. No deception about that,—no 'cross' there. She can't bring up grooms and jockeys and stable-helpers against me now. It will all be done amongst ourselves,—a family party, and no mistake!"

All things considered, Annesley Beecher, it was just as well for you that you had not that "one moment" you wished for.

CHAPTER XXIV
A DEAD HEAT

Some eight or ten days have elapsed since the scene we have Just recorded,—not one of whose incidents are we about to relate,—and we are still at Holbach. As happens so frequently in the working of a mathematical question, proofs are assumed without going over the demonstrations; so, in real life,—certain postulates being granted,—we arrive at conclusions which we regard as inevitable.

We are at Holbach, but no longer strolling along its leaf-strewn alleys, or watching the laughing eddies of its circling river,—we are within doors. The scene is a small, most comfortably furnished chamber of the little inn, where an ample supper is laid out on a sideboard, a card-table occupying the centre of the room, at which two players are seated, their somewhat "charged" expressions and disordered dress indicating a prolonged combat,—a fact in part corroborated by the streak of pinkish dawn that has pierced between the shutters, and now blends with the sickly glare of the candles. Several packs of cards litter the floor around them, thrown there in that superstitious passion only gamblers understand, and a decanter and some glasses stand on the table beside the players, who are no others than our acquaintances Grog Davis and Paul Classon.

There is a vulgar but not unwise adage that tells us "dogs do not eat dogs," and the maxim has a peculiar application to gamblers. All sorts and manners of men love to measure their strength with each other,— swordsmen, swimmers, pedestrians, even hard drinking used to have its duels of rivalry,—gamblers never. Such an employment of their skill would seem to their eyes about as absurd as that of a sportsman who would turn his barrel against his companion instead of the cock-pheasant before him. Their "game" is of another order. How, then, explain the curious fact we have mentioned? There are rivalries that last life-long; there are duels that go on from year to year of existence, and even to the last leave the question of superiority undetermined. The game of piquet formed such between these two men. At every chance meeting in life,—no matter how long the interval or how brief the passage might be,—they recurred to the old-vexed question, which fortune seemed to find a pleasure in never deciding definitively. The fact that each had his own separate theory of the game, would have given an interest to the encounter; but besides there was now another circumstance whose import neither were likely to undervalue. Davis had just paid over to Paul Classon the sum of two hundred napoleons,—the price of a secret service he was about to perform,—and the sight of that glowing heap of fresh gold—for there it lay on the corner of the table—had so stimulated the acquisitiveness of Grog's nature that he could not resist the temptation to try and regain them. The certainty that when he should have won them it would only be to restore them to the loser, for whose expenses on a long Journey they were destined, detracted nothing from this desire on his part A more unprofitable debtor than Holy Paul could not be imagined. His very name in a schedule would reflect discredit on the bankruptcy! But there lay the shining pieces, fresh from the mint and glittering, and the appeal they made was to an instinct, not to reason. Was it with the knowledge of this fact that Paul had left them there instead of putting them up in his pocket? Had he calculated in his own subtle brain that temptations are least resistible when they are most tangible? There was that in his reverence's look which seemed to say as much, and the thoughtless wantonness of his action as his fingers fiddled with the gold may not have been entirely without a purpose. They had talked together, and discussed some knotty matters of business, having concluded which, Davis proposed cards.

"Our old combat, I suppose?" said Paul, laughing. "Well, I 'm always ready."

And down they sat, hour after hour finding them still in the same hard straggle, fortune swinging with its pendulous stroke from side to side, as though to elicit the workings of hope and fear in each alternately. Meanwhile they drank freely, and from time to time arose to eat at the side-table in that hurried and greedy way that only gamblers eat, as though vexed at the hanger that called them from their game. They were both too great proficients in play to require that absorption of faculties inferior gamblers need. They could, and did, talk of everything that came uppermost, the terms of the game dropping through the conversation like the measured booming of great guns amid the clattering crash of musketry. Luck for some time had favored Holy Paul; and while he became blander, softer, and more benign of look, Grog grew fierce, his eyes fiery, and his words sharp and abrupt. Classon's polished courtesy chafed and irritated him, but he seemed determined to control his anger as far as he might, and not give his adversary the transient advantage of temper. Had spectators been admitted to the lists, the backers would have most probably taken the Churchman.

His calm countenance, his mild, unexcited eye, his voice so composed and gentle, must have made Paul the favorite.

"We shall scarcely have time for another game, Kit,"—he'd have called him Grog, but that he was losing,—"I perceive the day is beginning to break."

"So am I, for the matter of that," said Davis, with a bitter laugh. "You have won—let me see—forty-six, and twenty-seven, and a hundred and twelve,—that was a 'thumper,'—and thirty-four, besides that loose cash there,—about two hundred and forty or fifty naps, Master Paul. A very pretty-night's work, and more profitable than preaching, I take it."

"Regarding the matter as a mere monetary question—"

"No gammon,—cut the cards," broke in Davis; "one game must finish us. Now, shall we say double or quits?"

"If you really wish me to speak my candid mind, I'd rather not."

"I thought as much," muttered Grog to himself; and then, in a louder voice, "What shall it be then.—one-hundred and fifty? Come, even if you should lose, you'll get up winner of a clean hundred."

"Would that it were at the expense of some one I love less!"

"Answer my question," said Davis, angrily. "Will you have a hundred and fifty on the last game,—yes or no?"

"Yes, of course, Kit, if you desire it."

"Cut again; there is a faced card," said Davis. And now he dealt with a slow deliberation that showed what an effort his forced composure was costing him.

Classon sat back in his chair watching the cards as they fell from the dealer's hand, but affecting in his half-closed eyes and folded arms the air of one deep in his own musings.

"I will say this, Davis," said he, at last, with the slow utterance that announces a well-matured thought, "you have managed the whole of this business with consummate skill; you have done it admirably."

"I believe I have," said Davis, with a sort of stern decision in his tone; "and there was more difficulty in the case than you are aware of."

"There must have been very considerable difficulty," rejoined Paul, slowly. "Even in the very little I have seen of him I can detect a man whose temperament must have presented the greatest embarrassments. He is proud, very proud, suspectful to any extent. I have five cards—forty-seven."

"Not good."

"Three queens."

"Four tens."

"So, then, my tierce in spades is not good, of course. I play one."

"Fifteen and five, twenty, and the tens ninety-four. The first honor I have scored this hour. The difficulty I allude to was with my daughter; she would n't have him."

"Not have him?—not accept a peer of the realm?"

"Who told her he was a peer? She only knows him as the Honorable Annesley Beecher."

"Even so. As the Honorable Annesley Beecher, he is a man of high connections,—related to some of the first people. A dub—play a club. I take it that such a man is a very high mark indeed."

"*She* wasn't of your mind, that's clear," said Davis, abruptly; "nor do I believe it would have signified in the least to have told her that he *was* a Lord."

"Romantic!" muttered Paul.

"No, not a bit."

"Loved another, perhaps."

"How should she? She never saw any other except a one-eyed Pole, that taught her music at that Belgian school, and a sort of hairy dwarf, that gave lessons in drawing! A hundred and seventeen. It's your deal."

"And he himself has no suspicion of his brother's death?" said Classon, as he gave out the cards.

"Not the slightest. He was trying to write a letter to him, to break the news of his marriage, only yesterday."

"Cleverly done,—most cleverly done," said Paul, in ecstasy. "If he had come to the knowledge, he might very possibly have refused *her*."

"I rather—suspect—not," said Grog, dwelling slowly on each word, while his countenance assumed an expression of fierce and terrible determination. "A lucky take in, that,—the queen of diamonds: it gives me seven cards. Refuse her! by Heaven, he'd have had a short experience of his peerage! Kings and knaves—six, and seven I play—twenty-three. Piqued again, Holy Paul! No, no; he'd never have dared that."

Classon shook his head doubtingly.

"You might just as well tell me, Paul Classon, that you 'd refuse to marry them," said Davis, as he struck the table with his clenched fist, "and that I would bear it! I have a way of not being denied what I have determined on; that has done me good service in life. That blear-eyed boy—the Attaché at the Legation in Frankfort—wanted to refuse me a passport for the Honorable Annesley Beecher and Mrs. Beecher, saying that, until the marriage, there was no such person. But I whispered a word to him across the table, and he gave it, and there it is now."

"Going to Italy!" said Classon, as he read from the document which Grog had thrown down before him; "wonderful fellow,—wonderful fellow,—forgets nothing!" muttered he to himself.

"Yes, but he does, though; he has just forgotten four kings and suffered *you* to count four queens, Master Paul,—a tribute to your agreeability somewhat too costly."

"Even to the travelling-carriage, Kit," resumed Classon, not heeding the sarcasm; "and a more complete thing I never saw in my life. You picked it up at Frankfort."

"Yes, at the Hôtel de Russie; got it for two thousand two hundred francs,—it cost ten, six months ago. A quint in spades, and the cards divided; I score thirty-one."

"And when is he to learn that he has succeeded to the title?"

"When he's across the Alps,—when he is out of the land of rouge et noir and roulette; he may know it then, as soon as he pleases. I 'm to join them at Como, or Milan, as I can't well 'show' at Baden, even at this late time of year. Before I come up he 'll have heard all about Lacking-ton's death."

"Will it ever occur to him, Kit, to suspect that you were aware of it?"

"I don't know; perhaps it may," said Grog, doggedly.

"If so, will the impression not lead to a very precarious state of relations between you?"

"Maybe so,—seven hearts and five spades, you are 'capoted.' There, Paul, that doesn't leave so much between us, after all. What if he does suspect it? The world suspects fifty things about me that no man has ever yet dared to lay to my charge. If you and I, Master Paul, were to fret ourselves about the suspicions that are entertained of us, we'd have a pleasant life of it. Your good health."

"To yours, my dear Kit; and may I never drink it in worse tipple would be the only additional pleasure I could suggest to the toast. It is wonderful Madeira!"

"I have had it in the London Docks since the year '81; every bottle of it now, seeing that the vines are ruined in the island, is worth from thirty shillings to five-and-thirty. I won it from Tom Hardiman; he took the invoice out of his pocket-book and flung it across the table to me. 'Grog,' says he, 'when you take it out of bond, mind you ask me to dinner, and give me a bottle of it?' But he's gone, 'toes up,' and so here's to his memory."

"'Drunk in solemn silence,' as the newspapers say," broke in Paul, as he drained his glass.

"Yes," said Davis, eying the wine by the light, "that's a tipple this little inn here is not much accustomed to see under its roof; but if I were to stay a little longer, I'd make something of this place. They never heard of Harvey's sauce, Chili vinegar, Caviare, Stilton; even Bass and British gin were novelties when I came. There, as well as I can make it up, you are a winner of fifteen naps; there they are."

"Dear me, I fancied I stood safe to come off with a hundred!" said Paul, lugubriously.

"So you did, without counting the points; but you've lost five hundred and sixty-four,—ay, and a right good thing you've made of it, Master Paul. I'd like to know how long it is since you earned such a sum honestly."

Classon sighed heavily as he swept the cash into his pocket, and said, "I'm unable to tell you; my memory grows worse every day."

"When you go back to England, you can always brush it up by the Police sheet,—that's a comfort," said Davis, with a savage laugh.

"And what will the noble Viscount have to spend yearly?" asked Classon, to change the theme.

"Something between eight and ten thousand."

"A snug thing, Kit,—a very snug thing indeed; and I take it that by this time o' day he knows the world pretty well."

"No; nothing of the kind!" said Grog, bluntly; "he's a fool, and must stay a fool!"

"The more luck his, then, to have Christopher Davis for his father-in-law."

"I'll tell you what's better still, Holy Paul,—to have Lizzy Davis for his wife. *You* think she's going to make a great match of it because he's the Lord Viscount and she is *my* daughter; but *I* tell you, and I'm ready to maintain it too, I never met the man yet was worthy of her. There may be girls as handsome, though I never saw them,—there may be others as clever, that

I'm no judge of; but this I do know,—that for pluck, real pluck, you 'll not find her equal in Europe. She'd never have married him for his rank; no, if it was a dukedom he had to offer her. She 'd never have taken him for his fortune, if it had been ten times the amount. No, she would n't consent to it, even to take *me* out of my difficulties and set me all straight with the world, because she fancied that by going on the stage, or some such trumpery, she could have done that just as well. She'd not have had him for himself, for she knows he's a fool, just as well as I do. There was only one thing I found she could n't get over: it was the thought she *dare* not marry him; that to thrust herself into the station and rank *he* occupied would be to expose herself to insults that must crush her. It was by a mere chance I discovered that this was a challenge she 'd have rather died than decline. It was for all the world like saying to myself, 'Don't you go into the ring there, Kit Davis; my Lords and the gentlemen don't like it.' 'Don't they? Well, let's see how they'll take it, for I *am* a-going!' It was *that* stung her, Paul Classon. *She* did n't want all those fine people; *she* did n't care a brass farthing about their ways and their doings! *She* 'd not have thought it a hard lot in life just to jog on as she is. She did n't want to be called a countess, nor live like one; but when it was hinted to her, that if she *did* venture amongst them, it would be to be driven back with shame and insult, then her mind was made up at once. Not that she ever confessed as much to me; no, I found out her secret by watching her closely. The day I told her I forget what anecdote about some outrageous piece of insolence played off on some new intruder into the titled class, she suddenly started as if something had stung her, and her eyes glared like a tiger's; then, catching me by the hand, she said, 'Don't tell me these things; they pain me more to hear than real, downright calamities!' That was enough for *me*. I saw her cards, Paul, and I played through them!"

Classon heaved a deep sigh, and was silent.

"What are you sighing over, Paul?" asked Davis, half morosely.

"I was just sorrowing to myself to think how little all her pluck will avail her."

"Stuff and nonsense, sir! It is the very thing to depend on in the struggle."

"Ay, if there were a struggle, Kit, but that is exactly what there will not be. You, for instance, go into Brookes's to-morrow, you have been duly elected. It was a wet day, only a few at the ballot, and somehow you got in. Well, you are, to all intents, as much a member as his Grace there, or the noble Marquis. There's no commotion, no stir when you enter the room. The men at their newspapers look up, perhaps, but they read away immediately with only increased attention; the group at the window talks on too; the only thing noticeable is that nobody talks to *you*. If you ask for the 'Globe' or the 'Chronicle,' when the reader shall have finished, he politely hands it at once, and goes away."

"If he did, I'd follow him —"

"What for? — to ask an explanation where there had been no offence? To make yourself at once notorious in the worst of all possible ways? There's nothing so universally detested as the man that makes a 'row;' witness the horror all well-bred people feel at associating with Americans, they're never sure how it's to end. Now, if all these considerations have their weight with men, imagine how they mast be regarded by women, fifty times more exacting as they are in all the exigencies of station, and whose freemasonry is a hundred times more exclusive."

"That's all rot!" broke in Davis, his passion the more violent as the arguments of the other seemed so difficult to answer. "You think to puzzle *me* by talking of all these grand people and their ways as if they weren't all men and women. That they are, and a rum lot, too, some of them! Come," cried Davis, suddenly, as though a happy thought had just flashed across his mind, "it was the turn of a straw one day, by your own account, that you were not a bishop. Now, I 'd like to know, if that lucky event had really taken place, wouldn't you have been the same Holy Paul Classon that sits there?"

"Perhaps not, entirely," said Classon, in his oiliest of voices. "I trust that I should, in ascending to that exalted station, have cast off the slough of an inferior existence, and carried up little of my former self except the friendships of my early years."

"Do you fancy, Master Paul, that gammon like this can impose upon a man of my sort?"

"My dear and worthy friend," rejoined Classon, "the tone in which I appeal to you is my tribute to your high ability. To an inferior man I had spoken very different language. Sentiments are not the less real that they are expressed with a certain embroidery, just as a Bank post-bill would be very good value though a Choctaw Indian might deem it a piece of waste-paper."

"I 'd like to see you try it on with Lizzy in this fashion," said Davis. "I don't think even your friend the Choctaw Indian would save you."

"I should be proud of even defeat at such hands!" exclaimed Paul, rapturously.

"You 'd have little to be proud of when she 'd have done with you," cried Grog, all his good-humor restored by the mere thought of his daughter.

"Have you spoken to his Lordship about what I mentioned?" said Paul, half diffidently.

"No," said Grog; "on reflection, I thought it better not. I 'm sure, besides, that there's no Church preferment in his gift; and then, Classon, he knows you, as who does not?"

"'Quæ regio terræ non plena est?' Ay, Grog, you and I have arrived at what the world calls Fame."

"Speak for yourself, sir; I acknowledge no partnership in the case. When I have written letters, they have not been begging ones; and when I have stretched out my hand, there was no pistol in the palm of it!"

"Very true, Kit; *I* never had a soul above petty larceny, and *you* had a spirit that aspired to transportation for life."

Davis bounded on his chair, and glowered with a fearful stare at the speaker, who meanwhile drained the decanter into his glass with an unmoved serenity.

"Don't be angry, my ancient friend," said he, blandly. "The cares of friendship, like the skill of a surgeon, must often pain to be serviceable. Happy let us call ourselves when no ruder hand wields the probe or the bistoury!"

"Make an end of canting, I want to speak to you about matters of moment. You will set out to-day, I hope."

"Immediately after the marriage."

"What road do you take?"

"Strasburg, Paris, Marseilles, whence direct to Constantinople by the first steamer."

"After that?"

"Across the Black Sea to Balaklava."

"But when do you reach the Crimea?"

"Balaklava is *in* the Crimea."

Davis flushed scarlet. The reflection on his geography wounded him, and he winced under it.

"Are you quite clear that you understand my instructions?" said he, testily.

"I wish I was as sure of a deanery," said Paul, smacking his lips over the last glass.

"You can scarcely wish over-well to the Church, when you desire to be one of its dignitaries," said Davis, with a sarcastic grin.

"Why so, my worthy friend? There is a wise Scotch adage says, 'It taks a' kind of folk to mak a warld;' and so, various orders of men, with gifts widely differing, if not discrepant, are advantageously assembled into what we call corporations."

"Nonsense,—bosh!" said Grog, impatiently. "If you have no better command of common-sense where you are going, I have made a precious bad choice of an agent."

"See how men misconstrue their own natures!" exclaimed Classon, with a sort of fervor. "If any one had asked me what gift I laid especial claim to possess, I protest I should have said 'common-sense;' a little more common-sense than any one else I ever met."

"You are modest too."

"Becomingly so, I hope and believe."

"Have you any other remarkable traits that you might desire to record?"

"A few, and a very few," said Paul, with a well-assumed air of humility. "Nature has blessed me with the very best of tempers. I am never rash, hasty, or impetuous; I accept the rubs of life with submission; I think well of every one."

"Do you, faith!" exclaimed Davis, with a scornful laugh.

"Knowing well that we are all slaves of circumstances, I take motives where others demand actions, just as I would take a bill at three months from him who has no cash. It may be paid, or it may not."

"You'd have passed it ere it became due, eh, Master Paul?"

"Such is possible; I make no claims above human frailty."

"Is sobriety amongst your other virtues?"

"I rarely transgress its limits, save when alone. It is in the solitary retirement where I seek reflection that I occasionally indulge. There I am, so to say, 'Classo cum Classone.' I offer no example to others,—I shock no outward decorum. If the instinctive appreciation of my character—which I highly possess—passes that of most men, I owe it to those undisguised moments when I stand revealed to myself. Wine keeps no secrets; and Paul Classon drunk appeals to Paul Classon sober. Believe me, Kit, when I tell you no man knows half the excellent things in his own heart till he has got tipsy by himself!"

"I wish I had never thought of you for this affair," said Davis, angrily.

"Pitt made the same speech to Wolfe, and yet that young general afterwards took Quebec."

"What do I care about Wolfe or Quebec? I want a particular service that a man of moderate brains and a firm purpose can accomplish."

"And for which Paul Classon pledges himself with his head? Ay, Grog Davis, that is my bond."

"The day you come back to me with proof of success, I hand you five hundred pounds."

"Cash?"

"Cash,—and more, if all be done to our entire satisfaction. *He*—" here he jerked up his thumb towards Beecher's room—"*he* sha'n't forget you."

Paul closed his eyes, and muttered something to himself, ending with, "And 'five pounds for the Cruelty to Animals,—from the Reverend Paul Classon.' I shall be in funds for them all."

"Ah, Kit!" said he at last, with a deep-drawn sigh, "what slaves are we all, and to the meanest accidents too,—the veriest trifles of our existence. Ask yourself, I beseech you, what is it that continually opposes your progress in life,—what is your rock ahead? Your name! nothing but your name!—call yourself Jones, Wilkins, Simpson, Watkins, and see what an expansion it will give your naturally fine faculties. Nobody will dare to assert that you or I are the same men we were five-and-twenty or thirty years ago, and yet *you* must be Davis and *I* must be Classon, whether we will or not. I call this hard,—very hard indeed!"

"Would it be any benefit to me if I could call myself Paul Classon?" said Grog, with an insolent grin.

"It is not for the saintly man who bears that name to speak boastfully of its responsibilities—"

"In bills of exchange, I O U's, promissory notes, and so forth," laughed in Grog.

"I have, I own, done a little in these ways; but what gifted man ever lived who has not at some time or other committed his sorrows to paper. The misfortune in my case was that it was stamped."

"Do you know, Holy Paul, I think you are the greatest 'hemp' I ever met."

"No, Kit, don't say so,—don't, my dear and valued friend; these words give me deep pain."

"I do say it, and I maintain it!"

"What good Company you must have kept through life, then!"

"The worst of any man in England. And yet," resumed he, after a pause, "I 'm positively ashamed to think that my daughter should be married by the Reverend Paul Classon."

"A prejudice, my dear and respected friend,—a prejudice quite beneath your enlarged and gifted understanding! Will it much signify to you if he, who one of these days shall say, 'The sentence of this court, Christopher Davis, is transportation beyond the seas,' be a Justice of the Common Pleas or a Baron of the Exchequer? No, no, Kit; it is only your vain, conceited people who fancy that they are not hanged if it was n't Calcraft tied the noose!"

More than once did Davis change color at this speech, whose illustrations were selected with special intention and malice.

"Here 's daybreak already!" cried Grog, throwing open the window, and admitting the pinkish light of an early dawn, and the fresh sharp air of morning.

"It's chilly enough too," said Classon, shivering, as he emptied the gin into his glass.

"I think you 've had enough already," said Grog, rudely, as he flung both tumbler and its contents out of the window. "Go, have a wash, and make yourself a little decent-looking; one would imagine, to see you, you had passed your night in the 'lock-up'!"

"When you see me next, you 'll fancy I 'm an archdeacon." So saying, and guiding himself by the chairs, Paul Classon left the room.

With a quiet step, and firm, neither "overtaken" by liquor nor fatigued by the night's debauch, Davis hastened to his chamber. So long as he was occupied with the cares of dressing, his features betrayed no unusual anxiety; he did, indeed, endeavor to attire himself with more than ordinary care; and one cravat after another did he fling on the floor, where a number of embroidered vests were already lying. At length the toilet was completed, and Grog surveyed himself in the large glass, and was satisfied. He knew he didn't look like Annesley Beecher and that "lot," still less did he resemble the old "swells" of Brookes's and the Carlton; but he thought there was something military, something sporting,—a dash of the "nag," with "Newmarket,"—about him, that might pass muster anywhere! "At all events, Lizzy won't be ashamed of me," muttered he to himself. "Poor, poor Lizzy!" added he, in a broken tone; and he sank down into a chair, and leaned his head on the table.

A gentle tap came to the door. "Come in," said he, without raising his head; and she entered.

As the rich robe of silk rustled across the floor, he never raised his head; nor even when, bending over, she threw an arm around his neck and kissed his forehead, did he stir or move.

"I want you to look at me, dearest papa," said she, softly.

"My poor Lizzy,—my own dear Lizzy!" murmured he, half indistinctly; then, starting suddenly up, he cried aloud, "Good heavens! is it worth all this—"

"No, indeed, papa," burst she in; "it is *not*—it is *not* worth it!"

"What do you mean?" asked he, abruptly. "What were you thinking of?"

"It was *your* thoughts I was following out," said she, drearily.

"How handsome,—how beautiful you are, girl!" exclaimed he, as, holding both her hands, he surveyed her at full length. "Is this Brussels lace?"

She nodded assent

"And what do you call these buttons?"

"They are opals."

"How it all becomes you, girl! I'd never like to see you less smartly dressed! And now.—and now I am to lose you!" And he fell upon her neck, and clasped her fondly to his heart.

"Oh, my dear father, if you knew—" She could not continue.

"And don't I know!" broke he in. "Do you think that all my hard, bad experience of life has left me so bereft of feeling! But I 'll tell you another thing I know, Lizzy," said he, in a deep, calm voice; "that what we fancy must break our hearts to do we can bear, and bear patiently, and, what's more, so learn to conform to, that after a few years of life we wonder that we ever thought them hardships!"

"We do not change so much without heavy suffering!" said she, sorrowfully.

"That is possible too," said he, sighing. Then, suddenly rallying, he said, "You'll write to me often, very often, Lizzy; I 'll want to hear how you get on with these great folk; not that I fear anything, only this, girl, that their jealousy will stimulate their rancor. You are so handsome, girl! so handsome!"

"I 'm glad of it," said she, with an air of proud exultation.

"Who's there?" cried Davis, impatiently, as a sharp knock came to the door. It was the Reverend Paul come to borrow a white neckcloth, none of his own being sufficiently imposing for such an occasion.

"I am scarcely presentable, Miss Davis. I am sure I address Miss Davis," said he, pushing into the room, and bowing ceremoniously at each step. "There can be but only one so eminently beautiful!"

"There, take what you want, and be off!" cried Davis, rudely.

"Your father usurps all the privileges of long friendship, and emboldens me to claim some, too, my dear young lady. Let me kiss the fairest hand in Christendom." And with a reverential homage all his own, Paul bent down and touched her hand with his lips.

"This is the Reverend Paul Classon, Lizzy," said Davis,—"a great dignitary of the Church, and an old schoolfellow of mine."

"I am always happy to know a friend of my father's," said she, smiling gracefully. "You have only just arrived?"

"This moment!" said he, with a glance towards Grog.

"There, away with you, and finish your dressing," broke in Davis, angrily; "I see it is nigh seven o'clock."

"Past seven, rather; and the company assembled below stairs, and Mr. Beecher—for I presume it must be he—pacing the little terrace in all the impatience of a bride-groom. Miss Davis, your servant." And with a bow of deep reverence Paul retired.

"There were so many things running in my mind to say to you, Lizzy," said Davis, "when that Classon came in." It was very hard for him not to add an epithet; but he *did* escape that peril.

"I own, papa, he did not impress me very favorably."

"He's a first-rate man, a great scholar, a regular don amongst the shovel-hats," said Grog, hastily; "that man was within an ace of being a bishop. But it was not of *him* my head was full, girl. I wanted to talk to you about Beecher and that haughty sister-in-law of his. *She* 'll 'try-it on' with you, Lizzy; I 'm sure she will!"

"Dearest papa, how often have you told me that in preparing for the accidents of life we but often exaggerate their importance. I'll not anticipate evil."

"Here's Beecher!—here he is!" cried Davis, as he clasped her once more to his heart; and then, opening the door, led her down the stairs.

There was a full assemblage of all the folk of the little inn, and the room was crowded. The landlord and his wife, and four buxom daughters and two sons, were there; and a dapper waiter, with very tight-fitting trousers, and a housemaid, and three farm-servants, all with big bouquets in their hands and huge bows of white ribbon on their breasts; and Mademoiselle Annette, Lizzy's maid, in a lilac, silk and a white crape bonnet; and Peters, Beecher's man, in a most accurate blue frock, except his master, looking far more like a gentleman than any one there.

As for Annesley Beecher, no man ever more accurately understood how to "costume" for every circumstance in life; and whether you saw him lounging over the rail in Rotten Row, strolling through the Park at Richmond, sunning himself at Cowes, or yawning through a wet day in a country-house, his "get-up" was sure to be faultless. Hundreds tried in vain to catch the inimitable curl of his hat, the unattainable sweep of his waistcoat-collar; and then there were shades and tones of his color about him that were especially his own. Of course, I am not about to describe his appearance on this morning; it is enough if I say that he bestowed every care upon it, and succeeded. And Paul,—Holy Paul,—how blandly imposing, how unctuously serene he looked! Marriage was truly a benediction at such hands. He faltered a little, his dulcet accents trembled with a modest reluctance, as he asked, "'Wilt thou take—this woman—'" Could he have changed the Liturgy for the occasion, he had said, "this angel;" as it was, his voice compensated for the syllables, and the question was breathed out like air from the Garden of Eden.

And so they were married; and there was a grand breakfast, where all the household were assembled, and where Paul Classon made a most effective little speech to "the health of the bride," interpolating his English and German with a tact all his own; and then they drove away with four posters, with all the noise and whip-cracking, the sighs and smiles and last good-byes, just as if the scene had been Hanover Square, and the High Priest a Canon of Westminster!

CHAPTER XXV
STUNNING TIDINGS

A telegram, duly despatched, had prepared the hotel of the Cour de Bade for the arrival of the Honorable Annesley and Mrs. Beecher; and when the well-appointed travelling-carriage came clattering into the *porte-cochère* at nightfall, there was a dress parade of landlord and waiters ready to receive them.

It was a very long time since Beecher had felt the self-importance of being deemed rich. For many a year back life had been but a series of struggles, and it was a very delightful sensation to him to witness once more all the ready homage, all the obsequious attention which are only rendered to affluence. Herr Bauer had got the despatch just in time to keep his handsomest suite of rooms for him; indeed, he had "sent away the Margraf of Schweinerhausen, who wanted them." This was gratifying; and, limited as Beecher's German was, he could catch the muttered exclamations of "Ach Grott, wie schön!" "Wie leiblich!" as his beautiful wife passed up the stairs; and this, too, pleased him. In fact, his was just then the glorious mood that comes once in a lifetime to the luckiest of us,—to be charmed with everything.

To enjoy the sunshine one must have sojourned in shadow; and, certainly, prosperity is never so entrancing as after some experience of its opposite, and Beecher was never wearied of admiring the splendor of the apartment, the wonderful promptitude of the waiters, and the excellence of everything. It must be owned the dinner was in Bauer's best style,— the bisque, the raebraten, the pheasant, all that could be wished for; and when the imposing host himself uncorked a precious flask of a "Cabinet Steinberger," Beecher felt it was a very charming world when one had only got to the sunny side of it. Mr. Bauer—a politeness rarely accorded, save to the highest rank—directed the service in person, and vouchsafed to be agreeable during the repast.

"And so your season was a good one, Bauer?" said Beecher.

"Reasonably so, your Excellency. We had the King of Wurtemberg, the Queen of Greece, a couple of archdukes, and a crown prince of something far north,—second rate ones all, but good people, and easily satisfied."

Beecher gave a significant glance towards Lizzy, and went on: "And who were your English visitors?"

"The old set, your Excellency: the Duke of Middleton, Lord Headlam and his four daughters, Sir Hipsley Keyling, to break the bank, as usual—"

"And did he?"

"No, Excellency; it broke *him*."

"Poor devil! it ain't so easy to get to windward of those fellows, Bauer; they are too many for us, eh?" said Beecher, chuckling with the consciousness that *he* had the key to that mysterious secret.

"Well, Excellency, there's nobody ever does it but one, so long as I have known Baden."

"And who is he, pray?"

"Mr. Twining,—Adderley Twining, sir; that's the man can just win what and when and how he pleases."

"Don't tell *me* that, Bauer; *he* has n't got the secret. If Twining wins, it 's chance,—mere chance, just as you might win."

"It may be so, your Excellency."

"I tell you, Bauer,—I know it as a *fact*,—there's just one man in Europe has the martingale, and here's to his health."

Mr. Bauer was too well skilled in his calling not to guess in whose honor the glass was drained, and smiled a gracious recognition of the toast.

"And your pretty people, Herr Bauer," broke in Lizzy,—"who were your great beauties this season?"

"We had nothing remarkable, Madame," said he, bowing.

"No, Master Bauer," broke in Beecher; "for the luck and the good looks I suspect you should have gone somewhere else this summer."

Bauer bowed his very deepest acknowledgment. Too conscious of what became him in his station to hazard a flattery in words, he was yet courtier enough to convey his admiration by a look of most meaning deference.

"I conclude that the season is nigh over," said Lizzy, half languidly, as she looked out on the moonlit promenade, where a few loungers were lingering.

"Yes, Madame; another week will close the rooms. All are hastening away to their winter quarters,—Rome, Paris, or Vienna."

"How strange it is, all this life of change!" said Lizzy, thoughtfully.

"It is not what it seems," said Beecher; "for the same people are always meeting again and again, now in Italy, now in England. Ah! I see the Cursaal is being lighted up. How jolly it looks through the trees! Look yonder, Lizzy, where all the lamps are glittering. Many a sad night it cost me, gay as it appears."

Mr. Bauer withdrew as the dessert was placed on the table, and they were alone.

"Rich fellow that Bauer," said Beecher; "he lends more money than any Jew in Frankfort. I wonder whether I could n't tempt him to advance me a few hundreds?"

"Do you want money, then?" asked she, unsuspectingly.

"Want it? No, not exactly, except that every one wants it; people always find a way to spend all they can lay their hands on."

"I don't call that wanting it," said she, half coldly.

"Play me something, Lizzy, here's a piano; that Sicilian song, — and sing it." He held out his hand to lead her to the piano, but she only drew her shawl more closely around her, and never moved. "Or, if you like better, that Styrian dance," continued he.

"I am not in the humor," said she, calmly.

"Not in the humor? Well, be in the humor. I was never in better spirits in my life. I would n't change with Davis when he won the Czarewitch. Such a dinner as old Bauer gave us, and such wine! and then this coffee, not to speak of the company, — eh, Lizzy?"

"Yes, Mr. Bauer was most agreeable."

"I was n't talking of Mr. Bauer, *ma chère*, I was thinking of some one else."

"I did n't know," said she, with a half-weary sigh.

Beecher's cheek flushed up, and he walked to the window and looked out; meanwhile she took up a book and began to read. Along the alley beneath the window troops of people now passed towards the rooms. The hour of play had sounded, and the swell of the band could be heard from the space in front of the Cursaal. As his eyes followed the various groups ascending the steps and disappearing within the building, his imagination pictured the scene inside.

There was always a kind of rush to the tables on the last few nights of the season. It was a sort of gamblers' theory that they were "lucky," and Beecher began to con over to himself all the fortunate fellows who had broken the bank in the last week of a season. "I told old Grog I 'd not go," muttered he; "I pledged myself I'd not enter the rooms; but, of course, that meant I 'd not play,—it never contemplated mere looking in and seeing who was there: rather too hard if I were not to amuse myself, particularly when"—here he turned a glance towards Lizzy—"I don't perceive any very great desire to make the evening pass pleasantly here. Ain't you going to sing?" asked he, half angrily.

"If you wish it," said she, coldly.

"Nor play?" continued he, as though not hearing her reply.

"If you desire it," said she, rising, and taking her place at the piano.

He muttered something, and she began. Her fingers at first strayed in half-careless chords over the instrument; and then, imperceptibly, struck out into a wild, plaintive melody of singular feeling and pathos,—one of those Hungarian airs which, more than any other national music, seem to dispense with words for their expression.

Beecher listened for a few moments, and then, muttering indignantly below his breath, he left the room, banging the door as he went out. Lizzy did not seem to have noticed his departure, but played on, air succeeding air, of the same character and sentiment; but at last she leaned her head upon the instrument and fell into a deep revery. The pale moonlight, as it lay upon the polished floor, was not more motionless. Beecher, meanwhile, had issued forth into the street, crossed the little rustic bridge, and held his way towards the Cursaal. His humor was not an enviable nor an amiable one. It was such a mood as makes a courageous man very dangerous company, but fills an individual of the Beecher type with all that can be imagined of suspicion and distrust. Every thought that crossed his mind was a doubt of somebody or something. He had been duped, cheated, "done," he did n't exactly know when, how, or by whom, with what object, or to what extent. But the fact was so. He entered the rooms and walked towards the play-table. There were many of the old faces he remembered to have seen years ago. He exchanged bows and recognitions with several foreigners whose names he had forgotten, and acknowledged suitably the polite obeisance of the croupiers, as they rose to salute him. It was an interesting moment as he entered, and the whole table were intently watching the game of one player, whose single Louis d'or had gone on doubling with each deal, till it had swelled into a sum that formed the limit of the bank. Even the croupiers, models as they are of impassive serenity, showed a touch of human sentiment as the deal began, and seemed to feel that they were in presence of one who stood higher in Fortune's favor than themselves.

"Won again!" cried out a number of voices; "the thirteenth pass! Who ever saw the like? It is fabulous, monstrous!" Amid the din of incessant commentaries, few of them uttered in the tone of felicitation, a very tall man stretched his arm towards the table, and began to gather in the gold, saying, in a pleasant but hurried voice: "A thousand pardons. I hope you 'll excuse me; would n't inconvenience you for worlds. I think you said"—this was to the banker—"I think you said thirty-eight thousand francs in all; thank you, extremely obliged; a very great run of luck, indeed,—never saw the like before. Would you kindly exchange that note, it is a Frankfort one; quite distressed to give you the trouble; infinitely grateful;" and, bashfully sweeping the glittering coins into his hat, as if ashamed to have interrupted the game, he retired to a side table to count over his winnings. He had just completed a little avenue of gold columns, muttering to himself little congratulations, interspersed with "What fun!" when Beecher, stepping up, accosted him. "The old story, Twining! I never heard nor read of a fellow with such luck as yours!"

"Oh, very good luck, capital luck!" cried Twining, rubbing his lean hands, and then slapping them against his leaner legs. "As your Lordship observes, I do occasionally win; not always, not always, but occasionally. Charmed to see you here,—delighted,—what fun! Late,—somewhat late in the season,—but still lovely weather. Your Lordship only just arrived, I suppose?"

"I see you don't remember me, Twining," said Beecher, smiling, and rather amused to mark how completely his good fortune had absorbed his attention.

"Impossible, my Lord-!—never forget a face,—never!"

"Pardon me if I must correct you this once; but it is quite clear you *have* forgotten me. Come, for whom do you take me?"

"Take you, my Lord,—take you? Quite shocked if I could make a blunder; but really, I feel certain I am speaking with Lord Lackington."

"There, I knew it!" cried Beecher, laughing out "I knew it, though, by Jove! I was not quite prepared to hear that I looked so old. You know he's about eighteen years my senior."

"So he was, my Lord,—so he was," said Twining, gathering up his gold. "And for a moment, I own, I was disposed to distrust my eyes, not seeing your Lordship in mourning."

"In mourning? and for whom?"

"For the late Viscount, your Lordship's brother!"

"Lackington! Is Lackington dead?"

"Why, it's not possible your Lordship hasn't heard it? It cannot be that your letters have not brought you the tidings? It happened six—ay, seven weeks ago; and I know that her Ladyship wrote, urgently entreating you to come out to Italy." Twining continued to detail, in his own peculiar and fitful style, various circumstances about Lord Lackington's last illness. But Beecher never heard a word of it, but stood stunned and stupefied by the news. It would be too tangled a web were we to inquire into the complicated and confused emotions which then swayed his heart. The immense change in his own fortunes, his sudden accession to rank, wealth, and station, came, accompanied by traits of brotherly love and affection bestowed on him long, long ago, when he was a Harrow boy, and "Lack" came down to see him; and then, in after life, the many kind things he had done for him,—helping him out of this or that difficulty,—services little estimated at the time, but now remembered with more than mere gratitude. "Poor Lackington! and that I should not haver been with you!" muttered he; and then, as if the very words had set another chord in vibration, he started as he thought that he had been duped. Davis knew it all; Davis had intercepted the letters. It was for this he had detained him weeks long in the lonely isolation of that Rhenish village. It was for this his whole manner had undergone such a marked change to him. Hence the trustfulness with which he burned the forged acceptances; the liberality with which he supplied him with money, and then—the marriage! "How they have done me!" cried he, in an agony of bitterness,—"how they have done me! The whole thing was concerted,—a plant from the very beginning; and *she* was in it!" While he thus continued to mutter to himself imprecations upon his own folly, Twining led him away, and imperceptibly induced him to stroll along one of the unfrequented alleys. At first Beecher's questions were all about his brother's illness,—how it began, what they called it, how it progressed.

Then he asked after his sister-in-law,—where she then was, and how. By degrees he adverted to Lackington's affairs; his will,—what he had left, and to whom. Twining was one of the executors, and could tell him everything. The Viscount had provided handsomely, not extravagantly, for his widow, and left everything to his brother! "Poor Lackington, I knew he loved me always!" Twining entered into a somewhat complicated narrative of a purchase the late Viscount had made, or intended to make, in Ireland,—an encumbered estate,—but Beecher paid no attention to the narrative. All his thoughts were centred upon his own position, and how Davis had done him.

"Where could you have been, my Lord, all that time, not to have heard of this?" asked Twining.

"I was in Germany, in Nassau. I was fishing amongst the mountains," said the other, in confusion.

"Fishing?—great fun, capital fun; like it immensely,—no expense, rods and hooks,—rods and hooks; not like hunting,—hunting perfectly ruinous,—I mean for men like myself, not, of course, for your Lordship."

"Poor Lackington!" muttered Beecher, half unconsciously.

"Ah!" sighed Twining, sympathetically.

"I was actually on my way out to visit him, but one thing or another occurred to delay me!"

"How unfortunate, my Lord; and, really, his anxieties about *you* were unceasing. You have not to be told of the importance he attached to the title and name of your house! He was always saying, 'If Beecher were only married! If we could find a wife for Annesley—'"

"A wife!" exclaimed the other, suddenly.

"Yes, my Lord, a wife; excellent thing, marriage,—capital thing,—great fun."

"But it's done, sir; I 'm booked!" cried Beecher, vehemently. "I was married on Sunday last."

"Wish your Lordship every imaginable joy. I offer my felicitations on the happy event Is the Viscountess here?"

"She *is* here," said Beecher, with a dogged sternness.

"May I ask the name of Lady Lackington's family?" said Twining, obsequiously.

"Name,—name of her family!" echoed Beecher, with a scornful laugh. Then, suddenly stopping, he drew his arm within Twining's, and in the low voice of a secret confidence, said, "You know the world as well as most men,—a deal better, I should say; now, can you tell me, is a marriage of this kind binding?"

"What kind of marriage do you mean?"

"Why, a private marriage in an inn, without banns, license, or publication of any kind, the ceremony performed by a fellow I suspect is a degraded parson,—at least, I used to hear he was 'scratched' years ago,—Classon."

"Paul Classon,—Holy Paul?—clever fellow, very ingenious. Tried to walk into me once for a subscription to convert the Mandans Indians,—did n't succeed,—what fun!"

"Surely no ministration of his can mean much, eh?"

"Afraid it does, my Lord; as your late brother used to observe, marriage is one of those bonds in which even a rotten string is enough to bind us. Otherwise, I half suspect some of us would try to slip our cables,—slip our cables and get away! What fun, my Lord,—what fun!"

"I don't believe such a marriage is worth a rush," went on Beecher, in that tone of affirmation by which he often stimulated his craven heart to feel a mock confidence. "At least, of this I am certain, there are five hundred fellows in England would find out a way to smash it."

"And do you want to 'cryoff my Lord?" asked Twining, abruptly.

"I might, or I might not; that depends. You see, Twining, there's rather a wide line of country between Annesley Beecher with nothing, and Viscount Lackington with a snug little estate; and if I had only known, last Sunday morning, that I was qualified to run for a cup I'd scarcely have entered for a hack stakes."

"But then, you are to remember her connections."

"Connections!" laughed out Beecher, scornfully.

"Well, family,—friends; in short, she may have brothers,—a father?"

"She *has* a father, by Jove!—she *has* a father!"

"May I be so bold as to ask—"

"Oh, you know him well!—all the world knows him, for the matter of that. What do you say to Kit Davis,—Grog!"

"Grog Davis, my Lord?—Grog Davis!"

"Just so," said Beecher, lighting a cigar with an affected composure he intended to pass off for great courage.

"Grog—Grog—Grog!—wonderful fellow! astonishing fellow! up to everything! and very amusing! I must say, my Lord,—I must say, your Lordship's father-in-law is a very remarkable man."

"I rather suspect he is, Twining."

"Under the circumstances,—the actual circumstances, I should say, my Lord, keep your engagement,—keep your engagement."

"I understand you, Twining; you don't fancy Master Grog. Well, I know an opinion of that kind is abroad. Many people are afraid of him; I never was,—eh?" The last little interrogative was evoked by a strange smile that flickered across Twining's face. "You suspect that I *am* afraid of him, Twining; now, why should I?"

"Can't possibly conceive, my Lord,—cannot imagine a reason."

"He is what is called a dangerous fellow."

"Very dangerous."

"Vindictive."

"To the last. Never abandons a pursuit, they tell me."

"But we live in an age of civilization, Twining. Men of his stamp can't take the law in their own hands."

"I 'm afraid that is exactly the very thing they do, my Lord; they contrive always to be in the wrong, and consequently have everything their own way;" and so Mr. Twining rubbed his hands, slapped his legs, and laughed away very pleasantly.

"You are rather a Job's comforter, Twining," said Beecher, tartly.

"Not very like Job, your Lordship; very little resemblance, I must say, my Lord! Much more occasion for pride than patience,—peerage and a fine property!"

"I 'm sure I never coveted it; I can frankly say I never desired prosperity at the price of—the price of—By the way, Twining, why not compromise this affair? I don't see why a handsome sum—I'm quite willing it should be handsome—would n't put all straight. A clever friend might be able to arrange the whole thing. Don't you agree with me?"

"Perfectly, my Lord; quite convinced you have taken the correct view."

"Should you feel any objection to act for me in the matter,—I mean, to see Davis?"

Twining winced like a man in pain.

"Why, after all, it is a mere negotiation."

"Very true, my Lord."

"A mere experiment."

"Just so, my Lord; so is proving a new cannon; but I'd just as soon not sit on the breech for the first fire."

"It's wonderful how every one is afraid of this fellow, and I wind him round my finger!"

"Tact, my Lord,—tact and cleverness, that's it."

"You see, Twining," said Beecher, confidentially, "I'm not quite clear that I'd like to be off. I have n't regularly made up my mind about it. There's a good deal to be said on either side of the question. I'll tell you what to do: come and breakfast with us to-morrow morning,—I'd say dine, but I mean to get away early and push on towards the South; you shall see her, and then—and then we 'll have a talk afterwards."

"Charmed, my Lord,—delighted,—too happy. What 's your hour?"

"Let us say eleven. Does that suit you?"

"Perfectly; any hour,—eleven, twelve, one,—whenever your Lordship pleases."

"Well, good-night, Twining, good-night."

"Good-night, my Lord, good-night. What fun!" muttered he, slapping his legs as he stepped out to his lodgings.

It was not till he had smoked his fourth cigar, taking counsel from his tobacco, as was his wont, that the new Viscount returned to his hotel. It was then nigh morning, and the house was so buried in sleep that he knocked full half an hour before he gained admittance.

"There's a gentleman arrived, sir, who asked after you. He didn't give his name."

"What is he like,—old, young, short, or tall?"

"Middle-aged, sir, and short, with red beard and moustaches. He drank tea with the lady upstairs, sir, and waited to see you till nigh two o'clock."

"Oh, I know him," muttered Beecher, and passed on. When he reached his dressing-room, he found the table covered with a mass of letters addressed to Lord Viscount Lackington, and scrawled over with postmarks; but a card, with the following few words, more strongly engaged his attention: "It's all right, you are the Viscount—C. D."

A deep groan burst from Beecher as he dropped the card and sank heavily into a seat. A long, long time slipped over ere he could open the letters and examine their contents. They were almost all from lawyers and men of business, explanation of formalities to be gone through, legal details to be completed, with here and there respectful entreaties to be continued in this or that agency. A very bulky one was entirely occupied with a narrative of the menaced suit on the title, and a list of the papers which would be hereafter required for the defence. It was vexatious to be told of a rebellion ere he had yet seated himself on the throne; and so he tossed the ungracious document to the end of the room, his mood the very reverse of that he had so long pictured to himself it might be.

"I suppose it's all great luck!" muttered he to himself; "but up to this I see no end of difficulty and trouble."

CHAPTER XXVI
UNPLEASANT EXPLANATIONS

Beecher had scarcely dropped off to sleep when he was awoke by a heavy, firm tread in the room; he started up, and saw it was Davis.

"How is the noble Viscount?" said Grog, drawing a chair and seating himself. "I came over here post haste when I got the news."

"Have you told her?" asked Beecher, eagerly.

"Told her! I should think I have. Was it not for the pleasure of that moment that I came here,—here, where they could arrest me this instant and send me off to the fortress of Rastadt? I shot an Austrian officer in the garrison there four years ago."

"I heard of it," groaned Beecher, from the utmost depth of his heart "So that she knows it all?"

"She knows that you are a peer of England, and that she is a peeress."

Beecher looked at the man as he spoke, and never before did he appear to him so insufferably insolent and vulgar. Traits which he had in part forgotten or overlooked now came out in full force, and he saw him in all the breadth of his coarseness. As if he had read what was passing in Beecher's mind, Davis stared fully at him, resolute and defiant.

"I suppose," resumed Grog, "it was a pleasure you had reserved for yourself to inform her Ladyship of her step in rank, but I thought she'd just like to hear the news as well from her father."

Beecher made no answer, but sat buried in thought; at last he said: "Mr. Twining, whom I met accidentally last night, told me of my brother's death, and told me, besides, that it had occurred fully eight weeks ago."

"So long as that!" said Davis, dryly.

"Yes, so long as that," said Beecher, fixing his eyes steadfastly on the other. "He tells me, too, that Lady Lackington wrote twice, or even thrice, to urge me to come on to Italy; that my arrival was looked for hourly. Many other letters were also sent after me, but not one reached my hand. Strange, very strange!"

"I suppose you have them all there now," said Grog, defiantly, as he pointed to the mass of letters on the dressing-table.

"No, these are all of recent dates, and refer, besides, to others which I have never got."

"What has become of the others, then?" asked Grog, resolutely.

"That's the very point *I* cannot decide, and it is the very question I was about to ask of *you*."

"What do you mean?" said Grog, calmly.

"What I mean is this," said Beecher, "that I am curious to learn how long it is since you knew of my brother's death?"

"If you'd like to hear when I suspected that fact, perhaps I can tell you," said Grog.

"Well, let me hear so much."

"It was shortly after your arrival at Holbach."

"Ah! I thought so—I thought as much!" cried Beecher triumphantly.

"Wait a bit,—wait a bit; don't be sure you have won the game, I've a card in my hand yet. When you endorsed certain large bills for Lazarus Stein at Aix, you signed your name 'Lackington.' Oh, there's no denying it, I have them here in this pocket-book. Now, either your brother was dead, or you committed a forgery."

"You know well, sir," said Beecher, haughtily, "at whose instance and persuasion I wrote myself Lackington.'"

"*I* know it! I know nothing about it. But before we carry this controversy further, let me give you a hint: drop this haughty tone you have just taken with me,—it won't do,—I tell you it won't. If you're the Lord Viscount to the world, you know deuced well what you are to me, and what, if you push me to it, I could make you to *them*."

"Captain Davis, I am inclined to think that we had better come to an understanding at once," said Beecher, with a degree of firmness he could rarely assume. "Our relations cannot be what they have hitherto been. I will no longer submit to dictation nor control at your hands. Our roads in life lie in opposite directions; we need seldom to meet, never to cross each other. If Lady Lackington accepts the same view of these matters as myself, well; if not, it will not be difficult to suggest an arrangement satisfactory to each of us."

"And so you think to come the noble Lord over me, do you?" said Grog, with an irony perfectly savage in look and tone. "I always knew you were a fool, but that you could carry your stupid folly that far I never imagined. You want to tell me—if you had the pluck you would tell me—that you are ashamed of having married *my* daughter, and I tell *you* that out of your whole worthless, wretched, unmanly life, it is the one sole redeeming action. That *she* stooped to marry *you* is another matter,—she that, at this very moment, confers more honor upon your rank than it can ever bestow upon *her!* Ay! start if you will, but don't sneer; for if you do, by the eternal Heaven above us, it will be the last laugh you 'll ever indulge in!" A sudden movement of his hand towards the breast of his coat gave such significance to the words that Beecher sprang from his seat and approached the bell-rope. "Sit down there,—there, in that chair," cried Grog, in the thickened accents of passion. "I have n't done with you. If you call a servant into the room, I' ll fling *you* out of the window. If you imagined, when I burned your forged acceptances, that I had n't another evidence against you stronger than all, you mistook Kit Davis. What! did you think to measure yourself against *me?* Nature never meant you for that, my Lord Viscount,—never!"

If Davis was carried away by the impetuosity of his savage temper in all this, anger never disabled him from keenly watching Beecher and scanning every line in his face. To his amazement, therefore, did he remark that he no longer exhibited the same extent of fear he had hitherto done. No, he was calmer and more collected than Grog had ever seen him in a moment of trial.

"When your passion has blown over," said Beecher, quietly, "you will perhaps tell me what it is you want or require of me."

"Want of you,—want of you!" reiterated Davis, more abashed by the other's demeanor than he dared to confess, even to himself,—"what can *I* want of you? or, if I do want anything, it is that you will remember who you are, and who am I. It is not to remember that you are a Lord, and I a leg,—it is not that I mean,—you 're not very like to forget it; it is to call to mind that I have the same grip of you I have had any day these ten years, and that I could show up the Viscount Lackington just as easily as the Honorable Annesley Beecher."

If Beecher's cheek grew paler, it was only for a moment, and, with an amount of calm dignity of which Grog had not believed him capable, he said,—

"There's not any use in your employing this language towards me,—there's not the slightest necessity for me to listen to it. I conclude, after what has passed between us, we cannot be friends: there's no need, however, of our being enemies."

"Which means, 'I wish you a very good-morning, Kit Davis,' don't it?" said Grog, with a grin.

Beecher gave a smile that might imply anything.

"Ah! so that's it?" cried Davis, endeavoring, by any means, to provoke a reply.

Beecher made no answer, but proceeded in most leisurely style with his dressing. #

"Well, that's candid, anyhow," said Grog, sternly. "Now, I 'll be as frank with *you*: I thought a few days back that I 'd done rather a good thing of it, but I find that I backed the wrong horse after all. You are the Viscount, now, but you won't be so this day six months."

Beecher turned his head round, and gave a smile of the most insolent incredulity.

"Ay, I know you'll not believe it, because it is I that tell you; but there came out a fellow from Fordyce's with the same story, and when you open your letters you 'll see it again."

Beecher's courage now deserted him, and the chair on which he leaned shook under his grasp.

"Here's how it is," said Grog, in a calm, deliberate tone: "Dunn—that same fellow we called on one day together—has fallen upon a paper—a title, or a patent, or a writ, or something—that shows you have no claim to the Viscounty, and that it ought to go, along with the estates, to some man who represents the elder branch. Now Dunn, it seems, was some way deep with your brother. He had been buying land for him, and not paying, or paying the money and not getting the land,—at all events, he was n't on the square with him; and seeing that you might probably bring him to book, he just says, 'Don't go into accounts with me, and here's your title; give me any trouble, and I 'll go over to the enemy.'"

"But there can be no such document."

"Fordyce's people say there is. Hankes, Dunn's own agent, told them the substance of it; and it seems it was on the list of proofs, but they never could lay a hand on it."

Beecher heard no more, but taking up the lawyer's letter, which he had thrown so indignantly from him the night before, he began patiently to read it.

"Who can make head or tail of all this?" cried he, in angry impatience. "The fellow writes as if I was a scrivener's clerk, and knew all their confounded jargon. Mere schemes to extort money these!"

"Not always. There's now and then a real charge in the gun, and it's too late to know it when you 're hit," cried Grog, quietly.

"Why do not Fordyce's people send out a proper person to communicate with myself directly," said Beecher, haughtily. "They did, and I saw him," said Grog, boldly.

Beecher grew crimson, and his lip trembled with a convulsive movement. It was very hard indeed to restrain himself, but, with an effort, he succeeded, and simply said, "And then—"

"And then," resumed Davis, "I packed him off again."

"What authority had you to thrust yourself forward in this manner?" cried Beecher, passionately. "What authority?—the interest of my daughter, the Viscountess Lackington," said Grog, with a mingled insolence and mockery. "You may safely swear it was out of no special regard for *you*. What authority?" And with this he burst out into a laugh of sarcastic defiance.

"It need not offend you," said Beecher, "if I say that a question like this must be intrusted to very different hands from yours."

"You think so, eh?"

"I'm sure of it."

"Well, I am not; so far from it, that I'm ready to declare if I can't pull you through, there's not that man living who can. Lawyers can meet lawyers. If one wins a trick here, the other scores one there. This fellow has a deed,— that one has a codicil. It is always the same game; and they 're in no hurry to finish, for they are playing on velvet. What 's really wanting is some one that does n't care a rush for a little risk,—ready to bribe this man,—square the other,—burn a parish register, if need be, and come at—at any document that may be required,—at the peril of passing his days at Norfolk Island."

"You fancy that the whole world is like the ring at Ascot," said Beecher, sneeringly.

"And ain't it? What's the difference, I'd like to know? Is it noble lords like yourself would prove the contrary?"

"I will see Fordyce myself," said Beecher, coldly.

"You needn't be at the trouble," said Davis, calmly. "There's two ways of doing the thing: one is a compromise with the claimant, who turns out to be that young Conway, the 'Smasher.'"

"Young Conway, the one-armed fellow?"

"Just so. The other is, to get hold of Dunn's papers. Now, I have despatched a trusty hand to the Crimea to see about the first of these plans. As for the other, I 'll do it myself."

"How so?"

"Just this way: you shall give me a written authority to demand from Dunn all your family papers and documents, making me out to be your agent for the Irish estates." Beecher started, and a slight cast of derision marked his lip; but there was that in Grog's face that speedily suppressed every temptation to sneer, and he grew sick with terror. "Dunn will be for holding out," resumed Davis. "He 'll be for writing to yourself for explanations, instructions, and so forth; and if I were a fellow of his own sort, I 'd have to agree; but, being what I am,—Kit Davis, you see,—I'll Just say: 'No gammon, my old gent. We don't mean to lose this match, nor don't mean to let *you* nobble *us*. Be on the square, and it will be all the better for yourself.' *We 'll* soon understand each other."

A gentle tap at the door here interrupted Davis, and Beecher's servant, with a most bland voice, said, "Her Ladyship is waiting breakfast, my Lord," and disappeared.

"Who told *him*?" asked Beecher, a strange sense of pleasure vibrating through him as this recognition reminded him of his newly acquired station.

"I told him last night," said Davis, with a look that seemed to say, "And of whatever I do, let there be no farther question."

As they entered the breakfast-room, they found Lizzy—I must ask pardon if I return at times to their former names in speaking of her and her husband—in conversation with Mr. Twining, that gentleman having presented himself, and explained how he came to be there.

"Do you know Captain Davis, Twining? Let me present him to you," said Beecher, blushing deeply as he spoke.

"Charmed, my Lord,—much honored,—fancy we have met before,—met at York Spring Meet. Rataplan beat by a neck,—great fun!"

"It was n't great fun for me," growled out Grog; "I stood to win on Bruiser."

"Excellent horse,—capital horse,—wonderful stride!"

"I'll tell you what he was," said Grog, sternly,—"a rare bad 'un!"

"You surprise—amaze me, Captain Davis,—quite astonish me! Always heard a great character of Braiser!"

"You did, did you?" said Grog, with a jocose leer.

"Well, the information wasn't thrown away, for you laid heavily against him."

"Most agreeable man, your father-in-law, my Lord," said Twining, slapping his legs and laughing away in high good humor; then, turning again to Davis, he engaged him in conversation.

Meanwhile Beecher had drawn Lizzy into a recess of the window, and was whispering anxiously to her.

"Did this piece of news take you by surprise?" asked he, scanning her closely as he spoke.

"Yes," said she, calmly.

"It was quite unexpected," said he, half in question,—"at least by me," added he, after a pause.

She saw that some suspicion—she knew not of what, and as possibly cared as little—agitated him, and she turned away to the breakfast-table without speaking. Beecher, however, led her back again to the window. "I 'd like much to ask you a question," said he, half timidly; "that is, if I did not fear you might take it ill."

"And there is such a risk, is there?" asked she.

"Well, it is just possible," faltered he.

"In that case, take my advice, and do not hazard it." There was a calm resolution in her tone that carried more weight with it than anything like passion, and Beecher felt in his heart that he dared not reject her counsel.

Lizzy had now taken her place at the breakfast-table, her air, look, and manner being all that could denote a mind perfectly easy and contented. So consummate, too, was her tact, that she gradually led the conversation into that tone of pleasant familiarity when frank opinions are expressed and people talk without restraint; and thus, without the semblance of an effort, she succeeded, while developing any agreeability Beecher possessed, in silencing her father, whose judgments of men and events were not always the safest. As for Twining, she perfectly fascinated him. He was no mean critic in all that regards dress and manners; few men could more unerringly detect a flaw in breeding or a solecism in address. Mere acting, however good, would never have imposed upon him, and all the polish of manner and the charm of a finished courtesy would have failed with him if unaccompanied by that "sentiment" of good breeding which is its last and highest captivation. How subdued was all the flippant mockery of his manner! how respectful the tone in which he accosted her! It was the Viscountess, and not Grog Davis's daughter, he saw before him. Now Beecher saw all this, and a sense of pride swelled his heart, and made him almost forget his distrusts and suspicions. When breakfast was over, Lizzy, passing her arm within her father's, led him away. She had many things to say to him, and he to her, so that Beecher and Twining were left alone together.

"Well, Twining," said Annesley, as he lighted a cigar, "tell me frankly,—don't you think I might have done worse?"

"Impossible to have done better,—impossible!" said Twining. "I don't speak of her Ladyship's beauty, in which she surpasses all I have ever seen, but her manner—her courtesy—has a blending of grace and dignity that would confer honor on the most finished Court in Europe."

"I'm glad you say so, Twining; men quote *you* as an authority on these things, and I own frankly I am delighted to have my own judgment so ratified."

"Her appearance in the world will be such a success as one has not seen for years!" exclaimed Twining.

"She'll be sharply criticised," said Beecher, puffing his cigar.

"She can well afford it, my Lord."

"What will the women say, Twining? She is *so* good-looking,—what will the women say?"

"Where there's no rivalry, there will be no dispraise. She is so surpassingly beautiful that none will have courage to criticise; and if they should, where can they detect a fault?"

"I believe you are right, Twining,—I believe you are right," said Beecher, and his face glowed with pleasure as he spoke. "Where she got her manners I can't make out," added he, in a whisper.

"Ay, my Lord, these are Nature's own secrets, and she keeps them closely."

"It is the father—old Grog—is the difficulty," whispered Beecher, still lower; "what can be done with *him?*"

"Original, certainly; peculiar,—very peculiar,—what fun!" And Twining in an instant recovered all his wonted manner, and slapped away at his legs unmercifully.

"I don't exactly see the fun of it,—especially for me," said Beecher, peevishly.

"After all, a well-known man, my Lord,—public character,—a celebrity, so to say."

"Confound it!" cried Beecher, angrily, "don't you perceive there lies the whole annoyance? The fellow is known from one end of England to the other. You can't enter a club of a rainy day, when men sit round the fire, without hearing a story of him; you don't get to the third station on a railroad till some one says, 'Have you heard old Grog's last?' There's no end to him?"

"Wonderful resources!—astonishing!—great fun!"

"I'll be hanged if it *is* great fun, though you are pleased to say so," said Beecher, angrily.

Twining was far too good-tempered to feel hurt by this peevishness, and only rubbed his hands and laughed joyfully.

"And the worst of all," resumed Beecher,—"the worst of all is, he *will* be a foreground figure; do what you may, he *will* be in the front of the Stand-house."

"Get him a situation abroad, my Lord,—something in the colonies," broke in Twining.

"Not a bad thought that, Twining; only he is so notorious."

"Doesn't signify in the least, my Lord. Every office under the Crown has its penal settlements. The Foreign Office makes its culprits consuls; the Colonial sends their chief justices to the Gold Coast; and the Home Secretary's Botany Bay is Ireland."

"But would they really give me something,—I mean something he 'd take?"

"I have n't a doubt of it, my Lord; I wanted to get rid of a poor relation t' other day, and they made him a Boundary Commissioner at Baffin's Bay. Baffin's Bay!—what fun!" And he laughed immoderately.

"How am I to set about this, Twining? You are aware that up to this I have had no relations with politics or parties."

"Nothing easier, my Lord; always easy for a peer,—proxy often of great consequence. Write to the Premier,—hint that you are well disposed to adopt his views,—due maintenance of all the glorious privileges of our Constitution, with progressive improvement,—great fun, capital fun! all the landmarks firm and fixed, and as much of your neighbor's farm as possible. Or if you don't like to do this, set Davenport Dunn at them; he is your Lordship's Irish agent,—at least, he was the late Viscount's,—he 'll do it,—none better, none so well!"

"That might be the best way," said Beecher, musing.

"He'll be charmed—delighted—overjoyed at this proof of your Lordship's confidence. He 'll go to work at once, and before your Lordship begins to receive, or go out, your amiable and most highly gifted father-in-law may be Income-tax Collector in Cochin-China."

"Now, there's only one thing more, Twining, which is, to induce Davis to agree to this. He likes Europe,—likes the life of England and the Continent."

"Certain he does,—quite sure of it; no man more calculated to appreciate society or adorn it. Capital fun!"

"Do you think," resumed Beecher, "that you could just throw out a hint—a slight suggestion—to see how he'd take it?"

"Come much better from your Lordship."

"Well, I don't know—that is, I half suspect—"

"Far better, infinitely better, my Lord; your own tact, your Lordship's good taste—Oh dear me, one o'clock already, and I have an appointment!" And with the most profuse apologies for a hurried departure, and as many excuses to be conveyed to her Ladyship, Mr. Twining disappeared.

Although Twining's reluctance to carry into execution the tone of policy he suggested did not escape Beecher's penetration, the policy itself seemed highly recommendable. Grog out of Europe,—Grog beyond the seas, collecting taxes, imprisoning skippers, hunting runaway negroes, or flogging Caffres,—it mattered not, so that he never crossed his sight again. To be sure, it was not exactly the moment to persuade Davis to expatriate himself when his prospects at home began to brighten, and he saw his daughter a peeress. Still, Dunn was a fellow of such marvellous readiness, such astonishing resources! If any man could "hit off" the way here, it was he. And then, how fortunate! Grog was eagerly pressing Beecher to be accredited to this same

Davenport Dunn; he asked that he might be sent to confer and negotiate with him about the pending action at law. What an admirable opportunity was this, then, for Dunn to sound Davis and, if occasion served, tempt him with an offer of place! Besides these reasons, valid and sound so far as they went, there was another impulse that never ceased to urge Beecher forward, and this was a vague shadowy sort of impression that if he could only succeed in his plan he should have outwitted Grog, and "done" *him.* There was a sense of triumph associated with this thought that made his heart swell with pride. In his passion for double-dealing, he began to think how he could effect his present purpose,—by what zigzag and circuitous road, through what tangled scheme of duplicity and trick. "I have it,—I have it," cried he at length; and he hastened to his dressing-room, and, having locked the door, he opened his writing-desk and sat down to write. But it is not at the end of a chapter I can presume to insert his Lordship's correspondence.

CHAPTER XXVII
OVERREACHINGS

Beecher did not amongst his gifts possess the pen of a ready writer; but there was a strange symmetry observable between the composition and the manual part. The lines were irregular, the letters variously sized, erasures frequent, blots everywhere, while the spelling displayed a spirit that soared above orthography. A man unused to writing, in the cares of composition, is pretty much in the predicament of a bad horseman in a hunting-field. He has a vague, indistinct motion of "where" he ought to go, without the smallest conception as to the "how." He is balked or "pounded" at every step, always trying back, but never by any chance hitting off the right road to his object.

Above a dozen sheets of paper lay half scrawled over before him after two hours of hard labor, and there he still sat pondering over his weary task. His scheme was simply this: to write a few lines to Dunn, introducing his father-in-law, and instructing him to afford him all information and details as to the circumstances of the Irish property, it being his intention to establish Captain Davis in the position of his agent in that country; having done which, and given to Grog to read over, he meant to substitute another in its place, which other was confidentially to entreat of Dunn to obtain some foreign and far-away appointment for Davis, and by every imaginable means to induce him to accept it. This latter document Dunn was to be instructed to burn immediately after reading. In fact, the bare thought of what would ensue if Davis saw it, made him tremble all over, and aggravated all the difficulties of composition. Even the mode of beginning puzzled him, and there lay some eight or ten sheets scrawled over with a single line, thus: "Lord Lackington presents his compliments" — "The Viscount Lackington requests" — "Lord Lackington takes the present opportunity" — "Dear Dunn" — "Dear Mr. Dunn" — "My dear Mr. Dunn" — "Dear D." How nicely and minutely did he weigh over in his mind the value to be attached to this exordium, and how far the importance of position counterbalanced the condescension of close intimacy! "Better be familiar," said he, at last; "he 's a vulgar dog, and he 'll like it;" and so he decided for "My dear Dunn."

"My dear Dunn,—As I know of your influence with the people in power—too formal that, perhaps," said he, re-reading it—"as I know what you can do with the dons in Downing Street—that 's far better—I want you to book the bearer—no, that is making a flunkey of him—I want you to secure me a snug thing in the Colonies—or better, a snug Colonial appointment—for my father-in-law—no, for my friend—no, for my old and attached follower, Captain Davis—that's devilish well-rounded, 'old and attached follower, Captain Davis.' When I tell you that I desire he may get something over the hills and far away, you 'll guess at once—you 'll guess at once why—no, guess the reason—no, you 'll see with half an eye how the cat jumps." He threw down his pen at this, and rubbed his hands in an ecstasy of delight. "Climate does n't signify a rush, for he's strong as a three-year-old, and has the digestion of an 'ostrage;' the main thing, little to do, and opportunities for blind hookey. As to outfit, and some money in hand, I 'll stand it. Once launched, if there's only a billiard-table or dice-box in the colony, he 'll not starve."

"Eh, Grog, my boy," cried he, with a laugh, "as the parsons say, 'Salary less an object than a field of profitable labor!' And, by Jove! the grass will be very short, indeed, where you can't get enough to feed on! There 's no need to give Dunn a caution about reserve, and so forth with him,—he knows Grog well."

Having finished this letter, and placed it carefully in his pocket, he began the other, which, seeing that it was never to be delivered, and only shown to Davis himself, cost him very little trouble in the composition. Still it was not devoid of all difficulty, since, by the expectations it might create in Grog's mind of obtaining the management of the Irish property, it would be actually throwing obstacles in the way of his going abroad. He therefore worded the epistle more carefully, stating it to be his intention that Captain Davis should be his agent at some future time not exactly defined, and requesting Dunn to confer with him as one enjoying his own fullest confidence.

He had but finished the document when a sharp knock at the door announced Davis. "The very man I wanted," said Beecher; "sit down and read that."

Grog took his double eye-glass from his pocket,—an aid to his sight only had recourse to when he meant to scrutinize every word and every letter,—and sat down to read. "Vague enough," said he, as he concluded. "Small credentials for most men, but quite sufficient for Kit Davis."

"I know that," said Beecher, half timidly; for no sooner in the redoubted presence than he began to tremble at his own temerity.

"This Mr. Dunn is a practical sort of man, they say, so that we shall soon understand each other," said Davis.

"Oh, you'll like him greatly."

"I don't want to like him," broke in Grog; "nor do I want him to like *me*."

"He's a fellow of immense influence just now; can do what he pleases with the Ministry."

"So much the better for him," said Grog, bluntly.

"And for his friends, sir," added Beecher. "He has only to send in a name, and he's sure to get what he asks for, at home or abroad."

"How convenient!" said Grog; and whether it was an accident or not, he directed his eyes full on Beecher as he spoke, and as suddenly a deep blush spread over the other's face. "Very convenient, indeed," went on Grog, while his unrelenting glance never wavered nor turned away. As he stared, so did Beecher's confusion increase, till at last, unable to endure more, he turned away, sick at heart "My Lord Viscount," said Grog, gravely, "let me give you a word of counsel: never commit a murder; for if you do, your own fears will hang you."

"I don't understand you," faltered out Beecher.

"Yes, you do; and right well too," broke in Grog, boldly. "What rubbish have you got into your head now, about 'a place' for me? What nonsensical scheme about making me an inspector of this or a collector of that? Do you imagine that for any paltry seven or eight hundred a year I 'm going to enter into recognizance not to do what's worth six times the amount? Mayhap you 'd like to send me to India or to China. Oh, that's the dodge, is it?" exclaimed he, as the crimson flush now extended over Beecher's forehead to the very roots of his hair. "Well, where is it to be? There 's a place called Bogota, where they always have yellow fever; couldn't you get me named consul there? Oh dear, oh dear!" laughed he out, "how you *will* go on playing that little game, though you never score a point!"

"I sometimes imagine that you don't know how offensive your language is," said Beecher, whose angry indignation had mastered all his fears; "at least, it is the only explanation I can suggest for your conduct towards myself!"

"Look at it this way," said Grog; "if you always lost the game whenever you played against one particular man, wouldn't you give in at last, and own him for your master? Well, now, that is exactly what you are doing with me,—losing, losing on, and yet you won't see that you're beaten."

"I'll tell you what I see, sir," said Beecher, haughtily,—"that our intercourse must cease."

Was it not strange that this coarse man, reckless in action, headstrong and violent, felt abashed, for the instant, in presence of the dignified manner which, for a passing moment, the other displayed. It was the one sole weapon Grog Davis could not match; and before the "gentleman" he quailed, but only for a second or two, when he rallied, and said, "I want the intercourse as little as you do. I am here for the pleasure of being with my daughter."

"As for that," began Beecher, "there is no need—" He stopped abruptly, something terribly menacing in Grog's face actually arresting his words in the utterance.

"Take you care what you say," muttered Grog, as he approached him, and spoke with a low, guttural growl. "I have n't much patience at the best of times; don't provoke me *now*."

"Will you take this letter,—yes or no?" said Beecher, resolutely.

"I will: seal and address it," said Grog, searching for a match to light the taper, while Beecher folded the letter, and wrote the direction. Davis continued to break match after match in his effort to strike a light. Already the dusk of declining day filled the room, and objects were dimly descried. Beecher's heart beat violently. The thought that even yet, if he could summon courage for it, he might outwit Grog, sent a wild thrill through him. What ecstasy, could he only succeed!

"Curse these wax contrivances! the common wooden ones never failed," muttered Davis. "There goes the fifth."

"If you 'll ring for Fisher—"

An exclamation and an oath proclaimed that he had just burned his finger; but he still persevered.

"At last!" cried he,—"at last!" And just as the flame rose slowly up, Beecher had slipped the letter in his pocket, and substituted the other in its place.

"I'll write 'Private and confidential,'" added Beecher, "to show that the communication is strictly for himself alone." And now the document was duly sealed, and the name "Lackington" inscribed in the corner.

"I 'll start to-night," said Davis, as he placed the letter in his pocket-book; "I may have to delay a day in London, to see Fordyce. Where shall I write to you?"

"I'll talk that over with my Lady," said the other, still trembling with the remnant of his fears. "We dine at six," added he, as Davis arose to leave the room.

"So Lizzy told me," said Davis.

"You don't happen to know if she invited Twining, do you?"

"No! but I hope she didn't," said Grog, sulkily.

"Why so? He's always chatty, pleasant, and agreeable," said Beecher, whose turn it was now to enjoy the other's irritation.

"He's what I hate most in the world," said Davis, vindictively; "a swell that can walk into every leg in the Ring,—that's what he is!" And with this damnatory estimate of the light-hearted, easy-natured Adderley Twining, Grog banged the door and departed.

That social sacrament, as some one calls dinner, must have a strange, mysterious power over our affections and our sympathies; for when these two men next met each other, with napkins on their knees and soup before them, their manner was bland, and even cordial. You will probably say, How could they be otherwise? that was neither the time nor place to display acrimony or bitterness, nor could they carry out in Lizzy's presence the unseemly discussion of the morning. Very true; and their bearing might, consequently, exhibit a calm and decent courtesy; but it did more,—far more; it was familiar and even friendly, and it is to the especial influence of the dinner-table that I attribute the happy change. The blended decorum and splendor—that happy union of tangible pleasure with suggestive enjoyment, so typified by a well-laid and well-spread table—is a marvellous peacemaker. Discrepant opinions blend into harmonious compromise as the savory odors unite into an atmosphere of nutritious incense, and a wider charity to one's fellows comes in with the champagne. Where does diplomacy unbend? where do its high-priests condescend to human feelings and sympathies save at dinner? Where, save at Mansion House banquets, are great Ministers facetious?

Where else are grave Chancellors jocose and Treasury Lords convivial?

The three who now met were each in their several ways in good spirits: Grog, because he had successfully reasserted his influence over Beecher; Beecher, because, while appearing to be defeated, he had duped his adversary; and Lizzy, for the far better reason that she was looking her very best, and that she knew it. She had, moreover, passed a very pleasant morning; for Mr. Twining had made it his business—doubtless, with much hand-rubbing and many exclamations of "What fun!"—to go amongst all the tradespeople of Baden, proclaiming the arrival of a "millionnaire

Milor," and counselling them to repair with all the temptations of their shops to the hotel. The consequence was that Lizzy's drawing-room was like a fair till the hour of dressing for dinner. Jewelry in its most attractive forms, rich lace, silks, velvets, furs, costly embroideries, inlaid cabinets, gems, ancient and modern,—all the knick-knackeries which a voluptuous taste has conceived, all the extravagant inventions of a fashion bent on ruinous expenditure,—were there; fans sparkling with rubies, riding-whips incrusted with turquoises, slippers studded over with pearls. There was nothing wanting; even richly carved meerschaums and walking-sticks were paraded, in the hope that as objects of art and elegance they might attract her favor. Her father had found her dazzled and delighted by all this splendor, and told her that one of the first duties of her high station was the encouragement of art. "It is to you, and such as you, these people look for patronage," said he. "An English peeress is a princess, and must dispense her wealth generously."

I am bound to acknowledge, her Ladyship did not shrink from this responsibility of her station. Without caring for the cost,—as often without even inquiring the price,—she selected what she wished; and rows of pearls, diamond bracelets, rings, and head ornaments covered her dressing-table, while sable and Astrakan cloaks, cashmeres, and Genoa velvets littered every corner of the room. "After all," thought she, as she fixed a jewelled comb in her hair, "it is very nice to be rich; and while delighting yourself you can make so many others happy."

Doubtless, too, there was some reason in the reflection; and in the smiling faces and grateful glances around her she found a ready confirmation of the sentiment. Happily for her at the moment, she did not know how soon such pleasures pall, and, as happily for ourselves, too, is it the law of our being that they should do so, and that no enjoyment is worth the name which has cost no effort to procure, nor any happiness a boon which has not demanded an exertion to arrive at. If Beecher was startled at the sight of all these costly purchases, his mind was greatly relieved as Grog whispered him that Herr Koch, the banker, had opened a credit for him, on which he might draw as freely as he pleased. The word "Lackington" was a talisman which suddenly converted a sea of storm and peril into a lovely lake only ruffled by a zephyr.

At last the pleasant dinner drew to a close; and as the coffee was brought in, the noise of a carriage beneath the windows attracted them.

"That's *my* trap," said Davis; "I ordered it for half past eight, exactly."

"But there 's no train at this hour," began Lizzy.

"I know that; but I mean to post all night, and reach Carlsruhe for the first departure in the morning. I 'm due in London on Monday morning,— eh, my Lord?"

"Yes, that you are," said Beecher; "Dublin, Tuesday evening."

"Just so," said Davis, as he arose; "and I mean to keep my time like a pendulum. Can I do any little commission for your Ladyship as I pass through town,—anything at Howell and James's, anything from Storr's?"

"I never heard of them—"

"Quite time enough, Lizzy," broke in Beecher; "not to say that we might stock a very smart warehouse with the contents of the next room. Don't forget the courier,—he can join us at Rome; and remember, we shall want a cook. The 'Mowbray' have an excellent fellow, and I 'm sure an extra fifty would seduce him, particularly as he hates England, detests a club, and can't abide the 'Sundays;' and my Lady will require something smarter than Annette as a maid."

"Oh, I could n't part with Annette!"

"Nor need you; but you must have some one who can dress hair in a Christian fashion."

"And what do you call that?" asked Grog, with a stare of insolent meaning.

"My Lord is quite right in the epithet; for I copied my present coiffure from a picture of a Jewish girl I bought this morning, and I fancy it becomes me vastly."

There was in the easy coquetry of this speech what at once relieved the awkwardness of a very ticklish moment, and Beecher rewarded her address with a smile of gratitude.

"And the house in Portland Place to be let?" murmured Davis, as he read from his note-book. "What of that box in the Isle of Wight?"

"I rather think we shall keep it on; my sister-in-law liked it, and might wish to go there."

"Let her buy it or take a lease of it, then," said Grog. "You 'll see, when you come to look into it, she has been left right well off."

Beecher turned away impatiently, and made no reply.

"All that Herefordshire rubbish of model farm and farming-stock had better be sold at once. You are not going into that humbug like the late Lord, I suppose?"

"I have come to no determination about Lackington Court as yet," said Beecher, coldly.

"The sooner you do, then, the better. There's not a more rotten piece of expense in the world than southdowns and shorthorns, except it be Cochin-China hens and blue tulips."

"Let Fordyce look to my subscriptions at the clubs."

"Pure waste of money when you are not going back there."

"But who says that I am not?" asked Beecher, angrily.

"Not yet a bit, at all events," replied Davis, and with a grin of malicious meaning so significant that Beecher actually sickened with terror.

"It will be quite time enough to make further arrangements when I confer with the members of my family," said Beecher, haughtily.

To this speech Davis only answered by another grin, that spoke as plain as words could, "Even the high tone will have no effect upon *me*." Luckily this penance was not long to endure, for Lizzy had drawn her father aside, and was whispering a few last words to him. It was in a voice so low and subdued they spoke that nothing could be heard; but Beecher imagined or fancied he heard Grog mutter, "'Pluck' will do it; 'pluck' will do anything." A long, affectionate embrace, and a fondly uttered "Good-bye, girl," followed, and then, shaking hands with Beecher, Davis lighted his cigar and departed.

Lizzy opened the window, and, leaning over the balcony, watched the carriage as it sped along the valley, the lights appearing and disappearing at intervals. What thoughts were hers as she stood there? Who knows? Did she sorrow after him, the one sole being who had cared for her through life; did her heart sadden at the sense of desertion; was the loneliness of her lot in life then uppermost in her mind; or did she feel a sort of freedom in the thought that now she was to be self-guided and self-dependent? I know not. I can only say that, though a slight flush colored her cheek, she shed no tears; and as she closed the window and returned into the room, her features were calm and emotionless.

"Why did not papa take the route by Strasburg? It is much the shortest?"

"He couldn't," said Beecher, with a triumphant bitterness,—"he could n't. He can't go near Paris."

"By Verviers, then, and Belgium?" said she, reddening.

"He'd be arrested in Belgium and tried for his life. He has no road left but down the Rhine to Rotterdam."

"Poor fellow!" said she, rising, "it must be a real peril that turns *him* from his path." There was an accent on the pronoun that almost made the speech a sarcasm; at all events, ere Beecher could notice it, she had left the room.

"Now, if Fortune really meant to do me a good turn," said Beecher to himself, "she 'd just shove my respected father-in-law, writing-desk, pocket-book, and all, into the 'Rheingau,' never to turn up again." And with this pious sentiment, half wish, half prayer, he went downstairs and strolled into the street.

As the bracing night air refreshed him, he walked along briskly towards Lindenthal, his mind more at ease than before. It was, indeed, no small boon that the terror of Grog's presence was removed. The man who had seen him in all his transgressions and his shortcomings was, in reality, little else than an open volume of conscience, ever wide spread before him. How could he presume in such a presence to assert one single high or honorable motive? What honest sentiment dare be enunciate? He felt in his heart that the Viscount Lackington with ten thousand a year was not the Honorable Annesley Beecher with three hundred. The noble Lord could smile at the baits that to the younger son were irresistible temptations. There was no necessity that *he* should plot, scheme, and contrive; or if he did, it should be for a higher prize, or in a higher sphere and with higher antagonists. And yet Grog would not have it so. Let him do what he would, there was the inexorable Davis ever ready to bring down Lackington to the meridian of Beecher! Amidst all the misfortunes of his life, the ever having known this man was the worst,—the very worst!

And now he began to go over in his mind some of the most eventful incidents of this companionship. It was a gloomy catalogue of debauch and ruin. Young fellows entrapped at the very outset in life, led on to play, swindled, "hocussed," menaced with exposure, threatened with who knows what perils of public scandal if they refused to sign this or that "promise to pay." Then all the intrigues to obtain the money; the stealthy pursuit of the creditor to the day of his advancement or his marriage; the menaces measured out to the exigencies of the case,—now a prosecution, now a pistol. What a dreadful labyrinth of wickedness was it, and how had he threaded through it undetected! He heaved a heavy sigh as he muttered a sort of thanksgiving that it was all ended at last,—all over! "If it were not for Grog, these memories need never come back to me," said he. "Nobody wants to recall them against me, and the world will be most happy to dine with the Viscount Lackington without a thought of the transgressions of Annesley Beecher! If it were not for Grog,—if it were not for Grog!" and so ran the eternal refrain at the close of each reflection. "At all events," said he, "I 'll 'put the Alps between us;'" and early on the following morning the travelling-carriage stood ready at the door, and amidst the bowings and reverences of the hotel functionaries, the "happy pair" set out for Italy.

Do not smile in any derision at the phrase, good reader; the words are classic by newspaper authority; and whatever popular preachers may aver to the contrary, we live in a most charming world, where singleness is blessed and marriage is happy, public speaking is always eloquent, and soldiery ever gallant. Still, even a sterner critic might have admitted that the epithet was not misapplied; for there are worse things in life than to be a viscount with a very beautiful wife, rolling pleasantly along the Via Mala on Collinge's best patent, with six smoking posters, on a bright day of November. This for his share; as to hers, I shall not speak of it. And yet, why should I not? Whatever may be the conflict in the close citadel of the heart, how much of pleasure is derivable from the mere aspect of a beautiful country as one drives rapidly along, swift enough to bring the changes of scene agreeably before the eye, and yet not too fast to admit of many a look at some spot especially beautiful. And then how charming to lose oneself in that-dreamland, where, peopling the landscape with figures of long, long ago, we too have our part, and ride forth at daybreak from some deep-vaulted portal in jingling mail, or gaze from some lone tower over the wide expanse that forms our baronial realm,—visions of ambition, fancies of a lowly, humble life, alternating as the rock-crowned castle or the sheltered cot succeed each other! And lastly, that strange, proud sentiment we feel as we sweep past town and village, where human life goes on in its accustomed track,—the crowd in the market-place, the little group around the inn, the heavy wagon unloading at the little quay, the children hastening on to school,—all these signs of a small, small world of its own, that we, in our greatness, are never again to gaze on, our higher destiny bearing us ever onward to grander and more pretentious scenes.

"And this is Italy?" said Lizzy, half aloud, as, emerging from the mists of the Higher Alps, the carriage wound its zigzag descent from the Splügen, little glimpses of the vast plain of Lombardy coming into view at each turn of the way, and then the picturesque outlines of old ruinous Chiavenna, its tumble-down houses, half hid in trellised vines, and farther on, again, the head of the Lake of Como, with its shores of rugged rock.

"Yes, and this miserable dog-hole here is called Campo Dolcino!" said Beecher, as he turned over the leaves of his "John Murray." "That's the most remarkable thing about these Italians; they have such high-sounding names for everything, and we are fools enough to be taken in by the sound."

"It is a delusion that we are rather disposed to indulge in, generally," said Lizzy. "The words, 'your Majesty' or 'your Highness,' have their own magic in them, even when the representatives respond but little to the station."

"It was your father, I fancy, taught you that lesson," said he, peevishly.

"What lesson do you mean?"

"To hold people of high rank cheaply; to imagine that they must be all cheats and impositions."

"No," said she, calmly but resolutely. "If he taught me anything on this subject, it was to attribute to persons of exalted station very lofty qualities. What I have to fear is that my expectation will be far above the reality. I can imagine what they might be, but I 'm not so sure it is what I shall find them."

"You had better not say so to my sister-in-law," said Beecher, jeeringly.

"It is not my intention," said she, with the same calm voice.

"I make that remark," resumed he, "because she has what some people would call exaggerated notions about the superiority of the well-born over all inferior classes; indeed, she is scarcely just in her estimate of low people."

"Low people are really to be pitied!" said she, with a slight laugh; and Beecher stole a quick glance at her, and was silent.

He was not able long to maintain this reserve. The truth was, he felt an invincible desire to recur to the class in life from which Lizzy came, and to speak disparagingly of all who were humbly born. Not that this vulgarity was really natural to him, — far from it. With all his blemishes and defects he was innately too much a gentleman to descend to this. The secret impulse was to be revenged of Grog Davis; to have the one only possible vengeance on the man that had "done him;" and even though that was only to be exacted through Davis's daughter, it pleased him. And so he went on to tell of the prejudices — absurd, of course — that persons like Lady Georgina would persist in entertaining about common people. "You 'll have to be so careful in all your intercourse with her," said he; "easy, natural, of course, but never familiar; she would n't stand it."

"I will be careful," said Lizzy, calmly.

"The chances are, she 'll find out some one of the name, and ask you, in her own half-careless way, 'Are you of the Staffordshire Davises? or do you belong to the Davises of such a place?'"

"If she should, I can only reply that I don't know," said Lizzy.

"Oh! but you must n't say that," laughed out Beecher, who felt a sort of triumph over what he regarded as his wife's simplicity.

"You would not, surely, have me say that I was related to these people?"

"No, not exactly that; but, still, to say that you didn't know whether you were or not, would be a terrible blunder! It would amount to a confession that you were Davises of nowhere at all."

"Which is about the truth, perhaps," said she, in the same tone.

"Oh! truth is a very nice thing, but not always pleasant to tell."

"But don't you think you could save me from an examination in which I am so certain to acquit myself ill, by simply stating that you have married a person without rank, station, or fortune? These facts once understood, I feel certain that her Ladyship will never allude to them unpleasantly."

"Then there 's another point," said Beecher, evidently piqued that he had not succeeded in irritating her, — "there 's another point, and you must be especially careful about it, — never, by any chance, let out that you were educated at a school, or a pensionnat, or whatever they call it. If there 's anything she cannot abide, it is the thought of a girl brought up at a school; mind, therefore, only say, 'my governess.'"

She smiled and was silent.

"Then she'll ask you if you had been 'out,' and when you were presented, and who presented you. She 'll do it so quietly and so naturally, you 'd never guess that she meant any impertinence by it."

"So much the better, for I shall not feel offended."

"As to the drawing-room," rejoined Beecher, "you must say that you always lived very retiredly, — never came up to town; that your father saw very little company."

"Is not this Chiavenna we 're coming to?" asked Lizzy, a slight—but very slight—flush rising to her cheek. And now the loud cracking of the postilions' whips drowned all other sounds as the horses tore along through the narrow streets, making the frail old houses rock and shiver as they passed. A miserable-looking vetturino carriage stood at the inn door, and was dragged hastily out of the way to make room for the more pretentious equipage. Scarcely had the courier got down than the whole retinue of the inn was in motion, eagerly asking if "Milordo" would not alight, if his "Eccellenza" would not take some refreshment.

But his "Eccellenza" would do neither; sooth to say, he was not in the best of humors, and curtly said, "No, I want nothing but post-horses to get out of this wretched place."

"Is n't that like an Englishman?" said a voice from the vetturino carriage to some one beside him.

"But I know him," cried the other, leaping out. "It's the new Viscount Lackington." And with this he approached the carriage, and respectfully removing his hat, said, "How d'ye do, my Lord?"

"Ah, Spicer! you here?" said Beecher, half haughtily. "Off to England, I suppose?"

"No, my Lord, I 'm bound for Rome."

"So are we, too. Lady Lackington and myself," added be, correcting at once a familiar sort of a glance that Spicer found time to bestow upon Lizzy. "Do you happen to know if Lady Georgina is there?"

"Yes, my Lord, at the Palazzo Gondi, on the Pintian;" and here Spicer threw into his look an expression of respectful homage to her Ladyship.

"Palazzo Gondi; will you try and remember that address?" said Beecher to his wife. And then, waving his hand to Spicer, he added, "Good-bye,— meet you at Rome some of these days," and was gone.

CHAPTER XXVIII
AT ROME

In a small and not very comfortably furnished room looking out upon the Pintian Hill at Rome, two ladies were seated, working,—one in deep mourning, whose freshness indicated a recent loss; the other in a strangely fashioned robe of black silk, whose deep cape and rigid absence of ornament recalled something of the cloister. The first was the widowed Viscountess Lackington; the second the Lady Grace Twining, a recent convert to Rome, and now on her way to some ecclesiastical preferment in the Church, either as "Chanoinesse," or something equally desirable. Lady Lackington looked ill and harassed; there were not on her face any traces of deep sorrow or affliction, but the painful marks of much thought. It was the expression of one who had gone through a season of trial wherein she had to meet events and personages all new and strange to her. It was only during the last few days of Lord Lackington's illness that she learned the fact of a contested claim to the title, but, brief as was the time, every post brought a mass of letters bearing on this painful topic. While the lawyers, therefore, showered their unpleasant and discouraging tidings, there was nothing to be heard of Beecher; none knew where he was, or how a letter was to reach him. All her own epistles to him remained unacknowledged. Fordyce's people could not trace him, neither could Mr. Dunn, and there was actually the thought of asking the aid of that inquisitorial service whose detective energies are generally directed in the pursuit of guilt.

If Annesley Beecher might be slow to acknowledge the claims of fraternal affection, there was no one could accuse him of any lukewarmness to his own interests, and though it was now two months and upwards since the Viscount's death, yet he had never come forward to assert his new rank and station. Whatever suspicions might have weighed down the mind of the Viscountess regarding this mysterious disappearance, the language of all the lawyers' letters was assuredly ill calculated to assuage. They more than hinted that they suspected some deep game of treachery and fraud. Beecher's long and close intimacy with the worst characters of the turf— men notorious for their agency in all the blackest intrigues—was continually brought up. His life of difficulty and strait, his unceasing struggle to meet his play engagements, driving him to the most ruinous compacts, all were quoted to show that to a man of such habits and with such counsellors any compromise would be acceptable that offered present and palpable advantages in lieu of a possible and remote future.

The very last letter the Viscountess received from Fordyce contained this startling passage: "It being perfectly clear that Mr. Beecher would only be too ready to avail himself of his newly acquired privileges if he could, we must direct our sole attention to those circumstances which may explain why he could not declare himself the Viscount Lackington. Now, the very confident tone lately assumed by the Conway party seems to point to this mysterious clew, and everything I learn more and more disposes me to apprehend a shameful compromise."

It was with the letter that contained this paragraph before her Lady Lackington now sat, affecting to be engaged in her work, but in reality reading over, for the fiftieth time, the same gloomy passage.

"Is it not incredible that, constituted as the world now is, with its railroads and its telegraphs, you cannot immediately discover the whereabouts of any missing individual?" said Lady Lackington.

"I really think he must have been murdered," said Lady Grace, with the gentlest of accents, while she bent her head over the beautiful altar-cloth she was embroidering.

"Nonsense,—absurdity! such a crime would soon have publicity enough."

Lady Grace gave a smile of compassionate pity at the speech, but said nothing.

"I can't imagine how you could believe such a thing possible," said the Viscountess, tartly.

"I can only say, my dear, that no later than last night Monsignore assured me that, through M. Mazzini and the Bible societies, you can make away with any one in Europe, and, indeed, in most parts of the world besides. Don't smile so contemptuously, my dear. Remember who it is says this. Of course, as he remarks, the foolish newspapers have their own stupid explanations always ready, at one moment calling it a political crime, at another the act of insanity, and so on. They affected this language about Count Rossi, and then about the dear and sainted Archbishop of Paris; but what true believer ever accepted this?"

"Monsignore would not hold this language to me," said Lady Lackington, haughtily.

"Very probably not, dearest; he spoke in confidence when he mentioned it to me."

"I mean, that he would hesitate ere he forfeited any respect I entertain for his common-sense by the utterance of such wild absurdity. What is it, Turner?" asked she, suddenly, as her maid entered.

"Four packing-cases have just come, my Lady, with Mr. Spicer's respectful compliments, and that he will be here immediately,—he has only gone to change his dress."

"Why don't he come at once? I don't care for his dress."

"No, my Lady, of course not," said Turner, and retired.

"I must say he has made haste," said Lady Lackington, languidly. "It was only on the eighth or the ninth, I think, he left this, and as he had to get all my mourning things,—I had actually nothing,—and to go down to Lackington Court, and then to Wales, and after that to the Isle of Wight, what with lawyers and other tiresome people to talk to, he has really not done badly."

"I hope he has brought the chalice," sighed Lady Grace.

"I hope he has brought some tidings of my respectable brother-in-law," said the Viscountess, in a tone that seemed to say where the really important question lay.

"And the caviare,—I trust he has not forgotten the caviare. It is the only thing Monsignore eats at breakfast in Advent."

An insolent gesture of the head was all the acknowledgment Lady Lackington vouchsafed to this speech. At last she spoke: "When he can get horse-racing out of his head, Spicer is a very useful creature."

"Very, indeed," said Lady Grace.

"The absurd notion that he is a sporting character is the parent of so many other delusions; he fancies himself affluent, and, stranger still, imagines he's a gentleman." And the idea so amused her Ladyship that she laughed aloud at it.

"Mr. Spicer, my Lady," said a servant, flinging wide the door; and in a most accurate morning-dress, every detail of which was faultless, that gentleman bowed his way across the room with an amount of eagerness that might possibly exact a shake of the hand, but, if unsuccessful, might easily subside into a colder acceptance. Lady Lackington vouchsafed nothing beyond a faint smile, and the words, "How d'ye do?" as with a slight gesture she motioned to him the precise chair he was to seat himself on. Before taking his place, Mr. Spicer made a formal bow to Lady Grace, who, with a vacant smile, acknowledged the courtesy, and went on with her work.

"You have made very tolerable haste, Spicer," said Lady Lackington. "I scarcely expected you before Saturday."

"I have not been to bed for six nights, my Lady."

"You 'll sleep all the better for it to-night, perhaps."

"We had an awful gale of wind in crossing to Calais,—the passage took eight hours."

"You relished land travelling all the more for it afterwards."

"Not so, my Lady; for at Lyons the whole country was flooded, and we were obliged to march eleven miles afoot on a railway embankment, and under a tremendous storm of rain; but even that was not the worst, for in crossing the St. Bernard—"

"I really don't care for such moving accidents; I always skip them in the newspapers. What of my mourning,—is much crape worn?"

"A great deal of crape, my Lady, and in 'bouffes' down the dress."

"With bugles or without? I see by your hesitation, sir, you have forgotten about the bugles."

"No, my Lady, I have them," said he, proudly; "small acorns of Jet are also worn on points of the flounces, and Madame Frontin suggested that, as your Ladyship dislikes black so much—"

"But who said as much, sir?" broke she in, angrily.

"And the caviare, Mr. Spicer,—have you remembered the caviare?" lisped out Lady Grace.

"Yes, my Lady; but Fortnum's people are afraid some of it may prove a failure. There was something, I don't know what, happened to the fish in the Baltic this year."

"Who ventured to say black was unbecoming to me?" asked Lady Lackington, changing her question, and speaking more angrily.

"It was Frontin, my Lady, who remarked that you once had said nothing would ever induce you to wear that odious helmet widows sometimes put on."

"Oh dear; and I have such a fancy for it," exclaimed Lady Grace.

"You mistake, my dear; you are confounding the occasion with the costume," said Lady Lackington; and her eyes sparkled with the malice of her remark.

Mr. Spicer's face exhibited as much enjoyment of the wit as he deemed decorous to the party satirized.

"And now, sir, for the important part of your mission r have you obtained any information about my brother-in-law?"

"Yes, my Lady, I saw him at Chiavenna. He drove up to the post-house to change horses as we were there; he told me, in the few minutes we spoke together, that they were on their way to Rome."

"Whom do you mean, sir, when you say 'they'?"

"Lord and Lady Lackington, my Lady."

"Is he married? Did you say he was married, sir?'" exclaimed she, in a voice discordant above all her efforts to restrain.

"Yes, my Lady; I was, in a manner, presented to her Ladyship, who was, I must say, a very beautiful person—"

"I want no raptures, sir; are you quite certain she was his wife?"

"His Lordship told me so, my Lady; and when they reached the Hôtel Royal, at Milan, I took occasion to question the courier! whom I knew before, and he told me all about it."

"Go on, sir."

"Well, my Lady, they were just married about ten or twelve days when I met them; the ceremony had been performed in some little out-of-the-way spot in the Rhine country, where Mr. Beecher had been staying for the summer, and where, as it happened, he never received any tidings of the late Lord's death, or the presumption is, he had never made this unfortunate connection."

"What do you mean by 'unfortunate connection'?"

"Why, one must really call it so, my Lady; the world, at least, will say as much."

"Who is she, sir?"

"She's the daughter of one of the most notorious men in England, my Lady,—the celebrated leg, Grog Davis."

Ah, Mr. Spicer, small and insignificant as you are, you have your sting, and her Ladyship has felt it. These words, slowly uttered in a tone of assumed sorrow, so overcame her they were addressed to, that she covered her face with her handkerchief and sat thus, speechless, for several minutes. To Spicer it was a moment of triumph,—it was a vengeance for all the insults, all the slights she showered upon him, and he only grieved to think how soon her proud spirit would rally from the shock.

Lady Lackington's face, as she withdrew her handkerchief, was of ashy paleness, and her bloodless lips trembled with emotion. "Have you heard what this man has said, Grace?" whispered she, in a voice so distinct as to be audible throughout the room.

"Yes, dearest; it is most distressing," said the other, in the softest of accents.

"Distressing! It is an infamy!" cried she. Then suddenly turning to Spicer, with flaring eyes and flushed face, she said, "You have rather a talent for blundering, sir, and it is just as likely this is but a specimen of your powers. I am certain she is not his wife."

"I can only say, my Lady, that I took pains enough to get the story accurately; and as Kuffner, the courier, was at the marriage—"

"Marriage!" broke she in, with a sarcastic irony; "why, sir, it is not thus a peer of England selects the person who is to share his dignity."

"But you forget, my Lady," interposed Spicer, "that he did n't know he was a peer—he had not the slightest expectation of being one—at the time. Old Grog knew it—"

"Have a care, sir, and do not *you* forget yourself. These familiar epithets are for your associates in the ring, and not for *my* ears."

"Well, the Captain, my Lady,—he is as well known by that name as the other,—he had all the information, and kept back the letters, and managed the whole business so cleverly that the first Mr. Beecher ever knew of his. Lordship's death was when hearing it from Mr. Twining at Baden."

"I thought Mr. Twining was in Algiers, or Australia, I forget which," said Lady Grace, gently.

"Such a marriage must be a mockery,—a mere mockery. He shall break it,—he must break it!" said Lady Lacking-ton, as she walked up and down with the long strides and the step of a tigress in a cage.

"Oh dear! they are so difficult to break!" sighed Lady-Grace. "Mr. Twining always promised me a divorce when the law came in and made it so cheap, and now he says that it's all a mistake, and until another Bill, or an Act, or something or other, is passed, that it's a luxury far above persons of moderate fortune."

"Break it he shall," muttered Lady Lackington, as she continued her march.

"Of course, dearest, expense doesn't signify to *you*," sighed out Lady Grace.

"And do you mean to tell me, sir," said Lady Lacking-ton, "that this is the notorious Captain Davis of whose doings we have been reading in every newspaper?"

"Yes, my Lady, he is the notorious"—he was going to say "Grog," but corrected himself, and added—"Captain Davis, and has been for years back the intimate associate of the present Lord Lackington."

Mr. Spicer was really enjoying himself on this occasion, nor was it often his fortune to give her Ladyship so much annoyance innocuously. His self-indulgence, however, carried him too far; for Lady Lackington, suddenly turning round, caught the expression of gratified malice on his face.

"Take care, sir,—take care," she cried, with a menacing gesture of her finger. "There may chance to be a flaw somewhere in your narrative; and if there should, Mr. Spicer,—if there should,—I don't *think* Lord Lackington would forget it,—I am *sure I* sha'n't." And with this threatening declaration her Ladyship swept out of the room in most haughty fashion.

"This is all what comes of being obliging," exclaimed Spicer, unable to control himself any longer. "It was not *I* that threw Beecher into Grog's company,—it was not *I* that made him marry Grog's daughter. For all that *I* cared, he might go and be a monk at La Trappe, or marry as many wives as Brigham Young himself."

"I hope you brought me Lady Gertrude Oscot's book, Mr. Spicer,— 'Rays through Oriel Windows'?" said Lady Grace, in one of her sweetest voices. "She is such a charming poetess."

"I'd lay my life on't, she's just as wide-awake as her father," muttered Spicer to himself.

"As wide-awake? Dear me, what can you mean?"

"That's she's fly—up to trap—oh, isn't she!" went he on, still communing to himself.

"Lady Gertrude Oscot, sir?"

"No; but Grog Davis's daughter,—the new Viscountess Lackington,— my Lady. I was thinking of *her*," said Spicer, suddenly recalled to a sense of where he stood.

"I protest, sir, I cannot understand how two persons so totally dissimilar could occur to any mind at the same moment." And with this Lady Grace gathered up the details of her embroidery, and courtesying a deep and formal adieu, left the room.

"Haven't I gone and done it with both of them!" said Spicer, as he took out his cigar-case to choose a cigar; not that he had the slightest intention of lighting it in such a place,—no profanity of the kind ever occurred to him,—all he meant was the mock bravado to himself of an act that seemed to imply so much coolness, such collected courage. As to striking a light, he 'd as soon have done it in a magazine.

And sticking his cigar in his mouth, he left the house; even in the street he forgot to light it, and strolled along, turning his weed between his lips, and revolving no very pleasant thoughts in his mind: "All the way to England, down to Wales, then the Isle of Wight, seeing no end of people,— lawyers, milliners, agents, proctors, jewellers, and dressmakers—eternal explainings and expostulatings, begging for this, deprecating that; asking this man to be active and the other to be patient; and then back again over the whole breadth of Europe in atrocious weather, sea-sick and land-sick, tossed, Jolted, and shaken,—and all for what,—ay, for what? To be snubbed, outraged, and insulted, treated like a lackey,—no, but ten times worse than any lackey would bear. And why should I bear it? That's the question. Why should I? Does it signify a brass farthing to me whether the noble house of Lackington quarters its arms with the cogged dice and the marked king of the Davises? What do I care about their tarnished shield? It's rather cool of my lady to turn upon *me!*" Well reasoned and true, Mr. Spicer; you have but forgotten one small item in the account, which is the consideration accorded to you by your own set, because you were seen to mingle with those so much above you.

We are told that when farthings are shaken up a sufficiently long time with guineas in a bag, they acquire a sort of yellow lustre, which, though by no means enabling them to pass for guineas, still makes them wonderfully bright farthings, and doubtless would render them very intolerant in the company of their equals. Such was, in a measure, what had happened to Mr. Spicer; and though at first sight the process would seem a gain, it is in reality the reverse, since, after this mock gilding, the coin—whether it be man or farthing—has lost its stamp of truthfulness, and will not "pass" for even the humble value it once represented.

"At all events," thought Mr. Spicer, as he went along, "her Ladyship has not come off scot free for all her impertinence. I have given her materials for a very miserable morning, and irritated the very sorest spot in all her mind.

It was just the very lesson she wanted; there's nothing will do her so much good in the world."

It is by no means an uncommon delusion for ill-natured people to fancy that they are great moral physicians, and that the bitters they drop into *your* wine-glass and *my* teacup are admirable tonics, which our constitutions require. The drug is not always an evil, but the doctor is detestable.

As Spicer drew nigh one of the great hotels in the Piazza di Spagna, he recognized Beecher's travelling-carriage just being unloaded at the door. They had arrived at that moment, and the courier was bustling about and giving his orders like one whose master was likely to exact much and pay handsomely.

"The whole of the first floor, Freytag," said the courier, authoritatively; "every room of it. My Lord cannot bear the disturbance of people lodged near him."

"He used not to be so particular in the 'Bench,'" muttered Spicer. "I remember his sleeping one of three in a room."

"Ah, Mr. Spicer, my Lord said, if I should meet you, to mention he wishes to see you."

"Do you think he'd receive me now, Kuffner?"

"Well, I 'll go and see."

Mr. Kuffner came speedily back, and, beckoning to Spicer to follow, led the way to Lord Lackington's room. "He is dressing for dinner, but will see you," added he, as he introduced him.

The noble Viscount did not turn from the mirror at which he was elaborately arranging his neckcloth as Spicer entered, but satisfied himself with calling out, "Take a chair, Spicer; you 'll find one somewhere."

The tone of the salutation was not more significant than the aspect of this room itself. All the articles of a costly dressing-case of silver-gilt were ranged on one table Essence-bottles, snuff-boxes, pipe-heads, with rings, jewelled buttons, and such-like knick-knackeries covered another; whatever fancy could suggest or superfluity compass of those thousand-and-one trinkets the effeminacy of our age has introduced into male costume, all abounded. Quantities, too, of the most expensive clothes were there,—rich uniforms, fur-lined pelisses, and gold-embroidered waistcoats. And as Mr. Spicer quickly made the tour of these with his eye, his gaze rested at last on my Lord himself, whose dressing-gown of silver brocade would have made a state robe for a Venetian Doge.

"Everything is in confusion just now; but if you 'll throw down some of those things, you 'll get a chair," said Beecher, carelessly.

Spicer, however, preferred to take his place at the chimney, on which he leaned in an attitude that might take either the appearance of respect or familiarity, as the emergency required.

"When did you arrive?" asked my Lord.

"About two hours ago," was the short reply.

Beecher turned to gaze at the man, who answered without more semblance of deference, and now, for the first time, their eyes met. It was, evidently, Spicer's game, by a bold assertion of former intimacy, to place their future intercourse on its old footing; and just as equally decided was Beecher that no traditions of the past should rise up and obtrude themselves on the present, and so he threw into this quiet, steady stare an amount of haughty resolution, before which Spicer quailed and struck his flag.

"Perhaps I should say three hours, my Lord," added Spicer, flurriedly; and Beecher turned away with a slight curl on his lip, as though to say, "The conflict was not a very long one." Spicer marked the expression, and vowed vengeance for it.

"I thought you 'd have got here two or three days before," said Beecher, carelessly.

"Vetturino travelling is not like extra-post, my Lord," said Spicer, fawningly. "You could cover your hundred miles between breakfast and a late dinner, while we thought ourselves wonderful to get over forty from sunrise to midnight."

"That's true," yawned out Beecher; "vetturino work must be detestable."

"No man could give you a better catalogue of its grievances than your father-in-law, my Lord; he has had a long experience of them. I remember, one winter, we started from Brussels in the deep snow,—there was Baring, Hope, Fisk, Grog, and myself."

"I don't care to hear your adventures; and it would be just as agreeable to me were you to call my relative Captain Davis, as to speak of him by a vulgar nickname."

"Faith, my Lord, I did n't mean it. It slipped out quite unconsciously, Just as it did awhile ago,—far more awkwardly, by the bye,—when I was talking to Lady Lacking-ton. The dowager, I mean."

"And what occasion, sir, had you to refer to Captain Davis in *her* company?" asked Beecher, fiercely.

"She asked me plumply, my Lord, what was her Ladyship's name, what family she came of, who her connections were, and I told her that I never heard of any of them, except her father, popularly known as Grog Davis,—a man that every one on the turf was acquainted with."

"You are a malicious scoundrel, Spicer," said Beecher, whose pale cheek now shook and trembled with passion.

"Well, I don't think so, my Lord," said the other, quietly. "It is not, certainly, the character the world gives me. And as to what passed between her Ladyship and myself this afternoon, I did my very best to escape difficulties. I told her that the Brighton affair was almost forgotten now,— it was fully eighteen years since it happened; that as to Charles Herbert's death, there were two stories,—some averring that poor Charley had actually struck Grog; and then, though the York trial was a public scandal— Well, my Lord, don't look so angrily at me; it was by no fault of *mine* these transactions became notorious."

"And what have you been all your whole life to this Davis but his cad and errand-boy,—a fellow he has sent with a bad horse,—for he would not have trusted you with a good one,—to run for a hack stakes in an obscure county, a lounger about stables and the steps of club-houses, picking up scraps of news from the jocks and selling them to the gentlemen? Does it become you to turn out Kit Davis and run full cry after him?"

It was but rarely that Beecher's indignation could warm up to the temperature of downright passion; but when it did so, it gave the man a sort of power that few would have recognized in his weak and yielding nature; at all events, Spicer was not the man to stem such a torrent, and so he stared at him with mingled terror and anger.

"I tell you, Mr. Spicer," added Beecher, more passionately still, "if you hadn't known Davis was a thousand miles away, you 'd never have trusted yourself to speak of him in this fashion; but, for your comfort I say it, he 'll be here in a day or two."

"I never said a word of him you 'd not find in the newspapers," said Spicer, doggedly.

"When you come to settle accounts together, it will surprise me very much if there won't be matter for another paragraph in them," said Beecher, with a sneer.

Spicer winced; he tried to arrange his neckcloth, and then to button his glove, but all his efforts could not conceal a tremor that shook him from head to foot. Now, when Beecher got his "man down," he never thought he could trample enough upon him; and as he walked the room in hasty strides to and fro, he jeeringly pictured to Spicer the pleasures of his next meeting with Davis: not, indeed, but that all his eloquence was superfluous; it needed no descriptive powers to convince any who enjoyed Grog's *friendship* what his enmity might imply.

"I know him as well as *you* do, my Lord," said Spicer, as his patience at last gave way; "and I know, besides, there's more than half the Continent where he can't set a foot."

"Perhaps you mentioned that, also, to my sister-in-law," said Beecher, derisively.

"No, I said nothing about it!" muttered the other.

There was now a pause; each only waited for any, the slightest show of concession to make advances to the other; for although without the slightest particle of good feeling on either side, they well knew the force of the adage that enjoins friendship among knaves. My Lord thoroughly appreciated the utility of a Spicer; well did Spicer understand all the value of a peer's acquaintance.

Each ruminated long over the situation; and at last Beecher said, "Did poor Lackington leave you anything in his will?"

"A racing snaffle and two whips, my Lord."

"Poor fellow, he never forgot any one, I 'm sure," sighed Beecher.

"He had a wonderful memory, indeed, my Lord; for I had borrowed twenty pounds of him at the Canterbury races some ten years ago, and he said to me, just before he took to bed, 'Never mind the trifle that's between us, Spicer; I shall not take it.'"

"Good-hearted, generous fellow!" muttered Beecher.

Spicer's mouth twitched a little, but he did not speak.

"There never was a better brother, never!" said Beecher, far more intent upon the display of his own affectionate sorrow than in commemorating fraternal virtues. "We never had a word of disagreement in our lives. Poor Lackington! he used to think he was doing the best by me by keeping me so tight, and always threatening to cut me down still lower; he meant it for the best, but you know I could n't live upon it, the thing was impossible. If I had n't been one of the 'wide-awakes,' I 'd have gone to the wall at once; and let me tell you, Master Spicer, it wasn't every fellow would have kept his head over water where I was swimming."

"That I 'm convinced of," said Spicer, gravely.

"Well, it's a long lane has no turning, Spicer," said he, oomplacently looking at himself in the glass. "Even a runaway pulls up somewhere; not but I'm sorry from the bottom of my heart for poor Lack, but it will be our own turn one of these days; that's a match there's no paying forfeit on, eh, Spicer? it must come off whether we will or not!"

"So it must, my Lord," sighed out Spicer, sympathetically.

"Ay, by Jove! whether a man leaves twelve thousand a year or only two hundred behind him," sighed out Beecher, who could not help making the application to himself.

Again did Spicer sigh, and so profoundly, it might have represented grief for the whole peerage.

"I say, old fellow," said Beecher, clapping him familiarly on the shoulder, "I wish you had n't told Georgy all that stuff about Davis; these things do no good."

"I assure you solemnly, my Lord, I said it with the best motives; her Ladyship would certainly learn the whole history somewhere, and so I thought I 'd just sketch the thing off in a light, easy way."

"Come, come, Spicer,—no gammon, my lad; you never tried any of your light, easy ways with *my* sister-in-law. At all events, it's done, and can't be undone now," sighed he, drearily. Then, after a moment, he added, "How did she take the news?"

"Well, at first, my Lord, she wouldn't believe it, but went on, 'She's not his wife, sir; I tell you they're not married,' and so on."

"Well,—and then?"

"Then, my Lord, I assured her that there could be no doubt of the matter; that your Lordship had done me the honor of presenting me—"

"Which I never did, Master Spicer," laughed in Beecher,—"you know well enough that I never did; but a fib won't choke you, old fellow."

"At all events, I made it clear that you were really married, and to the daughter of a man that would send you home on a shutter if you threw any doubt on it."

"Wouldn't he, by Jupiter!" exclaimed Beecher, with all the sincerity of a great fact "Well, after *that*, how did she take on?"

"She did n't say a word, but rocked from side to side, this way,—like one going to faint; and, indeed, her color all went, and she was pale as a corpse; and then she took long breaths, and muttered below her voice, 'This is worst of all!' After that she rallied, and certainly gave it to your Lordship in round style, but always winding it up with, 'Break it he shall, and must, if it was the Archbishop of Canterbury married them.'"

"Very fine talking, Master Spicer, but matrimony is a match where you can't scratch and pay forfeits. I wish you could," muttered he to himself. "I wish you had the presence of mind and the pluck to have told her that it was *my* affair, and not *hers*. As to the honor of the Lackingtons and all that lot, she is n't a Lackington any more than you are,—she 's a De Tracey; good blood, no better, but she isn't one of us, and you ought to have told her so."

"I own I 'd not have had courage for that!" said Spicer, candidly.

"That's what I'd have said in your place, Spicer. The present Viscount Lackington is responsible to himself, and not to the late Lord's widow; and, what's more, he is no flat, without knowledge of men and the world, but a fellow with both eyes open, and who has gone through as smart a course of education as any man in the ring. Take up the Racing Calendar, and show me any one, since Huckaback beat Crim. Con., that ever got it so 'hot' as I have. No, no, my Lady, it won't do, preaching to me about 'life.' If *I* don't know a thing or two, who does? If you 'd have had your wits about you, Spicer, that's what you 'd have told her."

"I'm not so ready at a pinch as you are, my Lord," muttered Spicer, who affected sullenness.

"Few are, Master Spicer,—very few are, I can tell you;" and in the pleasure of commending and complimenting himself and his own great gifts, Beecher speedily ceased to remember. What so lately had annoyed him. "Dine here at seven, Spicer," said he, at last, "and I'll present you to my Lady. She 'll be amused with *you*." Though the last words were uttered in a way that made their exact significance somewhat doubtful, Mr. Spicer never sought to canvass them; he accepted the invitation in good part, for he was one of those men who, though they occasionally "quarrel with their bread-and-butter," are wise enough never to fall out with their truffles.

CHAPTER XXIX
THE TWO VISCOUNTESSES

When the new Viscount had dismissed Mr. Spicer, he set out to visit his sister-in-law. Any one who has been patient enough to follow the stages of this history will readily imagine that he did not address himself to the task before him with remarkable satisfaction. If it had been a matter to be bought off by money, he would readily have paid down a good round sum as forfeit. It was no use fortifying himself, as he tried to do, by all the commonplaces he kept repeating to his own heart, saying, "She ain't my guardian. I'm no ward to be responsible to *her*. She can exercise no control over me or my property. She 's the dowager, and no more." All the traditions of his younger brother life rose up in rebellion against these doctrines, and he could think of her as nothing but the haughty Viscountess, who had so often pronounced the heaviest censures upon his associates and his mode of living. A favorite theory of his was it, also, in olden time, to imagine that, but for Georgina, Lackington would have done this, that, and t'other for him; that she it was who thwarted all his brother's generous impulses, and brought him to look with stern disfavor on his life of debt and dissipation. These memories rushed now fully to his mind, and, assuredly, added no sentiment of pleasure to his expectation of the meeting. More than once did he come to a halt, and deliberate whether, seeing how unpleasant such an interview must prove, he need incur the pain of it. "I could write to her, or I could send Lizzy to say that I was confined to bed, and ill. Would n't that be a flare up! By Jove! if I could only see the match as it came off between them, I 'd do *that*. Not but I know Georgy would win; she 'd come out so strong as 'Grande Dame;' the half-bred 'un would have no chance. Still, there would be a race, and a close one, for Lizzy has her own turn of speed; and if she had the breeding—" And as he got thus far in his ruminations, he had reached the Palazzo Gondi, where his sister-in-law lived. With a sort of sullen courage he rang the bell, and was shown in; her Ladyship was dressing, but would be down in a moment.

Beecher had now some minutes alone, and he passed them scrutinizing the room and its appurtenances. All was commoner and more homely than he looked for. Not many indications of comfort; scarcely any of luxury. What might this mean? Was her settlement so small as to exact this economy, or was it a voluntary saving? If so, it was the very reverse of all her former tastes, for she was essentially one who cultivated splendor and expense. This problem was still puzzling him, when the door opened, and she entered. He advanced rapidly to meet her, and saluted her on each cheek. There was a strange affectation of cordiality on each side. Prize-fighters shake hands ere they double them up into catapults for each other's heads; but the embrace here was rather more like the kiss the victim on the scaffold bestows upon his executioner.

Seated side by side on the sofa, for a few minutes neither uttered a word; at last she said, in a calm, low voice, "We had hoped to see you before this, — *he* looked anxiously for your coming."

Beecher heaved a heavy sigh; in that unhappy delay was comprised all the story of his calamities. And how to begin—how to open the narrative?

"I wrote as many as five letters," resumed she; "some addressed to Fordyce's, others to the care of Mr. Davenport Dunn."

"Not one of them ever reached me."

"Very strange, indeed," said she, with the smile of faintest incredulity; "letters so seldom miscarry nowadays. Stranger, still, that none of your other correspondents should have apprised you of your brother's state; there was ample time to have done it."

"I know nothing of it I vow to Heaven I had not the slightest suspicion of it!"

"Telegraphs, too, are active agencies in these days, and I wrote to Fordyce to use every exertion to acquaint you."

"I can only repeat what I have said already, that I was utterly ignorant of everything till I arrived at Baden; there I accidentally met Twining—"

"Spicer told me about it," said she abruptly, as though it was not necessary to discuss any point conceded on both sides. "Your coming," continued she, "was all the more eagerly looked for because it was necessary you should be, so far as possible, prepared for the suit we are threatened with; actions at law for ejectments on title are already announced, and great—the very greatest—inconvenience has resulted for want of formal instructions on your part."

"Is the thing really serious, Georgy?" asked he, with an unfeigned anxiety of manner.

"If you only will take the trouble of reading Fordyce's two last letters, — they are very long, I confess, and somewhat difficult to understand, —you will at least see that his opinion is the reverse of favorable. In fact, he thinks the English estates are gone."

"Oh, Georgy dearest! but *you* don't believe that?"

"The Irish barony and certain lands in Cork," resumed she, calmly, "are not included in the demand they profess to make; nor, of course, have they any claim as to the estates purchased by Lord Lackington through Mr. Dunn."

"But the title?"

"The Viscounty goes with the English property."

"Good heavens! a title we have held undisturbed, unquestioned, since Edward the Third's time. I cannot bring myself to conceive it!"

"Great reverses of condition can be borne with dignity when they are not of our own incurring," said she, with a stern and pointed significance.

"I'm afraid I cannot boast of possessing all your philosophy," said he, touchily.

"So much the worse. You would need it, and even more, too, if all that I have heard be true."

There was no mistaking this inference, and Beecher only hesitated whether he should accept battle at once, or wait for another broadside.

"Not but," broke she in, "if you could assure me that the rumors were untrue,—that *you* have been calumniated, and I misinformed,—if, I say, you were enabled to do this, the tidings would help greatly to sustain me through this season of trouble."

"You must speak more plainly, Georgina, if I am to understand you."

"Are you married, Annesley?" said she, abruptly.

"Yes. I hope I am of an age to enter the holy estate without leave from my relations."

"It is true, then?" said she, with a deep, full voice.

"Perfectly true. And then?" There was an open defiance in this tone of questioning which seemed actually to sting her.

"And then?" repeated she, after him,—"'and then?' You are right to say, 'and then?'—if that means 'What next?'"

Beecher turned pale and red, as fear and passion swayed him alternately; but he never spoke.

"Is it really a marriage?" broke she in again, "or is it some mockery enacted by a degraded priest, and through the collusion of some scheming sharpers. Oh, Annesley! tell me frankly how you have been tricked into this ignominious contract!" And her accents, as she spoke this, assumed a tone of imploring affection that actually moved him. To this a sense of offended dignity quickly succeeded with him, and he said, —

"I cannot permit you to continue in this strain; I am rightfully, legally married, and the lady who shares my lot is as much the Viscountess Lackington as you are."

She covered her face with both her hands, and sat thus for several minutes.

"Perhaps it is all for the best," muttered she, in a low but audible accent, — "perhaps it is all for the best. Loss of rank, station, and name will fall the more lightly on those who so little understood how to maintain them with dignity."

"And if I am threatened with the loss of my title and fortune," cried Beecher, passionately, "is it exactly the time to heap these insults on me?"

Partly from the firmness of his manner as he uttered these words, partly that they were not devoid of truthful meaning, she accepted the reproof almost submissively.

"You must go over to England at once, Beecher," said she, calmly. "You must place yourself immediately in Fordyce's hands, and secure the best advice the Bar affords. I would go with you myself, but that—" The deep flush that spread over Beecher's face as she paused here made the moment one of intense pain to each. "No matter," resumed she; "there is only one danger I would warn you against. You dropped the word 'compromise;' now, Annesley, let nothing induce you to descend to this. Such a suggestion could only have come from those whose habits of life accept expediency in lieu of principle. Maintain your rights proudly and defiantly so long as they pertain to you; if law should at last declare that we are only usurpers—" She tried to finish, but the words seemed as if they would choke her, and after an effort almost convulsive she burst into tears. Scarcely less moved, Beecher covered his face with his hands and turned away.

"I will do whatever you advise me, Georgina," said he at length, as he seated himself on the sofa at her side. "If you say I ought to go to England, I'll set off at once."

"Yes; you must be in London; you must be where you can have daily, hourly access to your lawyers; but you must also determine that this contest shall be decided by law, and law alone. I cannot, will not, believe that your rights are invalid. I feel assured that the House of Lords will maintain the cause of an acknowledged member of their order against the claims of an obscure pretender. This sympathy, however, will only be with you so long as you are true to yourself. Let the word 'compromise' be but uttered, and the generous sentiment will be withdrawn; therefore, Annesley," —here she dropped her voice, and spoke more impressively, — "therefore, I should say, go over to England *alone*; be free to exercise untrammelled your own calm judgment, —keep your residence a secret from all save your law advisers, — see none else."

"You mean, then, that I should go without my wife?"

"Yes!" said she, coldly; "if she accompany you, her friends, her father, with whom she will of course correspond, will know of your whereabouts, and flock round you with their unsafe counsels; this is most to be avoided."

"But how is it to be managed, Georgina; she cannot surely stop here, at an hotel too, while I am away in England?"

"I can see nothing against such an arrangement; not having had the pleasure of seeing and knowing Lady Lack-ington, I am unable to guess any valid reasons against this plan. Is she young?"

"Not twenty."

"Handsome, of course?" said she, with a slight but supercilious curl of the lip.

"Very handsome, —beautiful," answered he, but in a voice that denoted no rapture.

Lady Lackington mused for a moment or two; it seemed as if she were discussing within her own mind a problem, stating and answering objections as they arose, for she muttered such broken words as, "Dangerous, of course—in Rome especially—but impossible for her to go to England—all her relations—anything better than that—must make the best of it;" then turning to Beecher with an air of one whose determination was taken, she said: "She must stay with me till you return." Before he had rallied from his surprise at this resolution, she added, "Come over to tea this evening, and let me see her."

Beecher pressed her hand cordially, as though to imply a gratitude above words; but in reality he turned away to conceal all the emotions this new position of difficulty occasioned, merely calling out, "We 'll come very early," as he departed.

Lizzy heard that Spicer was to be their guest at dinner, and they themselves to take tea with the Viscountess. Lackington, with equal indifference. She had scarcely *seen* Mr. Spicer, and was not over-pleased with her brief impression; of her Ladyship she had only *heard*, but even that much had not inspired her to anticipate a pleasant meeting.

There was, however, in her husband's manner, a sort of fidgety anxiety that showed he attached to the coming interview an amount of importance she could by no means understand. He continued to throw out such hints as to "Georgina's notions" on this or that point; and, while affecting a half ridicule, really showed how seriously he regarded them. Even to Lizzy's dress his cares extended; and he told her to be mindful that nothing in her costume should attract special criticism or remark.

Beecher was far more uneasy than even his looks betrayed. He dreaded to dwell upon the haughty demeanor his sister-in-law would so certainly assume, and the sort of inspection to which his wife was to be subjected. In his heart he wished that Lizzy had been less beautiful, less attractive, or, as he ungraciously styled it to himself, "less showy." He well knew how damaging would all her brilliant qualities become to the eyes of one herself a belle and a beauty in times past. He discussed over and over with himself whether it might not be better to acquaint Lizzy of the kind of dress parade that awaited her, or leave wholly to chance the events of the interview. For once in his life he took a wise resolve, and said nothing on the matter.

The dinner passed off somewhat heavily,—Beecher silent and preoccupied, Lizzy thoughtful and indisposed to converse, and Spicer vexed, in spite of all his resolutions to the contrary, by what he had insultingly called to himself "the airs of Grog Davis's daughter;" and yet nothing could be less just than to stigmatize by such a phrase a manner quiet, calm, and unpretentious, and totally removed from all affectation.

For a while Beecher bestowed a watchful attention on Spicer, uneasy lest by some adroit piece of malice he might either irritate Lizzy or lead her covertly into some imprudent disclosures; but he soon saw that it would have required a hardier spirit than Mr. Spicer's to have adventured on impertinence in that quarter, and, lighting his cigar, he sat moodily down by the window to think on the future.

Left with the field thus open, Spicer canvassed within himself how best to profit by the opportunity. Should he declare himself an old friend of her father's,—his associate and his colleague? Should he dexterously intimate that, knowing all about her family and antecedents, she could not do better than secure his friendship? Should he not also slyly suggest that, married to a man like Beecher, the counsels of one prudent and wily as himself would prove invaluable? "Now or never," thought he, as he surveyed her pale features, and interpreted their expression as implying timidity and fear.

"Your first visit to Rome, I believe?" said he, as he searched for a cigar amidst the heap on the table.

A cold assent followed.

"Wonderful place; not merely for its old monuments and ruins, though they are curious too, but its strange society,—all nations and all ranks of each mixed and mingled together: great swells and snobs, grand ladies, princes, cardinals and ambassadors, thrown together with artistes, gamblers, and fast ones of either sex,—a regular fair of fine company, with, plenty of amusement and lots of adventure."

"Indeed!" said she, languidly.

"Just the place your father would like," said he, dropping his voice to a half-whisper.

"In what way, pray?" asked she, quietly.

"Why, in the way of trade, of course," said he, laughing. "For the fine-lady part of the matter he 'd not care for it,—that never was his line of country,—but for the young swells that thought themselves sporting characters, for the soft young gents that fancied they could play, Grog was always ready. I ask your pardon for the familiar nickname, but we 've known each other about thirty years. He always called me Ginger. Haven't you heard him speak of old Ginger?"

"Never, sir."

"Strange that; but perhaps he did not speak of his pals to you?"

"No, never."

"That was so like him. I never saw his equal to hunt over two different kinds of country. He could get on the top of a bus and go down to St. John's Wood, or to Putney, after a whole night at Crawley's, and with an old shooting-jacket and Jim-crow on him, and a garden-rake in his hand, you 'd never suspect he was the fellow who had cleared out the company and carried off every shilling at billiards and blind-hookey. Poor old Kit, how fond I am of him!"

A stare, whose meaning Spicer could not fathom, was the only reply to the speech.

"And he was so fond of *me!* I was the only one of them all he could trust. He liked Beech—I mean his Lordship there; he was always attached to him, but whenever it was really a touch-and-go thing, a nice operation, then he'd say, 'Where's Ginger? give me Ginger!' The adventures we've had together would make a book; and do you know that more than once

I thought of writing them, or getting a fellow to write them, for it's all the same. I'd have called it 'Grog and Ginger.' Wouldn't that take?"

She made no reply; her face was, perhaps, a thought paler, but unchanged in expression.

"And then the scenes we've gone through!—dangerous enough some of them; he rather liked that, and *I* own it never was my taste."

"I am surprised to hear you say so, sir," said she, in a low but very distinct voice; "I'd have imagined exactly the reverse."

"Indeed! and may I make so bold as to ask why?"

"Simply, sir, that a gentleman so worldly-wise as yourself must always be supposed to calculate eventualities, and not incur, willingly at least, those he has no mind for. To be plain, sir, I 'm at a loss to understand how one not fond of peril should hazard the chance of being thrown out of a window,—don't start, I 'm only a woman, and cannot do it, nor, though I have rung for the servant, am I going to order *him*. For this time it shall be the door." And, rising proudly, she walked toward the window; but ere she reached it, Spicer was gone.

"What's become of Spicer, Lizzy?" said Beecher, indolently, as his eyes traversed the room in search of him.

"He has taken his leave," said she, in a voice as careless.

"He's tiresome, I think," yawned he; "at least, I find him so."

She made no reply, but sat down to compose her thoughts, somewhat ruffled by the late scene.

"Ain't it time to order the carriage? I told Georgy we'd come early," added he, after a pause.

"I almost think I'll not go to-night," said she, in a low voice.

"Not go! You don't mean that when my sister-in-law sends you a message to come and see her that you 'll refuse!" cried he, in a mixture of anger and astonishment.

"I'm afraid I could be guilty of so great an enormity," said she, smiling superciliously.

"It's exactly the word for it, whatever you may think," said he, doggedly. "All I can say is, that you don't know Georgina, or you'd never have dreamt of it."

"In that case it is better I *should* know her; so I'll get my bonnet and shawl at once."

She was back in the room in a moment, and they set out for the Palazzo Gondi.

What would not Beecher have given, as they drove along, for courage to counsel and advise her,—to admonish as to this, and caution as to that? And yet he did not dare to utter a word, and she was as silent.

It would not be very easy to say exactly what sort of person Lady Georgina expected in her sister-in-law; indeed, she had pictured her in so many shapes to herself that there was not an incongruity omitted in the composition, and she fancied her bold, daring, timid, awkward, impertinent, and shy alternately, and, in this conflict of anticipation, it was that Lizzy entered. So utterly overcome was Lady Georgina by astonishment, that she actually advanced to meet her in some confusion, and then, taking her hand, led her to a seat on the sofa beside her.

While the ordinary interchange of commonplaces went on,—and nothing could be more ordinary or commonplace than the words of their greeting,—each calmly surveyed the other. What thoughts passed in their minds, what inferences were drawn, and what conclusions formed in this moment, it is not for me to guess. To women alone pertains that marvellous freemasonry that scans character at a glance, and investigates the sincerity of a disposition and the value of a lace flounce with the same practised facility. If Lady Georgina was astonished by the striking beauty of her sister-in-law, she was amazed still more by her manner and her tone. Where could she have learned that graceful repose,—that simplicity, which is the very highest art? Where and how had she caught up that gentle quietude which breathes like a balmy odor over the well-bred world? How had she acquired that subtlety by which wit is made to sparkle and never to startle; and what training had told her how to weave through all she said the flattery of a wish to please?

Woman of the world as she was, Lady Lackington had seen no such marvel as this. It was no detraction from its merit that it might be all acting, for it was still "high art." Not a fault could she detect in look, gesture, or tone, and yet all seemed as easy and unstudied as possible. Her Ladyship knew well that the practice of society confers all these advantages; but here was one who had never mixed with the world, who, by her own confession, "knew no one," and yet was a mistress of every art that rules society.

Lady Georgina had yet to learn that there are instincts stronger than all experience, and that, in the common intercourse of life, Tact is Genius.

Though Lizzy was far more deeply versed in every theme on which it was her Ladyship's pleasure to talk than herself,—though she knew more of painting, of music, and of literature, than the Viscountess, she still seemed like one gleaning impressions as they conversed, and at each moment acquiring nearer and clearer views; and yet even this flattery was so nicely modulated that it escaped detection.

There was a mystery in the case her Ladyship determined to fathom. "No woman of her class," as she phrased it, could have been thus trained without some specific object. The stage had latterly been used as a sort of show mart where young girls display their attractive graces, at times with immense success. Could this have been the goal for which she had been destined? She adroitly turned the conversation to that topic, but Lizzy's answers soon negatived the suspicion. Governesses, too, were all-accomplished in these days; but here there was less of acquirement exhibited than of all the little arts and devices of society.

"Is my trial nearly over?" whispered Lizzy in Beecher's ear as he passed beside her chair. "I'd rather hear a verdict of Guilty at once than to submit to further examining."

A look of caution, most imploringly given, was all his reply.

Though Lady Lackington had neither heard question nor answer, her quick glance had penetrated something like a meaning in them, and her lip curled impatiently as she said to Beecher, "Have you spoke to Lady Lackington of our plans for her,—I mean during your absence?"

He muttered a sullen "No, not yet," and turned away.

"It was an arrangement that will, I hope, meet your approval," said Lady Georgina, half coldly, "since Beecher must go over to England for some weeks; and as you could not with either comfort or propriety remain alone in your hotel, our plan was that you should come here."

Lizzy merely turned her eyes on Beecher, but there was that in their expression that plainly said, "Is this *your* resolve?" He only moved away, and did not speak.

"Not but if any of your own family," continued Lady Lackington, "could come out here, and that you might prefer *their* company,—that would be an arrangement equally satisfactory. Is such an event likely?"

"Nothing less so, my Lady," said Lizzy. "My father has affairs of urgency to treat at this moment."

"Oh, I did not exactly allude to your father,—you might have sisters."

"I have none."

"An aunt, perhaps?"

"I never heard of one."

"Lizzy, you are aware, Georgina," broke in Beecher, whose voice trembled at every word, "was brought up abroad,—she never saw any of her family."

"How strange! I might even say, how unfortunate!" sighed her Ladyship, superciliously.

"Stranger, and more unfortunate still, your Ladyship would perhaps say, if I were to tell you that I never so much as heard of them."

"I am not certainly prepared to say that the circumstance is one to be boastful of," said Lady Lackington, who resented the look of haughty defiance of the other.

"I assure your Ladyship that you are mistaken in attributing to me such a sentiment. I have nothing of which to be boastful."

"Your present position, Lady Lackington, might inspire a very natural degree of pride."

"It has not done so yet, my Lady. My experience of the elevated class to which I have been raised has been too brief to impress me; a wider knowledge will probably supply this void."

"And yet," said Lady Georgina, sarcastically, "it is something,—the change from Miss Davis to the Viscountess Lackington."

"When that change becomes more real, more actual, my Lady," said Lizzy, boldly, "it will, assuredly, bear its fruits; when, in being reminded of what I was and whence I came, I can only detect the envious malevolence that would taunt me with what is no fault of mine, but a mere accident of fortune,—when I hear these things with calm composure, and in my rank as a peeress feel the equal of those who would disparage me,—then, indeed, I may be proud."

"Such a day may never come," said Lady Georgina, coldly.

"Very possibly, my Lady. It has cost me no effort to win this station you seem to prize so highly; it will not exact one to forego all its great advantages."

"What a young lady to be so old a philosopher! I'm sure Lord Lackington never so much as suspected the wisdom he acquired in his wife. It may, however, be a family trait."

"My father was so far wise, my Lady, that he warned me of the reception that awaited me in my new station; but, in his ignorance of that great world, he gave me, rather, to believe that I should meet insinuated slights and covert impertinences than open insults. Perhaps I owe it to my vulgar origin that I really like the last the best; at least, they show me that my enemies are not formidable."

"Your remarks have convinced me that it would be quite superfluous in me to offer my protection to a lady so conversant with life and the world."

"They will, at least, serve to show your Ladyship that I would not have accepted the protection."

"But, Lizzy dearest, you don't know what you are saying. Lady Georgina can establish your position in society as none other can."

"I mean to do that without aid."

"Just as her father, Mr. Grog, would force his way into the stand-house," whispered Lady Lackington, but still loud enough for Lizzy to overhear.

"Not exactly as your Ladyship would illustrate it," said Lizzy, smiling; "but, in seeing the amount of those gifts which have won the suffrages of society, I own that I am not discouraged. I am told," said she, with a great air of artlessness, "that no one is more popular than your Ladyship."

Lady Lackington arose, and stared at her with a look of open insolence; and then turning, whispered something in Beecher's ear.

"After all," muttered he, "*she* did not begin it. Get your shawl, Lizzy," added he, aloud; "my sister keeps early hours, and we must not break in on them."

Lady Lackington and Lizzy courtesied to each other like ladies of high comedy; it seemed, indeed, a sort of rivalry whose reverence should be most formal and most deferential.

"Have n't you gone and done it!" cried Beecher, as they gained the street. "Georgina will never forget this so long as she lives."

"And if she did I 'd take care to refresh her memory," said Lizzy, laughing; and the mellow sounds rang out as if from a heart that never knew a care.

"I shall require to set out for England to-morrow," said Beecher, moodily, so soon as they had reached the hotel. The speech was uttered to induce a rejoinder, but she made none.

"And probably be absent for several weeks," added he.

Still she never spoke, but seemed busily examining the embroidered coronet on the corner of her handkerchief.

"And as circumstances require—I mean, as I shall be obliged to go alone, and as it would be highly inconvenient, not to say unusual, for a young married woman, more especially in the rank you occupy, to remain in an hotel alone, without friends or relatives, we have thought—that is, Georgy and I have considered—that you should stay with her."

Lizzy only smiled; but what that strange smile might signify it was far beyond Beecher's skill to read.

"There is only one difficulty in the matter," resumed he; "and as it is a difficulty almost entirely created by yourself, you will naturally be the more ready to rectify it." He waited long enough to provoke a question from her, but she seemed to have no curiosity on the subject, and did not speak.

"I mean," added he, more boldly, "that before accepting my sister's hospitality, you must necessarily make some *amende* for the manner in which you have just treated her."

"In which *I* treated *her!*" said Lizzy, after him, her utterance being slow and totally passionless.

"Yes, these were my words," said he.

"Have you forgotten how *she* treated *me?*" asked Lizzy, in the same calm tone.

"As to that," said he, with a sort of fidgety confusion,—"as to that, you ought to bear in mind who she is—what she is—and then it's Georgy's way; even among her equals—those well born as herself—she has always been permitted to exercise a certain sort of sway; in fact, the world of fashion has decreed her a sort of eminence. You cannot understand these things yet, though you may do so, one day or other. In a word, *she* can do what *you* cannot, and must not, and the sooner you know it the better."

"And what is it you propose that I should do?" asked she, with seeming innocence.

"Write her a note,—brief if you like, but very civil,—full of excuses for anything that may have given her offence; say all about your ignorance of life, newness to the world, and so on; declare your readiness to accept any suggestions she will kindly give you for future conduct,—for she knows society like a book,—and conclude by assuring her—Well!" cried he, suddenly, for she had started from him so abruptly that he forgot his dictation.

"Go on,—go on," said she, resuming her calm tone.

"You 've put me out," cried he; "I can't remember where I was. Stay—I was saying—What was it? it was something like—"

"Something like 'I 'll not do it any more,'" said Lizzy, with a low laugh; while, at the same instant, she opened her writing-desk and sat down to write.

Now, although Beecher would have preferred seeing her accept this lesson with more show of humility, he was, on the whole, well satisfied with her submission. He watched her as her pen moved across the paper, and saw that she wrote in a way that indicated calm composure and not passion. The note was quickly finished; and as she was folding it, she stopped, and said, "But perhaps you might like to read it?"

"Of course I 'd like to read it," said he, eagerly, taking it op and reading aloud:—

> "'The Viscountess Lackington having received Lord
> Lackington's orders to apologize to Georgina, Viscountess
> Lackington, for certain expressions which may have offended
> her, willingly accepts the task as one likely to indicate to
> her Ladyship the propriety of excusing her own conduct to
> one who had come to claim her kindness and protection.'

"And would you presume to send her such a note as this?" cried he, as he crushed it up and flung it into the fire.

"Not now," said she, with a quiet smile.

"Sit down, and then write—"

"I'll not write another," said she, rising. She moved slowly across the room; and as she gained the door, she turned and said, "If you don't want Kuffner, I 'd be glad to have him here;" and without awaiting his reply, she was gone.

"Haven't I made a precious mess of it?" cried Beecher, as he buried his head between his hands, and sat down before the fire.

CHAPTER XXX
MRS. SEACOLE'S

In a dense fog, and under a thin cold rain, the "Tigris" steamed slowly into the harbor of Balaklava. She had been chartered by the Government, and sent out with some seventy thousand pair of shoes, and other like indispensables for an army much in want, but destined to be ultimately re-despatched to Constantinople,—some grave omissions in red tapery having been discovered,—whereby she and the shoes remained till the conclusion of the war, when the shoes were sold to the Russians, and the ship returned to England.

Our concern is not, however, with the ship or the shoes, or the patent, barley, the potted meats, or the "printed instructions" with which she was copiously provided, but with two passengers who had come up in her from Constantinople, and had, in a manner, struck up a sort of intimacy by the way. They were each of them men rather advanced in life; somewhat ordinary in appearance, of that commonplace turn in look, dress, and bearing that rarely possesses attraction for the better-off class of travellers, but, by the force of a grand law of compensations, as certainly disposes them to fraternize with each other. There are, unquestionably, some very powerful affinities which draw together men past the prime of life, when they wear bad hats, seedy black coats very wide in the skirt, and Berlin gloves. It is not alone that if they smoke the tobacco is of the same coarse kind, and that brandy-and-water is a fountain where they frequently meet, but there are mysterious points of agreement about them which develop rapidly into close intimacy, and would even rise to friendship if either of them was capable of such a weakness.

They had met, casually, at "Miseri's" at Constantinople, and agreed to go up the Black Sea together. Now, though assuredly any common observer passing them might not readily be able to distinguish one from the other again, both being fat, broad-shouldered, vulgar-looking men of about fifty-four or more, yet each was a sort of puzzle to the other; and in the curiosity thus inspired, there grew up a bond between them that actually served to unite them.

If we forbore any attempt at mystification with our valued reader in an early stage of this history, it is not now, that we draw to its close, we would affect any secrecy. Let us, therefore, at once announce the travellers by their names; one being Terry Driscoll, the other the Reverend Paul Classon.

Driscoll had dropped hints—vague hints only—that he had come out to look after a nephew of his, a kind of scapegrace who was always in trouble; but in what regiment he served, or where, or whether he was yet alive, or had been broke and sent home, were all little casualties which he contemplated and discussed with a strange amount of composure. As for Paul, without ever entering directly upon the personal question, he suffered his ministerial character to ooze slowly out, and left it to be surmised that he was a gentleman of the press, unengaged, and a Christian minister, unattached.

Not that these personal facts were declared in the abrupt manner they are here given to the reader. Far from it; they merely loomed through the haze of their discourse as, walking the deck for hours, they canvassed the war and its objects, and its probable results. Upon all these themes they agreed wonderfully, each being fully satisfied that the whole campaign was only a well-concerted roguery,—a scheme for the dismemberment of Turkey, when she had been sufficiently debilitated by the burden of an expensive contest to make all resistance impossible. Heaven knows if either of them seriously believed this. At all events, they said it to each other, and so often, so circumstantially, and so energetically that it would be very rash in us to entertain a doubt of their sincerity.

"I have been recommended to a house kept by a Mrs. Seacole," said Classon, as they landed on the busy quay, where soldiers and sailors and land-transport men, with Turks, Wallachs, Tartars, and Greeks, were performing a small Babel of their own.

"God help me!" exclaimed Terry, plaintively, "I 'm like a new-born child here; I know nobody, nor how to ask for anything."

"Come along with me, then. There are worse couriers than Paul Classon." And bustling his way through the crowd, his Reverence shouldered his carpet-bag, and pushed forward.

It was, indeed, a rare good fortune for Terry to have fallen upon a fellow-traveller so gifted and so accomplished; for not only did Paul seem a perfect polyglot, but he possessed that peculiar bustling activity your regular traveller acquires, by which, on his very entrance into an inn, he assumes the position less of guest than of one in authority and in administration. And so now Paul had speedily investigated the resources of the establishment, and ordered an excellent supper, while poor Driscoll was still pottering about his room, or vainly endeavoring to uncord a portmanteau which a sailor had fastened more ingeniously than necessary.

"I wish I knew what he was," muttered Terry to himself. "He 'd be the very man to help me in this business, if I could trust him."

Was it a strange coincidence that at the same moment Paul Classon should be saying to himself, "That fellow's simplicity would be invaluable if I could only enlist him in our cause; he is a fool well worth two wise men at this conjuncture"?

The sort of coffee-room where they supped was densely crowded by soldiers, sailors, and civilians of every imaginable class and condition. Bronzed, weather-beaten captains, come off duty for a good dinner and a bottle of real wine at Mother Seacole's, now mingled with freshly arrived subs, who had never even seen their regiments; surgeons, commissaries, naval lieutenants, Queen's messengers, and army chaplains were all there, talking away, without previous acquaintance with each other, in all the frankness of men who felt absolved from the rule of ordinary etiquette; and thus, amid discussions of the campaign and its chances, were mingled personal adventures, and even private narratives, all told without the slightest reserve or hesitation: how such a one had got up from his sick-bed, and reported himself well and fit for duty, and how such another had pleaded urgent private affairs to get leave to go home; what a capital pony Watkins had bought for a sovereign, what execrable bitter beer Jones was paying six shillings the bottle for; sailors canvassing the slow advances of landsmen, soldiers wondering why the blue-jackets would n't "go in" and blow the whole mock fortifications into the air; some boasting, some grumbling, many ridiculing the French, and all cursing the Commissariat.

If opinions were boldly stated, and sentiments declared with very little regard for any opposition they might create, there was, throughout, a tone of hearty good-fellowship that could not be mistaken. The jests and the merriment seemed to partake of the same hardy character that marked each day's existence; and many a story was told with a laugh, that could not be repeated at the "Rag," or reported at the Horse Guards. Classon and Driscoll listened eagerly to all that went on around them. They were under the potent spell that affects all men who feel themselves for the first time in a scene of which they have heard much. They were actually in the Crimea. The men around them had actually just come off duty in the trenches: that little dark-bearded fellow had lost his arm in the attack of the Mamelon; that blue-eyed youth, yonder, had led a party in assault on the Cemetery; the jovial knot of fellows near the stove had been "plotting" all night at the

Russians from a rifle-pit. There was a reality in all these things that imparted a marvellous degree of interest to individuals that might otherwise have seemed commonplace and ordinary.

Amidst the noisy narratives and noisier commentaries of the moment, there seemed one discussion carried on with more than usual warmth. It was as to the precise species of reward that could be accorded to one whose military rank could not entitle him to the "Bath."

"I tell you, Chidley," cried one of the speakers, "if he had been a Frenchman there would have been no end of boasting amongst our amiable allies, and he 'd have had Heaven knows what grade of the Legion and a pension, besides! Show me the fellow amongst them could have done the feat! I don't speak of the pluck of it,—they have plenty of pluck; but where's the rider could have sat his horse over it?"

"What height was it?" asked another, as he leisurely puffed his cigar.

"Some say six feet,—call it five, call it four, anything you please: it was to go at a breastwork with two nine-pounders inside, that was the feat; and I say, again, I don't know another fellow in the army that would have thought of it but himself!"

"Dick Churchill once jumped into a square and out again!"

A hearty roar of laughter announced the amount of credit vouchsafed to the story; but the speaker most circumstantially gave time and place, and cited the names of those who had witnessed the fact.

"Be it all as you say," interposed the first speaker, "Churchill did a foolhardy thing, without any object or any result; but Conway sabred three gunners with his own hand."

If the story, up to this moment, had only interested our two travellers by its heroic claims, no sooner was the name of Conway uttered than each started with astonishment. As for Classon, he arose at once, and, drawing near the narrator, politely begged to know if the Conway mentioned was a one-armed man.

"The same, sir,—Charley the Smasher, as they used to call him long ago; and, by George, he has earned some right to the title!"

"And he escaped unhurt after all this?" asked Classon.

"No, I never said that; he was almost hacked to pieces, and his horse had four bullets in him and fell dead, after carrying him half-way back to our lines."

"And Conway, is he alive? Is he likely to recover?" asked Paul, eagerly.

"The doctors say it is impossible; but Charley himself declares that he has not the slightest intention of dying, and the chances are, he 'll keep his word."

"Dear me! only think of that!" muttered Driscoll, as, with a look of intense simplicity, he listened to this discourse. "And where is he now, sir, if I might make so bould?"

"He's up at the Monastery of St George, about eight miles off."

"The Lord give him health and strength to go and fight the Russians again!" said Terry; and the speech, uttered in a tone so natural and so simple, was heard with a general laugh.

"Come over to this table, my old buck, and we 'll drink that toast in a bumper!" cried one of the officers; and with many a bashful expression of pleasure Mr. Driscoll accepted the invitation.

"Won't your friend join us?" asked another, looking towards Classon.

"I must, however reluctantly, decline, gentlemen," said Paul, blandly. "*I* cannot indulge like my respected friend here; *I* stand in need of rest and repose."

"He doesn't look a very delicate subject, notwithstanding," said a subaltern, as Classon retired.

"There 's no judging from appearances," observed Driscoll. "You 'd think *me* a strong man, but I 'm weak as a child. There's nothing left of me since I had the 'faver,' and I 'll tell you how it happened."

CHAPTER XXXI
THE CONVENT OF ST. GEORGE

Day broke heavily and dull through the massively barred windows of the Convent of St George, and dimly discovered a vast crowd assembled in the great hall of waiting: officers—sailor and soldier—come to inquire news of wounded comrades, camp-followers, sutlers, surgeons, araba-drivers, Tartar-guides, hospital nurses, newspaper correspondents, Jew money-changers, being only some of the varieties in that great and motley crowd.

Two immense fireplaces threw a ruddy glare over two wide semicircles of human faces before them; but here and there throughout the hall, knots and groups were gathered, engaged in deep and earnest converse. Occasionally, one speaker occupied the attention of a listening group; but, more generally, there was a sort of discussion in which parties suggested this or that explanation, and so supplied some piece of omitted intelligence.

It is to this dropping and broken discourse of one of these small gatherings that I would now draw my reader's attention. The group consisted of nigh a dozen persons, of whom a staff-officer and a naval captain were the principal speakers.

"My own opinion is," said the former, "that if the personal episodes of this war come ever to be written, they will be found infinitely more strange and interesting than all the great achievements of the campaign. I ask you, for instance, where is there anything like this very case? A wounded soldier, half cut to pieces by the enemy, is carried to the rear to hear that his claim to a peerage has just been established, and that he has only to get well again to enjoy fifteen thousand a year."

"The way the tidings reach him is yet stranger," broke in another.

"What is *your* version of that?"

"It is the correct one, I promise you," rejoined he; "I had it from Colthorpe, who was present When the London lawyer—I don't know his name—reached Balaklava, he discovered, to his horror, that Conway was in the front; and when the fellow summons pluck enough to move on to head-quarters, he learns that Charley has just gone out with a party of eight, openly declaring they mean to do something before they come back. Up to this, the man of parchment has studiously kept his secret; in fact, the general belief about him was that he was charged with a writ, or some such confounded thing, against the poor Smasher, and, of course, the impression contributed little to secure him a polite reception. Now, however, all his calm and prudential reserve is gone, and he rushes madly into the General's tent, where the General is at breakfast with all the staff and several guests, and, with the air of a man secure of his position, he flings down upon the table a letter to the General Commanding-in-chief from a Minister of State, saying, 'There, sir! may I reckon upon your assistance?' It was some time before the General could quite persuade himself that the man was in his senses, he talked away so wildly and incoherently, repeatedly saying, 'I throw it all upon you, sir. Remember, sir, I take none of the responsibility,— none!'

"'I wish you would kindly inform me as to the precise service you expect at my hands, sir,' said the General, somewhat haughtily.

"'To have this document deposited in the hands of Lieutenant Charles Conway, sir,' said he, pompously, laying down a heavily sealed package; 'to convey to him the news that his claim to the title and estates of his family has been declared perfect; that before he can reach England he will be Lord Viscount Cackington and Conway.'

"'Bad news from the front, sir,9 said an aide-de-camp, breaking in. 'After a successful attack on a small redoubt near the Cemetery; two squadrons of the —th have been surprised, and nearly all cut up. Conway, they say, killed.'

"'No, not killed,' broke in another; 'badly wounded, and left behind.'

"There was, as you may imagine, very little thought bestowed on the lawyer after this. Indeed, the party was scattered almost immediately, and Colthorpe was just going out, when one of Miss Nightingale's ladies said to him, 'Will you do me a great favor, Major Colthorpe,—a very great favor? It is to let me have my saddle put on your gray charger for half an hour.' Colly says, if she had n't been the very prettiest girl he had ever seen since they left England, he 'd have shirked it, but he could not; and in less than ten minutes, there she was, cantering away through the tents and heading straight for the front. It was not, however, only the gray Arab she carried off, but the great letter of the lawyer was gone too; and so now every one knew at once she was away to the front."

"And after that,—after that?" asked three or four together, as the narrator paused.

"After that," resumed he, "there is little to be told. Colthorpe's Arab galloped back with a ball in his counter, and the saddle torn to rags with shot. The girl has not been heard of."

"I can supply this portion of the story," said a young fellow, with his arm in a sling. "She had come up with Conway, whom they had placed on a horse, and were leading him back to the lines, when a Russian skirmishing-party swept past and carried the girl off, and she is now in Sebastopol, under the care of the Countess Woronzoff."

"And Conway?"

"Conway's here; and though he has, between shot and sabre-cuts, eight severe wounds, they say that, but for his anxiety about this girl's fate, his chances of recovery are not so bad. Here comes Dr. Raikes, however, who could give us the latest tidings of him."

The gentleman thus alluded to moved hastily down the hall, followed by a numerous train of assistants, to whom he gave his orders as he went He continued, at the same time, to open and run his eyes over various letters which an assistant handed to him, one by one.

"I will not be tormented with these requests, Parkes," said he, peremptorily. "You are to refuse all applications to see patients who are not in the convalescent wards. These interviews have, invariably, one effect, — they double *our* labor here."

By this time the doctor was hemmed closely in by a dense crowd, eagerly asking for news of some dear friend or kinsman. A brief "Badly," "Better," "Sinking," "Won't do," were, in general, the extent of his replies; but in no case did he ever seem at a loss as to the name or circumstance of the individual alluded to.

And now, at last, the great hall began to thin. Wrapping themselves well in their warm cloaks, securing the hoods tightly over their heads, men set out in twos and threes, on foot, on horseback, or in arabas, some for the camp, some for Balaklava, and some for the far-away quarter at the extreme right, near the Tchernaya. A heavy snow was falling, and a cold and cutting wind came over the Black Sea, and howled drearily along the vaulted corridors of the old Convent.

Matter enough for story was there beneath that venerable roof! It was the week after the memorable fight of Inkermann, and some of the best blood of Britain was ebbing in those dimly lighted cells, whose echoes gave back heart-sick sighs for home from lips that were soon to be mute forever. There are unlucky days in the calendar of medicine, — days when the convalescent makes no progress, and the sick man grows worse; when medicaments seem mulcted of half their efficacy, and disastrous chances abound. Doctors rarely reject the influence of this superstition, but accept it with calm resignation.

Such, at least, seemed the spirit in which two army surgeons now discussed the events of the day, as they walked briskly for exercise along one of the corridors of the Convent.

"We shall have a gloomy report to send in to-morrow, Parkes," said the elder. "Not one of these late operation cases will recover. Hopeton is sinking fast; Malcolm's wound has put on a treacherous appearance; that compound fracture shows signs of gangrene; and there's Conway, we all thought so well of last night, going rapidly, as though from some internal hemorrhage."

"Poor fellow! it's rather hard to die just when he has arrived at so much to live for. You know that he is to have a peerage."

"So he told me himself. He said laughingly to me, 'Becknell, my boy, be careful, you are cutting up no common sort of fellow; it's all lordly flesh and blood here!' We were afraid the news might over-excite him, but he took it as easily as possible, and only said, 'How happy it will make my poor mother;' and, after a moment, 'If I only get back to tell it to her!'"

"A civilian below," said an hospital sergeant, "wishes to see Mr. Conway."

"Can't be,—say so," was the curt reply, as the doctor tore, without reading, the piece of paper on which a name was written.

"The lawyer, I have no doubt," said the other; "as if the poor fellow could care to hear of title-deeds and rent-rolls now. He 'd rather have twenty drops of morphine than know that his estate covered half a county."

The sergeant waited for a second or two to see if the doctor should reconsider his reply, and then respectfully retired. The stranger, during the short interval of absence, had denuded himself of great-coat and snow-shoes, and was briskly chafing his hands before the fire.

"Well, Sergeant, may I see him?" asked he, eagerly.

"No. The doctors won't permit it."

"You did n't tell them who I was, then, that's the reason. You did n't say I was the confidential agent of his family, charged with a most important communication?"

"If I didn't, it was, perhaps, because I didn't know it," said the man, laughing.

"Well, then, go back at once, and say that I've come out special,—that I must see him,—that the ten minutes I 'll stay will save years and years of law and chancery,—and that"—here he dropped his voice—"there's a hundred pounds here for the same minutes."

"You'd better keep that secret to yourself, my good friend," interposed the sergeant, stiffly.

"Well, so I will, if you recommend it," said the other, submissively; "but surely, a ten-pound note would do you no harm yourself, Sergeant."

An insolent laugh was the only answer the other vouchsafed, as he lighted his cigar and sat down before the fire.

"They won't let me see him for the mischief it might do him," resumed the other, "and little they know that what I have to tell him might be the saving of his life."

"How so?"

"Just that I 've news for him here that would make a man a'most get out of his coffin,—news that would do more to cure him than all the doctors in Europe. There's paper in that bag there that only wants his name to them' to be worth thousands and thousands of pounds, and if he dies without signing them there's nothing but ruin to come of it; and when I said a ten-pound note awhile ago to you, it was a hundred gold sovereigns I meant, counted into the hollow of your fist, just as you sat there. See now, show me your hand."

As if in a sort of Jocular pantomime, the man held out his hand, and the other, taking a strong leather purse from his pocket, proceeded to untie the string, fastened with many a cunning device. At length it was opened, and, emptying out a quantity of its contents into one hand, he began to deposit the pieces, one by one, in the other's palm. "One, two, three, four," went he on, leisurely, till the last sovereign dropped from his fingers with the words "one hundred!"

Secret and safe as the bargain seemed, a pair of keen eyes peering through the half-snowed-up window had watched the whole negotiation, following the sergeant's fingers as they closed upon the gold and deposited it within his pocket.

"Wait here, and I'll see what can be done by and by," said the sergeant, as he moved away.

Scarcely was the stranger left alone than the door opened, and a man entered, shaking the snow from his heavy boots and his long capote.

"So, my worthy friend," cried he, in a rich, soft voice, "you stole a march on me,—moved off without beat of drum, and took up a position before I was stirring!"

"Ah, my reverend friend, *you* here!" said the other, in evident confusion. "I never so much as suspected you were coming in this direction."

Paul Classon and Terry Driscoll stared long and significantly at each other. Of all those silences, which are more eloquent than words, none can equal that interval in which two consummate knaves exchange glances of recognition, so complete an appreciation is there of each other's gifts, such an honest, unaffected, frank interchange of admiration.

"You are a clever fellow, Driscoll, you are!" said Paul, admiringly.

"No, no. The Lord help me, I'm a poor crayture," said Terry, shaking his head despondingly.

"Don't believe it, man,—don't believe it," said Paul, clapping him on the shoulder; "you have great natural gifts. Your face alone is worth a thousand a year, and you have a shuffling, shambling way of coming into a room that's better than an account at Coutts's. Joe Norris used to say that a slight palsy he had in one hand was worth twelve hundred a year to him at billiards alone."

"What a droll man you are, Mr. Classon!" said Terry, wiping his eyes as he laughed. And again they looked at each other long and curiously.

"Driscoll," said Paul, after a considerable pause, "on which side do you hold your brief?"

"My brief! God knows it's little I know about brief and parchments," sighed Terry, heavily.

"Come, come, man, what's the use of fencing? I see your hand; I know every trump in it."

Driscoll shook his head, and muttered something about the "faver that destroyed him entirely."

"Ah!" sighed Classon, "I cannot well picture to my mind what you might have been anterior to that calamity, but what remains is still remarkable,—very remarkable. And now I ask again, on which side are you engaged?"

"Dear me,—dear me!" groaned out Terry; "it's a terrible world we live in!"

"Truly and well observed, Driscoll. Life is nothing but a long and harassing journey, with accidents at every stage, and mischances at every halt; meanwhile, for whom do you act?"

The door at the end of the long gallery was slightly and noiselessly opened at this instant, and a signal with a hand caught Driscoll's attention. Rapid and stealthy as was the motion, Classon turned hastily round and detected it.

"Sit still, Driscoll," said he, smiling, "and let us talk this matter over like men of sense and business. It's clear enough, my worthy friend, that neither you nor I are rich men."

Driscoll sighed an assent.

"That, on the contrary, we are poor, struggling, hard-toiling fellows, mortgaging the good talents Fortune has blessed us with to men who have been born to inferior gifts but better opportunities."

Another sigh from Terry.

"You and I, as I have observed, have been deputed out here to play a certain game. Let us be, therefore, not opponents, but partners. One side only can win, let us both be at that side."

Again Terry sighed, but more faintly than before.

"Besides," said Classon, rising and turning his back to the fire, while he stuck his hands in his pockets, "I'm an excellent colleague, and, unless the world wrongs me, a most inveterate enemy."

"Will he live, do you think?" said Terry, with a gesture of his thumb to indicate him of whom he spoke.

"No; impossible," said Classon, confidently; "he stands in the report fatally wounded, and I have it confidentially that there's not a chance for him."

"And his claim dies with him?"

"That's by no means so sure; at least, we'd be all the safer if we had his papers, Master Driscoll."

"Ay!" said Driscoll, knowingly.

"Now, which of us is to do the job, Driscoll? That's the question. I have my claim to see him, as chaplain to the—I 'm not sure of the name of what branch of the service—we'll say the 'Irregular Contingent' Legion. What are you, my respected friend?"

"A connection of the family, on the mother's side," said Terry, with a leer.

"A connection of the family!" laughed out Classon. "Nothing better."

"But, after all," sighed Terry, despondingly, "there's another fellow before us both,—that chap had brought out the news to the camp, Mr. Reggis, from the house of Swindal and Reggis."

"He's cared for already," said Classon, with a grin.

"The Lord protect us! what do you mean?" exclaimed Driscoll, in terror.

"He wanted to find his way out here last night, so I bribed two Chasseurs d'Afrique to guide him. They took him off outside the French advance, and dropped him within five hundred yards of a Cossack picket, so that the worthy practitioner is now snug in Sebastopol. In fact, Driscoll, my boy, I 'm—as I said before—an ugly antagonist!"

Terry laughed an assent, but there was little enjoyment in his mirth.

"The girl,—one of those hospital ladies," continued Classon,—"a certain Miss Kellett, is also a prisoner."

"Miss Kellett!" cried Driscoll, in amazement and terror together. "I know her well, and if she's here she 'll outwit us both."

"She's in safe hands this time, let her be as cunning as she will. In fact, my dear Driscoll, the game is our own if we be but true to each other."

"I 'm more afraid of that girl than them all," muttered Driscoll.

"Look over those hills yonder, Driscoll, and say if that prison-house be not strong enough to keep her. Mr. Reggis and herself are likely to see Moscow before they visit Cheapside. Remember, however, if the field be our own, it is only for a very brief space of time. Conway is dying. What is to be done must be done quickly; and as there is no time for delay, Driscoll, tell me frankly what is it worth to you?" Terry sneezed and wiped his eyes, and sneezed again,—all little artifices to gain time and consider how he should act.

"My instructions are these," said Classon, boldly: "to get Conway to sign a bond abdicating all claim to certain rights in lieu of a good round sum in hand; or, if he refuse—" S.

"Which he certainly would refuse," broke in Driscoll.

"Well, then, to possess myself of his papers, deeds, letters, whatever they were,—make away with them, or with any one holding them. Ay, Driscoll, it is sharp practice, my boy; but we 're just now in a land where sudden death dispenses with a coroner's inquest, and the keenest inquirer would be puzzled whether the fatal bullet came from a Russian rifle or a

Croat carbine. Lend me a helping hand here, and I 'll pledge myself that you are well paid for it. Try and dodge me, and I'll back myself to beat you at your own game."

"Here's an order for one of you gentlemen," said an hospital orderly, "coming up to see Lieutenant Conway."

"It is for me," said Driscoll, eagerly; "I'm a relation of his."

"And I am his family chaplain," said Classon, rising; "well go together." And before Driscoll could interpose a word, Paul slipped his arm within the other's and led him away.

CHAPTER XXXII
SHOWING "HOW WOUNDS ARE HEALED"

On a low little bed in a small chamber, once a cell of the Convent, Charles Conway lay, pale, bloodless, and breathing heavily. The surgeon's report of that morning called him "mortally wounded," and several of his comrades had already come to bid him farewell. To alleviate in some measure his sufferings, he was propped up with pillows and cushions to a half-sitting posture, and so placed that his gaze could rest upon the open sea, which lay calm and waveless beneath his window; but even on this his eyes wandered vaguely, as though already all fixity of thought was fled, and that the world and its scenes had ceased to move or interest him. He was in that state of exhaustion which follows great loss of blood, and in which the brain wanders dreamily and incoherently, though ready at any sudden question to arouse itself to an effort of right reason.

A faint, sad smile, a little nod, a gesture of the hand, were tokens that one by one his comrades recorded of their last interview with him; and now all were gone, and he was alone. A low murmur of voices at his door bespoke several persons in earnest conversation, but the sounds never reached the ears of the sick man.

"He spoke of making a will, then?" said Classon, in a whisper.

"Yes, sir," replied the sergeant. "He asked several times if there was not some one who could take down his wishes in writing, and let him sign it before witnesses."

"That will do admirably," said Paul, pushing his way into the room, closely followed by Terry Driscoll. "Ah, Driscoll," said Paul, unctuously, "if we were moralists instead of poor, frail, time-serving creatures as we are, what a lesson might we not read in the fate of the poor fellow that lies there!"

"Ay, indeed!" sighed out Terry, assentingly.

"What an empty sound 'my Lord' is, when a man comes to that!" said Paul, in the same solemn tone, giving, however, to the words "my Lord" a startling distinctness that immediately struck upon the sick man's ear. Conway quickly looked up and fixed his eyes on the speaker.

"Is it all true, then,—am I not dreaming?" asked the wounded soldier, eagerly.

"Every word of it true, my Lord," said Classon, sitting down beside the bed.

"And I was the first, my Lord, to bring out the news," interposed Terry. "'Twas myself found the papers in an old farm-house, and showed them to Davenport Dunn."

"Hush, don't you see that you only confuse him?" whispered Classon, cautiously.

"Dunn, Dunn," muttered Conway, trying to recollect. "Yes, we met at poor Kellett's funeral,—poor Kellett! the last of the Albueras!"

"A gallant soldier, I have heard," chimed in Classon, merely to lead him on.

"Not a whit more so than his son Jack. Where is he?—where is Jack?"

None could answer him, and there was a silence of some minutes.

"Jack Kellett would never have deserted me in this way if he were alive and well," muttered Conway, painfully. "Can no one give me any tidings of him?"

Another silence ensued.

"And I intended he should have been my heir," said Conway, dreamily. "How strangely it sounds, to be sure, the notion of inheriting anything from Charley Conway! How little chance there was a month or two back that my best legacy might not have been a shabrack or a pair of pistols; and now I'm the Lord Viscount—what is it?—Viscount—"

A wild gust of wind—one of those swooping blasts for which the Euxine is famous—now struck the strong old walls, and made the massive casements rattle. The sick man started at the noise, which recalled at once the crash of the battle-field, and he cried out vigorously, "Move up, men,—move up; keep together, and charge! Charge!" and with bent-down head and compressed lips he seemed like one prepared to meet a murderous onslaught. A sudden faintness succeeded to this excitement, and he lay back weak and exhausted. As he fell back, a letter dropped from his hand to the ground. Classon speedily caught it up, and opened it. He had, however, but time to read the opening line, which ran thus—"My dearest Charley, our cause is all but won—"

"From his mother," interposed Driscoll, leaning over his shoulder.

"Ay, my mother," murmured Conway, whose ear, preternaturally acute from fever, caught the word; "she will see that my wishes are carried out, and that all I leave behind me goes to poor Jack."

"We'll take care of that, sir," said Classon, blandly; "only let us know what it is you desire. We have no other object here than to learn your wishes."

With all the alacrity of one accustomed to such emergencies, Paul drew a small portfolio from his pocket provided with all materials for writing, and arrayed them neatly before him; but already the sick man had dropped off into a sleep, and was breathing heavily.

"That box must contain all the papers," said Classon, rising stealthily and crossing the room; "and see, the key is in the lock!" In a moment they were both on the spot, busily ransacking the contents. One glance showed their suspicions to be correct: there were heaps of legal documents, copies of deeds, extracts of registries, with innumerable letters of explanation. They had no time for more than the most hurried look at these; in fact, they turned in terror at every movement, to see if the sick man had recovered from his swoon.

"This is all; better than I ever looked for," said Classon. "Fill your pockets with them: we must divide the spoil between us, and be off before he rallies."

Driscoll obeyed with readiness. His eager eye scrutinized hastily so much as he could catch of the import of each document; but he did not venture, by any attempt at selection, to excite Classon's suspicions.

"If we cannot make our own terms after this night's work, Driscoll, my name is not Paul Classon. The poor fellow here will soon be past tale-telling, even if he were able to see us. There you have dropped a large parchment."

"I' ll put it in the pocket of my cloak," said the other, in a whisper; while he added, still more stealthily, "would n't you swear that he was looking at us this minute?"

Classon started. The sick man's eyes were open, and their gaze directed towards them; while his lips, slightly parted, seemed to indicate a powerless attempt to speak.

"No," said Classon, in a scarcely audible whisper; "that is death."

"I declare I think he sees us," muttered Driscoll.

"And if he does, man, what signifies it? He's going where the knowledge will little benefit him. Have you everything safe and sure now? There, button your coat well up; we must start at once."

"May I never! if I can take my eyes off him," said Driscoll, trembling.

"You had better take yourself off bodily, my worthy friend; there's no saying who might chance to come in upon us here. Is not that a signet-ring on his finger? It would only be a proper attention to carry it to his mother, Driscoll." There was a half-sarcasm about the tone of this speech that made it sound strangely ambiguous, as, stooping down, he proceeded to take off the ring.

"Leave it there,—leave it there! it will bring bad luck upon us," murmured Driscoll, in terror.

"There is no such bad luck as not to profit by an opportunity," whispered Classon, as he tried, but in vain, to withdraw the ring. A sharp, half-suppressed cry suddenly escaped him, and Driscoll exclaimed,—

"What is it? What's the matter?"

"Look, and see if he has n't got hold of me, and tightly too."

The affected jocularity of his tone accorded but ill with the expression of pain and fright so written upon his features, for the dying man had grasped him by the wrist, and held him with a grip of iron.

"That's what they call a dead man's grip, I suppose?" said Classon, in assumed mockery. "Just try if you cannot unclasp his fingers."

"I wouldn't touch him if you offered me a thousand guineas for it," said Driscoll, shuddering.

"Nonsense, man. We cannot stand fooling here, and I shall only hurt him if I try it with one hand. Come, open his fingers gently. Be quick. I hear voices without, and the tramp of horses' feet in the court below. Where are you going? You're not about to leave me here?"

"May I never! if I know what to do," muttered Driscoll, in a voice of despair. "And did n't I tell you from the first it would bring bad luck upon us?"

"The worst of all luck is to be associated with a fool and a coward," said Classon, savagely. "Open these fingers at once, or give me a knife and I 'll do it myself."

"The Lord forgive you, but you 're a terrible man!" cried Driscoll, moving stealthily towards the door.

"So you *are* going?" muttered Paul, with a voice of intense passion. "You would leave me here to take the consequences, whatever they might be?"

Driscoll made no reply, but stepped hastily out of the room, and closed the door.

For a moment Classon stood still and motionless; then bending down his head, he tried to listen to what was passing outside, for there was a sound of voices in the corridor, and Driscoll's one of them. "The scoundrel is betraying me!" muttered Paul to himself. "At all events, these must not be found upon me." And with this, and by the aid of his one disengaged hand, he proceeded to strew the floor of the room with the various papers he had abstracted from the box. Again, too, he listened; but now all was still without. What could it mean? Had Driscoll got clear away, without even alluding to him? And now he turned his gaze upon the sick man, who lay there calm and motionless as before. "This will end badly if I cannot make my escape," muttered he to himself; and he once more strove with all his might to unclasp the knotted fingers; but such was the rigid tenacity of their grasp, they felt as though they must sooner be broken than yield. "Open your hand, sir. Let me free," whispered he, in Conway's ear. "That fellow has robbed you, and I must follow him. There, my poor man, unclasp your fingers," said he, caressingly, "or it will be too late!"

Was it a delusion, that he thought a faint flickering of a smile passed over that death-like countenance? And now, in whispered entreaty, Classon begged and implored the other to set him free.

"There is nothing for it, then, but this," said Paul, with a muttered curse, "and your own fault is it that I am driven to it!" And, so saying, he drew a powerful clasp-knife from his pocket, and tried to open it with his teeth; but the resistance of the spring still defied all his efforts for some time, and it was only after a long struggle that he succeeded. "He's insensible; he'll never feel it," muttered Paul below his breath; "and even if he should, self-preservation is the first of all cares." And with this he grasped the knife vigorously in his strong hand, and gazed at the sick man, who seemed to return his stare as fixedly. There was in Conway's look even a something of bold defiance, that seemed to say, "I dare and defy you!" so at least did Classon read it, and quailed before its haughty meaning. "What wretched cowardice is over me, and at a time when minutes are worth days!" muttered Classon. "Here goes!" But now a confused noise of many voices, and the steps of advancing feet were heard in the corridor; and Classon sank down beside the bed, a cold sweat covering his forehead and face, while he trembled in every limb.

The room was speedily filled with staff officers and surgeons, in the midst of whom was a civilian, travel-stained and tired-looking, who pressed eagerly forward, saying, as he beheld Classon, "Who is this man,—what is he doing here?"

"An humble missionary,—a weak vessel," said Paul, whiningly. "In a paroxysm of his pain he caught me thus, and has held me ever since. There—at last I am free!" And as he said these words, the sick man's fingers unclasped and liberated him.

"There has been foul play here," said Mr. Reggie, the stranger in civilian dress. "See! that box has been rifled; the floor is covered with papers. This man must be detained."

"In bonds or in a dungeon, it matters not," said Paul, holding up his hands as if about to open a lengthy discourse; but he was hurried away ere he could continue.

"He is certainly no worse," said one of the surgeons, as he felt Conway's pulse and examined the action of his heart; "but I am far from saying that he will recover!"

"If I do not greatly mistake," said Reggis, "our friend the missionary is the man through whose kind offices I was betrayed within the Russian lines; but I' ll look to this later. As it was, I have had little to complain of my treatment in Sebastopol, and my detention was of the shortest."

"And Miss Kellett,—is she free also?" asked one of the bystanders.

"Yes; we came back together. She is up at headquarters, giving Lord Raglan an account of her capture."

"What is it, Conway?" asked one of the surgeons, suddenly startled by the intensity of the anxiety in his face. "Are you in pain?"

He shook his head in dissent.

"You are thirsty, perhaps? Will you have something to drink?"

"No," said he, with the faintest possible utterance.

"What is it, then, my poor fellow?" said he, affectionately.

"So it was not a dream!" gasped out Conway.

"What was it you fancied to be a dream?"

"All,—everything but this!" And he pointed to a deep wound from a sabre-cut in his shoulder.

"Ay, and that, too, will be as a dream some years hence!" said the other, cheeringly.

It was evident, now, that the excitement of talking and seeing so many persons about him was injurious, and the surgeons silently motioned to the bystanders to retire.

"May I remain with him?" asked the lawyer. "If he could give his consent to certain measures, sign one or two papers, years of litigation might be saved."

Conway had meanwhile beckoned to the surgeon to approach him; and then, as the other leaned over the bed, he whispered,—

"Was it true what I have just heard,—was she really here?"

"Miss Kellett, do you mean? Yes; she carried up the news to you herself? It was she that tied the handkerchief on your wounded artery, too, and saved your life."

"Here,—in the Crimea? It cannot—cannot be!" sighed Conway.

"She is not the only noble-hearted woman who has left home and friends to brave perils and face hardships, though, I own, she stands alone for heroism and daring."

"So, then, it was not a delusion,—I did actually see her in the trenches?" said Conway, eagerly.

"She was in the advanced parallel the night the Russians surprised the 5th. She was the first to give the alarm of the attack."

"Only think, doctor, of what happened to me that night! I was sent up at speed to say that reinforcements were coming up. Two companies of the Royals were already in march. My horse had twice fallen with me, and, being one-armed, I was a good deal shaken, and so faint when I arrived that I could scarcely deliver my message. It was just then a woman—I could only perceive, in the darkness, that she seemed young—gave me her brandy-flask; after drinking, I turned to give it back to her, but she was gone. There was no time to search for her at such a moment, and I was about to ride away, when a 'carcasse,' exploding on one of the redoubts, lit up the whole scene for a considerable space around, and whom should I see but Jack Kellett's sister, cheering the men and encouraging them to hold their ground?

I could have sworn to her features, as I could now to yours; but that she could really be there seemed so utterly impossible that I fancied it was a delusion. Nay," added he, after a pause, "let me tell the whole truth. I thought it was a warning! Ay, doctor, the weight is off my heart now that I have confessed this weakness." As Conway spoke, he seemed, indeed, as though he had relieved himself of some mighty care; for already his eye had regained its lustre, and his bold features recovered their wonted expression. "Now," cried he, with a renovated vigor, "I have done with false terrors about second sight, and the rest of it I am myself again."

"You can listen to my tidings, then," said Reggis, seating himself at the bedside, and at once beginning a narrative, to which I am obliged to own Conway did not always pay a becoming attention, his thoughts still reverting to very different scenes and incidents from those which the lawyer recounted. Indeed, more than once was the narrator's patience sorely tried and tested. "I am doing my very best to be brief, sir. I am limiting myself strictly to a mere outline of the case," said he, in something of piqué: "It *might* interest you,—it *ought* to interest you!"

"If the doctor yonder will promise me health and years to enjoy all this same good fortune, so it will interest me," cried Conway. "What does the income amount to?"

"If we only recover the English estates, it will be something under twelve thousand a year. If we succeed with, the Irish, it will be about three more."

"And how far are we on the road to this success?" "One verdict is already won. The first action for ejectment on title has been brought, and we are the victors. Upon this, all your counsel are agreed, your claim to the Viscounty rests."

"I can scarcely credit—scarcely picture it to myself," said Conway, half aloud. "My mind is confused by the thought of all the things I wish to do, if this be true. First of all, I want to purchase Jack Kellett's commission."

"If you mean Miss Kellett's brother, he is already gazetted an ensign, and on his way to join his regiment in India."

"And how do you know this?"

"She told me so herself."

"She! When and where have you seen her?"

"Here, at headquarters; in Sebastopol, where we were prisoners together; at the camp yesterday, where we parted."

"My poor head cannot bear this," said Conway, painfully; "I am struggling between the delight of all these good tidings and a terrible dread that I am to awake and find them but a dream. You said that she was here in the camp?"

"That she is. If you but heard the cheer that greeted her arrival! It began at the advanced pickets, and swelled loader and louder, till, like the roar of the sea, it seemed to make the very air tremble. There, hear that! As I live, it is the same shout again."

"Here comes the General and his staff into the court below," said the doctor, hurrying away to receive them.

As the sounds of a distant cheer died away, the noise of horses' feet resounded through the courtyard, and the clank of musketry in salute announced the arrival of an officer of rank.

"I declare they are coming this way," cried Mr. Reggis, rising in some confusion, "and I heard your name spoken. Coming, I have no doubt, to see *you.*"

"The General of your division, Conway, come to ask after you," said an aide-de-camp, entering, and then standing aside to make place for a venerable, soldier-like man, whose snow-white hair would have graced a patriarch.

"I have come to shake your hand, Conway," said he, "and to tell you we are all proud of you. There is nothing else talked of through our own or the French camp than that daring feat of yours; and England will soon hear of it."

A deep blush of manly shame covered Conway's face as he listened to these words; but he could not speak.

"I have been talking the matter over with the General Commanding-in-chief," resumed he, "who agrees with me that the Horse Guards might, possibly, recognizing your former rank of Captain, make you now a Brevet-major, and thus qualify you for the Bath."

"Time enough, General, for that," said Conway. "I have a very long arrear of folly and absurdity to wipe out ere I have any pretension to claim high rewards."

"Well, but if all that I hear be true, we are likely to lose your services here; they have a story abroad about a peerage and a vast fortune to which you have succeeded. Indeed, I heard this moment from Miss Kellett—"

"Is she here, sir?—can I see her?" cried Conway, eagerly.

"Yes. She has come over to say good-bye; for, I regret to say, she too is about to leave us to join her brother at Calcutta."

A sickly paleness spread itself over Conway's cheeks, and he muttered, "I must see her—I must speak with her at once."

"So you shall, my poor fellow," said the other, affectionately; "and I know of no such recompense for wounds and suffering as to see her gentle smile and hear her soft voice. She shall come to you immediately."

Conway covered his face with his hand, to conceal the emotion that stirred him, and heard no more. Nor was he conscious that, one by one, the persons around him slipped noiselessly from the room, while into the seat beside his bed glided a young girl's figure, dressed in deep black, and veiled.

"Such a fate!" muttered he, half aloud. "All this, that they call my good fortune, comes exactly when I do not care for it."

"And why so?" asked a low, soft voice, almost in his very ear.

"Is this, indeed, you?" cried he, eagerly. "Was it *your* hand I felt on my temples as I lay wounded outside the trenches? Was it your voice that cheered me as they carried me to the rear?"

She slightly bent her head in assent, and murmured, "Your old comrade's sister could not do less."

"And now you are about to leave me," said he, with an overwhelming sorrow in the tone.

She turned away her head slightly, and made no answer.

"I, who am utterly alone here," said he, in a broken voice. "Is this, too, like my old comrade's sister?" There was a peevishness in the way he spoke this of which he seemed himself to be ashamed the moment the words were uttered; and he quickly added, "What a fellow I am to say this to you!—you, who have done so much for me,—you, who promised to be a daughter to my poor mother when I am gone!"

"But you are not to take this gloomy view," said she, hastily; "the surgeons all pronounce you better; they agree that your wounds progress favorably, and that, in a week or two, you may be removed to Constantinople, and thence to England."

He gave a faint, sickly smile of most melancholy meaning.

"And what will not the cheery, bracing air of those Welsh mountains do, aided by the kind care of that best of nurses, a fond mother?"

"And where will you be by that time?" asked he, eagerly.

"Journeying away eastward to some far away land, still more friendless!" said she, sadly.

"This, then, is the sum of all my good fortune, that when life opens fairly for me, it shall be bereft of all that I care for!" cried he, wildly.

Terrified by the excited tone in which he spoke, as well as by the feverish lustre of his eyes, Sybella tried to calm and soothe him, but he listened—if, indeed, he heard her—with utter apathy.

"Come!" cried he, at last, "if your resolve be taken, so is mine. If you leave for India, I shall never quit the Crimea."

"It is not thus I expected one to speak who loves his mother as you do," said she, reproachfully.

"Ah, Sybella, it would indeed have been a happy day for me when I should have returned to her in honor, could I but have said, 'You have not alone a son beneath your roof, but a dear daughter also.' If all that they call my great luck had brought this fortune, then had I been indeed a fellow to be envied. Without that hope there is not another that I want to cling to.'"

She tried gently to withdraw her hand from his, but he held it in his grasp, and continued,—

"You, who never heard of me till the first day we met, know little of the stored-up happiness your very name has afforded me for many a day,—how, days long, Jack talked of you to me as we rambled together, how the long nights of the trenches were beguiled by telling of you,—till at length I scarcely knew whether I had not myself known and loved you for years. I used to fancy, too, how every trait of poor Jack—his noble ardor, his generous devotion—might be displayed amidst the softer and more graceful virtues of womanhood; and at last I came to know you, far and away above all I have ever dreamed of."

"Let me go,—let me say good-bye," said she, in a faint whisper.

"Bear with me a few moments longer, Sybella," cried he, passionately. "With all their misery, they are the happiest of my life."

"This is unfair,—it is almost ungenerous of you," said she, with scarcely stifled emotion, and still endeavoring to withdraw her hand.

"So it is!" cried he, suddenly; "it is unmanly and ignoble both, and it is only a poor, selfish sick man could stoop to plead so abjectly." He relinquished her hand as he spoke, and then, grasping it suddenly, he pressed it to his lips, and burst into tears. "A soldier should be made of better stuff, Sybella," said he, trying to smile. "Goodbye,—good-bye."

"It is too late to say so now," said she, faintly; "I will not go."

"Not go,—not leave me, Sybella?" cried he. "Oh that I may have heard you aright! Did you say you would remain with me, and for how long?"

"Forever!" said she, stooping down and kissing his forehead. The next moment she was gone.

"Come, Conway," said the doctor, "cheer up, my good fellow; you 'll be all right in a week or so. You 've got something worth living for, too, if all accounts be true."

"More than you think for, doctor," said Conway, heartily,—"far more than you think for."

"The lawyer talks of a peerage and a fine estate."

"Far more than that," cried Conway; "a million times better."

The surgeon turned a look of half apprehension on the sick man, and, gently closing the shutters, he withdrew.

Dark as was that room, and silent as it was, what blissful hopes and blessed anticipations crowded and clustered around that low "sick-bed"! What years of happiness unfolded themselves before that poor brain, which no longer felt a pang, save in the confusion of its bright imaginings! How were wounds forgotten and sufferings unminded in those hours wherein a whole future was revealed!

At last he fell off to sleep, and to dream of a fair white hand that parted the hair upon his forehead, and then gently touched his feverish cheek. Nor was it all a dream; she was at his bedside.

CHAPTER XXXIII
"GROG" IN COUNCIL

"What dreary little streets are those that lead from the Strand towards the Thames! Pinched, frail, semi-genteel, and many-lodgered are the houses, mysteriously indicative of a variously occupied population, and painfully suggesting, by the surging conflict of busy life at one end, and the dark flowing river at the other, an existence maintained between struggle and suicide." This, most valued reader, if no reflection of mine, but was the thought that occupied the mind of one who, in not the very best of humors, and of a wet and dreary night, knocked, in succession, at half the doors in the street in search after an acquaintance.

"Yes, sir, the second back," said a sleepy maid-servant at last; "he is just come in."

"All right," said the stranger. "Take that carpet-bag and writing-desk upstairs to his room, and say that Captain Davis is coming after them.'"

"You owe me a tip, Captain," said the cabman, catching the name as he was about to mount his box. "Do you remember the morning I drove you down to Blackwall to catch the Antwerp boat, I went over Mr. Moss, the sheriff's officer, and smashed his ankle, and may I never taste bitters again if I got a farthing for it."

"I remember," said Davis, curtly. "Here's a crown. I 'd have made it a sovereign if it had been his neck you 'd gone over."

"Better luck next time, sir, and thank you," said the man, as he drove away.

The maid was yet knocking for admission when Grog arrived at the door. "Captain Fisk, sir,—Captain Fisk, there 's a gent as says—"

"That will do," said Davis, taking the key from her hand and opening the door for himself.

"Old Grog himself, as I'm a living man!" cried a tall, much whiskered and moustached fellow, who was reading a "Bell's Life" at the fire.

"Ay, Master Fisk,—no other," said Davis, as he shook his friend cordially by the hand. "I 've had precious work to find you out I was up at

Duke Street, then they sent me to the Adelphi; after that I tried Ling's, in the Hay-market, and it was a waiter there—"

"Joe," broke in the other.

"Exactly. Joe told me that I might chance upon you here."

"Well, I 'm glad to see you, old fellow, and have a chat about long ago," said Fisk, as he placed a square green bottle and some glasses on the table. How well you 're looking, too; not an hour older than when I saw you four years ago!"

"Ain't I, though!" muttered Grog. "Ay, and like the racers, I 've got weight for age, besides. I'm a stone and a half heavier than I ought to be, and there's nothing worse than that to a fellow that wants to work with his head and sleep with one eye open."

"You can't complain much on that score, Kit; you never made so grand a stroke in your life as that last one,—the marriage, I mean."

"It was n't bad," said Davis, as he mixed his liquor; "nor was it, exactly, the kind of hazard that every man could make. Beecher was a troublesome one,—a rare troublesome one; nobody could ever say when he 'd run straight."

"I always thought him rotten," said the other, angrily.

"Well, he is and he isn't," said Grog, deliberately.

"He has got no pluck," said Fisk, indignantly.

"He has quite enough."

"Enough—enough for what?"

"Enough for a lord. Look here, Master Fisk, so long as you have not to gain your living by anything, it is quite sufficient if you can do it moderately well. Many a first-rate amateur there is, who wouldn't be thought a tenth-rate artist."

"I 'd like to know where you had been to-day if it was n't for your pluck," said Fisk, doggedly.

"In a merchant's office in the City, belike, on a hundred and twenty pounds a year; a land steward down in Dorsetshire, at half the salary; skipper of a collier from North Shields, or an overseer in Jamaica. These are the high prizes for such as you and me; and the droll part of the matter is, they *will* talk of us as 'such lucky dogs,' whenever we attain to one of these brilliant successes. Gazette my son-in-law as Ambassador to Moscow, and nobody thinks it strange; announce, in the same paper, that Kit Davis has been made a gauger, and five hundred open mouths exclaim, 'How did he obtain that? Who the deuce got it for him? Does n't he fall on his legs!' and so on."

"I suppose we shall have our turn one of these days," muttered the other, sulkily.

> "I hope not. I 'd rather have things as they are," said Grog, gravely.

"Things as they are! And why so, I 'd wish to ask?"

"Look at it this way, Tom Fisk," said Grog, squaring his arms on the table and talking with slow deliberation; "if you were going to cut into a round game, wouldn't you rather take a hand where the players were all soft ones, with plenty of cash, or would you prefer sitting down with a set of downy coves, all up to every dodge, and not a copper farthing in the company? Well, that's exactly what the world would be if the Manchester fellows had their way; that's exactly what it is, this very hour we 're sitting here, in America. There's nobody on the square there. President, judges, editors, Congressmen, governors, are all rogues; and they've come to that pass, that any fellow with a dash of spirit about him must come over to Europe to gain his livelihood. I have it from their own lips what I 'm telling you, for I was a-thinking about going over there myself; but they said, 'Don't go, sir,'—they always say 'sir,'—'don't go, sir. Our Western fellows are very wide awake; for every trump you 'd have up your sleeve, they 'd have two in their boots!'"

"For my own part," said Fisk, "I 'd not go live amongst them if you 'd make me Minister at Washington, and so I told Simmy Hankes this morning, when he came in such high feather about his appointment as consul—I forget where to."

"Hankes—Hankes! The same fellow that used to be with Robins?"

"Just so; and for some years back Davenport Dunn managing man."

Grog gave a very slight start, and then asked, carelessly, why he was leaving Dunn's employment.

"Dunn's going to shut up shop. Dunn is to be a peer, next week, and retires from business. He is to be in Tuesday's 'Gazette,' so Hankes tells me."

"He has done the thing well, I suppose?" said Davis, coolly.

"Hankes says something like two millions sterling. Pretty well for a fellow that started without a sixpence."

"I wonder he could n't have done something better for Hankes than that paltry place."

"So he might, and so he would; but you see, Simmy did n't like waiting. He's a close fellow, and one can't get much out of him; but I can perceive that he was anxious to get off the coach."

"Did n't like the pace,—didn't trust the tackle overmuch," said Grog, carelessly.

"Something of that kind, I 've no doubt," rejoined Fisk.

"Have you any pull over this same Hankes, Tom?" said Grog, confidentially.

"Well, I can't say I have. We were pals together long ago; we did a little in the racing line,—in a very small way, of course. Then he used to have a roulette-table at Doncaster; but somehow there was no 'go' in him: he was over-cautious, and always saying, 'I 'd rather take to "business;"' and as I hated business, we separated."

"It's odd enough that I can't remember the fellow. I thought I knew every one that was on the 'lay' these five-and-thirty years."

"He wasn't Hankes at the time I speak of; he was a Jew at that period, and went by the name of Simeon."

"Simeon, Simeon,—not the fellow that used to come down to Windsor, with the Hexquite Habannar cigars?"

And Grog mimicked not alone the voice, but the face of the individual alluded to, till Fisk burst into a roar of laughter.

"That's Simmy,—that's the man," cried Fisk, as he dried his eyes.

"Don't I know him! I had a class at that time,—young fellows in the Blues. I used to give them lessons in billiards; and Simmy, as you call him, discounted for the mess on a sliding scale,—ten per cent for the Major, and sixty for cornets the first year they joined. He was good fun, Simmy; he fancied he would have been a first-rate actor, and used to give scenes out of 'Othello,' in Kean's manner: that was the only soft thing about him, and many a fellow got a bill done by applauding 'Now is the winter of our discontent'!" And Grog gave a low growling sort of a laugh at his reminiscences.

"You 'll see him to-morrow; he's to breakfast here," said Fisk, rather amused at the prospect of a recognition between such men.

"He would never play 'Shylock,'" continued Grog, following out his reminiscences, "though we all told him he 'd make a great hit in the part.

The Jew, you see,—the Jew couldn't stand *that*. And so Mr. Simmy Hankes is no other than Simeon! It was an old theory of mine, whenever I saw a fellow doing wonderfully well in the world, without any help from friends or family, to fancy that one time or other he must have belonged to what they are so fond of calling 'the Hebrew persuasion'!"

"I wouldn't rake up old memories with him, Grog, if I were you," said Fisk, coaxingly.

"It ain't my way, Tom Fisk," said Davis, curtly.

"He 'll be at his ease at once when he perceives that you don't intend to rip up old scores; and he 'll be just as delicate with *you*."

"Delicate with me?" cried Grog, bursting out into a fit of immoderate laughter. "Well, if that ain't a good one! I wonder what he is! Do you imagine Fitzroy Kelly is ashamed of being thought a lawyer, or Brodie of being a surgeon? You must be precious soft, my worthy friend, if you suppose that I don't know what the world thinks and says of *me*. No, no, there's no need of what you call delicacy at all. You used to be made of other stuff than this, Tom Fisk. It's keeping company with them snobs of half-pay officers, clerks in the Treasury, and Press reporters-has spoiled you; the demi-gents of the 'Garottaman Club' have ruined hundreds."

"The Garottaman is one of the first clubs in town," broke in Fisk.

"You 're too much like sailors on a raft for my fancy," said Grog, dryly.

"What do you mean by that?"

"Just that you are hungry and have got nothing to eat,—you 're eternally casting lots who is to be devoured next! But we 'll not fall out about that. I 've been turning over in my head about this Simmy Hankes, and I 'd like to have an hour in his company, all alone. Could you manage to be out of the way to-morrow morning and leave me to entertain him at breakfast?"

"It will suit my book to a trivet, for I want to go over to Barnes to look after a yearling I 've got there, and you can tell Hankes that the colt was taken suddenly ill."

"He 'll not be very curious about the cause of your absence," said Grog, dryly. "The pleasure of seeing me so unexpectedly will put everything else out of his head." A grim smile showed the spirit in which he spoke these words.

It was now very late, and Davis threw himself on a sofa, with his great-coat over him, and, wishing his friend a goodnight, was soon sound asleep; nor did he awake till aroused by the maid-servant getting the room into readiness and arranging the table for breakfast. Then, indeed, Grog arose and made his toilet for the day,—not a very elaborate nor a very elegant one, but still a disguise such as the most practised detective could not have penetrated, and yet removable in a moment, so that he might, by merely taking off eyebrows and moustaches, become himself at once.

Having given orders that the gentleman he expected should be shown in on his arrival, Grog solaced himself at the fire with a morning paper, in all the ease of slippers and an arm-chair. Almost the first thing that struck his eye was a paragraph informing the world that the marriage of a distinguished individual—whose approaching elevation to the peerage had been already announced—with one of the most beautiful daughters of the aristocracy would take place early in the ensuing week. And then, like a codicil to a will, followed a brilliant description of the gold dressing-case ordered by Mr. Davenport Dunn, at Storr's, for his bride. He was yet occupied with the paragraph when Mr. Hankes entered the room.

"I am afraid I have made a mistake," said that bland gentleman. "I thought this was Captain Fisk's apartment."

"You're all right," said Grog, leisurely surveying the visitor, whose "get up" was really splendid. Amethyst studs glittered on his shirt; his ample chest seemed a shrine in its display of amulets and charmed offerings, while a massive chain crossed and recrossed him so frequently that he appeared to be held together by its coils. Fur and velvet, too, abounded in his costume; and even to the immense "gland" that depended from his cane, there was an amount of costliness that bespoke affluence.

"I regret, sir," began Hankes, pompously, "that I have not the honor—"

"Yes, yes; you *have* the honor," broke in Grog. "You've had it this many a year. Sit down here. I don't wear exactly so well as you, but you 'll remember me presently. I 'm Kit Davis, man. You don't require me to say who you are."

"Davis,—Grog Davis," muttered Hankes to himself, while an ashy paleness spread over his face.

"You don't look overjoyed to meet with an old friend," said Grog, with a peculiar grin; "but you ought, man. There's no friendships like early ones. The fellows who knew us in our first scrapes are always more lenient to our last wickednesses."

"Captain Davis,—Captain Davis!" stammered out Hankes, "this is indeed an unexpected pleasure!"

"So much so that you can hardly get accustomed to it," said Grog, with another grin. "Fisk received a hasty message that called him away to the country this morning, and left me to fill his place; and I, as you may guess, was little loath to have a cosey chat with an old friend that I have not seen—how many years is it?"

"It must be nigh ten, or even twelve!"

"Say, seven or eight and twenty, man, and you 'll be nigher the mark. Let me see," said he, trying to remember, "the last time I saw you was at Exeter. You were waiting for your trial about those bills of George Colborne. Don't look so frightened; there's no one to hear us here. It was as narrow an escape there as ever man had. It was after that, I suppose, you took the name of Hankes?"

"Yes," said the other, in a faint whisper.

"Well, I must say Christianity does n't seem to have disagreed with you. You 're in capital case,—a little pluffy for work, but in rare health, and sleek as a beaver."

"Always the same. He will have his joke," muttered Hankes, as though addressing some third party to the colloquy.

"I can't say that I have committed any excesses in that line of late," said Grog, dryly. "I 've had rather a tough fight with the world!"

"But you've fought it well, and successfully," Davis said the other, with confidence. "Have n't you married your daughter to a Viscount?"

"Who told you that? Who knows it here?" cried Grog, hurriedly.

"I heard it from Fordyce's people a fortnight ago. It was I myself brought the first news of it to Davenport Dunn."

"And what did he say?"

"Well, he didn't say much; he wondered a little how it came about; hinted that you must be an uncommon clever fellow, for it was a great stroke, if all should come right."

"You mean about the disputed claim to the title?"

"Yes."

"He has his doubts about that, then, has he?"

"He has n't much doubt on the subject, for it lies with himself to decide the matter either way. If he likes to produce certain papers, Conway's claim is as good as established. You are aware that they have already gained two of their actions on ejectment; but Dunn could save them a world of time and labor, and that's why he's coming up to-morrow. Fordyce is to meet him at Calvert's Hotel, and they 're to go into the entire question."

"What are his terms? How much does he ask?" said Grog, bluntly.

"I can't possibly say; I can only suspect."

"What do you suspect, then?"

"Well," said Hankes, drawing a long breath, "my impression is that if he decide for the present Viscount, he 'll insist upon an assignment of the whole Irish property in his favor."

"Two thousand a year, landed property!" exclaimed Grog.

"Two thousand eight hundred, and well paid," said Hankes, coolly; "but that is not all."

"Not all! what do you mean?"

"Why, there's another hitch. But what am I saying?" cried he, in terror. "I don't believe that I'd speak of these things on my death-bed."

"Be frank and open with me, Simeon. I am a true pal to the man that trusts me, and the very devil to him that plays me false."

"I know it," said the other, gloomily.

"Well, now for that other hitch, as you called it What is it?"

"It's about an estate that was sold under the 'Encumbered Court,' and bought by the late Lord Lackington—at least in his name—and then resold at a profit—" Here he stopped, and seemed as though he had already gone too far.

"I understand," broke in Grog; "the purchase-money was never placed to the Viscount's credit, and your friend Dunn wants an acquittance in full of the claim."

"You've hit it!"

"What's the figure,—how much?"

"Thirty-seven thousand six hundred pounds."

"He 's no retail-dealer, this same Davenport Dunn," said Grog, with a grin; "that much I *will* say of him."

"He has a wonderful head," said Hankes, admiringly.

"I 'll agree with you, if it save his neck!" said Davis-, and then added, after a moment, "He's bringing up all these documents and papers with him, you said?"

"Yes; he intends to make some settlement or other of the matter before he marries. After that he bids farewell to business forever."

"He'll go abroad, I suppose?" said Davis, not attaching any strong signification to his remark; but suddenly perceiving an expression of anxiety in Hankes's face, he said, "Mayhap it were all as well; he'd be out of the way for a year or so!"

The other nodded an assent.

"He has 'realized' largely, I take it?"

Another nod.

"Foreign funds and railways, eh?"

"Not railways,—no, scrip!" said Hankes, curtly.

"Won't there be a jolly smash!" said Davis, with a bitter laugh. "I take it there's not been any one has 'done the trick' these fifty years like this fellow."

"I suspect you 're right there," murmured Hankes.

"I have never seen him but once, and then only for a few minutes, but I read him like a printed book. He had put on the grand integrity and British-mercantile-honesty frown to scowl me down, to remind Davis, 'the leg,' that he was in the presence of Dunn, the Unimpeachable, but I put one eye a little aslant, this way, and I just said, 'Round the corner, old fellow,—round the corner!' Oh, didn't he look what the Yankees call 'mean ugly'!"

"He 'll never forget it to you, that's certain."

"If he did, I 'd try and brush up his memory a bit," said Davis, curtly. "He must be a rare sharp one," added he, after a pause.

"The cleverest man in England, I don't care who the other is," cried Hankes, with enthusiasm. "When the crash comes,—it will be in less than a month from this day,—the world will discover that they're done to the tune of between three and four millions sterling, and I defy the best accountant that ever stepped to trace out where the frauds originated,—whether it was the Railways smashed the Mines, the Mines that ruined the Great Ossory, the Great Ossory that dipped the Drainage, or the Drainage that swamped the Glengariff, not to speak of all the incidental confusion about estates never paid for, and sums advanced on mock mortgage, together, with cancelled scrip reissued, preference shares circulated before the current ones, and dock warrants for goods that never existed. And that ain't all" continued Hankes, to whom the attentive eagerness of Grog's manner vouched for the interest his narrative excited,—"that ain't all; but there isn't a class nor condition in life, from the peer to the poorest laboring-man, that he has n't in some way involved in his rogueries, and made him almost a partner in the success. Each speculation being dependent for its solvency on the ruin of some other, Ossory will hate Glengariff, Drainage detest Mines, Railways curse Patent Fuel, and so on. I 'll give the Equity Court and the Bankrupt Commissioners fifty years and they'll not wind up the concern."

Grog rubbed his hands gleefully, and laughed aloud.

"Then all the people that will be compromised!" said Hankes; "Glumthal himself is not too clean-handed; lords and fine ladies that lent their names to this or that company, chairmen of committees in the House that did n't disdain to accept five hundred or a thousand shares as a mark of grateful recognition for pushing a bill through its second reading; ay, and great mercantile houses that discounted freely on forged acceptances, owning that they thought the best of all security was the sight of a convict-hulk and a felon's jacket, and that no man was such prompt pay as he that took a loan of a friend's signature. What a knockdown blow for all that lath-and-plaster edifice we dignify by the name of Credit, when the world sees that it is a loaf the rogue can take a slice out of as well as the honest man!"

"Won't we have stunning leaders in the 'Times' about it!" cried Grog. "It will go deuced hard with the Ministry that have made this fellow a peer."

"Yes, they'll have to go out," said Hanked, gravely; "a cabinet may defend a bad measure,—they 'll never fight for a bad man."

"And they can't hang this fellow?" said Grog, after a pause.

"Hang! I should think not, indeed."

"Nor even transport him?"

"No, not touch a hair of his head. He'll have to live abroad for a year or two,—in Paris or Rome,—no great hardship if it were Naples; he 'll make a surrender of his property,—an old house somewhere and some brick-fields, a mine of Daryamon coal, and a flax-mill on a river that has scarcely any water, together with a sheaf of bad bills and Guatemala bonds. They 'll want to examine him before the Court, and he'll send them a sick-certificate, showing how agitation and his recent losses have almost made him imbecile; and even Mr. Linklater will talk feelingly about his great reverse of condition."

"It's as good as a play to hear about this," said Grog; "it beats Newmarket all to sticks."

"If it's a play, it won't be a benefit to a good many folk," said Hankes, grinning.

"Well, he *is* a clever fellow,—far and away cleverer than I ever thought him," said Grog. "Any man—I don't care who he is—can do the world to a short extent, but to go in at them on this scale a fellow must be a genius."

"He *is* a genius," said Hankes, in a tone of decision. "Just think for a moment what a head it must have been that kept all that machinery at work for years back without a flaw or a crack to be detected, started companies, opened banks, worked mines, railroads, and telegraphs, built refuge harbors, drained whole counties, brought vast tracts of waste land into cultivation, equalizing the chances of all enterprises by making the success of this come to the aid of the failure of that: the grand secret of the whole being the dexterous application of what is called 'Credit.'"

"All that wouldn't do at Doncaster," said Grog; "puff your horse as much as you like, back him up how you will in the betting-ring, if he has n't the speed in him it won't do. It's only on 'Change you can 'brag out of a bad hand.' Dunn would never cut any figure on the turf."

"There you are all wrong; there never yet was the place, or the station, where that man would n't have distinguished himself. Why, it was that marvellous power of his kept me with him for years back. I knew all that was going on. I knew that we hadn't—so to say—coals for one boiler while we had forty engines in full stroke; but I could n't get away. It was a sort of fascination; and when he 'd strike out a new scheme, and say carelessly, 'Call the capital one million, Hankes,' he spoke like a man that had only to put his hand in a bag and produce the money. Nothing daunted, nothing deterred him. He'd smash a rival company as coolly as you 'd crush a shell under your heel, and he 'd turn out a Government with the same indifference he 'd discharge a footman."

"Well," grumbled out Grog, at last, for he was getting irritable at the exaggerated estimate Hankes formed of his chief, "what has it all come to? Ain't he smashed at last?"

"*He* smashed!" cried Hankes, in derision. "*He* smashed! *You* are smashed! I am smashed! any one else you like is smashed, but *he* is not! Mind my words, Davis, Davenport Dunn will be back here, in London, before two years are over, with the grandest house and the finest retinue in town. His dinners will be the best, and his balls the most splendid of the season. No club will rival his cook, no equipage beat his in the Park. When he rises in the Lords,—which he 'll do only seldom,—there will be a most courteous attention to his words; and, above all, you'll never read one disparaging word about him in the papers. I give him two years, but it's just as likely he 'll do it in less."

"It may be all as you say," said Grog, sullenly, "though I won't say I believe it myself; but, at all events, it does n't help *me* on my way to my own business with him. I want these papers of Lackington's out of his hands! He may 'walk into' the whole world, for all that I care: but I want to secure *my* daughter as the Viscountess,—that's how it stands."

"How much ready money can you command? What sum can you lay your hand on?"

Grog drew his much-worn pocket-book from his breast, and, opening the leaves, began to count to himself.

"Something like fifty-seven pounds odd shillings," said he, with a grin.

"If you could have said twelve or fourteen thousand down, it might be nearer the mark. Conway's people are ready with about ten thousand."

"How do you know?" asked Grog, savagely.

"Dunn told me as much. But he does n't like to treat with them, because the difficulty about the Irish estate would still remain unsettled."

"Then what am I to do? How shall I act?" asked Grog.

"It's not an easy matter to advise upon," said Hankes, thoughtfully, "for Dunn holds to one maxim with invariable tenacity, which is never to open any negotiation with a stranger which cannot be completed in one interview. If you couldn't begin by showing the bank-notes, he'd not discuss the question at all."

Grog arose and walked the room with hasty steps: he tried to seem calm, but in the impatient gesture with which he threw his cigar into the fire might be read the agitation he could not conquer nor conceal.

"What could you yourself do with him, Hankes?" said he, at last.

"Nothing,—absolutely nothing," said the other. "He never in his life permitted a subordinate to treat, except on his own behalf; that was a fixed law with him."

"Curse the fellow!" burst out Davis, "he made rules and laws as if the world was all his own."

"Well, he managed to have it pretty much his own way, it must be confessed," said Hankes, with a half-smile.

"He is to be in town to-morrow, you said," muttered Grog, half aloud. "Where does he stop?"

"This time it will be at Calvert's, Upper Brook Street. His house in Piccadilly is ready, but he 'll not go there at present."

"He makes a mystery of everything, so far as I can see," said Grog, angrily. "He comes up by the express-train, does n't he?" grumbled he, after a pause.

"If he has n't a special engine," said Hankes. "He always, however, has his own *coupé* furnished and fitted up for himself and never, by any chance, given to any one else. There 's a capital bed in it, and a desk, where he writes generally the whole night through, and a small cooking-apparatus, where he makes his coffee, so that no servant ever interrupts him at his work. Indeed, except from some interruption, or accident on the line, the guard would not dare to open his door. Of course *his* orders are very strictly obeyed. I remember one night Lord Jedburg sent in his name, and Dunn returned for answer, 'I can't see him.'"

"And did the Prime Minister put up with that?" asked Davis.

"What could he do?" said the other, with a shrug of the shoulder.

"If I were Lord Jedburg, I'd have unkennelled him, I promise you *that*, Simmy. But here, it's nigh twelve o'clock, and I have a mass of things to do. I say, Hankes, could you contrive to look in here to-morrow evening, after nightfall? I may have something to tell you."

"We were strictly confidential,—all on honor, this morning, Kit," said the other, whispering.

"I think you know *me*, Mister Simmy," was all Grog's reply. "I don't think my worst enemy could say that I ever 'split' on the fellow that trusted me."

A hearty shake-hands followed, and they parted.

CHAPTER XXXIV
THE TRAIN

The up-train from Holyhead was a few minutes behind time at Chester, and the travellers who awaited its arrival manifested that mixture of impatience and anxiety which in our railroad age is inseparable from all delay. One stranger, however, displayed a more than ordinary eagerness for its coming, and compared the time of his watch repeatedly with the clock of the station.

At length from the far-away distance the wild scream of the engine was heard, and with many a cranking clash and many a heavy sob the vast machine swept smoothly in beneath the vaulted roof. As the stranger moved forward to take his place, he stopped to hear a few words that met his ear. It was a railroad official said: "Mr. Davenport Dunn delayed us about a quarter of an hour; he wanted to give a look at the new pier, but we have nearly made it up already." "All right!" replied the station-master. The stranger now moved on till he came in front of a coupé carriage, whose window-blinds rigidly drawn down excluded all view from without. For an instant he seemed to fumble at the door, in an endeavor to open it, but was speedily interrupted by a guard calling out, "Not there, sir,—that's a private carriage;" and thus warned, the traveller entered another lower down the line. There were two other travellers in the same compartment, apparently strangers to each other. As the stranger with whom we are immediately concerned took his place, he slipped into his pocket a small latch-key, of which, in the very brief attempt to try the door of the private carriage, he had successfully proved the utility, and, drawing his rug across his knees, lay calmly back.

"Here we are, detained again," grumbled out one of the travellers. "I say, guard, what is it now?"

"Waiting for a telegram for Mr. Davenport Dunn, sir. There it comes! all right" A low bell rings out, a wild screech following, and with many a clank and shock the dusky monster sets out once more.

"Public convenience should scarcely be sacrificed in this manner," grumbled out the former speaker. "What is this Mr. Dunn to you or to me that we should be delayed for his good pleasure?"

"I am afraid, sir," replied the other, whose dress and manner bespoke a clergyman, "that we live in an age when wealth is all-powerful, and its possessors dictate the law to all poorer than themselves."

"And can you tell me of any age when it was otherwise?" broke in the last arrival, with a half-rude chuckle. "It's all very fine to lay the whole blame of this, that, and t' other to the peculiar degeneracy of our own time; but my notion is, the world grows neither worse nor better." There was that amount of defiance in the tone of the speaker that seemed to warn his companions, for they each of them maintained a strict silence. Not so with him; he talked away glibly about the influence of money, pretty plainly intimating that, as nobody ever met the man who was indifferent to its possession, the abuse showered upon riches was nothing but cant and humbug. "Look at the parsons," said he; "they tell you it is all dross and rubbish, and yet they make it the test of your sincerity whenever they preach a charity sermon. Look at the lawyers, and they own that it is the only measure they know by which to recompense an injury; then take the doctors, and you 'll see that their humanity has its price, and the good Samaritan charges a guinea a visit."

The individuals to whom these words were addressed made no reply; indeed, there was a tone of confident assumption in the speaker that was far from inviting converse, and now a silence ensued on all sides.

"Do either of you gentlemen object to tobacco?" said the last speaker, after a pause of some duration; and at the same time, without waiting for the reply, he produced a cigar-case from his pocket, and began deliberately to strike a light.

"I am sorry to say, sir," responded the clergyman, "that smoking disagrees with me, and I cannot accustom myself to endure the smell of tobacco."

"All habit," rejoined the other, as he lighted his cigar. "I was that way myself for years, and might have remained so, too, but that I saw the distress and inconvenience I occasioned to many jolly fellows who loved their pipe; and so I overcame my foolish prejudices, and even took to the weed myself."

The other travellers muttered some low words of dissatisfaction; and the clergyman, opening the window, looked out, apparently in search of the guard.

"It's only a cheroot, and a prime one," said the smoker, coolly; "and as you object, I 'll not light another."

"A vast condescension on your part, sir, seeing that we have already signified our dislike to tobacco," said the lay traveller.

"I did not remark that *you* gave any opinion at all," said the smoker; "and my vast condescension, as you term it, is entirely in favor of this gentleman."

There was no mistaking the provocation of this speech, rendered actually insulting by the mode in which it was delivered; and the traveller to whom it was addressed, enveloping himself in his cloak, sat moodily back, without a word. The train soon halted for a few seconds; and, brief as was the interval, this traveller employed it to spring from his place and seek a refuge elsewhere, — a dexterous manœuvre which seemed to excite the envy of the parson, now left alone with his uncongenial companion. The man of peace, however, made the best of it, and, drawing his travelling-cap over his eyes, resolved himself to sleep. For a considerable while the other sat still, calmly watching him; and at last, when perfectly assured that the slumber was not counterfeited, he gently arose, and drew the curtain across the lamp in the roof of the carriage. A dim, half-lurid light succeeded, and by this uncertain glare the stranger proceeded to make various changes in his appearance. A large bushy wig of black hair was first discarded, with heavy eyebrows, and whiskers to match; an immense overcoat was taken off, so heavily padded and stuffed that when denuded of it the wearer seemed half his size; large heels were unscrewed from his boots, reducing his height by full a couple of inches; till, at length, in place of a large, unwieldy-looking man of sixty, lumbering and beetle-browed, there came forth a short, thick-set figure, with red hair and beard, twinkling eyes of a fierce gray, and a mouth the very type of unflinching resolution. Producing a small looking-glass, he combed and arranged his whiskers carefully, re-tied his cravat, and bestowed a most minute scrutiny on his appearance, muttering, as he finished, to himself, "Ay, Kit, you 're more like yourself now!" It is, perhaps, unnecessary to say this speech was addressed to our acquaintance Grog Davis, nor was it altogether what is called a "French compliment;" he *did* look terribly like himself. There was in his hard, stern face, his pinched-up eyes, and his puckered mouth, an amount of resolute vigor that showed he was on the eve of some hazardous enterprise. His toilet completed, he felt in his breastpocket, to assure himself that something there was not missing; and then, taking out his watch, he consulted the time. He had scarcely time to replace it in his pocket, when the train entered a deep cutting between two high banks of clay. It was, apparently, the spot he had waited for; and in an instant he had unfastened the door by his latch-key, and stood on the ledge outside. One more look within to assure himself that the other was still asleep, and he closed the door, and locked it.

The night was dark as pitch, and a thin soft rain was falling, as Davis, with a rapidity that showed this was no first essay in such a walk, glided along from carriage to carriage, till he reached a heavy luggage van, immediately beyond which was the *coupé* of Mr. Davenport Dunn.

The brief prayer that good men utter ere they rush upon an enterprise of deadly peril must have its representative in some shape or other with those whose hearts are callous. Nature will have her due; and in that short interval—the bridge between two worlds—the worst must surely experience intense emotion. Whatever those of Davis, they were of the briefest. In another second he was at the door of Dunn's carriage, his eyes glaring beneath the drawn-down blind, where, by a narrow slip of light, he could detect a figure busily employed in writing. So bent was he on mastering every portion and detail of the arrangement within, that he actually crept around till he reached the front windows, and could plainly see the whole *coupé* lighted up brilliantly with wax candles.

Surrounded with papers and letters and despatch-boxes, the man of business labored away as though in his office, every appliance for refreshment beside him. These Davis noted well, remarking the pistols that hung between the windows, and a bell-pull quite close to the writing-table. This latter passed through the roof of the carriage, and was evidently intended to signalize the guard when wanted. Before another minute had elapsed Davis had cut off this communication, and, knotting the string outside, still suffered it to hang down within as before.

All that *precaution* could demand was now done; the remainder must be decided by *action*. Noiselessly introducing the latch-key, Davis turned the lock, and, opening the door, stepped inside. Dunn started as the door banged, and there beheld him. To ring and summon the guard was the quick impulse of his ready wit; but when the bell-rope came down as he pulled it, the whole truth flashed across him that all had been concerted and plotted carefully.

"Never mind your pistols. I'm armed too," said Davis, coolly. "If it was your life I wanted, I could have taken it easily enough at any minute during the last ten or twelve."

"What do you mean, then, sir, by this violence? By what right do you dare to enter here?" cried Dunn, passionately.

"There has been no great violence up to this," said Davis, with a grin. "As to my right to be here, we'll talk about that presently. You know *me*, I believe?"

"I want to know why you are here," cried Dunn, again.

"And so you shall; but, first of all, no treachery. Deal fairly, and a very few minutes will settle all business between us."

"There is no business to be settled between us," said Dunn, haughtily, "except the insolence of your intrusion here, and for that you shall pay dearly."

"Don't try bluster with me, man," said Grog, contemptuously. "If you just stood as high in integrity as I know you to stand low in knavery, it would n't serve you. I've braved pluckier fellows than ever you were."

With a sudden jerk Dunn let down the window; but Grog's iron grip held him down in his place, as he said sternly, "I 'll not stand nonsense. I have come here for a purpose, and I 'll not leave it till it's accomplished. You know *me*."

"I do know you," said Dunn, with an insolent irony.

"And I know *you*. Hankes—Simmy Hankes—has told me a thing or two; but the world will soon be as wise as either of us."

Dunn's face became deadly pale, and, in a voice broken And faint, he said, "What do you mean? What has Hankes said?"

"All,—everything. Why, bless your heart, man, it was no secret to me that you were cheating, the only mystery was *how* you did the trick; now Hankes has shown me that. I know it all now. You had n't so many trumps in your hand, but you played them twice over,—that was the way you won the game. But that's no affair of mine. 'Rook' them all round,—only don't 'try it on' with Kit Davis! What brought me here is this: *my* daughter is married to Annesley Beecher that was, the now Viscount Lackington; there's another fellow about to contest the title and the estates. *You* know all about his claim and his chances, and you can, they tell me, make it all 'snag' to either party. Now, I 'm here to treat with you. How much shall it be? There's no use in going about the bush,—how much shall it be?"

"I can be of no use to you in this business," said Dunn, hesitatingly; "the papers are not in my keeping. Conway's suit is in the hands of the first men at the bar—"

"I know all that, and I know, besides, you have an appointment with Fordyce at Calvert's Hotel, to arrange the whole matter; so go in at once, and be on the square with me. Who has these papers? Where are they?"

Dunn started at the sudden tone of the question, and then his eyes turned as quickly towards a brass-bound despatch-box at the bottom of the carriage. If the glance was of the speediest, it yet had not escaped the intense watchfulness of Davis, who now reiterated his question of "Where are they?"

"If you 'd come to me after my interview with Fordyce," said Dunn, with a slow deliberation, as though giving the matter a full reflection, "I think we might hit upon something together."

"To be sure, we might," said Grog, laughing; "there 's only one obstacle to that pleasant arrangement,—that I should find an inspector and two constables of the police ready waiting for my visit. No, Master Dunn, what we 're to do we 'll do *here* and *now*."

"You appear to measure all men by your own standard, sir," said Dunn, indignantly; "and let me tell you that in point of honor it is a scant one."

"We're neither of us fit for a grenadier-company of integrity, that's a fact, Dunn; but, upon my solemn oath, I believe I 'm the best man of the two. But what's the use of this 'chaff'? I have heard from Hankes how it stands about that Irish estate you pretended to buy for the late Lord, and never paid for. Now you want to stand all square upon that, naturally enough; it is a pot of money,—seven-and-thirty thousand pounds. Don't you see, old fellow, I have the whole story all correct and clear; so once more, do be business-like, and say what's your figure,—how much?"

Again did Dunn's eyes revert to the box at his feet, but it was difficult to say whether intentionally or not Davis, however, never ceased to watch their gaze; and when Dunn, becoming suddenly conscious of the scrutiny, grew slightly red, Grog chuckled to himself and muttered, "You're no match for Kit Davis, deep as you are."

"Until we learn to repose some trust in each other, sir," said Dunn, whose confusion still continued, "all dealing together is useless."

"Well, if you mean by that," retorted Davis, "that you and I are going to start for a ten years' friendship, I declare off, and say it's no match. I told you what brought me here, and now I want *you* to say how I 'm to go back again. Where are these same papers?—answer me that."

"Some are in the hands of Conway's lawyers; some are in the Crimea, carded away surreptitiously by a person who was once in my confidence; some are, I suspect, in the keeping of Conway's mother, in Wales—"

"And some are locked up in that red box there," said Grog, with a defiant look.

"Not one. I can swear by all that is most solemn and awful there's not a document there that concerns the cause." As Dunn spoke these words, his voice trembled with intense agitation, and he grew sickly pale.

"What if I wouldn't believe you on your oath?" broke in Grog, whose keen eyes seemed actually to pierce the other's secret thoughts. "It was n't to-day, or yesterday, that you and *I* learned how to dodge an oath. Open that box there; I 'll have a look through it for myself."

"That you never shall," said Dunn, fiercely, as he grasped the bundle of keys that lay before him and placed them in his breast-pocket.

"Come, I like your pluck, Dunn, though it won't serve your turn this time. I 'll either see that box opened before me now, or I'll carry it off with me,—which shall it be?"

"Neither, by Heaven!" cried Dunn, whose passion was now roused effectually.

"We 'll, first of all, get these out of the way; they're ugly playthings," said Davis, as with a spring he seized the pistols and hurled them through the open window; in doing so, however, he necessarily leaned forward, and partly turned his back towards Dunn. With a gesture quick as lightning, Dunn drew a loaded pistol from his breast, and, placing the muzzle almost close to the other's head, drew the trigger. A quick motion of the neck made the ball glance from the bone of the skull, and passing down amongst the muscles of the neck, settle above the shoulder. Terrible as the wound was, Davis sprang upon him with the ferocity of a tiger. Not a word nor a cry escaped his lips, as, in all the agony of his suffering, he seized Dunn by the throat with one hand, while, drawing from his breast a heavy life-preserver, he struck him on the head with the other. A wild scream,—a cry for help, half smothered in the groan that followed, rang out, and Dunn reeled from his seat and fell dead on the floor! Two fearful fractures had rent the skull open, and life was extinguished at once. Davis bent down, and gazed long and eagerly at the ghastly wounds; but it was not till he had laid his hand over the heart that he knew them to be fatal. A short shudder, more like the sense of sudden cold than any sentiment of horror, passed over him as he stood for a few seconds motionless; then, opening the dead man's coat, he drew forth his keys and searched for that one which pertained to the red box. He carefully placed the box upon the table and unlocked it The contents were title-deeds of the Glengariff family, but all in duplicate, and so artfully imitated that it would have been scarcely possible to distinguish original from copy. Of the Lackingtons there was nothing but a release of all claims against Davenport Dunn, purporting to have been the act of the late Lord, but of which the signature was only indicated in pencil.

"The discovery was n't worth the price," muttered Davis, as he turned a half-sickly look upon the lifeless mass at his feet. "I 'm not the first who found out that the swag did n't pay for the smash; not," added he, after a moment, "that I was to blame here: it was he began it!"

With some strange mysterious blending of reverence for the dead, with a vague sense of how the sight would strike the first beholders, Davis raised the corpse from the floor and placed it on the seat He then wiped the clotted gore from the forehead, and dried the hair. It was a gruesome sight, and even he was not insensible to its terrors; for, as he turned away, he heaved a short, thick sigh. How long he stood thus, half stunned and bewildered, he knew not; but he was, at length, recalled to thought and activity by the loud whistle that announced the train was approaching a station. The next minute they glided softly in beside a platform, densely crowded with travellers. Davis did not wait for the guard, but opened the door himself, and slowly, for he was in pain, descended from the carriage.

"Call the station-master here," said he to the first official he met "Let some one, too, fetch a doctor, for I am badly wounded, and a policeman, for I want to surrender myself." He then added, after a pause, "There's a dead man in that carriage yonder!"

The terrible tidings soon spread abroad, and crowds pressed eagerly forward to gaze upon the horrible spectacle. No sooner was it announced that the murdered man was the celebrated Davenport Dunn, than the interest increased tenfold, and, with that marvellous ingenuity falsehood would seem ever to have at her disposal, a dozen artfully conceived versions of the late event were already in circulation. It was the act of a maniac,—a poor creature driven mad by injustice and persecution. It was the vengeance of a man whose fortune had been ruined by Dunn. It was the father of a girl he had seduced and abandoned. It was a beggared speculator,—a ruined trustee,—and so on; each narrative, strangely enough, inferring that the fatal catastrophe was an expiation! How ready is the world to accept this explanation of the sad reverses that befall those it once has stooped to adulate,—how greedily does it seek to repay itself for its own degrading homage, by maligning the idol of its former worship! Up to this hour no man had ever dared to whisper a suspicion of Dunn's integrity; and now, ere his lifeless clay was cold, many were floundering away in this pseudo-morality about the little benefit all his wealth was to him, and wondering if his fate would not be a lesson! And so the train went on its way, the *coupé* with the dead body detached and left for the inspection of the inquest, And Davis on a sick-bed and in custody of the police.

His wound was far more serious than at first was apprehended; the direction the ball had taken could not be ascertained, and the pain was intense. Grog, however, would not condescend to speak of his suffering, but addressed himself vigorously to all the cares of his situation.

"Let me have some strong cavendish tobacco and a pint of British gin, pen, ink, and paper, and no visitors."

The remonstrances of the doctor he treated with scorn.

"I'm not one of your West-end swells," said he, "that's afraid of a little pain, nor one of your Guy's Hospital wretches that's frightened by the surgeon's tools; only no tinkering, no probing. If you leave me alone, I have a constitution that will soon pull me through."

His first care was to dictate a telegraphic despatch to a well-known lawyer, whose skill in criminal cases had made him a wide celebrity. He requested him to come down at once and confer with him. His next was to write to his daughter, and in this latter task he passed nearly half the night. Written as it was in great bodily pain and no small suffering of mind, the letter was marvellously indicative of the man who penned it. He narrated the whole incident to its fatal termination exactly as it occurred; not the slightest effort did he make at exculpation for his own share in it; and he only deplored the misfortune in its effect upon the object he had in view.

"If Dunn," said he, "hadn't been so ready with his pistol, I believe we might have come to terms; but there's no guarding against accidents. As matters stand, Annesley must make his own fight, for, of course, I can be of little use to him or to any one else till the assizes are over. So far as I can see, the case is a bad one, and Conway most likely to succeed; but there's yet time for a compromise. I wish you 'd take the whole affair into your own hands."

To enable her to enter clearly upon a question of such complication, he gave a full narrative, so far as he could, of the contested claim, showing each step he had himself taken in defence, and with what object he had despatched Paul Classon to the Crimea. Three entire pages were filled with this theme; of himself, and his own precarious fortunes, he said very little indeed.

"Don't be alarmed, Lizzy," wrote he; "if the coroner's inquest should find a verdict of 'Wilful Murder' against me, such a decision does not signify a rush; and as I mean to reserve all my defence for the trial, such a verdict is likely enough. There will be, besides this, the regular hue and cry people get up against the gambler, the leg, and who knows what else they 'll call me. Don't mind that, either, girl. Let the moralists wag their charitable tongues; we can afford to make a waiting race, and, if I don't mistake much, before the trial comes off, Davenport Dunn himself will be more ill thought of than Kit Davis. Above all, however, don't show in public; get away from Rome, and stay for a month or two in some quiet, out-of-the-way place, where people cannot make remarks upon your manner, and either say, 'See how this disgraceful affair has cut her up,' or, 'Did you ever see any one so brazen under an open shame?'

"I have sent for Ewin Jones, the lawyer, and expect him by the down train; if he should say anything worth repeating to you, I 'll add it ere I seal this."

A little lower down the page were scrawled, half illegibly, the following few words: —

"Another search for the ball, and no better luck; it has got down amongst some nerves, where they 're afraid to follow it, — a sort of Chancery Court Jones is here, and thinks 'we 'll do,' particularly if 'the Press' blackguards Dunn well in the mean time. Remember me to A. B., and keep him from talking nonsense about the business, — for a while, at least, — that is, if you can, and

"Believe me, yours, as ever,

"C. Davis."

CHAPTER XXXV
THE TRIAL

Scarcely had the town been struck by the large placards announcing the dreadful murder of Davenport Dunn, which paraded the streets in all directions, when a second edition of the morning papers brought the first tidings of the ruin that was to follow that event; and now, in quick succession, came news that the treasurer of the grand Glengariff Company had gone off with some fifty thousand pounds; that the great Ossory Bank had stopped payment; companies on every hand smashing'; misfortune and calamity everywhere. Terrible as was the detail which the inquest revealed, the whole interest of the world was turned to the less striking but scarcely less astounding news that society had for years back been the dupe of the most crafty and unprincipled knave of all Europe, that the great idol of its worship, the venerated and respected in all enterprises of industry, the man of large philanthropy and wide benevolence, was a schemer and a swindler, unprincipled and unfeeling. The fatal machinery of deception and falsehood which his life maintained crumbled to ruin at the very moment of his death; he was himself the mainspring of all fraud, and when he ceased to dictate, the game of roguery was over. While, therefore, many deplored the awful crime which had just been committed, and sorrowed over the stain cast upon our age and our civilization, there arose amidst their grief the wilder and more heartrending cry of thousands brought to destitution and beggary by this bold, bad man.

Of the vast numbers who had dealings with him, scarcely any escaped: false title-deeds, counterfeited shares, forged scrip abounded. The securities intrusted to his keeping in all the trustfulness of an unlimited confidence had been pledged for loans of money; vast sums alleged to have been advanced on mortgage were embezzled without a shadow of security. From the highest in the peerage to the poorest peasant, all were involved in the same scheme of ruin, and the great fortunes of the rich and the hardly saved pittance of the poor alike engulfed. So suddenly did the news break upon the world that it actually seemed incredible. It was not alone a shock given to mercantile credit and commercial honesty, but it seemed an outrage against whatever assumed to be high-principled and honorable. It could not be denied that this man had been the world's choicest favorite.

Upon *him* had been lavished all the honors and rewards usually reserved for the greatest benefactors of their kind. The favors of the Crown, the friendship and intimacy with the highest in station, immense influence with the members of the Government, power and patronage to any extent, and, greater than all these, because more wide-spread and far-reaching, a sort of acceptance that all he said and did and planned and projected was certain to be for the best, and that they who opposed his views or disparaged his conceptions were sure to be mean-minded and envious men, jealous of the noble ascendancy of his great nature. And all this because he was rich and could enrich others! Had the insane estimate of this man been formed by those fighting the hard battle of fortune, and so crushed by poverty that even a glimpse of affluence was a gleam of Paradise, it might have been more pardonable; but far from it. Davenport Dunn's chief adherents and his primest flatterers were themselves great in station and rolling in wealth; they were many of them the princes of the land. The richest banker of all Europe—he whose influence has often decided the fate of contending nations—was Dunn's tried and trusted friend. The great Minister, whose opening speech of a session was the *mot d'ordre* for half the globe, had taken counsel with him, stooping to ask his advice, and condescending to indorse his opinions. A proud old noble, as haughty a member of his order as the peerage possessed, did not disdain to accept him for a son-in-law; and now the great banker was to find himself defrauded, the great minister disgraced, and the noble Lord who had stooped to his alliance was to see his estate dissipated and his fortune lost!

What a moral strain did not the great monitors of our age pour forth; what noble words of reproof fell from Pulpit and Press upon the lust of wealth, the base pursuit of gold; what touching contrasts were drawn between the hard-won competence of the poor man and the ill-gotten abundance of the gambler! How impressively was the lesson proclaimed, that patient industry was a nobler characteristic of a people than successful enterprise, and that it was not to lucky chances and accidental success, but to the virtues of truthfulness, order, untiring labor, and economy, that England owed the high place she occupied amongst the nations of the earth. All this was, perhaps, true; the only pity was that the pæan over our greatness should be also a funeral wail over thousands reduced to beggary and want! For weeks the newspapers had no other themes than the misery of this man's cruel frauds. Magistrates were besieged by appeals from people reduced to the last destitution; public offices crowded with applicants, pressing to know if the titles or securities they held as the sole guarantees of a livelihood, were true or false. All confidence seemed gone. Men trembled at every letter they opened; and none knew whether the tidings of each moment might not be the announcement of utter ruin.

Until the event had actually occurred, it was not easy to conceive how the dishonesty of one man could so effectually derange the whole complex machinery of a vast society; but so it really proved. So intensely had the money-getting passion taken possession of the national mind, so associated had national prosperity seemed to be with individual wealth, that nothing appeared great, noble, or desirable but gold, and the standard of material value was constituted to be the standard of all moral excellence: intending to honor Industry, the nation had paid its homage to Money!

Of all the victims to Dunn's perfidy, there was one who never could be brought to believe in his guilt This was the old Earl of Glengariff. So stunned was he by the first news of the murder that his faculties never rightly recovered the shock, and his mind balanced between a nervous impatience for Dunn's arrival and a dreary despondency as to his coming; and in this way he lived for years, his daughter watching over him with every care and devotion, hiding with many an artifice the painful signs of their reduced fortune, and feeding with many a false hope the old man's yearnings for wealth and riches. The quiet old town of Bruges was their resting-place; and there, amidst deserted streets and grass-grown pavements, they lived, pitied and unknown.

The "Dunn Frauds," as by journalist phrase they were now recognized, formed for months long a daily portion of the public reading, and only at length yielded their interest to a case before the "Lords,"—the claim preferred by a Crimean hero to the title of Viscount Lackington, and of which some successful trials at Bar gave speedy promise of good result. Indeed, had the question been one to be decided by popular suffrage, the issue would not have been very doubtful. Through the brilliant records of "our own correspondent" and the illustrated columns of a distinguished "weekly," Charles Conway had now become a celebrity, and meetings were held and councils consulted how best to honor his arrival on his return to England. As though glad to turn from the disparaging stories of fraud, baseness, and deception which Dunn's fall disclosed, to nobler and more spirit-stirring themes, the nation seemed to hail with a sort of enthusiasm the character of this brave soldier!

His whole military career was narrated at length, and national pride deeply flattered by a record which proved that in an age stigmatized by late disclosures, chivalry and heroism had not died out, but survived in all their most brilliant and ennobling features. While municipal bodies voted their freedom and swords of honor, and public journals discussed the probable rewards of the Crown, another turn was given to popular interest by the announcement that, on a certain day, Christopher Davis was to be tried at the Old Bailey for the murder of Davenport Dunn. Had the hand which took away his life been that of some one brought down to beggary by his machinations, a certain amount of sympathy would certainly have been wrung from national feeling. Here, however, if any such plea existed, no token was given. Davis had maintained, at the coroner's inquest, a dogged, unbroken silence, simply declaring that he reserved whatever he meant to say for the time of his trial. He did not scruple, besides, to exhibit an insolent contempt for a verdict which he felt could exercise little influence on the future, while to his lawyer he explained that he was not going to give "Conway's people" the information that he had so totally failed in securing the documents he sought for, and his presumed possession of which might induce a compromise with Beecher.

In vain was he assured that his obstinate refusal to answer the questions of the jury would seriously endanger his safety by arming the public mind against him; he sternly resisted every argument on this score, and curtly said, "There are higher interests at stake than mine here, — it is my daughter, the Viscountess, is to be thought of, not me." Nor did his reserve end there. Through the long interval which preceded his trial, he confided very sparingly in his lawyer, his interviews with him being mainly occupied in discussing points of law, what was and what was not evidence, and asking for a history of such cases — if any there were — as resembled his own. In fact, it soon appeared that, having mastered certain details, Davis was determined to conduct his own defence, and address the jury in his own behalf.

The interest the public takes in a criminal trial is often mainly dependent on the rank of the persons implicated; not only is sympathy more naturally attracted to those whose condition in life would seem to have removed them from the casualties of crime, but, in such cases, the whole circumstances are sure to be surrounded with features of more dramatic interest. Now, although Davis by no means occupied that station which could conciliate such sympathy, he was widely known, and to men of the first rank in England. The habits of the turf and the ring establish a sort of acquaintanceship, and even intimacy, between men who have no other neutral territory in life; and, through these, Davis was on the most familiar terms with noble lords and honorable gentlemen, who took his bets and pocketed his money as freely as from their equals.

With these, his indomitable resolution, his "pluck" had made him almost a favorite. They well knew, too, how they could count upon these same faculties in any hour of need, and "Old Grog" was the resource in many a difficulty that none but himself could have confronted.

If his present condition excited no very warm anxiety for his fate, it at least created the liveliest curiosity to see the man, to watch how he would comport himself in such a terrible exigency, to hear the sort of defence he would make, and to mark how far his noted courage would sustain him in an ordeal so novel and so appalling. The newspapers also contributed to increase this interest, by daily publishing some curious story or other illustrating Davis's early life, and, as may be surmised, not always to his advantage on the score of probity and honor. Photographers were equally active; so that when, on the eventful morning, the clerk of the arraigns demanded of the prisoner whether he pleaded guilty or not guilty, the face and features of the respondent were familiar to every one in the Court. Some expected to see him downcast and crestfallen, some looked for a manner of insolent swagger and pretension. He was equally free from either, and in his calm but resolute bearing, as he surveyed bench and jury-box, there was unmistakable dignity and power. If he did not seek the recognitions of his acquaintances throughout the Court, he never avoided them, returning the salutations of the "swells," as he called them, with the easy indifference he would have accorded them at Newmarket.

I have no pretension to delay my reader by any details of the trial itself. It was a case where all the evidence was purely circumstantial, but wherein the most deliberate and deep-laid scheme could be distinctly traced. With all the force of that consummate skill in narrative which a criminal lawyer possesses, Davis was tracked from his leaving London to his arrival at Chester. Of his two hours spent there the most exact account was given, and although some difficulty existed in proving the identity of the traveller who had taken his place at that station with the prisoner, there was the strongest presumption to believe they were one and the same. As to the dreadful events of the crime itself, all must be inferred from the condition in which the murdered man was found and the nature of the wounds that caused his death. Of these, none could entertain a doubt; the medical witnesses agreed in declaring that life must have been immediately extinguished. Lastly, as to the motive of the crime, — although not essential in a legal point of view, — the prosecutor, in suggesting some possible cause, took occasion to dwell upon the character of the prisoner, and even allude to some early events in his life. Davis abruptly stopped this train of argument, by exclaiming, "None of these are in the indictment, sir. I am here on a charge of murder, and not for having horsewhipped *you* at Ascot, the year Comas won the Queen's Cup."

An interruption so insulting, uttered in a voice that resounded throughout the Court, now led to a passionate appeal from the counsel to the bench, and a rebuke from the Judge to Davis, who reminded him how unbecoming such an outrage was, from one standing in the solemn situation that he did.

"Solemn enough if guilty, my Lord, but only irksome and unpleasant to a man with as easy a conscience as mine," was the quick reply of Grog, who now eyed the Court in every part with an expression of insolent defiance.

The evidence for the prosecution having closed, Davis arose, and with a calm self-possession addressed the Court:—

"I believe," said he, "that if I followed the approved method in cases like the present, I'd begin by expressing the great confidence and satisfaction I feel in being tried by a Judge so just and a jury so intelligent as that before me; and then, after a slight diversion as to the blessings of a good conscience, I 'd give you fifteen or twenty minutes of pathetic lamentation for the good and great man whose untimely death is the cause of this trial. Now, I'm not about to do any of these. Judges are generally upright; juries are, for the most part, painstaking and fair. I conclude, therefore, that I'm as safe with his Lordship and yourselves as with any others; and as to Mr. Davenport Dunn and his virtues, why, gentlemen, like the character of him who addresses you, the least said the better! Not," added he, sternly, "that I fear comparison with him,—far from it; we were both adventurers, each of us traded upon the weakness of his fellows; the only difference was, that he played a game that could not but win, while I took my risks like a man, and as often suffered as I succeeded. *My* victims—if that's the phrase in vogue for them—were young fellows starting in life with plenty of cash and small experience: *his* were widows, with a miserable pittance, scarcely enough for support; orphan children, with a thousand or two trust money; or, as you might see in the papers, poor governesses eagerly seizing the occasion to provide for the last years of a toilsome life. But my opinion is you have no concern with *his* character or with *mine*; you are there to know how he came by his death, and I 'll tell you that."

In a narrative told calmly, without stop or impediment, and utterly free from a word of exaggeration or a sentiment of passion, he narrated how, by an appointment, the nature of which he refused to enter upon, he had met Davenport Dunn on the eventful night in question. The business matter between them, he said,—and of this, too, he declined to give any particular information,—had led to much and angry recrimination, till at length, carried beyond the bounds of all temper and reserve, Davis rashly avowed that he was in the possession of the secret history of all Dunn's frauds; he showed, by details the most exact, that he knew how for years and years this man had been a swindler and a cheat, and he declared that the time for unmasking him had arrived, and that the world should soon know the stuff he was made of. "There was, I suspected," continued he, "in the red box at my feet a document whose production in a trial would have saved a friend of my own from ruin, and which Dunn was then carrying up to London to dispose of to the opponent in the suit. I affected to be certain that it was there, and I quickly saw by his confusion that I guessed aright. I proposed terms for it as liberal as he could wish, equal to any he could obtain elsewhere. He refused my offers. I asked then to see and read it, to assure myself that it was the paper I suspected. This, too, he refused. The altercation grew warm; time pressed, for we were not far from the station where I meant to stop, and, driven to half desperation, I declared that I 'd smash the box, if he would not consent to unlock it. I stooped as I said this, and as my head was bent he drew a pistol and shot me. The ball glanced from my skull and entered my neck. This is the wound," said he, baring his throat, "and here is the bullet. I was scarcely stunned, and I sprang to my legs and killed him!".

The sensation of horror the last words created was felt throughout the Court, and manifested by a low murmur of terror and disgust. Davis looked around him with a cold, resolute stare, as if he did not shrink in the least from this show of disapprobation.

"I am well aware," said he, calmly, "there are many here at this moment would have acted differently. That lady with the lace veil yonder, for instance, would have fainted; the noble Lord next the Bench, there, would have dropped on his knees and begged his life. I see one of the jury, and if I can read a human countenance, his tells me he 'd have screamed out for the guard. Well, I have nothing to say against any of these ways of treating the matter. None of them occurred to *me*, and I killed him! The Crown lawyer has told you the rest; that I surrendered myself at once to the police, and never attempted an escape. A legal friend has mentioned to me that witnesses to character are occasionally called in cases like the present, and that I might derive benefit from such testimony. Nothing would be easier for me than this. There is a noble lord, a member of the Cabinet, knows me long and intimately; there's a venerable bishop now in town could also speak for me. He taught me chicken hazard thirty years ago, and I have never ceased to think affectionately of him. There 's a Judge in the adjoining Court who was my chum and companion for two years—Well, my Lord, I have done. I shall call none of them; nor have I anything more to observe."

The Jury, after a short address from the Judge, retired; and Davis's lawyer, rising, approached the dock and whispered something to the prisoner.

"What's the betting?" murmured Grog.

"Even as to the first charge. Two to one for a verdict of manslaughter."

"Take all you can get for me on the first," said Grog, "and I'll take the odds on the other in hundreds. It's a sort of a hedge for me. There, let's lose no time; they 'll be back soon."

In a few minutes after this brief conversation, the jury returned into Court. Their finding was Not Guilty of murder, Guilty of manslaughter only.

Davis listened to the decision calmly, and then, having pencilled down a few figures in his note-book, he muttered, "Not so bad, neither; seven hundred on the double event!" So occupied was he in his calculations, that he had not heard a recommendation to mercy, which the jury had appended, though somewhat informally, to their verdict.

"What a pot of money one might have had against that!" said Davis. "Is n't it strange none of us should ever have thought of it!"

The Judge reserved sentence till he had thought over the recommendation, and the trial was over.

CHAPTER XXXVI
THE END OF ALL THINGS

From the day of Davenport Dunn's death to the trial of Kit Davis three whole months elapsed,—a short period in the term of human life, but often sufficient to include great events. It only took three months, once on a time, for a certain great Emperor to break up his camp at Boulogne-sur-Mer and lay Austria at his feet! In the same short space the self-same Emperor regained and lost his own great empire. What wonder, then, if three months brought great and important changes to the fortunes of some of the individuals in this story!

I have not any pretension to try to interest my reader for the circumstances by which Charles Conway recovered the ancient title and the estates that rightfully belonged to him, nor to ask his company through the long and intricate course of law proceedings by which this claim was established. Enough to say that amidst the documents which contributed to this success, none possessed the same conclusive force as that discovered so accidentally by Sybella Kellett. It formed the connecting link in a most important chain of evidence, and was in a great measure the cause of ultimate success. It rarely happens that the great mass of the public feels any strong interest in the issue of cases like this; the very rank of the litigants removing them, by reason of their elevation, from so much of common-place sympathy, as well as the fact that the investigation so frequently involves the very driest of details, the general public regards these suits with a sentiment of almost indifference.

Far different was it on the present occasion. Every trial at Bar was watched with deep interest, the newspapers commenting largely on the evidence, and prognosticating in unmistakable terms the result. Crimean Conway was the national favorite, and even the lawyers engaged against him were exposed to a certain unpopularity. At length came the hearing before the Privilege Committee of the Lords, and the decision by which the claim was fully established and Charles Conway declared to be the Viscount Lackington. The announcement created a sort of jubilee. Whether the good public thought that the honors of the Crown were bestowed upon their favorite with a somewhat niggard hand, or whether the romance of the case—the elevation of one who had served in the ranks and was now a peer of the realm—had captivated their imaginations, certain it is they had adopted his cause as their own, and made of his success a popular triumph.

Few people of Europe indulge in such hearty bursts of enthusiasm as our own, and there is no more genuine holiday than that when they can honor one who has conferred credit upon his nation. Conway, whose name but a short time back was unknown, had now become a celebrity, and every paragraph about him was read with the liveliest interest. To learn that he had arrived safely at Constantinople, that he was perfectly recovered from his wounds, that he had dined on a certain day with the Ambassador, and that at a special audience from the Sultan he had been decorated with the first class of the Medjidié, were details that men interchanged when they met as great and gratifying tidings, when suddenly there burst upon the world the more joyful announcement of his marriage: "At the Embassy chapel at Pera, this morning, the Viscount Lackington, better known to our readers as Crimean Conway, was married to Miss Kellett, only daughter of the late Captain Kellett, of Kellett's Court. A novel feature of the ceremony consisted in the presence of Rifaz Bey, sent by order of the Sultan to compliment the distinguished bridegroom, and to be the bearer of some very magnificent ornaments for the bride. The happy couple are to leave this in H.M.S. 'Daedalus' to-morrow for Malta; but, intending to visit Italy before their return, will not probably reach England for two or three months."

Within a few weeks after, a passage in the "Gazette" announced that Viscount Lackington had been honored with the Bath, and named Aide-de-camp to the Queen. It is not for poor chroniclers like ourselves to obtrude upon good fortune like this, and destroy, by attempted description, all that constitutes its real happiness. The impertinence that presses itself in personal visits on those who seek seclusion is only equalled by that which would endeavor to make history of moments too sacred for recording.

Our story opened of a lovely morning in autumn,—it closes of an evening in the same mellow season, and in the self-same spot, too, the Lake of Como. Long motionless shadows stretched across the calm lake as, many-colored, from the tints of the surrounding woods, it lay bathed in the last rays of a rich sunset. It was the hour when, loaded with perfume, the air moves languidly through the leaves and the grass, and a sense of tender sadness seems to pervade nature. Was it to watch the last changes of the rich coloring, as from a rose pink the mountain summits grew a deep crimson, then faded again to violet, and, after a few minutes of deepest blue, darkened into night, that a small group was gathered silently on the lake terrace of the Villa d'Este? They were but three,—a lady and two gentlemen. *She*, seated a little apart from the others, appeared to watch the scene before her with intense interest, bending down her head at moments as if to listen, and then resuming her former attitude.

The younger of the men seemed to participate in her anxiety,—if such it could be called,—and peered no less eagerly through the gathering gloom that now spread over the lake. The elder, a short, thick-set figure, displayed his impatience in many a hurried walk of a few paces, and a glance, quick and short, over the water. None of them spoke a word. At last the short man asked, in a gruff, coarse tone, "Are you quite sure she said it was this evening they were to arrive?"

"Quite sure; she read the letter over for me. Besides, my sister Georgina makes no mistakes of this kind, and she 'd not have moved off to Lugano so suddenly if she was not convinced that they would be here to-night."

"Well, I will say your grand folk have their own notions of gratitude as they have of everything else. She owes these people the enjoyment of a capital income, which, out of delicacy, they have left her for her life, and the mode she takes to acknowledge the favor is by avoiding to meet them."

"And what more natural!" broke in the lady's voice. "Can she possibly forget that they have despoiled her of her title, her station, her very name? In her place, I feel I should have done exactly the same."

"That's true," burst out the younger man. "Lizzy is right. But for them, Georgina had still been the Viscountess Lackington."

"*You* have a right to feel it that way," laughed out the short man, scornfully. "You are both in the same boat as herself, only that they have n't left *you* twelve hundred per annum!"

"I hear a boat now; yes, I can mark the sound of the oars," said the lady.

"What a jolly change would a good squall now make in your fortunes!" said the short man. "A puff of wind and a few gallons of water are small things to stand between a man and twelve thousand a year!"

The suggestion did not seem to find favor with the others, for they made no reply.

"You never sent off your letter, I think?" resumed he, addressing the younger man.

"Of course not, father," broke in the female voice. "It was an indignity I could not stoop to."

"Not stoop to?" cried out Grog, for it is needless to say that it was himself, with his daughter and son-in-law, who formed the group. "I like that,—I like our not stooping when it's crawling we 're come to!"

"Ay, by Jove!" muttered Beecher, ruefully, "that it is, and over a rough road too!"

"Well, I'd have sent the letter," resumed Grog. "I'd have put it this way: 'You did n't deal harshly with the Dowager; don't treat *us* worse than *her.*'"

"Father, father!" cried Lizzy, imploringly, "how unlike you all this is!"

"I know it is, girl,—I know it well enough. Since that six months I passed in Newgate I don't know myself. I 'm not the man I was, nor I never shall be again. That same dull life and its dreary diet have broken up old Grog." A heavy sigh closed these words, and for some minutes the silence was unbroken.

"There comes a boat up to the landing-place," cried Beecher, suddenly.

"I must see them, and I will," said Lizzy, rising, and drawing her shawl around her. "I have more than a mere curiosity to see this Crimean hero and his heroic wife." It was hard to say in what spirit the words were uttered, so blended was the ardor and the sarcasm in their tone. "Are you coming, father?"

"I—no. Not a bit of it," said Grog, rudely. "I'd rather see a promising two-year-old than all the heroes and all the beauties in Europe."

"And you, Beecher?" asked she, with a half-smile.

"Well, I've no great wish on the subject. They have both of them cost me rather too heavily to inspire any warm interest in their behalf."

The words were scarcely uttered, when the large window of the room adjoining the terrace was flung open, and a great flood of light extended to where they stood: at the same moment a gentleman with a lady on his arm advanced towards them.

"Mr. Annesley Beecher is here, I believe?" said the stranger.

"Yes; that is my name, sir," was the answer.

"Let me claim a cousin's privilege to shake your hand, then," said the other. "You knew me once as Charles Conway, and my wife claims you as a still older friend."

"My father bore you the warmest affection," said Sybella, eagerly.

Beecher could but mutter some half-inarticulate words.

"I have done you what you must feel a cruel injury," said Conway, "but I believe the game was never yet found out where all could rise winners. There is, however, a slight reparation yet in my power. The lawyers tell me that a separate suit will be required to establish our claim to the Irish estates.

Take them, therefore;, you shall never be disturbed in their possession by me or mine. All I ask is, let there be no bad blood between us. Let us be friends."

"You may count upon me, at all events," said Lizzy, extending her hand to him. "I am, indeed, proud to know you."

"Nor would I be forgotten in this pleasant compact," said Sybella, advancing towards Lizzy. "We have less to forgive, my dear cousin, and we can be friends without even an explanation."

The acquaintance thus happily opened, they continued to walk the terrace together for hours, till at length the chill night air warned Conway that he was still an invalid.

"Till to-morrow, then," said Sybella, as she kissed Lizzy's cheek affectionately.

"Till to-morrow!" replied the other, as a heavy tear rolled down her cheek, for *hers* was a sad heart, as she followed with her eyes their retreating figures.

"Ain't he a trump!" cried Beecher, as he drew his wife's arm within his own, and led her along at his side. "He doesn't believe one syllable about our sending those fellows over to the Crimea to crib the papers; he fancies we were all 'on the square'—Oh, I forgot," broke he in, suddenly, "you were never in the secret yourself. At all events, he's a splendid fellow, and he's going to leave the Irish estates with us, and that old house at Kellett's Court. But where's your father? I 'm dying to tell him this piece of news."

"Here I am," said Grog, gruffly, as he came forth from a little arbor, where he had been hiding.

"We're all right, old boy," burst in Beecher, joyfully. "I tried the cousin dodge with Conway, rubbed him down smoothly, and the upshot is, he has offered us the Irish property."

Grog gave a short grunt and fixed his eyes steadfastly on his daughter, who, pale and trembling all over, caught her father's arm for support.

"He felt, naturally enough," resumed Beecher, "that ours was a deuced hard case."

"I want to hear what *your* answer was,—what reply *you* made him!" gasped out Lizzy, painfully.

"Could there be much doubt about that?" cried Beecher. "I booked the bet at once."

"No, no, I will not believe it," said she, in a voice of deep emotion: "you never did so. It was but last night, as we walked here on this very spot, I told you how, in some far-away colony of England, we could not fail to earn an honorable living; that I was well content to bear my share of labor, and you agreed with me that such a life was far better than one of dependence or mere emergency. You surely could not have forgotten this!"

"I did n't exactly forget it, but I own I fancied twelve hundred a year and a snug old house a better thing than road-making at Victoria or keeping a grammar-school at Auckland."

"And you had the courage to reason thus to the man who had descended to the ranks as a common soldier to vindicate a name to which nothing graver attached than a life of waste and extravagance! No, no, tell me that you are only jesting with me, Annesley. You never said this!"

"Lizzy's right—by Heaven, she's right!" broke in Grog, resolutely.

"If you mean that I refused him, you're both much mistaken; and to clinch the compact, I even said I 'd set out for Ireland to-morrow."

"I 'm for New Orleans," said Grog, with a rough shake, as though throwing a weight from his shoulders.

"Will you have a travelling-companion, father?" asked Lizzy, in a low voice.

"Who is it to be, girl?"

"Lizzy,—your own Lizzy!"

"That will I, girl," cried he, as he threw his arms about her, and kissed her in sincere affection.

"Good-bye, sir," said she, holding out her hand to Beecher. "Our compact was a hollow one from the first. It would be but a miserable deception to maintain it."

"I knew luck was going to turn with me!" muttered Beecher, as he watched her leaving the terrace, "but I 'd never have believed any one if he 'd told me that I 'd have booked an estate and scratched my marriage all on the same evening!"